D1826543

MASK

OF

DECEPTION

Copyright © 2024 Karen Furk

Karen Furk asserts the right to be identified as the author of this work.

ISBN: 978-1-912569-02-1

This novel is a work of fiction. Characters, names, places and incidents are a product of the author's imagination and are used fictitiously. Any resemblance to actual persons, living or dead, events or localities is entirely coincidental.

All rights reserved. No part of this document or the related files may be reproduced or transmitted in any form, by any means (including electronic, mechanical, photocopying, recording or otherwise) without prior written permission of the author.

Cover artwork by Reuben Lane

Also By Karen Furk

The Mask Chronicles
Mask of the Gods
Mask of Deception
Beneath the Mask – Coming soon

Flurry of Feathers (mailing list exclusive)
Now available!
Sign up at www.karenfurk.co.uk

MASK OF DECEPTION

BOOK TWO

KAREN FURK

For Rosa and Tom.

*For the blackcurrant and liquorice sweets that Grandma (never)
gave me, even though they made me look like a chipmunk when
I tried to hide them in my cheeks, turned my tongue purple and
made my breath stink!*

*For the endless cuddles and love and for teaching me that what
happens at Grandma and Grandad's stays at Grandma and
Grandad's…except the sweets.*

12 REALMS MAP

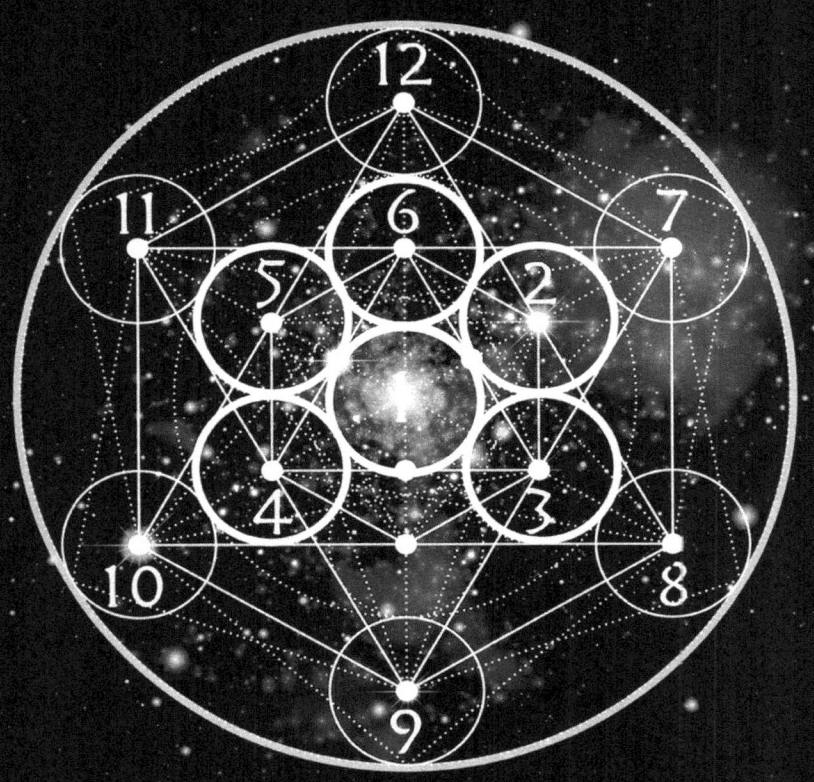

1. ACQUOROUS
2. ATIS
3. TOURANGA
4. AGALUCIA
5. AVEYAMARA
6. AMARAVEYA
   [5 & 6 TWINNED]

7. AVALONIA
8. PYLONARIA
9. DRAKE LEVANTINE
10. ORTALIS
11. ERDA
12. STORM LANDS

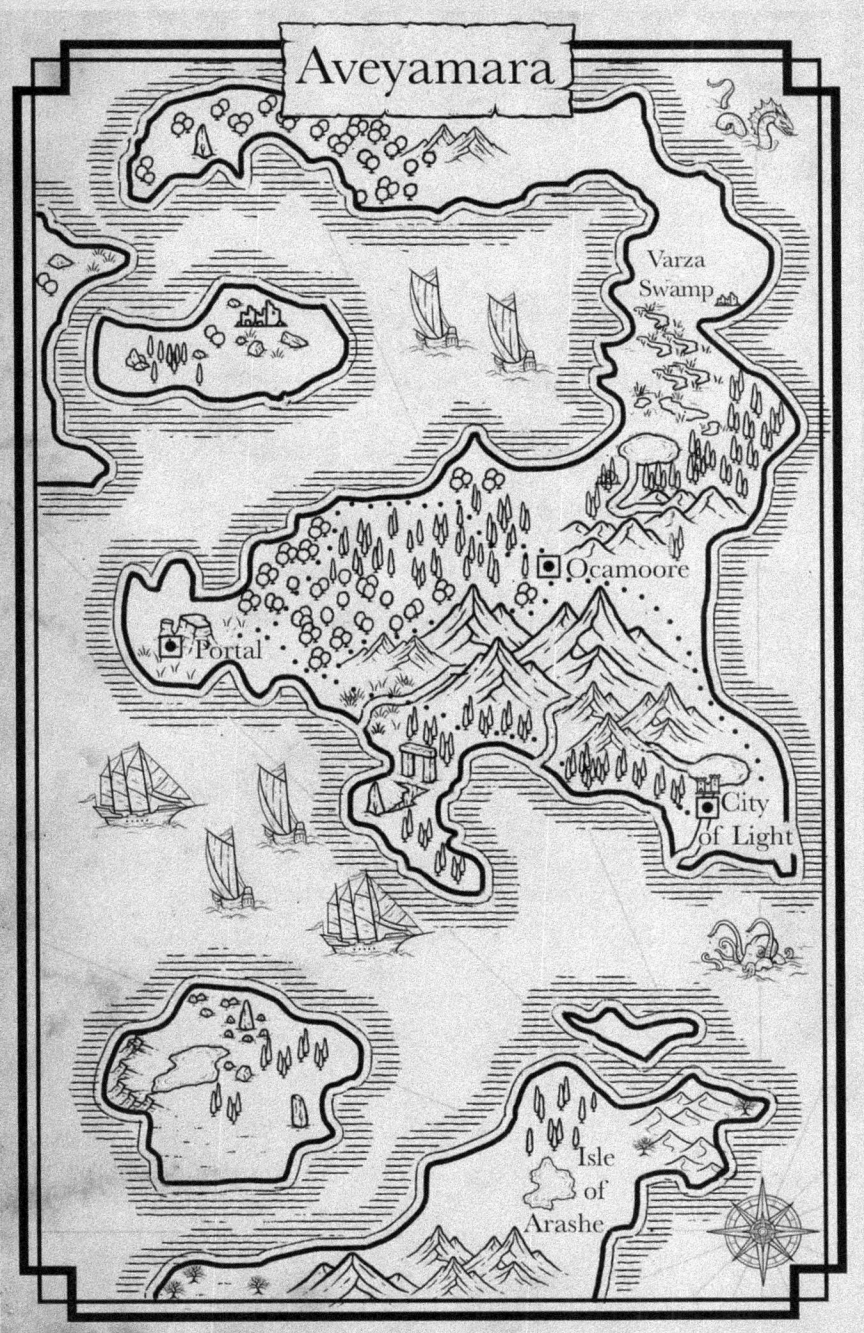

Welcome to the sea of souls

*Every storm rider leaves the sea of souls with a chosen one to love
them, a warrior to protect them and a curse around their neck
forged a long time ago.*

*The curse ensures many storm riders will not live to see their
twenty-first birthday.*

Their numbers dwindle.

They face an uncertain future.

One they may not survive.

*That's why they walk amongst humans in secret. They learnt long
ago not to trust any beyond their own people. Their survival and
that of their chosen ones and warriors depends on this.*

*Bonds forged between souls in the sea cannot be broken
in human form.*

*This is why to a storm rider their chosen one is precious. They
will give their life to protect that of their soulmate,
as will their warrior.*

The curse ensures they often do.

Bonding between the souls of a storm rider and chosen one is a beautiful, innocent ritual that happens once the chosen one reaches eighteen, sometimes before. It gifts a storm rider their full arsenal of defensive magic capabilities.

Bonding only happens with the consent of the chosen one.

Making chosen ones the more powerful of the three.

The survival of one, tied to the other two.

If one is lost, that loss will haunt every waking moment of the other two.

They will not find peace until all three reunite.

Three souls, created by magic, tied together eternally.

Chapter 1

Maya

A fierce storm raged beyond the thick glass and sturdy frames of the bifold doors. Rain pelted the glass, thrumming with an agitation that Maya found unsettling as she rested her head against the kitchen wall. For some reason, she was unable to stop thinking about the bracelet Haydan had given to her when she was a child. Sucking in a breath, she focused on a streak of lightning which struck a nearby tree, tearing the trunk apart.

Pulling her fleece wrap around her body tighter, Maya contemplated her options. Tallin, Haydan's grandfather, was growing irritated at her lack of response. The tenth heart-shaped charm that hung from the bracelet, the one gifted to her by Tallin that Haydan knew nothing about, had been burning, glowing and bouncing at various intervals for the last few weeks. She had ignored it and hidden it beneath her pillow, partly because she hoped Tallin would find something else to do, but also because she had no idea how to tackle the issue with Haydan. Since reaching her teens, their relationship had become strained.

Movement across the kitchen distracted Maya. She turned, drawn to the figure standing in the middle of the room. She hadn't felt his arrival thump in her chest, so it wasn't Haydan. For a moment, she feared Tallin had come to find her.

The kitchen spotlights sprang to life, blinding Maya with their intensity. She squinted, trying to make out who was loitering a safe distance away from her.

"Why are you in here in the dark? You can't hide from Tallin. He's been trying to contact you," Diego said.

Diego's distinctive green eyes locked onto Maya's with their customary intensity and focus that always left her feeling dazzled and overwhelmed by his presence. His voice sounded gruff and cold, suggesting she had irked him, but then relations between her and Haydan were frosty and he wouldn't like that. Her constant rejection of his son would not be well received.

When Maya didn't answer, Diego's brow creased. "Nothing to say for yourself, chosen one? You have a lot to say to my son, often when dismissing him. Personally, I don't know why he tolerates your belligerence. I would have dealt with your little rebellion by now, but it seems Haydan has more patience than I do. So, you have been ignoring Tallin."

How could Diego know that Tallin had a way to reach her, unless Tallin had told him? Maya finally found her voice. "What makes you think that? I was watching the storm. I like the storms. What do you want, Diego?"

The tiniest of movements tweaked the edge of Diego's mouth upwards, whether it was in amusement or annoyance Maya couldn't tell.

"I should think so too. You can only do that for so

long. Tallin would like Haydan to visit him. He wants to get to know his grandson. The fact you're ignoring Tallin means he has asked me to talk to you. This whole meeting is inappropriate, so don't ignore a request from the fae king, Maya. Tallin expects his wishes to be complied with. I suggest you don't annoy him further. If my visit is inappropriate, Tallin's will be even more so."

Diego's eyes tensed. For a moment Maya wondered if he was uncomfortable, then reminded herself that wasn't possible. "Why is this meeting inappropriate, Diego?" She kept her voice low and seductive, for some reason finding Diego's possible discomfort amusing. She stared at him, the small display of her own bravado making her feel empowered.

Any trace of amusement vanished from Diego's features as his brow furrowed. "Storm riders do not meet in private with chosen ones who are not their own. It's not considered etiquette."

Was Diego being serious? Maya bit back the laughter that threatened to surface at his formality, turning her head away to focus on the storm. With the lights on, she could see him reflected in the glass and that detracted from the storm outside. He had put the light on deliberately.

Maya had to get her emotions under control before Diego grew annoyed at her defiance. Apparently, she had a bad attitude. She was fed up with hearing Isaac, her stepfather, tell her at least every other day that she had a real problem with how she spoke to everyone.

"That amuses you, Maya? Be very careful. You may think right now that you are the one in charge where Haydan is concerned, but he tolerates your teenage bolshiness because he has to. As elder I have the right to discipline anyone I like with no concern for their status, so you might want to keep that in mind when trying to challenge me. Or maybe you would like that."

Diego took a step closer. Maya's heart pounded. For a moment she wondered how Katherine, her mother, had dealt with Diego when she got together with Isaac. Proper etiquette suggested Katherine would have had to request permission to be allowed to get involved with a human male. Katherine had a way of persuading people to give her what she wanted, so perhaps she had used her charm to talk Diego around.

Diego had a coldness to him that always alarmed Maya. When he made a threat like that he fully meant it, but she hated the idea of backing down in front of him. She brushed her hair behind her ear, buying time before a way to counter his threat sprang into her mind. She turned, unable to keep the glint of triumph out of her eyes as they clashed with his. "Yes, well I'm sure Haydan would like the humiliation of watching you discipline me. Did you 'discipline' my mother when she asked you if she could be with Isaac?"

Diego took another step closer. The skin across Maya's shoulders and back prickled and tingled as coldness brushed over her. "Oh, Haydan won't know about it. It can be our little secret. When you make contact with Tallin, via whatever means he has given you to do so, act respectfully. Challenges are even less welcome from Tallin, especially given your age now. He won't humour you with as much finesse as he did when you were younger. The fact you know how to tease and act provocatively merely makes your lack of bonding with Haydan more of a hindrance."

Maya shot Diego a questioning look. He scowled back. "Haydan keeps his physical contact with you to a bare minimum, but he is stronger and more capable bonded to you. It will also allow you to stay on Storm Lands with him. Tallin may be chosen one, but he will expect you to show support for Haydan at all times. Your refusal to bond is not supportive behaviour."

Maya huffed, finding Diego's lack of answer irritating. "So, are you going to answer my question? Did you 'discipline' my mother, whatever that means, when she asked you if she could move in with Isaac? I'm sure you didn't like that very much, the thought of one of our chosen ones with a human. I mean, storm rider males aren't known for understanding when it comes to other men being around their possessions, and since you're storm rider elder I'm certain you didn't like the thought of one of our chosen ones straying beyond the fold."

Diego's head tilted back, suggesting his displeasure at Maya's challenge. "I gave Katherine the permission she sought. She suffered enough when she lost your father and I'm not a monster. Isaac makes your mother happy and Katherine deserves to be happy. Plus, if Katherine's happy then you're happy. If you're happy then Haydan is usually happy, although at the moment you seem to enjoy proving that theory false. Maya, I am Haydan's father. I am elder. You would be wise to remember how dangerous I am and show me the respect I am due. You're not stupid. You challenge and push the boundaries but you know exactly how we operate, which does make me wonder about you. Haydan will be curious too. How much do you remember prior to and during your time in the sea?"

Something had hurt Maya badly before her soul had dropped into the depths of the sea, but the pain also made her decide to leave with Haydan. The reason for the discomfort remained elusive, but she had always felt that bonding with Haydan and gifting him the powers that accompanied the bond would prove to be the beginning of the end for them. She had no idea why she was so convinced about that, but she was in no rush to reach eighteen and find out if her gut instinct was correct.

"I don't remember the sea. Is it pretty?" Maya asked, wondering if Diego would talk about it.

His demeanour surprisingly relaxed, Diego rewarded her question with a warm smile. "It's beautiful, rather like the souls that live there. So, are you going to acknowledge Tallin's contact? You need to talk Haydan into returning. He says he will, but he's so far made no attempt to do so, not even with Kaleshar."

"It's not Tallin who bothers me," Maya said. She lowered her eyes to the dark boots Diego wore. He was standing within arm's reach. Not close enough to make her feel uncomfortable, but close enough to enhance her awareness of his power flooding the room. It brushed her skin, making it tingle as it swept around her. The pressure changed and her ears popped. He expected further explanation. Swallowing to clear the pressure, Maya dipped her head. "I find Haydan difficult to talk to right now. I'm not bonding anytime soon, Diego, so you may as well get used to the idea. I find his control over my life suffocating and Isaac encourages me to stand my ground. This is what I need right now."

Diego's tensed jaw didn't bode well. "You're taking advice from the meddlesome human who does not understand our ways?" The warning in his voice lent him a hint of menace as he folded his arms behind his back and stared Maya down.

"Isaac understands our ways better than you think. He's a quick learner for a human," Maya said.

"I will be speaking to your mother about this." The tension around Diego's eyes confirmed Maya had succeeded in irritating him. "I've always had concerns about Isaac's involvement with you. Arianna needs his direct, forceful manner, but you do not—"

"Go to hell."

Shocked at her interruption, Maya raised her eyes from Diego's chest to clash with his. She hadn't intended to say that out loud; it just slipped out raw and unfiltered. Diego's eyes widened. She tensed her bottom lip, waiting for him to touch her, daring him to lay a finger on her. The air around her changed as the temperature plummeted. Possibly connected to his powers, the room became arctic. Her breath formed plumes in front of her face as they glared each other down for what felt like an eternity, before Diego disappeared in a huge blast of air that shook the doors.

Maya released the breath she had been holding and turned back towards the window. She should have guessed Diego wouldn't let her belligerence go so easily. The figure that appeared behind her moments later confirmed that, the warm hands that slid around the back of her neck, even more so.

Haydan

Something flared within Haydan's mind; catching like wildfire it tugged at his consciousness, distracting him. Arianna took full advantage. Charging at him, she hooked a hand around the back of his neck. Her other hand slid under his arm, connecting with the one around his neck. Too late he realised her intent as she hauled him forwards and slammed a knee into his stomach. He twisted away. Switching knees, she sank another into his thigh, numbing everything from his hip downwards. The pain provided a diversion from his earlier distraction. He lost his footing and almost collapsed in the grass and dirt at her feet.

Arianna moved unnaturally fast, which explained why she was so capable. Haydan could under normal circumstances keep a step ahead of her, but not when Tallin was making his presence felt in his mind.

"Focus, storm rider. You're being outwitted by your warrior and I will not let you use your powers to evade her. Fight for it! You are still stronger than she is physically," Teeam said. He sounded furious, but then Haydan had been irritating both Diego and Teeam of late. This was just another epic fail to add to his expanding list.

Haydan's mind was consumed by thoughts of forests, thick grasses and the walled city of Ocamoore. He missed Arianna's fist swinging at his head. He staggered forwards, his vision swimming as her other fist connected with his jaw, sending him reeling into the grass. A metallic taste flooded his mouth.

With a feral snarl Haydan dragged himself up before wiping his mouth with the back of his hand. The sheen of magic in his blood shimmered against his skin adding a purplish tinge to it. Arianna's eyes focused on the blood as a smirk of triumph tugged at her mouth.

"Again, Arianna," Haydan said.

Arianna dropped into her fighting stance with her fists up.

Teeam strode across, stepping between them to stare Haydan down. "No, enough."

When Arianna didn't move, Teeam spun around, fixing her with a hard look. "Stand down, warrior. That's an order from an elder. You have just gained pleasure from inflicting pain on your storm rider. I need to talk to your storm rider in private. Go and fight one of the other warriors. Sandau is about, he usually challenges you."

"It's not my fault Haydan can't concentrate and goes off looking for a fight every other night. He should be able to focus regardless of Maya."

When Teeam's attention moved back to her, Arianna turned and stalked off.

Teeam switched his attention back to Haydan. "What just happened, storm rider? This is becoming habitual. Arianna is already overconfident in her abilities. I can sense the moment you disengage from being here. If I can sense it, so can she. Does she understand what's going on up here with you?" Teeam reached out to tap the side of Haydan's head with his fingertips.

The contact unwelcome, Haydan blocked Teeam's hand with a hard swipe of his forearm. "The only person who understands what's going on up here is Diego."

Teeam appeared to assess Haydan.

"And I don't want Diego here right now. He doesn't understand Maya at all. I'm on my own dealing with her."

Teeam's attention remained locked onto Haydan. The staring becoming unnerving, Haydan folded his arms. Teeam's eyebrow raised suggesting disapproval. "Have you tried talking to Diego about what's bothering you? He understands what it's like to be without a chosen one, so he has experienced something similar…"

"It's not just about Maya. I'm not comfortable talking about this right now." But he would. Teeam was good at getting him to open up. In any case, Teeam had a way of working things out for himself.

"I would imagine you feel the call of Tallin's realm from time to time and of course Kaleshar places demands upon you and opens up Acquorous to your curiosity. Frustrations and demands on all sides perhaps," Teeam said, still clearly evaluating Haydan's responses.

The man's uncanny knack for knowing exactly what the problem was proved irritating. "How do you do that? Are you reading my mind? If you are, stop it," Haydan snapped.

Teeam chuckled, the sound warm and enchanting. "It's intuition, Haydan. That and a lucky guess, which you have confirmed with your response. You are still entering the human realm at night to party and look for fights. Why?"

Teeam wasn't going to leave this alone. Haydan could tell by the way he was needling him about the issues that Teeam and Diego had no doubt discussed at leisure. "Because being in a writhing mass of bodies on a dance floor distracts me from everything else and I can lose myself in the beat of the music. The fighting afterwards focuses me on the pain. I prefer distractions to everything going on up here at the moment." Haydan smacked his temple with the palm of his hand. He was allowing his frustration to spill over and rewarding Teeam's goading, but he couldn't help himself any more. Gritting his teeth, he stilled his body, waiting for Teeam's response, which would as per usual be calm and conciliatory.

"Talk to Diego. You need to go and visit Tallin–"

"No!"

Haydan's sharp tone appeared to startle Teeam. He jerked his head away and blinked a few times.

"Where is Diego anyway? He's usually all over me at this point."

Teeam remained silent. Haydan's curiosity got the better of him. "Where is my father, Teeam?"

Teeam focused his attention on something else beyond Haydan's sight. "How did you discover these clubs that you frequent in the human realm? You continue to concern Diego and me with your wild behaviour. I understand why you're in free fall, but I do not like it. Neither does your father. It reflects badly on him too. Maybe you want to think on that."

"Isaac introduced me to the clubs. It's an effective distraction," Haydan said. He was rapidly tiring of being harassed from all sides and the idea of running away from everyone was starting to appeal to him. Maya might appreciate him more if he left too, or she might not care. His irritation flared as Teeam continued to survey him like a regal god. Haydan raked his hand through his hair. "I've told Diego to stay out of things with Maya and me. It's none of his business."

Teeam looked incensed as his eyes locked back on Haydan. "Why do you not want to go into the dark fae's realm? Tallin's your grandfather. You need to understand the dark fae's realm better, Haydan. Diego will not like hearing how much the human is stirring things up."

If Diego talked to Maya it would not end well. Her childhood had been a time of playful innocence, but Maya was in a stroppy teenage rebellion phase. Her mood swings were as legendary as Isaac's. They rarely spoke at the moment. She mostly greeted Haydan with a grunt or a glare and their curt conversations often ended in explosive arguments. In fact, she had challenged Isaac a few nights before at the kitchen table and Isaac had an epic temper when he was riled. Even Katherine had been caught out by it. Haydan had done nothing to upset Maya. To appease her he stepped away from her as soon as she turned, giving her the space she needed, but it was far from easy. Sometimes he felt that stepping back just succeeded in making her even more irate at him.

Diego would not tolerate Maya's flares of rebellion and the thought of him disciplining her made Haydan feel nauseous. Maya was a total contradiction. She would push to stir Haydan up, and to a point she seemed to enjoy it, but any hint of pulling her back in line resulted in a surge of panic from her. He had seen Maya totally lose it twice, but both times she had been beside herself and only Isaac could calm her.

Isaac's face had been a picture when Maya threw herself into his arms. She could barely breathe and had been in hysterics. Haydan had shouted at her. It hadn't been helped by his powers stirring and flooding the room at the same time as his threat of forcing her to bond. Maya reacted like a feral creature, screaming at him and calling him a 'control freak' and a 'psycho' amongst other things before bolting for the bedroom door, pounding down the stairs, yelling for Isaac and launching herself at him. Given that Maya often stirred Isaac and Katherine up in the same manner, her choice of protector appeared odd, but then Maya knew how much he hated other men touching her. "Isaac, Teeam. The human is called Isaac. Tell me Diego isn't talking to Maya."

Teeam's honey-flecked eyes hardened to the colour of dark, smouldering leaves. "Diego is elder and answers to no one. If he feels Maya needs a reset he will do so without your approval or permission."

"Maya will snap. Tell him to stand down," Haydan said.

Teeam's expression remained impassive.

"Maya will lose it. Both times I tried to pull rank on her it didn't end well. She's *my* chosen one. I don't presume to take issue with my father's choice of partner. He has no right to interfere in mine."

Teeam's expression remained disinterested. "Stand down, storm rider." Teeam moved in towards Haydan, resting his hand on his shoulder: a warning to stay where he was and not move to interfere.

Haydan had no intention of waiting around and doing nothing. He brushed Teeam's hand off his shoulder. Arianna wasn't an option; Diego would pull rank on her. "Fine, I'll send Kaleshar to intervene with Maya and Diego. He doesn't answer to anyone, least of all you and my father." A smug feeling of satisfaction darted through his mind. His father would be livid at the intrusion.

Chapter 2

Tallin

Tallin prowled the castle. He had left Lavinia sleeping, curled up in his bed with her hair cascading over his pillow. He had been careful not to wake her, but perhaps when he returned he would snuggle up to her and steal some of her warmth. Now he roamed the space unable to sleep, his mind a riot of conflicting emotions.

His son, Diego, still kept away from his realm, only visiting if it was essential, or Tallin requested he visit. Haydan had not returned at all. He focused on Maya and her defiant refusal to respond to his requests for her attention. Her final act of rebellion, hiding her bracelet under her pillow, had been her last chance before he sent Diego in. He would not have the chosen one to his own grandson ignoring his requests for an audience.

He had sent Diego a pixie post. The small creature Tallin bewitched had been annoying him for a while with constant gifts and demands for his attention, so sending it with a message for Diego had given him some respite. He didn't keep pets and being adopted by a pesky creature more suited to the woodland wasn't his idea of fun. He could have made direct contact with Diego, but he wasn't in a huge rush and didn't want to expend so much energy, so he took his time and a pixie post provided the perfect solution. Diego had met Tallin briefly inside the portal, returning the pixie to him with a look of displeasure on his face as he fished the creature out of his pocket and held it out by one of its legs. It had clung to Diego's fingers until Tallin relented and opened his hand to allow the creature to climb across onto his palm.

The rejection from his son would not be well received by the pixie. If Diego decided he needed the creature's assistance in future, it would not be as forthcoming. Tallin kept that to himself; his son had to learn certain things for himself.

Over the course of the conversation that followed, Diego had promised to visit Tallin more in the coming months. Tallin looked forward to getting to know his son better, his grandson even more so. His request to borrow Diego's warrior had been met with an odd mixture of curiosity and wariness, which flitted across Diego's face before he composed himself, swiftly disguising any emotion. Inevitably, Diego had claimed to have no idea what Tallin was talking about. Did he really think Tallin could be fooled by such attempts at nonchalance? He had wasted no time in putting Diego straight and ending the pretence. Lavinia had already told him that all the elders had a warrior. For security reasons, they kept the details veiled.

Tallin walked into the library. His skin prickled. Perhaps he had been too preoccupied to notice it in the hallways. The intensity increased as he stepped over the threshold and moved towards the restricted section.

The library was a huge room occupying a large part of the first floor of the castle. The wards placed on the restricted section gates were powerful, but in addition the private elven areas were guarded by his wolf. The eagle protected the fae restricted section.

Someone was in Tallin's restricted section of the library. Dread descended in his mind as he approached the gate knowing he would find it breached. He rounded the nearest bookshelf to find the gate sitting open. The room was shrouded in darkness; nothing moved within, but he felt watched. His skin continued to prickle. Whoever had broken in was still there.

"My kind cannot breach this part of the library, but the portal has not activated." Tallin took a step closer, scanning the balcony overhead for signs of any intruders. There was no one up there. "Which leaves me wondering who would be brave enough to take the liberty of forcing their way into the restricted section of the king's library." His voice echoed eerily off the walls, sounding louder than he expected. He returned his attention to the darkness of the restricted section and his breath caught. Small, glowing rings appeared as though hovering a good six feet off the ground. They disappeared for a moment as their owner blinked.

There, in front of him, stood a god.

Despite Tallin's surprise at the intrusion, his mind focused on the portal. It hadn't activated. How had a god breached his realm undetected? "My Lord, if I had known you planned on visiting, I would have been able to formally welcome you."

The glowing orbs moved closer as their owner took a step forwards. Tallin mirrored the move but in the opposite direction, maintaining the distance. He would not attack unprovoked, but given that his visitor had made no move to identify himself, caution seemed wise.

"Well, well, well, King Tallin, look at you."

The soft, teasing voice confirmed Tallin was standing in the presence of a male god, a powerful one, judging by his ability to hide from Tallin's detection.

"What a sight to behold you are." The god blinked again, the orbs disappearing into the darkness before flaring. "A chosen one who will no longer kneel in the presence of a god." There was an edge to the voice now, a ripple of dislike threading through the intruder's words.

"So, you know who I am, but I do not know who you are, My Lord. You have me at a disadvantage. If I knew who I was addressing, I could decide whether to kneel or not. As it stands, I have an intruder in my library, who has breached a private section, but appears to be a god. Without a name, I have no proof." Tallin had heard tales of the gods, stories from when he was a child, myths and legends, but to have one standing in his library confirmed they were not imaginary.

The glowing eyes mesmerised him. Tallin could understand why the gods had no problem attracting and keeping anyone who pleased them. The lure of such a powerful god was palpable. The glowing orbs narrowed as the intruder appeared to either grimace or smile, Tallin couldn't tell which.

"Oh, I think we should play a game, Tallin, fae king. You try and work out who I am and I will tell you if you are correct."

Tallin didn't like the sound of that, but had little choice. "Asanda is commander-in-chief. He would not enter a realm to speak to the ruler in such a manner. Few meet him and those who do rarely live to tell the tale. I have done nothing to draw Asanda's attention.

You are not Asanda."

The eyes narrowed again. "You are correct. I am not Asanda … thankfully."

Amusement laced the voice. The god was clearly enjoying keeping Tallin guessing. He couldn't work out if 'thankfully' was added because he should be thankful it wasn't Asanda in his library, or if the god was thankful that he wasn't Asanda.

"Although make no mistake, Asanda is very much aware of you, Tallin. You escaped the sea and found your parents, giving you a longer life than a normal mortal. Asanda notices such curiosities."

The implied threat hung over the room, making Tallin feel uneasy. A throat-clear indicated his intruder wanted another name.

"Asanda has a son Kai. He is reclusive. I am not sure Kai would have need of my restricted books section, or that he would lie in wait for me, if he did. Given that he does not like company, he would have left by now."

The intruder chuckled. "You like your restricted books section, Tallin. You have been doing your research. I'm impressed. Keep going."

"Kai has brothers who are dark gods and never named in our records. He also has sons, maybe daughters as well. Exact numbers are vague. The gods do not announce such events to the universe. One of Kai's sons is prophesized to prove himself more worthy than the others."

Tallin fell silent as the intruder straightened up and blinked a few times as though surprised. When the intruder rearranged himself into a more comfortable position he knew who was standing in his castle. "Well, well, well, Lord Theander, look at you."

ॐॐ

Arianna

Arianna stalked off in search of Sandau. He was one of the few warriors left that she could fight and feel challenged by. Now in her teens, she was starting to discover how much she could outperform the other warriors in training. She displayed fierce survival instincts, patience combined with a powerful, ruthless style of attack and a strong determination to succeed. She was so unlike any of the others that even Diego and Teeam found her a handful, although they could still outperform her in training with their brute force and magic, as could Haydan when he was on form.

Of late Haydan had become distracted. He didn't like talking about it, probably because it made him appear weak. Arianna had to prise information out of him, but it always felt as though Haydan regarded her with a certain amount of suspicion or distrust. A storm rider who distrusted his warrior. Given the secrets Haydan kept, that seemed ironic.

Sandau lounged on one of the spectacular tree arches. A tree trunk formed an archway across the valley and numerous trees grew out from that. Sandau perched on the edge of the main trunk with his back against one of the trees that sprouted from it and his foot braced on one of the trees that grew facing towards the ground. Amusement crinkled the edge of his eyes as he peered down at Arianna.

"Arianna has come to seek me out. I'm honoured. Maybe she would like a kiss for a change because I'm sure all the fighting hints at something else going on." Sandau raised a dark eyebrow at her as one of the other female warriors nearby chuckled at his teasing.

They always played these games. Sandau was mouthy. He was a handsome man, in a rugged way, but he still acted like a child. "In your dreams, Sandau. I've told you you're not my kind of boy. I prefer a man. Men know how to treat a lady."

Sandau roared with laughter before dropping to the ground in front of Arianna. The hair to the side of his head was now braided, the other side twisted into dreadlocks. A new tattoo covered his bulging upper arm lending him the edge of a wild warrior. Black stripes adorned his nose and ran down his cheeks. Fearsome. That's how you would describe his look. When he stood he had grown another inch or two because she tilted her head back to meet his strange-coloured dark eyes with the ghosting effect across the irises, eyes that always felt like they were looking directly into her soul.

"I don't see a lady. I see a warrior. A beautiful warrior. One who needs a strong man to take her in hand," Sandau said. He gave Arianna a heated look, pouting his lips suggestively as he studied her with a predatory expression.

His words pleased Arianna, but he was genuinely flirting with her again. She fought back the urge to cringe. Since she had moved into her mid-teens, Sandau had gained more height and bulk and had begun to treat her differently, teasing her when an opportunity arose. He was becoming more direct in his approaches, but then he was older than her and his storm rider was supposed to be bonded. His wild side needed locking back in its cage. She folded her arms, fixing him with a sassy stare. "I'm still on curfew, will be for a long time if Maya and Haydan's fighting is anything to go by, and no one is taking me in hand, especially not you. You couldn't handle me anyway. I can still best you in training."

Sandau's eyebrows shot into his hairline. "You beat me in training once, Arianna, and I was injured. Okay, you want to fight today? I'll fight, but when I win you're mine. I get your hand in marriage."

Arianna couldn't help laughing at his offer. Sandau seemed even more offended by her response; perhaps insulting him was unwise. "I'm fifteen, Sandau. I live on Earth. You've got no chance, my friend. You might get a date out of me, but you'll have to get past my father and storm rider first."

Sandau's eyes tensed, which was never a good sign. "Okay, I'll ask permission from Haydan if it makes you feel better. I'm a patient man, Arianna. I can behave and do a long engagement, but I will marry you."

Arianna rolled her eyes. "I'm not a possession. In Earth traditions, it's customary for a man to ask the father of his future bride for his blessing before asking his daughter for her hand in marriage. I didn't come to find you to play your stupid games. I came to train. Are you training or not?"

The smug expression Sandau gave Arianna confirmed he would definitely train with her. It also confirmed he was on form and training with him when he was on form was always a contest.

"*Stupid games*, Arianna? You should know better than to challenge me in such a way. I am master and commander and I will enjoy bringing you to your knees, child warrior."

෨ඏ

Maya

Diego's fingers slid around Maya's neck. He pressed his thumbs against the back of her neck, where her bond tattoo would sit. Her legs crumpled beneath her as she dropped to the ground, no longer in control of her body. His magic swirled around her, brushing her skin, making it tingle.

"Did you just defy an elder, Maya? I know you like to challenge but even you should know to pick your battles wisely." His words cold and detached, Diego lowered himself to Maya's level. He remained behind her with a firm grip of her neck. "Let's start at the beginning, chosen one. Who is your storm rider?"

The pressure against Maya's neck increased as Diego pressed his thumbs harder into her skin. The way he held her stirred something deep inside her. Her traitorous soul appeared to enjoy being close to so much protective power. Surprisingly, for once she didn't feel the need to rebel but the need to be reminded of who and what she should be focusing on.

"I am chosen one to Haydan, your son." Maya could close her eyes and stay where she was forever. It felt like being back in the sea; it was so warm, inviting and safe.

"Why do you rebel like you do? I know it strengthens your relationship to be like this and that when you do choose to bond, your relationship with Haydan will be so much better for it, but you are on a path of self-destruction with this." Diego's fingertips tightened again.

Maya gasped, shocked by how much she was enjoying this. If it had been Haydan touching her neck, she would have been fighting with every survival instinct she possessed. Now the fighting seemed exhausting.

"Haydan gives you space, yet you still push him away. You don't see him bleed, but I do."

Maya closed her eyes, fighting back tears. She could detect the pain in Diego's voice, hear the torture in his soul at seeing his son tormented. What was wrong with her? Why couldn't she just spend time with Haydan and let him enjoy the reassurance of her company? Their relationship remained chaste and Haydan only angered when she defied him and pushed him away with all her aggression and fury.

"Every single time you reject him, you hurt him. All he wants is your companionship, to be close to the only woman who can calm his mind and soul. You are a soothing balm in what is a hostile universe. He never hurts you. He never tries to even touch you, yet you won't tolerate him near you. Why not?"

When Maya didn't respond Diego continued, "He has never tried to force you to bond. I gather he never will. For some reason, he seems to humour your rebellions far more than I do. I am not your friend right now, yet you goad me too. Do you have anything to say for yourself before I reset you?"

Maya's head snapped up, fixing onto Diego's eyes in the reflection from the windows. "Reset me? What does that mean? I don't want resetting. I don't want you touching me." Her breathing was speeding up, coming in short gasps. Now his touch on her skin felt sinister. A burning need to escape her tormentor reared up inside her.

"As elder I can reset any of our souls who lose their way and you are most definitely losing your way. This is a gentle reminder of whose child you are tormenting. My son is not a plaything that you can discard when it suits you. He is Tallin's heir. You will treat him with the respect he's due."

Diego dragged Maya backwards, pressing his face closer to her ear. "Are you going to respond to Tallin, Maya? Answer me, chosen one, before I lose my patience and make your reset particularly uncomfortable."

Rearing up, Maya back-fisted Diego across the side of his head. He released an angry yell, momentarily losing his grip on her neck. She took full advantage of his surprise and jumped to her feet, before making for the bifold door at the end of the kitchen. She couldn't outrun him, but she could at least get away from him long enough to get Haydan to join her.

I need you. Where are you? She threw the thought out praying Haydan would intervene. At least if he defended her, she would stand a chance of calming Diego down. Reaching the door handle, Maya dragged the door open. It slammed back into place and she turned to face down a furious elder who looked ready to start a war.

Diego had dropped into his intimidating mode. He moved like a wildcat stalking prey as he strode across the kitchen towards her. "What is wrong with you? Maybe Haydan should force the bond on you and get you to understand how this works, chosen one. You've just assaulted an elder. Do you have any understanding of the severity of the consequences of your actions?"

I'm sending Kaleshar. Teeam has me contained too. Has he

hurt you? Show a tiny hint of submission to him and he may back down. Do not antagonise him further. I know that's hard for you to do, but try.

Relief flooded Maya's mind at Haydan's response. He hadn't abandoned her; he was sending Kaleshar.

He wants to reset me. What the hell does that mean?

Haydan had fallen silent, but then he would need to reach Kaleshar to help her. Calm detachment replaced her earlier panic as she stared Diego down. "I will tolerate Haydan if that's what you demand, but you're not resetting me."

"Tolerate my son?" Diego grimaced as he pushed his shoulders back. "You do not get to tell me what to do, chosen one. Not now and not ever." Diego reached for Maya's arm and throat.

Maya blocked Diego's attempt with a swing of her arm, dropping into her fighting stance with her fists up. She was in huge amounts of trouble and couldn't win a fight with him. Locked in a stand-off of epic proportions, her submission was a long way off. She wasn't in the mood for appeasing the furious elder in front of her. He had just rejected her only offer of capitulation. She was certain he wouldn't hurt her, but she wasn't going to let him reset her without putting up one hell of a battle first.

Chapter 3

Tallin

Theander moved out of the darkness of the restricted section with Tallin's silver and grey wolf at his side. It lowered its head when Tallin made eye contact with it. "So that is where you have gone, you little traitor. Did he bring you something special to make your treachery worthwhile?"

Theander chuckled. "I have a way of charming what I want from most creatures. Don't be too hard on him, he didn't have much choice."

Tallin sniffed, fixing another hard glare on the animal, which hung its head before peering up at him with wide, doleful eyes. "You are a long way off being forgiven. You are supposed to guard against intruders, not let in anyone who offers you a good ear scratch. Stop giving me that look and get back to guarding that gate," Tallin said with a huff of disapproval.

Sliding back around Theander's legs, the wolf slunk away. A flowing dark cape surrounded Theander. The cape moved in a manner that suggested it was bewitched. When Theander came to a halt, the cloak continued to twitch. The fabric that reached the floor rolled about as though it was more smoke than material. Perhaps it was possessed; that was the more likely explanation.

The presence of such powerful magic reminded Tallin that he was in the company of Asanda's youngest and most favoured heir. "My Lord," Tallin said. Hesitating for a moment, he dropped onto one knee. His attention was drawn to Theander's bare feet. Maybe that was how the god had crept into his realm undetected, but the portal hadn't activated to allow Theander access, which could only mean Theander had another route in. "It is a rare event to find a god in my library. If you wanted access to the private section you were in, you only had to ask. May I enquire how you ended up here, My Lord?"

"Enough of the 'My Lord' business, Tallin. I needed to check the contents of the restricted section. I can't ask Kai or Asanda what you have in there and time is of the essence. My absence is going to be noticed if I linger here and I don't want to be caught sneaking back. There are spies everywhere."

Theander pulled his hand out from beneath the cloak, producing one of the large volumes that usually remained locked away from sight. The book he held was ancient and littered with powerful charms, spells and enchantments designed to keep out any prying eyes. It was surrounded by a layer of water. Within the water were numerous locks, which appeared as the book was tilted around. Tallin owned the only key that unlocked it and only he knew which lock to use to open it. Using the wrong lock alerted not only his wolf and guards, but also him to the intruder. There were a few other ways to open the book that didn't involve the key. Tallin was keeping those to himself. Theander threw the volume down on the table. It landed with a soft thump. Water sloshed around before settling back into the book's cover.

"Haydan hasn't been back here since the unfortunate incident when he was younger, has he?" Theander asked before fixing Tallin with a curious look.

Lying would be unwise. The gods could easily sense lies and falsehood.

Tallin shook his head, focusing his attention back on Theander's bare feet. It seemed odd for Theander to be barefoot, but then perhaps he liked to creep about like that on Acquorous. "I am working to address that issue."

"Hmm," Theander mused. "I'm sure you are. Is Diego involved by any chance?" Choosing to ignore Tallin's staring, Theander spun one of the nearby high-backed chairs around and straddled it. Settling into the seat, he studied Tallin over the top of it. "Haydan will feel the call of your realm, but he will resist it for now, unless you can tempt him back. There are too many dangers in this realm and he is not comfortable with that. I can't say I blame him. Until Maya capitulates and bonds with him, he perceives himself and Arianna as weak. For now, he regards Kaleshar as an inconvenience, something to be fully embraced once he has gained the security of Maya at his side at all times. But he no longer has the luxury of waiting to fathom out that power."

The room had grown cold. Suppressing a shudder, Tallin rolled his shoulders trying to quell the uneasy feeling that crept into his mind. "What exactly do you mean by that, My Lord?"

Theander's eyes narrowed.

Tallin corrected himself. "Sorry, Theander. It

feels odd to call you by your first name, disrespectful somehow."

Theander refocused on the enchanted book. "What do you know about the gods? Do you know anything about our history?"

"I have studied the texts. I know there are light and dark gods. I gather Asanda does not like change much. Perhaps you could be more specific. I covered a lot of your history."

"Did you notice anything odd about Maya when you met her? Any unusual talents?"

Theander looked nonchalant, but he was asking for a reason, as though he was fishing for something pertinent.

"Things she noticed that were out of the ordinary when she was here perhaps."

There was the chain around Tallin's neck, the small gateway that he protected, which led to the main fae realm. Lavinia held the key. Tallin guarded the doorway. No doubt those who entered Tallin's realm wondered about the lack of fae around. There were fae in his realm; Lavinia was one of them. The majority kept a low profile, preferring to stay away from the main portal into his realm from Earth. However, the main part of the fae realm remained protected. "She saw the Kantobra."

When Tallin raised his attention from the book, Theander was staring straight back. His cape shuddered around him.

"You're sure?"

Tallin nodded. "She saw him. He came to the door and pushed his paw through as though trying to reach her ... or tempt her. Either is possible."

Theander's attention remained locked onto Tallin,

who couldn't tell if the god viewed the news as a good or a bad thing. Theander's expression remained impassive, but then the gods were well versed in giving little away of their true feelings.

"When the mask resurfaced for Haydan after lying dormant for so long, it created huge ripple effects." Theander's brow furrowed as he concentrated on his hands and twisted a ring around on his index finger, a chunky ring with ornate silver detailing that wrapped around a large stone. Imbued with magic, the ring glowed as he fiddled with it. "Asanda granted Haydan with Kaleshar the freedom of our realm, but he can't freely walk Acquorous until he deals with an obvious problem. The dark gods want the mask and its rightful owner to pledge allegiance to them. That was why we set the events in motion last time and sent Ackir. It will not have taken them long to work out that either we have hidden the mask from them, or the rightful owner has been found. Luckily few of us know about what happened, but the dark gods, like the rest of us, have spies and allies all over the place. At some point, they will work out who has the mask and when they do, they will come looking for him and anyone connected to him."

Theander fell silent letting the enormity of the problem sink in. "You need to get Haydan here with Maya and Arianna. He is safer here than he is on Storm Lands. Maya is a long way off bonding, leaving Haydan and Arianna in a more vulnerable position too. I don't want the dark gods to find Storm Lands. They will destroy anything in their paths to get at what they want. I do not want that realm to be a casualty." He straightened out his hands, steepling his fingers together as he peered across at Tallin. "I don't care how you get Haydan here, but use whatever means you have to. If Diego can't get them here, you will have to use force and your sneaky elven charms."

Before Tallin could move to deny that accusation, the edge of Theander's mouth slid into a crafty smile. "Please don't refute that you're capable of being devious and manipulative. You're not as obvious about it as Lavinia, but it runs in your blood." After studying Tallin for a moment longer with his glowing eyes, Theander returned his attention to the ring. "When he's here, he needs to start harnessing the power that Kaleshar wields and he needs to begin mastering the realms, starting with this one and the one around your neck. Only when he proves himself worthy of the task will they start to back off and respect his powers. Kaleshar's, and indirectly Haydan's, powers will increase with each realm that he masters. I'm not even sure Haydan realises that at this stage. Once he has these two, the addition of Storm Lands will buy him more time. Right now, the dark gods will perceive him as weak and vulnerable. To my kind that means easy to manipulate and force under their control. If they can't get him to bow to their wishes and he hasn't mastered any of the realms, they will solve the problem by killing him." Theander fell quiet, before adding, "He is my friend, but he has no idea of the enormity of the task ahead of him."

Theander pulled the ring from his finger. Holding it between his thumbs and index fingers, he studied it, then held it out to Tallin. The way he held it was an ancient way of passing small gifts from one race to another. Tallin had never seen anyone use the technique before.

"Your father returned this to me a while ago. He

didn't want the Arvellan stone in this realm any more. Now this realm has a new king and I'm returning it. I think you may find it useful. In the presence of dark magic, it turns a ruby colour."

Tallin's father had mentioned the ring. If Tallin hadn't already known about it he would have been wary. It was unusual for the gods to present gifts unless they were up to something. Theander seemed genuine and Tallin had no reason to question the god's sincerity. "Tallin, fae king, offers you his thanks." Tallin held out his hand allowing Theander to drop the ring into his palm. Lighter than he expected it to be, it felt warm and welcoming. "Why are you telling me all of this now? Has something happened to make you wary?" Tallin asked. The timing seemed significant. Six years since Haydan had last been in the realm, it was only now that Theander had entered his realm to warn him.

"The dark gods are starting to work it out. I can only protect Haydan for so long before I have to encourage him to embrace this. He won't talk to me about it. Every time I try he shuts me down. I'm sure I don't need to warn you to be on your guard when he enters this realm."

Tallin grimaced at the suggestion Haydan would be in danger in his realm. "Meaning what exactly?"

Theander swung his leg back across the chair and stood. "Were you aware that last time they came into the realm, Haydan found and returned the soul of Diego's former chosen one to the sea? I have her held in safety for Diego, should he decide he wants her back. She was taken captive by one of your people."

"Diego has a chosen one?" Theander was a fascinating being, one Tallin would like to get to know better. "I knew I had a problem with one of my healers called Leylani. A rumour reached me that she had captured power sources, but when I visited her, she had let them go. Why are you telling me this?"

Theander surveyed the library, scrutinising the space before settling his attention back on Tallin. "I'm sure she still seeks power sources and would love to get her hands on your grandson. She won't touch Diego. He's too close to you and too powerful, but Haydan? He's not essential to your throne succession right now and not bonded. I gather Lavinia played a hand in getting Haydan here last time. I've never quite figured her out. She adores her grandson but tried to separate him and Maya last time they came into the realm. Tread with caution. I heard a rumour Lavinia and Leylani are good friends. You wouldn't happen to know anything about that, would you?" An eyebrow raised before Theander's eyes tensed into glowing slits in the darkness.

Tallin sighed. "I did not know that, but Lavinia likes to keep me on my toes. She mixes with a lot of my court. That is how she finds out so much information."

Theander's stance relaxed, and he lowered his gaze to the floor as though amused. "I would also watch Rebekka. She is storm rider, used to getting her own way. If she hears about the soul that escaped Leylani last time she will come searching for her. She will not want Diego's former chosen one returning to him. You, me and Haydan are the only ones who know where the soul is. If this leaks, I know where from because I won't tell her and I know Haydan won't either."

Tallin chuckled. "Of course, because Lavinia would never talk to Leylani and find out about this, nor tell Rebekka to stir things up for Diego. A distracted Diego might be just what Lavinia needs to cause a diversion. In any case, I expect Rebekka is highly intelligent. She may work it out for herself."

Theander moved off towards the end of the room, back towards the restricted section. The doors opened to let him through. He disappeared into the darkness. "This is why I like you. You're sharp, but you know how to play the game. I like this realm with you at the helm. I may return. Farewell for now, Tallin, fae king."

Tallin already knew that if he went to investigate he would find the restricted section empty. Theander had left. His attention returned to the water book on the table. Full of details about the gods and their past, the ancient volume contained information about mystical artefacts, the twelve realms and secret ways into them along with maps. The book also held the locations of the twelve keystones, each one guarded and only accessible by one worthy of harnessing such power. He had trawled it many times and had never come close to understanding it. There was nothing coincidental about Theander leaving that particular book out. The information within was hugely significant to Haydan's future.

Maya

Maya ducked around the back of Diego and attempted to grab his wrist and elbow, forcing him down towards the floor. A quick thump of air shuddered towards her as Diego vanished from her grasp and the room.

Diego's storm cloud burst into the kitchen and his

arm wrapped around Maya's neck as he tried to contain her in a stranglehold, before bringing his free hand up to press his fingers against the future location of her bond tattoo. Maya grabbed for his arm and yanked down hard. Bending over and pushing the bottom half of her torso backwards past Diego, she managed to drop her head to Diego's waist. Her link to Haydan would ensure she started to feel ill if she didn't break physical contact soon. A quick swing of her free arm up to his face ensured she could jab a finger into his eye and wriggle free as he reflexively pulled away.

Spinning around, Maya almost ran straight into Kaleshar, who looked like he was enjoying the experience far more than she was. She gasped and raised her arms to place a barrier between them as momentum carried her forwards, pressing her against his chest. A swirl of nausea washed over her at Haydan's immediate dislike of their proximity to each other. The initial surprise wearing off, she pushed away from Kaleshar. Mischief glinted in his eyes as he regarded her then Diego. Maya took the opportunity to open up space between herself and the furious elder.

"Challenging storm rider elders, Maya? Interesting, even for you," Kaleshar said, raising an eyebrow as he assessed the stand-off that had arisen.

Diego drew himself up. "Let me guess, Haydan sent you because he won't directly defy me? Arianna won't either."

He didn't sound that surprised by the development, but then Haydan was smart enough to understand the rules of engagement and sending Kaleshar was clever.

"Maya needs a reset. This is in Haydan's interest, so why is he also defying me?" Diego asked looking perplexed.

Kaleshar appeared wary. He kept his cold stare locked on Diego, but Maya also sensed curiosity from him. He tilted his head, suggesting he hadn't decided who he was siding with. Maya began backing away.

"Haydan wants you to leave Maya alone. She is not your chosen one. He will deal with her rebellion," Kaleshar said.

Diego moved in closer to Kaleshar and lowered his head. It was a gesture that seemed conciliatory. "Haydan doesn't deal with Maya's rebellion though. He allows her to rebel whenever she feels like it. I'm growing tired of how she hurts him. Don't you wonder why he hasn't taken her in hand and sorted this out? Who is the master of your relationship with my son?"

Kaleshar bestowed another of his mysterious smiles upon Maya. Could she fully trust him?

Kaleshar returned his attention to Diego. "Haydan connects to Maya and Arianna. Only Haydan fully wields my power. I will protect whatever makes him happy. If you want to reset Maya you have to get past me. I am asking you to stand down."

"You think I'm afraid to take you on, Kaleshar? My son won't see me harmed. This is a battle you can't win. Haydan knows I'll punish him if he interferes. You might want to remind him of that," Diego said.

Diego remained tensed. Even as Maya edged towards the bifold doors, she could tell he was ready to fight to get what he wanted. Kaleshar glanced down at her side, before meeting her eyes and returning his attention to Diego.

The silent communication didn't go unnoticed. Maya reached a shaking hand down into the warmth of the pocket on her fleece, wrapping her fingers around a warm, solid object. The mask. Relief flooded her mind at the realisation as she mouthed a 'thank you' to Kaleshar and pulled the mask free.

Looking back up, Maya met Diego's furious expression as he turned from Kaleshar, who grinned at her before disappearing from the kitchen. Kaleshar rarely took human form and never liked to hang around; perhaps that was a god trait.

Maya's attention snapped back to Diego as he took a step forwards.

"Maya, surely you can't hope to control that yourself? Even Haydan struggles to control Kaleshar. He will suffocate you and knowing how you like to rebel against any and every oppressive force, trying it out seems … foolish, no?" His eyebrows raised as he continued to survey her every movement.

Diego did have a point. Maya had never worn the mask. In fact, she had never touched it before. Haydan hid Kaleshar away, not permitting her access, as though considering her too stupid to be allowed anywhere near it. Given that she was now clutching it in her hand and staring down Diego, he was probably correct.

Diego's eyes narrowed as his left hand flicked out and the mask flew out of Maya's hand. It bounced and skittered across the polished floor, coming to rest by the doors where it reflected in the glass as though taunting Maya. Swallowing hard, she turned back to Diego, who was studying the mask as though surprised by his achievement. He cocked his head to the side. When nothing happened, his attention returned to her with the speed of a hawk hunting prey.

"I think your moment of hesitation just cost you dearly, chosen one. Perhaps even Kaleshar is curious about this. Perhaps he too wants you to better understand the way your relationship with Haydan works or should work … come here, Maya, and kneel. Do it for Haydan if nothing else."

Maya's breathing returned to short bursts as panic wrapped around her mind. She didn't want resetting. "I'll kneel, but you're not resetting me." She could barely get the words out her throat was so tight.

Diego rewarded her with a cold look, the sort that made Maya's heart quail. He was a magnificent beast when he was riled, but also truly terrifying. She had just infuriated him. There was no way he was going to back down. Not now. She had pushed him too far. His headshake confirmed that. Power released from him, enveloping her as he moved forwards. The overwhelming scent of cinnamon flooded her senses. He had never done that around her before, but she now enjoyed the full force of an angry elder demonstrating why he was elder and why she would submit. He reached for her neck, wrapping warm fingers gently around her throat, as his other hand moved around the back of her neck.

When an elder reached for your throat full submission was the only response. To rebel at this stage would place Maya's soul in danger of being evicted from the sea, an outcome too terrible to contemplate. She couldn't breathe, which was nothing to do with the feather-light touch of Diego's fingertips against her skin. Teeam would most certainly have done the same thing to Haydan to keep him away. She was trapped whichever way she turned.

Terror clawed its way up inside her as Diego's fingertips found the spot on her neck where her bond tattoo would be. His powers flooded her body. She could no longer fight him. Her breath caught as she dropped to her knees in front of him and onto all fours. He lowered to his knees with her.

Weighted down, the only sound that penetrated Maya's mind as she tried to breathe was a high-pitched wail of so much pain that it infiltrated her consciousness as all her other senses failed her. Paralysis swept over her body as her vision swam and darkness engulfed her.

Chapter 4

Haydan

"**D**efiance will not gain you any favour, Haydan," Teeam said. His hand wrapped around Haydan's throat, possibly pre-empting Haydan's rebellion before it happened.

The thought had crossed Haydan's mind more than once and Teeam could easily predict future events, so his actions were perhaps justified. The contact was delicate but would only remain so if Haydan didn't fight him.

"You might not like this, but Maya needs a gentle reminder of her place. Diego will not hurt her. Kaleshar is unlikely to fully intervene. His battle is not with your father and he will recognise there are certain things he would be wise not to get involved in."

Teeam spoke with his usual reassurance, but Haydan still felt unsettled by his actions. "Maya will completely freak out. Why aren't you helping me? You understand she's different. I know she challenges, but it's something she needs. I can't really explain it. It will make my relationship with her stronger. I can tolerate what she throws at me as long as I know she will come around.

When she is ready to embrace me, she will capitulate.
You can see the future, you know this. Until she is
eighteen none of this matters anyway."

Teeam refused to meet Haydan's eyes; instead, his
amber irises locked on a spot behind Haydan.

"Or is there something you're not telling me?"
Haydan asked.

Teeam stilled, the slight tensing of his body an
obvious sign that Haydan had just hit a nerve.

"Is that why you're permitting this? You're
unsettling me. What are you hiding?" Haydan's vision
tightened and everything lurched around him. He
gasped for breath as though he had been landed in
freezing cold water. For a moment, he thought Teeam
had released his powers, then his mind pulsed as
though hit by a shock wave. Maya was in trouble. What
had Diego done?

Teeam's eyes widened and his head turned, his
attention locking back on Haydan. "Diego has a
situation that he needs your help with. Perhaps you
were right." Teeam lowered his hand from Haydan's
throat, granting him permission to leave. "I will speak
to Diego once this is resolved. Your way seems to work
better with Maya. In future, we will respect that more."

"I understand why it concerns him. Maya chose me
in the sea. I grant her freedom of choice and free will
out here, not the illusion of it. I respect her decisions.
I always have. I always will. She just can't see that for
what it is yet. Full, absolute, one hundred per cent trust.
It is not our way, but it is my way. It is what I have been
trying to tell my father, but he doesn't listen."

Teeam nodded his head in understanding. Haydan
jumped away from his home world, his mind a riot of
confused emotions. Whatever Diego had done it had

sent Maya into free fall and she was never easy to calm when that happened. He would have to try something new.

Haydan dropped straight into the kitchen. Given the severity of the situation, he didn't worry about the usual etiquette of arriving outside the house to enter via a formal entrance.

Diego stood over the collapsed figure of Maya with a look on his face of confusion mingled with steely resolve. An apology would not be forthcoming. The elders didn't apologise to anyone. On all fours, with her head down and her hands over her head, Maya wailed and sobbed. The sound wavered between terror and exhaustion.

His own soul quailed at the sight of her in so much distress. Diego's proximity would not be helping the situation. Haydan rushed towards Maya, pausing as he drew alongside Diego. "I need you to move back," he said. Fixing his father with a cold glare, he waited whilst Diego took two steps back and moved around the central kitchen island to give them space. Haydan dropped to the floor beside Maya unsure what type of welcome he would receive. Usually he had to deal with a hellcat, but when she was upset, she occasionally became clingier with him. Regardless, he always approached the situation with caution just in case he misjudged it. "Maya baby, it's me."

The strange, tortured sound stopped, making the hairs on Haydan's neck rise up. Maya knew he was there. He reached a shaking hand out to stroke her upper back, which quivered from her exertion. His vision still swam, snapping in and out of focus at will as though possessed. "Diego has moved away. You're safe. He didn't intend to hurt you." Her body still shook, twitching and spasming as she remained in a tight ball. "Let me in, Maya." She remained unresponsive. Settling back on his haunches, Haydan gave Diego a cold stare. "I've warned you enough times about this."

Leaning forwards against the kitchen island, with his elbows braced on the worktop, Diego furrowed his brow. "She told me to go to hell. Have you ever seen hell? That is not somewhere you tell an elder to go to."

Haydan took a breath in and refocused on trying to reach Maya. "Maya, do you trust me? Nod if you do."

Maya tensed, but after a moment nodded.

He had only one way to reach her and he wasn't sure she would like it. His altera arm raised slowly, his hand sliding onto her back beside the other. He could sense her soul; it was inches away from his soul buried in his wrist. Hers was in so much pain that awareness reached him from where his was resting. Maya shuddered, her neck drawing back towards her body, inching closer to his altera. He could take a risk and try it to see what happened. Her reaction if he got it wrong couldn't be any worse than the state she had been in when he arrived. Maya's body moved back more, meaning his wrist was even closer to her neck.

Too late to change his mind, Haydan slid his altera slowly towards Maya's neck. Running his hands into her hair, he slipped his altera into place against the warmth of her neck. They both inhaled sharply as the connection formed, linking their souls together. All the fight left Maya as she collapsed to the floor as if in relief at his intervention. Haydan's eyes slid shut, partly in response to the respite, but also in delight. He had expected fury, not the capitulation he was now experiencing.

Maya launched herself towards Haydan. Her arm

nearest to him reached for his knee, before she twisted her whole body around and crawled into his arms. He swung his altera arm over her head, keeping the connection formed as she cuddled right in against him, with her face by his neck and her arms wrapped around his torso. Tensing his body at her proximity, he then permitted himself to relax a little. It wouldn't do any harm for his father to witness this moment of intimacy, to understand that their souls connected on a deeper level this way, even if their physical forms didn't. Her warm body was still trembling but not as much as earlier.

Wrapping his arms around her, Haydan held Maya tight. He shouldn't be in contact with her soul like that. It reminded him of the connection they shared and how much he craved it. Until they bonded, that special link, along with any physical contact, remained forbidden. That innocence was something Isaac, Maya's stepfather, had struggled to get his head around for a long time. In recent years Isaac had come around to Haydan's ways much more so than previously, although what he would make of their current huddle if he walked into the kitchen right now, Haydan didn't know.

Maya continued snuggling against Haydan, like a small creature burrowing for warmth. He kissed her forehead in a moment of weakness, temporarily letting his barriers down around her. He never normally allowed her anywhere near him, although usually that wasn't a problem because she hated him.

Haydan had no idea how to deal with Diego or Kaleshar. What had started as blind fury in his mind now reduced to ashes and relief that Diego had managed to drive Maya into his arms. It would only be a temporary respite, but it was a welcome reprieve from all the fighting and reminded him of how loving she could be if the right situation presented itself. Diego and Kaleshar would of course tell him that had been the plan all along. Tilting his head back against the kitchen units, he debated how much longer he could bear to be in close contact with her soul before he had to bury all those feelings and push her away again. He wasn't sure his life could get any more complicated, but then everything in his life seemed to work the opposite of the way it was supposed to. Maya wrapped her arms all the way around his back, pulling him in closer. He could feel her breath on his neck. He had to break their connection. Her parents would return home soon and being caught in their current embrace would not do him any favours. Diego's presence would make the scenario appear even odder, to Isaac at least. Katherine, Maya's mother, wouldn't care. To her, this was normal.

Haydan pulled away from Maya, who tried to ignore him and press her head back into the warm spot she had found and taken a liking to at the base of his neck. "Maya, much as this is delightful, I can't stay like this with you all day."

Maya's bottom lip pushed out and she fixed her huge dark eyes onto him and tried to return to the spot that had become so popular. Her eye sockets were dark and her eyes red and watery.

"Maya, I can't do this. You know I can't. I had to get you back and this seemed to work, but I can't hold you like this any longer. Your soul has to crave mine enough to want to bond with me. You can't have the best of both worlds. You know how this works."

Her head lowered. Haydan loved her, but her moods swung on a knife edge. She pushed him away with her arm. Still connected by his altera she couldn't push him far, but her body language clearly indicated normal relations had been resumed. "Maya, don't be like this with me. I need to know you're okay."

Defiance glinted in Maya's eyes as her head raised. "You won't even cuddle me until you get your own way, will you? I'm fine. You can let me go now."

What exactly did Maya want from him? He could never please her. At least she was all right. The cold rebuff of his proximity confirmed that. "Okay, I'm removing my altera now, you can have your freedom back."

Maya released air from her nose rapidly, before sneering at Haydan. "Why thank you, so good of you. Can you get rid of Diego too?" She huffed at Diego as she pushed up from the floor and fled for the door. Her feet pounded up the stairs and a loud bang followed as her bedroom door slammed shut.

The front door opened. Isaac's keys clattered onto the sideboard, before he burst into the kitchen with a surprised look on his face and various shopping bags in his hands. Judging by the strong, pungent smell, they contained food, possibly Chinese or Indian.

"Haydan, Diego. Get Teeam here and we have a full storm on the loose in the kitchen. Where are the girls?" Isaac grinned, apparently entertained by his own joke.

Diego gave Isaac a withering look and returned his attention to Haydan. "We'll talk back home. I expect you will come and find me."

"You can count on it," Haydan said, glaring at Diego.

Diego vanished in an abrupt blast of air, probably to further demonstrate his displeasure at him.

Haydan had delighted in his earlier contact with Maya, but he wasn't willing to confirm that to Diego, especially not in front of Isaac. Diego's disapproval of his relationship with Maya proved a continual problem. Diego wanted him bonded. He could understand why, but he had no intention of trying to force the issue with Maya. She had just spectacularly demonstrated why. Even the presence of Kaleshar didn't give him much respite. Kaleshar had his own agenda, which didn't always tie in with his. Diego was fully aware of that.

Haydan returned his attention to Isaac, who had started unpacking the food. It smelt good. "Diego's not staying. Don't ask why, please."

"I've brought plenty, given that there are always a few spare mouths to feed. I take it you're staying?" Isaac said. He shoved some cans of beer in the fridge and turned back to study Haydan. "Are you going to find the girls for me?"

The idea of returning held some appeal. When on form, Isaac could be entertaining and he appeared to be in a good mood. Haydan rewarded Isaac with a playful grin intended to convey his agreement. A pull in his subconscious refocused his attention on Arianna. Sandau had just attempted to kiss his warrior. That wasn't happening. Arianna could handle herself, her irate father, not so much; plus he had no wish to land her in serious trouble at home. His sneaky elven traits surfaced brushing his mind with all manner of mischief. The human would be far more accepting if Arianna had instigated the kiss herself, rather than the other way around.

"Maya's upstairs in her room in a strop. Arianna has taken to trying to kiss one of our warriors. Or rather, she's not currently fighting him off."

Isaac's smile dropped away. "I take it you're about to

intervene in that."

Haydan shot Isaac an amused smirk. "Yeah, Sandau seems to think I might not realise he's trying to dishonour my warrior. I'm fairly certain Arianna's about to remind him, but I intend to make my presence felt, just to let him know that I'm aware of exactly what she's up to at all times."

Isaac grinned at Haydan. "Good man. I'll keep your food warm, hurry up."

᪥

Arianna

Sandau bowed low before bringing his fists up into a guard stance. His wild, unruly hair made him look rough and dangerous. "You always pick me to fight with. Why don't you just admit you find me irresistible?"

His tone remained teasing. Sandau acted like a free warrior, but he had a storm rider. It had never been made clear who his storm rider was, which simply added to his air of mystery, and Sandau played to that intrigue whenever he could. He moved between various storm riders, never giving away who his true master was. As far as Arianna was aware, he was the only warrior with that ability.

Arianna ignored his digs and focused on her attack. Moving in close, she tried a couple of punches to his face. Sandau easily blocked them. He slid around to her side, into her blind spot, before retaliating with a swift backfist to her face and jab to her waist. Arianna impeded his assault, raising her arm up to protect her face, leaving her ribs open to attack. The jab made it through her defences. Determined not to leave her back undefended, she spun around with Sandau. Her ribs ached, but she didn't bruise easily and he hadn't used much force.

Movement off to Sandau's side drew her attention as a figure approached from the nearby foliage. The figure blended in so well that it could only be shreken. The shreken were a race of warriors that covered their bodies in magical symbols and runes that when activated made them appear almost invisible to the naked eye. They occasionally found their way onto Storm Lands, usually when a storm rider or warrior had interfered in something they shouldn't have and one of their revenge teams had been sent out to deal with the offender. They were only visible by choice, unless they were injured, or the charms protecting them were broken. Sandau appeared oblivious; he still had his back to the creature.

"Sandau, shreken," Arianna said. She reached for her sword held on her back in its sheath.

Sandau still didn't seem to understand the level of threat. There was more movement overhead. It was definitely a revenge team, sent to deal with Sandau by the look of their assault. The nearest figure broke into a run, charging straight at Sandau with a weapon raised above its head.

Shreken warriors fought with swords, axes and twin blade knives. Twin blade knives were lethal. The handle swept into two huge curved blades that seriously maimed or killed anyone who came into contact with them. The warrior lunging for Sandau carried a curved blade.

Sandau grinned. "Oh, come on, Arianna, that's a lame attempt at—"

Ignoring Sandau, Arianna rushed past him and swung her sword, aiming to block the attack. The clash of metal as the blades met sent a jolt down her arm. Her sword skimmed along the curved edge of the shreken weapon. The hilt of her sword slid under the handle and jammed in place. With a yell of fury, she forced the weapon down and to the side, before turning and slamming her full body weight into the attacker. A swift elbow to the head stunned her opponent, who dropped his blade and staggered backwards.

A glance over Arianna's shoulder confirmed Sandau had taken on another two shreken warriors. One was already injured and visible. A huge gash in his arm had opened up and blood dripped onto the ground. Now Storm Lands would know they were under attack. Arianna dropped to her knee and spun, ensuring her leg met with the shreken warrior's ankle. The figure collapsed to the floor. She sank her sword into his body.

Haydan was at Arianna's house with Isaac. She mentally checked in on him, ensuring he was safe, before turning back to Sandau. He punched the shreken warrior he was fighting so hard in the head, she figured the man would be seeing stars for a long time. The injured one was already collapsed in a heap.

"Is your storm rider safe?" Arianna said.

Sandau gave Arianna a mischievous grin as more of their warriors arrived to sweep the surrounding area. "I've kept one of them alive … or just about. He'll be the one to question," he said to the approaching warriors, before turning his attention back to her. "My storm rider is safe, yes, is yours?" The response was accompanied by a smug smile of triumph.

Sandau never gave away the sex of his storm rider either. It was a long-standing joke. She had tried countless times to catch him out. Sandau never fell for her traps. He strode forwards and barged into her, sweeping his leg around hers to land her on the floor before she could do anything to stop him. He landed on top of her. Pinned beneath him, she kept her arms rigid forming a barrier between them. Sandau smirked, before pushing her hands away as though she was nothing more than an annoyance to him.

Up close Arianna could sense Sandau's thrill at fighting. His breathing remained heavy. His eyes glinted with the fire she usually witnessed in training, but there was something else in the depths of his unusual ghosted irises as well, an emotion she couldn't read.

"Thank you for intervening before, although I was just letting you show off a little, you know." Sandau's voice was warm and inviting. Arianna worked out what the intangible emotion was that she couldn't quite place – desire. He dropped his head to capture her mouth. For some strange reason she let him, resisting him for a brief moment, before allowing the kiss to continue longer than she should have. She had never kissed a man before. If truth be told, it wasn't an unpleasant first kiss. Sandau knew what he was doing.

A moment later Arianna came to her senses. Haydan would detect the intrusion. Her arms raised to push Sandau away. "No, get off me. Haydan will know, you idiot."

Sandau pulled away looking delighted by his accomplishment. A shadow loomed over them. Arianna turned her head to find boots next to her. She tracked upwards. Haydan stood glaring down at her with his coat blowing around, adding to his menacing edge. Her heart sank; he didn't look amused.

"We have a shreken revenge team on Storm Lands and you both decide to celebrate your success in taking–" Haydan surveyed the collapsed figures "–three of them out, by rolling about in the grass together. Really? I expected better behaviour from both of you and a sense of responsibility. Sandau, have you checked your storm rider is safe? I've a good mind to have you both disciplined."

Sandau stood. Pushing his shoulders back, he squared up to Haydan. He was taller than Haydan, although that didn't seem to bother Arianna's storm rider, who still looked incensed.

"I kissed Arianna," Sandau said, wiping the back of his hand across his mouth as though reminding himself that it had just been in contact with hers.

Haydan's nostrils flared. He had an enhanced sense of smell. He would be able to smell her on Sandau. The realisation made Arianna cringe.

"If you want to get anyone disciplined take it up with my storm rider, because you don't get to touch me." Sandau raised his eyebrow as his mouth turned down in a sneer. "No unbonded rider is touching me."

There was a flicker of hesitation on Haydan's face, a tiny flash of uncertainty, or dislike of Sandau's challenge perhaps. He disguised it quickly, but Arianna noticed it. Her fists clenched. That was what Maya didn't see: the fact that even other warriors looked down on Haydan, taking any opportunity to goad him.

"I would watch my mouth if I was you, Sandau. Unlike Arianna, I do know who your storm rider is and I will be having words about this, you can count on it." Haydan locked his steely glare onto Sandau, who narrowed his eyes but remained where he was.

"Arianna, get on your feet now." Haydan slid his cold stare to Arianna before walking off. He shot another glare at Sandau over his shoulder as Diego approached off to his side. "Stay away from my warrior," Haydan said to Sandau as he waited for Arianna to scramble to her feet, catch him up and walk past him, before ushering her away and following her.

Diego moved alongside Haydan as they walked. Sandau fell into line behind them. "I have to question the only remaining shreken and find out what their team was doing here," Diego said. "If we have shreken revenge teams on Storm Lands, you need to stay out of the main areas. Consider yourself confined to your snug for the time being. Arianna, you will return home and stay put unless an emergency arises."

"I will return to my snug after I have checked Maya is alright after earlier," Haydan said.

What was the point of being warrior when at the first hint of danger, she was told to stay put? "I just defended Sandau. He was too busy drooling at me to notice. I am more than capable of defending Haydan if the need arises," Arianna said.

Diego glared at Arianna. He didn't speak but he rested his cold, sinister eyes on her, ensuring they silently conveyed his displeasure, letting her experience his disapproval full force. "Get your women in hand. I'm getting fed up with their belligerence." With that Diego turned to Sandau and stalked off with him towards their new shreken prisoner.

Now Arianna would get a lecture from Haydan. She released a heavy sigh of resignation. Every time she took a wrong turn he descended on her like a ton weight.

Chapter 5

ᚻaydan

Arianna flinched as Haydan's eyes met hers. Her cold glare reflected her displeasure at his intervention.

"I did just protect Sandau. He was being overly confident. He took advantage of me. I'm fully aware that his actions were inappropriate, but that is down to Sandau's storm rider to deal with."

"You didn't appear to be in a rush to break it off. You only did so when you remembered I would know. I don't appreciate finding you rolling about in the grass with Sandau, Arianna." Haydan captured her gaze with his, holding it until she lowered her head and her face flushed.

"I know. I apologise for not dealing with him sooner and for putting you in an awkward position. Sandau spoke to you out of turn," Arianna said.

Haydan refused to show how much that comment got to him. Defending an elder from danger took a certain amount of bravery and bravado. Sandau enjoyed an unusual status. He was held in high regard and frequently took advantage of that situation. Sandau's strange ghosted irises also hinted at his unusual heritage, which was never openly discussed. It wasn't a subject Haydan could easily address with Diego either. Based on previous conversations, Diego would tell him to accept the situation, and that would only change when he bonded with Maya. He refocused on Arianna, who looked a tiny bit apologetic.

"Your actions reflect on me too. Keep that in mind in future, warrior."

Arianna nodded, focusing on the floor at Haydan's feet. "Understood, but Sandau kissed me." She raised her eyes to meet his.

It was no surprise that Arianna's belligerence had returned. It always did. For some inexplicable reason Haydan felt the need to return fire. Maybe it was just to see the look on her face when she realised her home wouldn't be a sea of tranquillity when she returned. "We're going back to your house. Isaac knows Sandau has just kissed you. I made sure he was aware of the transgression."

The tightening of Arianna's hands into fists added a small measure of victory to the moment as Haydan dropped his storm cloud around her to return them to her house. The brush of the breeze against his skin provided a tiny bit of comfort that morning and he needed plenty of that given how much antagonism he faced from every quarter.

Haydan's chat with Isaac, Katherine and Arianna was brief. He made his way through to the lounge. Maya was sitting on the smaller sofa with her head down. She looked sullen as he entered the room and refused to acknowledge him.

"There's food in the kitchen if you want some," Haydan said. Unsure what mood she was in, he moved to the other seat and threw himself onto the chaise longue, throwing his arms out along the back of it before he dropped his head forwards.

Maya remained silent but brooding. Uncomfortable silence stretched out and she raised her head to lock her eyes on Haydan's. "Right, because I want Isaac and Mum giving me grief over what happened earlier."

"Isaac doesn't *know* what happened earlier. It's up to you whether you tell him. You can't not eat, beautiful. Your parents are more likely to give you grief over not eating than they are stirring my father up. Are you okay? I don't like seeing you so upset, although I did enjoy the rare treat of having you helpless in my arms."

Haydan kept his tone playful, hoping to tease a smile out of Maya. The edge of her lips twitched and she smothered a grin. It was only slight, but it eased his fear of finding himself on the receiving end of one of her teenage strops. "I don't ask for much, Maya, but I would really appreciate it if you wouldn't antagonise my father. I need to speak to Diego, and Kaleshar too, the little traitor, but you have to help me out a little bit, yes?"

Maya shrugged before focusing on Haydan. It began to unnerve him. He raised his head, meeting her measured scrutiny with what he hoped was a conciliatory look.

"What now? I'm tired of the fighting, it's exhausting. I can't breathe without you turning on me at the moment. I don't know what you want from me. I've already told you I won't force the bond on you. We're nothing more than friends right now. You have all the space you need, but I still feel like you hate me. Then you go and rile my father, almost get yourself reset and in that moment when you absolutely lose it, it's my soul that brings you back from the brink. It's the most torment I have ever endured. I'm under no illusion that my respite is temporary, but how can you swing so violently from one extreme to the other?"

Haydan's altera still tingled from the contact with Maya's soul earlier that evening. It had been like a drug sliding into his system when he held her like he had, with his soul wrapped around hers. Now it was all he could think about. That was why he stepped away from her. That was why he put barriers up and maintained distance. Whenever he moved too close he could sense her soul. It called to him, taunting him with something he couldn't and wouldn't have for a long time. She was everything he desired, but her confused expression confirmed he was no closer to getting what he wanted from her.

Did he detect a hint of distrust or accusation in the manner in which Maya was studying him? His conscience prickled. Maybe he shouldn't have formed the temporary connection between their souls. It was too late to backtrack now. "You moved your soul towards mine when you were collapsed on the floor. I had to do something to stop you from destroying yourself. You wouldn't stop screaming."

Maya slid her hands underneath her legs, palm down, and leant forwards. The focus of her attention appeared to be the huge, fluffy, olive green rug that showcased the large driftwood and glass coffee table in the middle of the room. "Why do you never talk about your heritage?"

Maya's throaty, soft voice suggested she remained

in a calm, relaxed mood. Haydan found her change of subject disorientating. "My heritage?" He had no wish to get into a discussion about his family with her. If she wanted to open up a debate about Tallin, the conversation would sour quickly. Maya's attention shifted from the coffee table back to Haydan, but she didn't meet his eyes directly.

"Tallin, you never talk about him. I thought you might want to go back to see him at some point. I could come with you."

Maya finally met Haydan's stare. He didn't want to discuss Tallin, and Maya's prying felt unwelcome. This was the second time in twenty-four hours he had been challenged by someone close to him about the fae king. 'Why is everyone obsessed with Tallin today? Teeam was on my back about it earlier as well. Has my grandfather been in touch with you?"

Still not meeting Haydan's eyes, Maya glanced towards the window. "No. I just hoped you might think about it. Tallin wanted you to go back to visit him. What happens if he comes looking for you?" Maya chewed her bottom lip, apparently finding the coffee table fascinating again.

"I know you're lying to me. I'm just not sure why. Is Tallin harassing you, or did he give you something when we visited him last time so he can contact you?" That made sense; Tallin had spent time alone with Maya. She was Tallin's route to Haydan and like Lavinia, Tallin would use that to his advantage. Maya fidgeted before shaking her head, still not meeting his eyes.

Last time they visited the fae realm, Maya had been young. There was nothing she still had with her that she had taken into the realm ... except the bracelet Haydan gifted her before he left. She hadn't worn that for the last couple of weeks. "You're not wearing your bracelet."

Maya's eyes widened in surprise as her startled stare clashed with Haydan's. There was his answer.

"Where is your bracelet? Is there a reason why you've abandoned it?"

The thrum of Maya's heartbeat racing indicated her discomfort. The bracelet was Tallin's route to contact her. There was no other explanation for her sudden panic.

"I left it off. Do you really want to fall out over this?" Maya asked, rewarding Haydan with another resentful look. "It reminded me of the influence you like to exert over my life, so I ditched it for a bit. Is that a problem?"

Maya was being far too defensive over the bracelet, so much so it made Haydan even more suspicious. The thought of touching something Tallin had meddled with made him feel ill and, of course, Tallin could have booby-trapped it in case Haydan did find it.

"I liked Tallin. I'd like to go back and visit him. You never do what I want." Maya shot Haydan a disgruntled look and stood, moving towards the door.

Maya wasn't escaping Haydan that easily. He flicked his hand, slamming the door shut as she neared the escape route. "Now you're in a rush to leave me. Was it something I said?" He feigned innocence, wondering if she would trip herself up. "I don't like my grandfather's deviousness, or the fact that Lavinia planned to trap us both. Tallin is the other half of Lavinia's soul. Don't be fooled by his innocent act. He's used to getting his own way and likes playing games. That's never a good combination for me." Standing, he noticed the way she studied his movements. She remained very much aware of his physical presence. In such close proximity to her, he could sense the contented thrum of her soul. It intensified as he moved closer, luring him. The realisation that she remained submissive sent a thrill of delight through him as he advanced.

"You're not trapping me here."

Maya backed up against the oak door as Haydan approached until her entire body was pressed back against it. Her gaze darted to either side of him; perhaps she was reviewing escape routes.

Haydan held up his hands, palms facing her. "I haven't trapped you. My hands are up here. I've not laid a finger on you." Her eyes tracked the swirling underside of his altera. He moved his hand out slowly, aiming his palm towards the solid oak door. Maya followed his altera, as though mesmerised by it. The surface of the door felt cool to the touch. As he brought his palm to rest on the smooth wood he angled the altera towards her cheek and studied the myriad of emotions that flitted across her face at the proximity. Confusion and conflict mingled with desire and yearning. Her breathing quickened, soft breaths brushing his face as her eyes remained on his.

"I know what you're doing, Haydan."

Maya licked her lips, her tongue sweeping across her bottom lip in a way that drew his attention. What would she do if he did come in close enough to kiss her? He shouldn't allow himself the contact, although it was far too tempting. He wanted the bond first; only then would he lower his defences and let her beneath them, but what harm would a kiss do? Sure, Diego would be aware of their proximity to each other, but Diego wanted Haydan bonded, so anything that moved him towards that goal had to be a good thing. Of course,

Maya didn't know that Diego would be aware of any physical contact between them. The idea of his father being able to veto any impropriety was embarrassing and she would probably find that fact mortifying as well. He was in no rush to share the news with her and she would likely avoid any contact with him if she found out, which added to his desolation. Plus, it would give her more ammunition to use in their arguments about bonding. He slid his other arm up against the door, trapping her between his arms but still not touching her. Now she didn't know where to look. Her cheeks warmed as her eyes lowered to his mouth, then tracked up to his eyes. He couldn't help smiling at her innocence as he moved in closer.

Indignation fired in the depths of Maya's irises, igniting like wildfire. "You think this is funny now you've proved your point? I've told you why I'm not wearing the bracelet—"

Haydan didn't let Maya finish. He moved in and planted a gentle kiss on her mouth. Her intake of breath told him she liked that. He lingered. She tasted of cherry lip balm. Her lips were warm and soft. A quick pause when he studied her eyes for any sign of doubt or hesitancy confirmed she welcomed the contact as much as he did. He kissed her harder, deepening the kiss as his fingertips cupped her warm face.

Arianna exploded out of the kitchen with a squeal of laughter. "Daddy, that's so wrong," she said.

Haydan placed his palm against Maya's shoulder. Trapping her against the door, he braced his foot against the bottom of it. The door handle rattled as Arianna tried to enter the lounge.

"Give us a minute, Arianna."

Silence returned before Arianna giggled. "Why, what are you up to? You're not kissing as well, are you? If you are you're a total hypocrite, plus that's gross. You've got about three seconds until Daddy gatecrashes the party to commandeer the lounge."

Isaac understood the arrangement between Maya and Haydan, well aware Haydan maintained a no-contact policy with Maya, which was rigorously enforced by Diego until they bonded. Isaac had goaded him about it on a number of occasions, initially finding it amusing, before wisely letting it drop when he realised it was a touchy subject. His expression unamused, Haydan returned his attention to Maya, who rolled her eyes in response to Arianna's goading.

"You didn't think it gross when Sandau tried to give you the kiss of life earlier," Haydan said to Arianna.

Maya's eyes widened in shock at Haydan's announcement. "Who's Sandau? You need to let me go. I don't want Isaac teasing me. I'll never hear the last of it," she said.

With a grin of amusement, Haydan released his foot and moved back from Maya. "He's warrior. I'll see you soon."

"Thank you." Maya stepped towards him, placed warm fingers against his jaw and planted an unexpected gentle kiss on his mouth.

What was she thanking him for now? He had no clue, but a willing kiss would never be turned away.

"For earlier. For rescuing me from Diego." Her voice sounded shaky and bewildered. "I couldn't let him reset me." Her expression was one of rapt adoration. "No one is ever touching my soul again, except for you. You're the *only* exception."

Was it possible to love her more than he did already?

In moments like these, he did. Rewarding her with a cheeky grin, he blew her a kiss before he vanished.

ॐ

Maya

The following morning after breakfast, Maya ran back up to her room and slid her hand under her pillow. The bracelet warmed as she wrapped her fingers around it, before turning hotter as she picked it up and studied it. She bounced it between her hands. "Ouch, okay, okay, Tallin, I get that you're peeved at me. Let's talk." It immediately cooled. Gripping it tight, she ran out into the garden, making for the large oval pods hanging from the trees in the woodland area.

The autumnal air felt cool and damp. Haydan had placed magic on the large, metal, egg-shaped cocoons. They were padded inside so they felt cosy and warm no matter how cold it was outside. Maya's favourite was the white one, which was also the one furthest from the house. She clambered inside, comforted by the way the external sounds became muted as though she had just entered another world. Crouching down, she backed up against the side before holding the bracelet up and studying it as she searched for the hidden fae charm. The bracelet acquired a new heart every year she and Haydan were together. There were now fifteen visible charms and the fae charm was well disguised. It was only when the air distorted around the edge of the hidden one that she found it. Preparing herself for an experience that would no doubt be unwelcome, she flicked it with her fingertip three times.

Magic exploded out, distorting the air as it swirled around. Maya tensed, her heart pounding as Tallin materialised in front of her. He was at full height and banged his head on the roof before bracing his arms on either side of the pod. He wore a long slate-grey coat, with a huge hood, which was made from soft felt. The collar of a white shirt was visible beneath a light grey waistcoat which had military-style buttons across the front of it. The royal crest with the wolf and eagle covered the brushed metal buttons and ran down each side of the coat. Closer inspection confirmed the design on the coat was moving. The eagle swooped around, the wolf prowled. Shooting her an odd look, Tallin scanned his surroundings.

"Where are we?" Tallin asked, his tone sharp.

He didn't appear in a good mood. His elegant eyebrows quirked as he gave Maya a look that suggested she answer him and quickly.

"In a pod in my garden," Maya said, wondering why Tallin appeared confused. "If you sit down it stops swinging as badly."

"We are on Earth?" Tallin asked, still looking unsure.

"Yes, we're on Earth. Where else would we be?" Maya couldn't keep the curtness out of her response and it hadn't gone unnoticed. Tallin refocused on her with the intensity of a hawk.

That mysterious look was back, the one that suggested Tallin had either found something amusing, or he was irritated by something. The edge of his mouth twisted.

"Oh, I am sorry, for a minute I thought I was in a very small snug. So, you have been ignoring me. Care to explain why? There are occasions when I need to contact you urgently, to protect you and Haydan. I cannot do that so easily when you ignore me."

"You want me to bring Haydan back into your realm. That's not so straightforward right now. Relations between me and Control Freak aren't good at the moment. I don't want to spend time with him unless I have to." Was it really Tallin in the pod with Maya? A chunky silver ring glinted on his finger. The stone embedded in it shimmered as she studied it. He definitely hadn't been wearing that last time she saw him. Reaching out, she grabbed a handful of Tallin's long jacket. The soft, luxurious fabric crumpled. It felt real enough. She pulled on it. Tallin peered down at her, his expression fierce. "Could you sit down? It's hurting my neck to look up at you," she said.

Tallin gave a soft laugh and collapsed onto the padded floor, folding his legs underneath him. The pod rocked violently. He looked pleased with his achievement as he studied Maya. "Control Freak? I assume that is a derogatory way of accusing my grandson of being controlling?" His eyes narrowed as he tilted his head. "I sympathise, but you should learn to use that to your advantage. Haydan adores you. You really are fascinating, Maya, but do not touch me again, please." He arched an eyebrow as he scrutinised her. "I do not like being mauled and you would be wise to remember I am king of the fae realm, not one of your Earth friends."

Wow, Tallin was being really defensive. "Okay, I was just checking if this is definitely you or some illusion. You wanted to see me, I'm here. What do you want, Tallin?"

Tallin's head lowered as he interlinked his long,

elegant fingers together. "Are you trying to be amusing? No one speaks to me like that, not even Levi." He fixed her with a harsh glare, then sniffed, as he pushed his shoulders back. "Things have taken on some urgency since I first tried to contact you. I no longer have the luxury of time. You, Haydan and Arianna are all in danger because of the mask. That means I have to bring things forward a little. Control Freak won't like my plan…"

Her term of endearment for Haydan was stated with a strong hint of sarcasm or condescension. Tallin was up to something. Every sense Maya possessed warned her to be on her guard.

Calculation burned in Tallin's intense gaze as he added, "But I am counting on that."

A small purple head pushed out of the pocket on his jacket, followed by two small hands that grabbed the top of the pocket. Maya pointed towards it. Tallin glanced down and a devilish grin spread across his face. He reached a hand out, allowing the small creature to clamber across to his palm where it stood for a moment as Tallin brought the creature level with his face. It looked as though it had been electrocuted. All its purple hair stood to attention. "Go find the warriors. Arianna is Haydan's warrior. Sandau is Diego's. They deliberately act like they have nothing to do with each other, but do not be fooled by appearances, or what they tell you. Tell them what I am about to do and invite them and their storm riders to join us. I am hosting a grand masked ball and they are all invited."

The small creature frowned and cocked its head, before beckoning Tallin closer and whispering something to him that Maya couldn't catch. Tallin's smile softened. A playful twinkle in his eyes enhanced the mischievousness he exuded. He was acting more like the man she remembered from last time she visited his realm.

"Give them the royal invitation and include Princess Maya in that. My ego likes the formality and flamboyance and it will stir Haydan and Diego into immediate action." Tallin raised his shoulders up as though delighted by his achievement. He swiftly followed this up with another of his devilish grins.

"What is that and what do you mean, what you're about to do?" Maya asked. She glanced at the exit, which was to her side. Tallin sat facing her. She had no way out. As her attention returned to him, he gave her a calculating look and leant forwards resting his elbows on his knees. The small creature climbed off his palm and made for the door.

"Why, you're coming back with me, of course. The others will follow on. I like getting my own way. You should already understand that, and that is a bewitched pixie, or a pixie post as I like to call them. He is the fae equivalent of a delivery boy. Diego loves him." Mischief glinted in Tallin's dark eyes again suggesting he was being heavily sarcastic.

Throwing her head back, Maya faked a cold laugh. "Oh right, nice one. You're funny. You can't travel like the riders do. This is a trick, isn't it? I'm out of here."

Maya stood but Tallin sprang to his feet with unnatural speed. She had forgotten how tall he was. He couldn't stand full height as the top of the snug restricted his head, but even with his head forward, the fierceness of his expression confirmed she had underestimated him. He shook his head as she tried edging past him. His arm moved across blocking her only escape route.

"The benefit of being me is I like to keep everyone guessing and if I want to travel like the riders do, there is little to stop me." His voice laced with wickedness, Tallin leant in, a cunning smile tugging his cheeks upwards. "You should know better than to misjudge me."

Tallin was bluffing surely? But then he had just materialised in the pod with Maya. She had grabbed his jacket and it was as real as she was. "Haydan will be furious. You can't possibly expect to kidnap me and get away with it?"

Tallin's shoulders raised as his mouth turned down at the edges. "Oh, he is Haydan now, is he? He was Control Freak a moment ago. I do not tend to go for abduction. I am more of a master of persuasion, but the clock is ticking. I hope you have not eaten recently." He reached for her.

Maya squealed and tried to block Tallin as he moved in and slung an arm around her waist, pulling her against him. Before she could even register feeling nauseous at the contact, the air swirled around her and the interior of the garden pod vanished.

"Hold your breath, Maya. You are about to get very cold and wet."

Chapter 6

Haydan

Standing in his father's snug, with Arianna beside him, Haydan waited for Diego and Teeam to explain what was going on. He had been summoned to his father's side just as Storm Lands locked down. This meant no one could enter or leave. Diego was sitting on one of the padded, luxurious seats that surrounded the ornate metal fire basket that occupied the middle of the central sunken area. Teeam was positioned to the side, his expression grave. Sandau loitered behind Diego with his hands resting on the backrest. Haydan shuffled his feet, hoping someone would speak to break the intolerable silence that had descended. He cleared his throat and Diego looked up and waved his hand, indicating for Haydan to take a seat.

"Sit down, both of you. I feel suffocated enough right now, without you looking at me like that. Sandau, you too, please. Your pacing is becoming irritating. I'm safe here," Diego said.

"I'm comfortable where I am right now," Sandau said.

Sandau had a perfect view of Arianna and stood

guard over his storm rider looking pleased with himself. His announcement didn't surprise Haydan, although he did shoot Arianna a warning glare to ignore Sandau and his posturing.

Teeam cleared his throat. "We've managed to get the shreken warrior who survived his encounter with two of our finest to talk. Well, I was persuasive enough to convince him helping us would be wise. It seems the revenge shreken team were in fact a bounty team, attempting to capture Sandau and his storm rider for a very lucrative contract. He was wary of revealing who offered the bounty, but I would hazard a guess that the dark gods are involved."

"No one knows who Sandau's storm rider is and he's never been very forthcoming with the information," Arianna said. Her stare locked with Sandau's ghosted irises as though setting him a challenge.

Diego raised his head, his green eyes flaring with indignation. "That's because it's no one else's business. Sandau is *my* warrior. That information does not leave this snug. Is that clear?"

Blinking a few times, Arianna nodded. "Perfectly clear. I will not speak of it again, unless you do first."

That was a surprising reply from Arianna. It was the first time Haydan had heard her speak in such a mature and responsible way in front of an elder. Even Diego studied her for a moment longer than necessary, as though startled.

"It's not who Sandau answers to that concerns me right now. I'm more concerned by who placed a contract with a large bounty on my head and you should be too, because Haydan is next in line to me. If the dark gods want me, then you and Haydan are likely to be next on their list of acquisitions." Diego ran a hand over his jaw, studying Arianna with a long, hard look as the news sank in. "That was the first team to find Sandau. They probably thought he would be easier to capture than me. Once they work out the first team failed, they will soon send more. If they fail to deliver, then we may find the dark gods walking our land for the very first time."

"None of you are safe in this realm right now," Teeam said. He scanned the room, settling his attention on Haydan. "Especially not unbonded storm riders; if they find their way to you, Haydan, Diego will have no choice but to give himself up to protect you. I can't risk that happening. None of you can stay."

"Why do they want us?" Haydan asked. Diego looked pale, like he hadn't slept much the previous night. His father's concern was worrying. Haydan knew about the dark gods from Theander, but how much of that information he could share he didn't know.

Diego leant forwards, resting his elbows on his knees. "Haydan, you control an artefact that descends from the gods. The fact they have chosen to take me first suggests they either want me to get to you or, and this is what I'm hoping, they think I control the mask and haven't figured out your part in it yet."

Diego's focus flitted between Haydan and Arianna before resting on Haydan. The intensity made him feel uncomfortable.

"What do you know about the dark gods, Haydan?"

Haydan was certain Diego wouldn't like his answer. "I've already told you, I have to be careful about what I share from Acquorous…"

"Don't you dare stonewall me on this." Diego's tone terse, fury surfaced in his eyes like a tsunami. The various shades of green exploded in rapid succession, finishing with a flare of silvery green, flowing through the irises like a flash flood down a river, before settling back into their normal colour. "I asked a question of you as elder. Your life is in danger. Your warrior and chosen one, everyone connected to you is in danger. I need to know what you know about the dark gods, now."

Diego's flare of anger alarmed Haydan. He rarely raised his voice. The intense way he studied Haydan suggested he move to answer his father's question and quickly. "I can't walk freely on Acquorous because the dark gods don't know the mask has been found and that I'm its master. Theander keeps my presence concealed. If they find out, it would become problematic because they originally sought it when the mask surfaced the first time around. Theander has tried to talk to me about it since, but I always shut him down."

Diego's eyes narrowed. Sandau focused on Haydan as though trying to read his body language.

The staring became irritating. "Why are you looking at me like that, warrior? If you have something to say, say it," Haydan said, meeting Sandau's speculative glare with his own defiant one.

Sandau tilted his head, then smirked. "You shut Theander down? Let me give you a piece of advice. When a god wants to open a discussion, you would be wise to take the opportunity. Diego wants names from you. He needs to know if you understand exactly who you are up against and how many dark gods you are potentially taking on. They will tear Storm Lands apart to get to you and anyone they can use as leverage. Storm Lands locking down has bought you time, but once the first bounty team is considered missing, they will send more. If that doesn't prove productive, the dark gods themselves will enter the fray. That's the point when it gets interesting, storm rider. Have you ever met a dark god? Have you ever fought one?" Sandau's eyebrows lifted as he shot Haydan a quizzical look.

Diego and Teeam remained silent, leaving Haydan with an uncomfortable challenge from his father's warrior, which he was expected to respond to. "Kai has a brother. He has never been named in my presence. I have no idea how many children the unnamed god has fathered, so I don't know how many dark gods are potentially involved and I've never met one, Sandau, no. Have you?"

Sandau surveyed Haydan with that same irritating expression, part condescension, part arrogance. "I've met Iskar in a previous cycle, yes. He is Kai's brother. I've never fought him, but I've seen the destruction that being is capable of and it turns my blood cold just thinking about it," Sandau said.

Haydan blinked, rapidly readjusting his view of Sandau. Diego and Teeam's silence suggested they had bowed to Sandau's greater knowledge of the dark gods. As far as Haydan knew, no one had ever met a dark god and they were never named, not even by other gods.

"The dark gods are dark for a reason. They are beyond any form of persuasion or understanding. If they want something, they take it. If they want you dead, it's a matter of time to them. Asanda would prefer them all locked in his vaults. Unfortunately, they are not easy to catch. You are friends with Theander as I understand it. You had better hope you have a good, strong friendship and you matter to him, because the only gods powerful enough to take on Iskar and win are Theander, Kai and Asanda, although I doubt Asanda will intervene unless his two most favoured boys are in danger." Sandau's attention switched from Haydan to Arianna and back again, before returning to Diego. "Your boy needs to be bonded, or all three are in danger. His lack of bond makes you appear weak too and gives Iskar a route to hurt you."

Diego shook his head, meeting Haydan's wide-eyed stare with an understanding expression before focusing back on the snug floor. "I'm not going to order Haydan to force the bond on Maya. I've seen her reaction when she doesn't want to do something and let's just say it will spectacularly backfire, plus they can't spend bonding night here. It's too dangerous."

"You know where you have to send them. He's already spoken to you about it. You should go with them. That way this realm is out of harm's way and you, Lavinia and Tallin can protect them if the need arises. If the dark gods come looking for you here, it will become clear very quickly that you are not around," Teeam said. He sank down onto the seat beside Diego. Silence returned, the air growing oppressive again.

"I can't leave this realm open to the dark gods, Teeam. If I'm going, I have to make it obvious I'm going so, to draw their attention away from here." Diego raked a hand through his hair. "Ironically, I'm going to have to ask my father for help."

"What's wrong with my chantillian cave?" Haydan asked. That was their place of sanctuary. Each rider had their own chantillian cave where they could conceal themselves from the world and no one knew where it was except the storm rider who owned it.

Sandau sneered. "You think you can hide from the

dark gods here? You can't hide from them. Your only hope right now is to keep ahead of them and pray that when they find you, Theander or the mask manage to outsmart them somehow. If you stay here, you and anyone connected to you is potentially going to die."

Haydan stood and began pacing. "But why Tallin's realm? I don't like it there. He's overwhelming, controlling and…"

Diego brought the discussion to an end as he stood and glared across at Haydan, his expression cold and uncompromising. "You are going to Tallin whether you like it or not. That is an order from an elder, not just your father. Take Kaleshar and Arianna with you." Diego turned his attention to Teeam. "I need regular sweeps of Katherine's home to ensure their families are safe. If the dark gods work out there are wards on that property set by the gods it will draw their interest." He fell silent for a moment, letting that news sink in.

Haydan had known for a while that the wards on Maya's home were set by the gods. The reminder from Diego made him wonder once again who had set the wards and why. He would perhaps ask Theander, who must have noticed the unusual protection that the property Isaac owned carried. It was a new property, built when Maya was very young, which meant the gods had recently entered the vicinity of the property to set the wards. Unless Isaac happened to have picked a plot of land that already carried the wards, which was unlikely. The wards ended on the edge of the property itself as though deliberately set.

"I need talk to you about Maya and what happened yesterday. You've refused to meet me since and–"

"Enough. This is not the time to be discussing that."

Surveying everyone gathered, Diego drew himself up. "I will follow you with Sandau once I know the dark gods will bypass this realm and follow us into Tallin's. Teeam, you will have to help me with that."

Teeam nodded in response, his golden eyes alert and wary.

"Is there any sign of Rebekka yet?" Diego asked as though he was also unsure of his partner's whereabouts.

Teeam shook his head. "No, she's gone to ground recently." He turned his attention to Haydan. "You will have to keep your wits about you in Tallin's realm. There are many unresolved issues from our last visit. Trust no one beyond your closest connections."

Haydan scratched at his head, ruffling his hair. He hated being treated like a child. "I'm aware of the issues in Tallin's realm, Tallin being one of them as far as I'm concerned. He might have invited us back, but I'm not bonded, so I'm understandably wary. The woodland where we enter is safe, but beyond that…"

Diego made a noise, something akin to disagreement. "Arianna, talk to your storm rider, explain to him what Maya has told you about her time with Tallin. Haydan needs to understand that the woodland is a grey area as well. Tallin controls it and it may not be the same as last time you entered. There are those in his court who covet power sources. Tallin acts like he has full control, but that healer, Leylani, is still in that realm and I'm sure she's capable of hiding her deceit from Tallin. I do not want to hear you have been kidnapped because you were not fully aware of the dangers." Warning glinted in the steely cold green of Diego's intense stare. "She probably knows how to capture you and you would be a fitting form of recompense to a woman who was crossed last time we entered that realm. She wanted Teeam. He got away. You are a route to hurt the king and wield power over him."

"Haydan doesn't listen to me and doesn't like to talk about Tallin," Arianna said, not meeting Diego's eyes and instead opting to challenge Sandau's smug, contemptuous expression.

His ghosted irises glowed in response as though he approved of her belligerence. Haydan gritted his teeth in irritation at their flirting. Regardless of whether Arianna knew what she was doing, she was well aware of Sandau's taste for feisty, confident personalities.

That response from Arianna drew Diego's attention. He swung towards her, with his head lowered and his expression livid. "What is it with the two of you?" Diego's terse question left no doubt that he was in a bad mood. "I might disagree with Sandau on occasion, but I trust him with my life and that of my offspring and those closest to my children, but you two? You have a massive trust issue. You can't work together if you don't trust each other and I sense that, Haydan–" Diego's attention switched to Haydan, his glare icy "– you are always battling for supremacy with your own warrior. Does she not defer to you in a manner that pleases you? Do you not trust Arianna?"

Arianna's eyes locked on Haydan with the intensity of a predator stalking prey. The seconds ticked by as he debated his answer. He did trust Arianna, but he doubted her. Why did he question her? He was supposed to place his life in her hands and trust her to defend him to the death when he was in danger or under attack. She was his defence when his magic couldn't help him, or when he was too busy using his magic to worry about immediate danger. He always battled with her for supremacy, but then she never fully deferred to him in a manner that satisfied him. She never gave him her complete and utter respect and submission when he asked it of her and her defiance remained at all times. It rippled beneath the surface, ready to burst free at any opportunity and that always set him on edge.

Arianna's jaw flexed as she returned her sullen gaze to Diego. Haydan had hurt her with his silence. Her glassy eyes reflected her ire as she blinked a few times.

"Well, doesn't the silence speak volumes, my liege?" Arianna's cold tone dripped with animosity, every syllable carefully pronounced to convey her utter fury at Haydan. He had effectively just denounced her in front of two elders and another warrior.

"I do trust you, Arianna. I just…" How could Haydan put into words what he really thought without causing a massive argument with Arianna? "You eternally challenge me."

"You never show confidence in me!" Arianna glared across at Haydan, her mouth a thin line as she fixed him with one of her menacing looks usually reserved for battle. "What do you expect, storm rider, when you deflect me like you do? I will cease to challenge you when you grant me the respect I am due as warrior. Or am I not worthy?"

Haydan's skin prickled. Teeam, Diego and Sandau stood in silence watching their epic showdown, with a look on their faces of complete shock. His cheeks warmed as he debated how to respond. Arianna did have a point. He never allowed her to step up to the mark. He always pushed her to the side as though he didn't need her. It was disrespectful, but he didn't know how to resolve the current situation.

Diego's attention moved to Sandau. "You are taking Haydan into Tallin's realm. Arianna is following on with me." Before either of them could object, Diego folded his arms and raised his head, defiance and authority flowing from him. "I suggest no one challenge my decision at this point. You're not fit to travel together and I will not allow you to enter Tallin's realm whilst this festers. It will land either one of you or both of you in great danger. My decision is final."

Diego sank back down into the seat opposite. The strain showed in his face, which looked tired and drawn. He rubbed a hand across his jaw as Sandau moved forwards.

"I'm not happy at leaving your side to babysit your son. I appreciate the trust and honour placed in me for this task, but protecting you is my primary objective. I can't do that if I'm apart from you."

Diego stood and placed his hand on Sandau's shoulder. "You have to guard my eldest son. I can't trust Arianna with that responsibility when neither of them are ready to step up and respect their roles. I have to give you that responsibility."

"Why do you not understand? You know how Arianna defies me," Haydan said, not caring if he sounded belligerent. Diego was dismissing him with his usual finesse and he hated that.

Diego's nose wrinkled as he stared down Haydan with a ferocity that would have alarmed him if Diego wasn't his father. Diego looked like a wild thing stirring from slumber as he filled the snug with his physical presence and the energy that released from his body in a swift blast of aggression: a warning to Haydan to watch himself. "You chose to leave the sea with two of the most awkward, challenging females I've ever encountered. You chose one to protect you and one to love you. Neither seems to be doing either very successfully right now, or does the problem lie with you? There must be some reason for your choice. The gods believe women to be fierce protectors of their men, so I'm praying that's your logic."

Haydan remained silent.

Diego looked even more livid. "Storm alive, Haydan, I assume you know what you're doing because if you don't, you'll have more than a dark god, his pack of hellhounds and a mask to worry about. I'll throw you back in the sea and strip you of your storm rider status if you let me down."

It felt as though the floor lurched beneath Haydan. Pulling away from Diego, he spun and stared off into the distance trying to gauge what Maya was up to. His senses were assaulted by the strong masculine scent that engulfed Maya as she was dragged beyond his reach. For a brief second, he thought the dark gods had found Maya first. His stomach churned at her contact with another male. He doubled over and contemplated if he was about to land his breakfast on Diego's feet just to finish off his morning perfectly.

"Breathe, Haydan."

An arm around his shoulder brought him to his senses. His heart thundered. His body warm and disorientated, his vision lurched as he tried to familiarise himself with the odd sensation that had just assaulted him.

Diego had moved to his side. "Sit down and focus. What's just happened? Can you reach Maya?"

Haydan shook his head as his father pushed him down onto the seat. He couldn't reach her. The more he tried to contact her, the more his attempt amplified and bounced back to him. The jarring sensation added to his discomfort.

Arianna dropped down into a crouch in front of him, concern furrowing her brow as she peered up at Haydan. "She's activated that charm bracelet, hasn't she? Tallin gifted her a charm, a way to reach him when the need arose. I warned her about doing that without telling you first."

"You know about that? Why didn't you tell me?" Haydan demanded. Arianna had kept a secret from him, one that was important and he had a right to know. He should have taken the charm bracelet off Maya the previous night, but he hadn't wanted to touch anything that Tallin had meddled with.

"I hate being in the middle of the two of you, but Maya tells me things she won't share with you. I keep her trust for a reason. If it's important, I would rather know about it than both of us being in the dark. Trust me, storm rider, I'm on your side."

Something caught Haydan's eye before he could respond. A small purple explosion of fur crept in by the door and strode across to stand at his feet. Arianna followed his stare and moved away as the creature came to a halt. It had a small pudgy face and large hands and feet. Its body was covered in purple hair that stood on end and gave the odd impression that the creature had been hit by lightning.

Diego groaned, his expression exasperated. "Oh, wonderful timing, Tallin. You had to introduce the pixie to Storm Lands, didn't you?"

The creature gave Diego a little grin then turned back to Haydan and bowed low before clearing its throat. "Prince Diego and Prince Haydan, with his warrior Arianna and Diego's warrior Sandau, are duly invited by King Tallin, Queen Lavinia and Princess Maya to attend a masked ball at King Tallin's summer court. The king requests the pleasure of your company with immediate effect." The creature shot Haydan a funny look, partway between an apology and assessing his response. "King Tallin apologises for having to resort to kidnapping your lady, but she is in very safe hands."

Was there a hint of suggestion in the creature's tone? It raised its eyebrows. Haydan moved to throttle the pixie. It appeared to share its master's flair for mischief and dramatics. Just the thought of Tallin having the audacity to touch Maya was enough to send his pulse racing and the sassy look from the shock of purple hair infuriated him further. The creature shrieked and tried to dive behind Arianna, who shooed it away.

Diego braced a hand against Haydan's shoulder. "That is exactly the reaction Tallin was counting on. You need to go. Take that damned pixie with you too. I can't abide the little pest." Diego grabbed the creature, which tried to nip at his fingers with sharp little teeth, and handed it to Haydan, who couldn't bring himself to look at it. "Show Haydan and Sandau the way. I'll get the lockdown shifted to allow you off Storm Lands and I'll catch you up," Diego said, waving a dismissive hand towards the door. "You will explain to Katherine and Isaac what's going on as well, please."

Travelling into Tallin's realm again was bad enough, but having to take small furry passengers was a further aggravation Haydan could do without. Disapproval flooded off him as he stalked past Arianna and followed Sandau, who led the way. His mood dark and brooding, his thoughts were consumed by what was waiting for him in Tallin's realm.

∂∽⊸

Maya

The plunge into the faerie pools as Maya and Tallin were dragged into the portal snatched all the air out of her body. The nerve of the man was unbelievable. Haydan would be furious at the imposition, but then the king of the dark fae realm was used to getting what he wanted and apparently that morning she was on his to-do list.

The moment Maya landed on the pad on the other side of the portal, she sprang back up and checked her surroundings. The air smelt clean and fresh and the sounds of trickling water filtered through from the surrounding area. She swayed as she orientated herself. A moment later, the organic material at the top of the cocoon parted and Tallin dropped down into the space beside her. Crossing his legs, he sank onto the floor, before shooting her a quirky grin.

"So, welcome back to my realm. Make yourself at home because you will be here for a while yet. You are going to have to help Control Freak figure a few things out before you leave. Speaking of which, I am sure he will be here soon enough."

The man was infuriating. Tallin looked as though he had just invited Maya for tea rather than kidnapping her. The top few buttons on his shirt had been unbuttoned. His waistcoat had been fully unfastened.

On the coat, the wolf shook itself off and cleaned itself, as though unconcerned by its drowning. The eagle had disappeared. Tallin's casual, relaxed mood irritated her so much that all she could manage in response was a low, guttural growl.

Tallin's eyes widened. Far from looking concerned, mirth seemed to be his chosen response. His mouth quirked up, as though he were amused by Maya's reaction, before he leant in with a devilish look glinting in his eyes. "Are you feeling alright now, Maya? You look quite furious, although I have no idea why. You are safe here."

"You've just kidnapped me, you utter lunatic."

Tallin chuckled and Maya's irritation flared. That was his last chance to redeem himself. Before considering what she was doing she leant forwards and raised her hand as if to hit him. Peering up at her, Tallin lifted his arm to block her attack. His demeanour playful he still looked as though he found the whole adventure hysterical. With an annoyed huff, she smacked his arm a number of times with her palms. It was a mock attack, partway between frustration and displeasure. Tallin ducked down and drew his arms over his head, permitting her assault as he hunkered down and shook with laughter. It took Maya a moment to register why.

Nausea roiled around Maya's stomach. Retreating from him, she groaned and backed up against the side of the pod, bracing her hands against her knees as she fought back the urge to vomit.

When her attack stopped, Tallin raised his head. "If you are going to be sick, please do not aim anywhere near me. Contact with other males sets all of Control Freak's possessive instincts off, which you feel as nausea. You are in your teens and unbonded, that makes your storm rider particularly possessive. It is probably a bad idea to be hitting me. I will tolerate your attack on me because you are upset and, in all honesty, I find you quite refreshing. Do that again, or in the presence of anyone else, and I will not be so understanding. Is that clear?"

Maya managed a nod in response. She had totally underestimated how strong that sensation of touching other males had become. She still felt disorientated.

Seemingly unconcerned Tallin lay back on the pad and spread his arms out. "I am drying off. I suggest you do the same, or you can go and join my guards outside. You will be going to my summer court."

"No, the only place I'm going is back home. You can't keep me here like I'm some kind of prisoner," Maya said. Now she could stand up again without feeling faint.

Tallin stretched his arms out before ruffling his hair. He had left the plaits out. After Maya's soaking earlier, she now knew why. He looked relaxed and boyish. Tiny streams of mist released from his hair as he dried off, although the mist wasn't from his hair. It was from the bond tattoo on his neck. Was that his subtle reminder that she was in his realm? Tallin sat back up, all hint of his earlier playfulness evaporating like the swirling white mist that surrounded him, which shrank towards his neck, disappearing in amongst his curls.

"I think you will find that this is my realm and I will do what I like."

The small, delicate chain from around Tallin's neck slid out from underneath his shirt as he began fastening the buttons back up. Tallin pushed it aside, seemingly unconcerned as he focused on the buttons. The tiny doorway hanging on the chain slid around.

Something about the way it moved struck Maya as odd, as though it had come to greet her. She had forgotten about that doorway and the tiny paw she had seen last time she visited. Tallin finished arranging his shirt and waistcoat buttons and glanced back up at her, leaving the doorway hanging right in her eyeline. Blinking a few times, Maya refocused on Tallin, unable to shake the thought that he had just done that deliberately. Now her curiosity about the little doorway was aroused and returning home didn't seem as appealing as it had. She would never find out what was beyond that doorway back home. "Are you serious? You forced me to come here. What right have you got to keep me here? I don't belong to you." Why had she just said that? She wasn't a possession. "In fact, I don't belong to anyone."

Tallin raised his shoulders. "You and Control Freak belong to each other. Fact. Control Freak considers you his because of that. Fact. You are not going home anytime soon. Fact." Fixing Maya with a cold, regal glare, Tallin raised the pendant up nearer to her eyeline. "You seem to be taken with the entrance to the fae realm." With a small sphinx-like smile he stood. "Spend some time with me and I may take you there."

Tallin climbed out of the chamber with the same level of finesse he used when he arrived. He leant back in, extending an arm to help Maya climb out. He wasn't as tall as she remembered, but then she had only been nine when she was last with Tallin. He cast his eye over her attire before raising an eyebrow.

"You have grown and developed some interesting curves, young lady. We will have to do something about your clothing. I can get you some rather beautiful dresses made. You should look like a princess."

Maya fought back the urge to roll her eyes and make

an 'ugh' noise. Bracing his forearm across his lower chest, Tallin extended his elbow towards her. It took her a moment to realise Tallin was formally offering her his arm to escort her out of the caves. The old-fashioned but welcoming gesture seemed to be a form of grown-up politeness. With a small smile, Maya slid her arm through his, hoping Haydan wouldn't overreact to the contact. "Why are we going to your summer court? Where is your summer court? Where's Lavinia? She doesn't like me. She tried to barter my soul last time I was here."

Tallin wrapped warm fingers around Maya's as they walked out of the caves and descended the path to the waiting carriage. "I can mask the contact between us from Control Freak if I choose to. Oh, Lavinia regrets her actions from last time very much, although I am certain her true intentions were misunderstood. In any case, she was protecting Control Freak from you. Lavinia doesn't trust you, or Arianna, because she's suspicious of your motives for surfacing from the sea with Control Freak."

Tallin's repetitive use of Maya's term of endearment for Haydan grew annoying. She gritted her teeth for a moment. "His name is Haydan, not Control Freak. I was expressing my displeasure at Haydan's control over my life with that term. I find it too much to bear sometimes. I feel like I have no control over my connection to him."

Without meeting Maya's eye, Tallin continued descending the path and his eyes widened. "Why would you think such a thing when you chose him before you left the sea? That makes no sense. When Levi has opportunity, she will apologise for her past misdemeanours and make amends. For now, I want to spend a bit of time getting to know you. You are my grandson's future mate and I know next to nothing about you. I want to know if I should trust you with my grandson, or whether I should be trusting Lavinia's instincts more on this one."

They had reached the carriages by the time Tallin finished talking. He led Maya to the front one. Two others queued up behind the first. Unsure how to read his last statement, Maya tried to gauge Tallin's mood. His expression was enigmatic, giving her little to go off. Capturing her elbow, he released her arm and gestured to the carriage steps. On the outside, he was in a charming mood, but his topics of conversation suggested that inside he shared Lavinia's burning concern for Haydan. She had no idea how to respond in a manner that didn't look defensive and her description of Haydan as a control freak earlier had probably added to his worries. Hopefully he would opt for the other carriage and she would have a chance to escape at some point. Perhaps she could demand a toilet break and slip away when Tallin and his guards were distracted.

Maya climbed into the carriage. It was circular inside and more like a large egg. Padded seating swept around the interior. She opted for the left-hand side, seating herself to discover Tallin ascending the steps behind her. He slid into the seat opposite her.

"I am not letting you travel alone." Tallin's stare glided from Maya, to the view out of the window, before slowly returning to her. "I cannot have you trying to escape." He fixed her with another of his hard, unreadable looks.

Maya was learning to regard that as Tallin's astute, regal, but assessing countenance. Intelligence and

a keen eye for detail were strong parts of Tallin's
demeanour and he had the measure of her. Her
thoughts wandered to the other carriages and who the
occupants would be.

"The other carriages are for Haydan, Arianna,
Diego and Sandau."

Tallin disarmed her with a delightful grin before she
could respond.

"I am not reading your mind. I just have a knack
for knowing what you are going to ask before you
ask it." When she tilted her head Tallin broadened his
grin. "And no, that is not the same thing at all. Call it
intuition."

Reaching for one of the large fluffy blankets stacked
on the back of the seat, Maya wrapped herself up
trying to keep warm. She should have taken advantage
of the warm-up pads when she arrived. Tallin looked
as though he had dried off. His hair was curlier when
it dried naturally. He returned his attention to the
woodland beyond the windows, leaving her with the
annoying thought that he was rather pleased with
himself that morning. She hoped Haydan would be as
pleased at the thought of retrieving her, otherwise she
would be stuck there for far longer than she hoped.

Chapter 7

Diego

Haydan left the snug and Diego turned his attention to Arianna. Defiance flared in her mysterious hazel eyes as she clenched her fists at her side.

"What went on in the sea before you fled the depths, warrior?"

Arianna remained silent. Standing, Diego enjoyed the slight widening of her eyes, which confirmed he could still intimidate her if he needed to. At some point, she would regard him with a reverential confidence, born of her strong abilities. Her fear would be replaced by admiration and respect. At that point, he would treat her with the esteem due her role as his son's guardian. It hadn't happened yet. "Because I know something happened. I just don't know what. Did someone hurt you, or get to you somehow? Are you protecting someone? Or maybe they promised you something in return for your co-operation?"

Arianna lowered her attention to Diego's feet. Her brow furrowed as she considered her response, then shook her head. "I don't know what you're talking about." Her confused stare met his.

"Your continued difficulties with Haydan bother me. He shouldn't distrust you like he does." She didn't appear to be deceiving Diego, but then those from the depths always carried secrets and that bothered him more than he cared to admit outwardly. It always had and Lavinia's concerns merely played to those insecurities.

Now Maya was back in Tallin's realm and he had no idea how his mother would welcome a chosen one whom she obviously didn't fully trust either.

Anger flared again as Arianna straightened up. "It's Haydan who has the issue. He keeps me at arm's length and never lets me lead. With the greatest of respect, you don't help matters. You are elder, you are a prince. He feels he has to prove himself to you. He's in awe of you and doesn't consider himself worthy of his status. Please don't deflect this onto me, as though it's all my fault."

"You're blaming your storm rider? That's a brave and rather foolish move, warrior. The first rule of being warrior is you keep your mouth shut about what goes on between you and your storm rider, whilst honouring them and remaining loyal at all times." Diego let his challenge remain as he waited to see how Arianna responded.

Teeam stretched out his legs and nodded. "Arianna does raise a valid point. Haydan regards you as intimidating. What happened earlier with Maya won't have helped."

Diego had foolishly hoped Teeam would back him up in front of Arianna. The swift return surprised him. "Because I'm elder? Maya told me to go to hell earlier."

Arianna gasped at the news. The idea of telling a

storm rider or elder to go to hell would be an alien concept to a woman who had learnt to show respect at all times or pay the penalty. A disciplining was enough to deter any warrior from speaking out of turn to any of them.

"Yes, Arianna, that was what was going on yesterday between Haydan, Maya and me. I tried to reset Maya. She demonstrated one of her flares of hysteria. I won't have her talk to me like that. Haydan tolerates Maya's outbursts of anger. I do not."

Teeam nodded. "I understand that, but Maya is unusual. You would be better to temper your usual reactions around her."

"Why don't you stop Haydan going out and fighting at night, Arianna?" Diego asked. She was meant to be the voice of reason where Haydan was concerned. She either knew about his trips to the clubs and encouraged them or failed to stop him going. Either way it was an added irritation he could do without.

"Haydan vents his frustrations that way. We've discussed it. He knows I don't approve. His behaviour reflects on me too. I do think some of it is him getting used to being in close proximity to other bodies though. Like he's trying to prove Maya rejecting him doesn't bother him, which of course it does."

Teeam stood and his gaze swept the room. Next to Diego, Arianna tensed. Warriors could always tell when storm riders and elders were concerned by something.

"We've got guests and I don't think this is a friendly visit," Diego said. The numbers involved suggested they had sent an envoy to try to capture him and Sandau. When bounty teams failed the shreken sent an envoy. They were now faced with at least thirty shreken warriors and being the focus of their attention was the least of his concerns, especially if the dark gods were behind their incursion.

Diego could already sense his power amplifying as he strode towards the door. Arianna and Teeam followed. He was in no rush to reach the arrival area and since Storm Lands was locked down, the shreken were contained in the arrival area. He would have to lift the lockdown to allow Haydan and Sandau out of the realm. The last thing he needed was Haydan trying to prove himself.

"Arianna if I tell you to go with Haydan and Sandau, you go. Is that clear?"

Diego ignored Arianna's eye-roll.

"Crystal clear. To be fair, it's Haydan and Sandau you should be more concerned about. Well, at least you won't have to worry about leaving subtle hints. You can do it publicly," Arianna said.

Diego ignored Arianna's quips and Teeam's soft chuckle, concentrating instead on switching into his battle attire as he walked up to the plants that protected the snug area. He strode past Arianna with Teeam, clearing the possessed plants without any of them touching him, probably because the plants sensed his magic. Teeam had to wait a moment as the tendrils wrapped around his altera arm, extending out to brush his altera before rapidly retracting and moving on to Arianna.

Teeam grimaced as he moved forwards. "How do you do that?"

Diego chuckled and shrugged. "No idea, but it annoys the hell out of Haydan. Will you take a group up through the trees that way?" He pointed further up the hill away from them. "You know what shreken are like. Make sure you have a number of our archers with you and focus on the one who appears to be leader. I'll take the lower ground. When I'm close enough I'll let you know which one is actually the leader." Shreken were less coordinated if the leader was taken out. "I'm hoping we don't have to involve the spirit at this stage. I'd rather only use her if we have to fend off dark gods." The spirit protected Storm Lands. Right now, she was holding the planet in lockdown for him and he didn't want her distracted, not when he had to get Haydan away, although Tallin was due to put in an appearance soon. He didn't know the details. According to his father, the plan was more effective that way.

Teeam selected his group of warriors and storm riders and moved off.

A number of storm riders and warriors stood waiting for them in the arrival area. No one would attempt to speak to thirty shreken without an elder present. Relations between storm riders and shreken were often tense. Storm riders regularly disturbed shreken raids into other territories, protecting women, children and as many innocent parties as they could, often driving shreken off with a combination of magic and brute force.

Diego emerged from the trees to find that the shreken had unveiled themselves. The arrival area was a large sloped piece of land cut into the hillside. It was surrounded by forest on all sides and isolated: a deception that caught many out. It was the most heavily protected part of the planet. When the realm locked down the focus became the arrival area. It was the only area where visitors could enter the realm, and once in it, they couldn't leave until their level of threat was ascertained. Effectively it was a containment unit, not that the shreken seemed to understand that. They had spread out and moved to the edges in a battle formation. He faced a line of their most fearsome warriors with no obvious leader on show.

"Who's in charge?" Diego asked, raising his voice as he strode forwards. His sword sat in the sheath on his back, although he had no intention of reaching for it unless provoked. Shreken were twitchy at the best of times. For now, Diego would let them think he was warrior.

It was difficult to identify the shreken leader. Half the group consisted of males, the other half females. If he wanted to get their attention he had to find their leader and it would not be the one who spoke first.

"We came for one of your more experienced warriors and one of your leaders. There's a sizeable bounty on their heads, warrior."

The male who spoke was a large brute with dark blond hair anchored back from his head in tiny braids. The muscles in his biceps were so large that veins stood out. Diego walked around him assessing him, considering his response. The surrounding shreken followed Diego's movements, their weapons trained on him. The leader was usually the one furthest away from the first speaker, which meant the leader was standing on higher ground. The male he circled didn't smell of a leader; he smelt of sweat and testosterone. Diego headed further up the field, sweeping his gaze around the gathered group. If he moved close to the leader he would sense the pack's focus shift and right now they still didn't care.

"Who has put a bounty on the heads of my people? Who brought you here? Because shreken don't usually invade our realm." Diego lowered his voice. "You usually can't find it." Snickers filtered through to him from his own people hidden in the surrounding trees. The shreken remained oblivious. He raised his voice again, shouting to be heard clearly. "Why are you involved in this? More to the point, I need names of who you're seeking, not vague mentions of experienced warriors and leaders. You don't even know what our leaders look like."

Another male from nearby, with a scar down one side of his face and landing strips shaved into his dark hair, stepped out of formation. "No, but the first two we capture, we get to keep. They'll do for now, until we can get names."

One of the women nearby grimaced. Her nose twitched as though the oaf speaking annoyed her. She had unusually blonde hair braided back against her head. She was petite, curvy and deceptively slight given how lethal-looking she was. Leather shreken warrior clothing wrapped around her torso, holding her sword in place against her back. Her astute gaze concentrated on an area to the side of Diego, but that didn't fool him. As soon as he noticed her, he felt all the attention of the pack focus in. Downwind of her, he sniffed the air. Her pheromones confirmed that she was the leader. They all answered to her. Her small frame didn't fool him. He glanced across at Teeam, who was standing on the ridge surveying the gathering. Now Diego had the task of gaining the upper hand with the leader. If he didn't assert dominance fast she would regard him as weak and that definitely wasn't happening.

꩜

Maya

The day passed quickly enough as the carriage made steady progress through the woodland. Tallin spent the time looking agitated. Maya asked for around the twentieth time if the portal had activated yet. He shook his head appearing annoyed at her constant pestering. Haydan still hadn't entered the realm and that was unlike him. Time moved faster in Tallin's realm than on Earth, however, so a day in the realm was only a few hours back home.

They had veered right through the woodland, instead of taking a direct path as Maya had done with Teeam last time they entered the realm.

"So, why are we heading to your summer court? What's it like?" Maya asked, wondering if Tallin would start talking, or continue to stew in his bad mood. "Haydan is probably letting you wait to make you suffer. You annoyed him last time and you goaded him with the purple pixie post thing. Time passes slower beyond your realm. In any case, he doesn't like it here."

Tallin's nose wrinkled as he leant forwards and reached for Maya's hand, pulling her hand across and raising it up to his mouth before planting a soft, lingering kiss on the back of it. He ignored her small gasp of surprise as nausea flooded her stomach again. "Well, there is a gentle reminder for him." A flash of anger glinted in the elven king's eyes before he released her hand, settled back into the soft grey cushions and smirked. "My summer court is quite beautiful. Surrounded by water and secrets." Mysteries shimmered in his intense stare as he inclined forwards, rested his elbows on his knees and grinned at her. "I think you will be right at home there … now, when you meet Lavinia, you will play nicely, won't you?" He gave her a suspicious look as he leant back in the seat and closed his eyes. "You may as well make yourself comfortable. It is another couple of hours or so before we reach the castle and it will be dark soon. I will not sleep once darkness falls, so I suggest you take a nap."

Maya's question about why Tallin wouldn't sleep after dark died on her lips as she studied his face. If he was aware of her eyes resting on him he didn't show any concern. In repose, he looked handsome. His thick but elegant brows framed his face. Dark hair skimmed his top lip and jaw as though he was growing a moustache and beard. It made him appear more mature than last time she had seen him, like a proper adult rather than an impish, spirited young man. Somehow that realisation made her feel sad. "Don't lose your playfulness, Tallin. You seem so serious now."

The edge of Tallin's lips curled upwards in response, but he didn't open his eyes. The seat tilted back so he was more reclined as he lay there.

The chain around Tallin's neck slipped back out from his shirt as the carriage moved. Maya's eyes lowered to wait for the doorway to reappear. Her patience was rewarded a few minutes later. The carriage lurched and the doorway finally slid around, gradually working its way out from underneath his shirt. Maya pulled the thick, soft cashmere wrap from around her shoulders and draped it over Tallin's torso. Her eyes locked on the tiny gate as she slipped closer and dropped onto the cushions on his side of the carriage to get a closer look.

Mist released from the doorway as it had done last time. Maya was so close to it and Tallin that even the faint swirl of nausea didn't put her off. Tallin smelt divine, of fresh pine and cool mint. She leant in. If Tallin woke now, she would be beyond embarrassed but she couldn't pull her gaze away from the teasing fronds of white mist that danced up into the air from the small gap that had opened up at the bottom. Up close it looked like a tiny, delicate silvery-bronze gate, with a minute padlock hanging from the clasp.

Maya raised her hand, her fingertips shaking as she moved her index finger closer. What would happen if she touched it? The temptation proved too much. The tiny paw reappeared. Inches from contact with it, Maya jumped as Tallin jolted awake and grabbed her hand.

"Bold, but foolish, Maya." Tallin held Maya in place, so she couldn't pull away. Uncomfortably close to Tallin's face, her stare clashed with his. He studied her with the fierceness of a hawk, scaring and thrilling her in equal measures. "The Kantobra does not reach out from the fae realm doorway for just anyone, but if you touch him, you will be dragged into his realm and I have enough on my mind at the moment, without having to rescue you. Haydan will also be livid. Go to sleep and stop meddling in things you do not understand."

Tallin's other hand moved up to Maya's temple. She tried to push his hand away, but he had already made contact with her skin. Warmth flooded her body. A feeling of nausea rolled over her, replaced moments later by one of calm contentment as darkness consumed her.

☙❧

Haydan

It hadn't taken much to convince Sandau to accompany Haydan to the danger zone. Until the lockdown was released over the realm they couldn't leave and since Sandau's primary concern was guarding Diego, who was dealing with the shreken, that was a predictable way of persuading him to detour via the arrival area. On the perimeter of the arrival area the warrior enjoyed a prime view of Diego, whilst still honouring his orders to guard Haydan. The warrior dwarfed Haydan as he strode beside him into the woodland on the edge of the large field.

Sandau had met Iskar. Haydan had never before encountered anyone who had come across a dark god. Theander never talked about them. In fact, even referring to the disavowed gods in his presence usually elicited a terse grunt of displeasure followed by a long, tense period of silence.

Reaching the bottom of the arrival area, Sandau moved ahead, checking the surroundings were clear, even though the shreken were further up the field. Haydan waited as Sandau completed his checks. Before he could open his mouth to speak, Sandau rushed back towards him, with wide eyes and a finger over his lips. He made a rotating motion with his finger, glancing up into the trees above. Haydan looked up into the surrounding foliage, not sure what he was supposed to be searching for.

High up in the canopy, something caught his attention. When he focused it became clear there were guards up in the trees, guards with bows and arrows trained on the gathering in the arrival area. They blended in really well with the foliage because they wore green and brown clothing, but they weren't shreken. One of them smirked before staring back up the field. Haydan caught a glimpse of a pointed ear peeking out from the guard's hood. Elven and fae guards meant Tallin was on Storm Lands, but that made no sense. Tallin had Maya. Another swirl of nausea confirmed the elven king had just taken the liberty of kissing Maya's hand, probably to remind Haydan he still had her with him, which meant Tallin wasn't actually there. What was the elven king playing at?

Movement in Haydan's jacket pocket drew his attention. He glanced down, wondering if Kaleshar was trying to join in, although the mask was safe in his inside jacket pocket, not the outside one. He watched the small purple shock of hair clamber out of his pocket with something clutched in its hand. Before he could grab it, to find out what it had hold of, the pesky creature ran off into the trees. With a mutter of displeasure, he turned back to the gathering. He would have to track the purple fluff down before he left now.

Diego had focused on one of the females of the pack. Lowering and tilting his head, he glared at her. His elder powers surfaced with a huge flare of lightning around him, shooting up from the ground towards the sky in an incredible display of power. All the shreken around Diego scattered with yells of anger. A crack of thunder boomed overhead. It appeared Diego had found the pack leader.

The ground shuddered as Diego disappeared in

a blaze of lightning and reappeared just behind the shreken warrior, who shouted, "Rider" and spun with a fierce expression on her face. She tried to barge into Diego and take him down to the floor: a shreken show of power. Diego vanished, materialising behind her again as she spun back and aimed an elbow into his face. Diego ducked with a speed Haydan had never witnessed before and charged into the woman, landing her on the floor as he threw his full weight at her. She was a fierce little thing, but even she couldn't outmanoeuvre the bulk of a furious elder slamming into her.

The shreken took a step back. None of them would interfere in a challenge between one of their leaders and Diego, whom they perceived as a pack leader too. With her pinned beneath him, Diego straddled her as she fought for breath, trapping her body on the ground with his weight. His free hand wrapped around the base of her throat as he glared down at her. Power flared and arced around her ankles. She clawed at Diego's arm and power snaked up her arms before he dragged her arms back down to the ground, holding her helpless beneath him.

"Mine," Diego shouted. Raising his head, he targeted the nearest shreken pack members with a confrontational glare. "I control the pack. I control you. All of you. Teeam!"

On the ridge, warriors appeared with bows and arrows trained on the shreken pack leader and a number of her primary pack.

"Any of you challenge me and she dies along with a good few of you." After a moment of silence, Diego returned his attention to the woman beneath him. "Who sent you? Who put a price on the head of one of our riders and their warrior?"

It was rare for Haydan to witness one of Diego's true flares of power. Seeing his father control a pack of shreken, like he just had, was breathtaking. Even Sandau gazed across as though fascinated. Now Diego had asserted his authority, the pack leader would have no choice but to yield to him.

Glaring up at Diego for a moment, whilst still looking furious and trying to fight his restraints to claw at his hand again, she finally lowered her focus to his chest. A shuddering sigh of frustration released from her as all the fight left her body. Diego let go of one of her hands and offered up his closed fist, allowing her to wrap her hand around it, in an act of surrender.

"I don't know, someone much higher up than me. The rumour is the dark gods put a bounty on your head, because it is you they want, isn't it? I've never seen a rider move like you do."

Diego didn't answer; his expression victorious, he turned his attention to the nearest of her pack. "You're going back without your pack leader. Tell the dark gods she's now our prisoner and that Diego, storm rider elder, took her down. If they come looking for me, I will no longer be on Storm Lands. This realm is no longer safe. I am leaving. If they want me, they will have to find me."

Diego had just demonstrated how to bring a pack of shreken under his control. Haydan hadn't known such a thing was possible. Everyone around him seemed equally fascinated; no one interrupted.

An arm snaked around Haydan's neck. Before he could turn or move to defend himself, a delicate hand slid around the other side of his head. The palm opened and a ball of light appeared in the corner of his vision. It hurt his eyes and he tried to turn the other way, but found himself unable to move. Sandau spun back in surprise from the arrival area. His eyes widened then tensed as he glared at whoever had just attacked Haydan.

"If you try to move, or fight me, I will hurt you. You do what I say, when I say it, or you will very much regret it, Haydan. Until I let you go, this will feel like being really drunk and until you are safe from harm you answer to me. Do we understand each other?"

Haydan's fuddled brain struggled to make sense of the soft, delicate, feminine voice. It sounded like Lavinia, his grandmother … which explained the fae and elven guards hiding in the trees. He groaned at the realisation, although he had no idea how she had crept up on him. That earned him a tightening of her arm around his throat.

"You're kidnapping me?" Haydan's voice sounded lethargic and his vision felt woozy and fuzzy. "I'm going to Tallin's realm anyway."

A soft chuckle with a hard edge close to his ear confirmed Lavinia was unamused. "Not fast enough for Tallin you're not. My love likes to get his own way and is running out of patience with you, and apparently your father is still ignoring his instructions too. The elven king will not tolerate disobedience for long. Did you learn nothing last time you entered Tallin's realm?" She yanked on Haydan's neck, moving the light closer. His head throbbed in response. "Stand now. Sandau, you know how this works. Are you going to be a problem as well, or do I have to threaten Diego to get you to obey?"

Sandau glanced to the side as hooded figures started appearing from the surrounding foliage. "You brought elven mages with you? Diego is heading into Tallin's realm soon. You have no right–"

"I am Tallin's queen, Diego's mother. I have every right." Lavinia dragged Haydan up onto his feet. "Move," she said. A hard nudge of her elbow to his back shoved him forwards into the open. The surrounding shreken retreated as Lavinia pushed Haydan ahead.

He glanced up to meet Teeam's keen stare. Standing on the ridge, Teeam surveyed the development without so much as a hint of concern, almost like he was expecting the events that unfolded. Haydan was struck by the intense feeling that this was all part of a plan, one that he wasn't party to, but one that was playing out around him regardless.

Turning his head, Diego appeared to consider the new situation, then focused back on his captive, studying his quarry pinned beneath him as though she was more important. After another tense moment, he settled his weight back from his knees to his haunches and turned his head to the side. "Mother, what are you doing here and why is half of the fae's army hiding in the trees with weapons aimed in this direction? More to the point, when did you arrive and who let you all into the realm? Because it wasn't me." He eyed the cloaked mages, his expression one of distaste.

Given how relaxed Teeam looked, he already knew about it, and Haydan had an inkling that Sandau had been privy to it as well. Diego might not know specific details, but he was adding to the general air of discord. It felt like a perfectly tensioned spider's web of deceit and it displayed all the hallmarks of a Tallin plan.

"Your father wants you back in his realm. You're taking too long. You can come without a fuss, or I can use force. Either way, Haydan is coming with me. This realm can't help him right now," Lavinia said. Her voice held that air of authority that it always did when she was pleased with herself, and showing Diego up in front of everyone would delight her no end.

Diego's eyebrow lifted. "You're sure you want to do this so publicly, Mother? Anyway, you're forgetting someone."

A snicker confirmed Lavinia wasn't concerned. "No, I don't think so. Tallin's realm offers more protection than she does."

Did Lavinia really think so little of Arianna? Haydan had already spotted his warrior. Up on the high ground near Teeam, Arianna crouched watching developments with a curious look on her face. Movement in the grass near her feet caught his attention. The shock of purple hair that had escaped his pocket earlier wandered up to her and tapped her knee. She glanced down and held out her hand, accepting the item offered by the creature. After considering it for a moment, she tilted the item left then right, allowing it to fully take form in her hand before shooting Haydan a sassy grin. He tried to shake his head, but struggled to move. What was she doing? A couple of nearby shreken noticed it; they were staring across at Arianna. It looked like she had Kaleshar. He patted his jacket. The inside pocket felt empty. She did have Kaleshar – the pixie had taken the mask from his pocket earlier.

Unfolding her arms from her knees, Arianna stood. The mask was face down in her palm, glinting in the sunlight, so it drew even more attention as it bounced light around. With a little mischievous shrug, as though in agreement, Arianna raised the mask up to her face.

Chapter 8

Maya

A slight roll of the carriage brought Maya to. She opened her eyes to find Tallin asleep across from her. He had placed another blanket over her to keep her warm; the realisation made her smile. Despite her forced nap, she had slept soundly enough, but had no idea how long for. Outside it was dark. Mist crept around the forest that lined either side of the carriage's route through the trees. A quick glance confirmed it was the same dirt road as the one they had followed earlier.

Rubbing her eyes, Maya sat up and peered out of the window, wondering when they would reach the summer palace. The mist rolled around, crawling about the trees as though searching for something. With a shiver, she glanced back towards Tallin. So many mysteries hid inside his mind. What was he dreaming about? Why had he said he wouldn't sleep after dark? Mist released in a gentle flow from his neck. Curling around his hair, it made him look even more mysterious than usual. It drifted out towards the carriage windows as though reaching for the mist outside.

The speed with which the mist outside rushed up to the carriage windows set Maya's heart pounding. The forest vanished from sight in thick white plumes of mist. Staring at it, mesmerised, she felt certain that faces with bright, intense eyes were swirling around out there. There were a few shouts from Tallin's men and one of them rode his horse alongside the carriage and pounded on the window. The mist from outside started seeping in around the edge of the glass-panelled door. Maya pushed back in her seat, wondering if she would be better aiming for Tallin, rather than leaning away from him. Fingers of mist reached out to her, pulling at her wrap as they glided further into the carriage. Maya kicked out for Tallin's leg. He wouldn't thank her for the bruise, but she no longer cared. The pounding against the window intensified as Tallin's guards tried to get his attention.

Tallin finally jolted awake. Registering Maya's panicked expression and leaping to his feet, he released the catch on the door, shouting for the driver to stop, before stepping out of the carriage.

The mist from outside followed Tallin as he descended to the ground and disappeared from her view. Alone in the carriage Maya was unable to see anything beyond the confines of her cocoon. "Tallin?" she said. "Where are you? Don't you dare leave me alone, Tallin." If something happened to him she was alone with no route out of the realm.

A moment later, the mist that surrounded the carriage jumped back to the forest boundary. The eerie quality of the moment made the hairs on Maya's neck rise up. The mist wasn't natural, it was controlled, presumably by the wraithlike figures that hovered on the boundary of the forest staring down Tallin with a confidence and gall that felt challenging even to her.

Tallin's response was even more alarming. He stood on the edge of the track, his attention locked onto the mist-enshrouded forest. His feet were positioned in such a way that she was reminded of a box stance in martial arts, with his front leg facing forwards and his other leg angled to the side. His head cocked to the side, he met the lead creature's glowing, undead stare with his own defiant one.

"I am king of this realm. My realm. My forest. My lands. You challenge me and I will make you regret it."

The lead creature edged closer to Tallin. It drifted, without any visible feet to hold it up. Its head raised and it homed in on Maya with its eyes, before returning its attention to Tallin when he clicked his fingers and moved his head to block its view.

"When I find out who you are, and I will find out, I will kill you and anyone connected to you." Tallin cast his gaze over the other gathered creatures. "Family go first, so think on that before you cross me." When the creatures remained Tallin stamped his front foot and drew his shoulders back. With a low growl of utter fury, he threw his hand out. Balls of light cascaded downwards, before bouncing along the ground in both directions. Tallin turned his head. That explained his odd choice of stance. He could easily scan the forest behind him.

Maya turned and gasped at the creatures with bright eyes who had crept up behind the carriage and now peered inside, their glowing orbs fixed on her. They were close enough to touch her. She spun back towards Tallin with a surprised shriek as he threw more balls of light out from his hands, aiming behind the carriage.

Explosions erupted, tumbling coloured powder over

the creatures. It seemed to stick to them, as though marking them or perhaps hurting them. All of the strange, bright-eyed wraiths rushed back into the forest wailing. The sight of the unusual visitors fleeing eased Maya's chest and she drew in a shaky breath, moving to the steps and out of the carriage to get as close to Tallin as she could.

Tallin remained standing to attention, his head cocked to the side as though listening for any further movement in the woodland. The fog had vanished. "I told you not to let me sleep after dark," he said. He continued scanning the forest, his gaze sweeping the woodland, as if searching for any hint of anything out of the ordinary.

Tallin's terse tone proved a challenge Maya could do without. "No you didn't. You said you don't sleep after dark. What the hell was that? You told me you had control of the woodland. That didn't look like control."

Tallin's head turned, his hair flailing as his jaw clenched and his hands tightened into fists. "Not out here. The forest has ears and it is listening to everything you are saying right now. I have control of the woodland."

Tallin took a step closer. Maya took an involuntary step back. He looked ready to harm her. As though noticing his fury concerned her, he ran a hand through his hair, glanced around and gestured for her to step back into the carriage.

"We are not far from the castle now." He turned towards his men. "Is everyone alright?"

Up front it appeared that some of his men had been injured, two of them quite badly. Tallin surveyed their injuries. One was bleeding from his shoulder and another was holding his stomach. "We must get back to the castle so I can get my guards medical attention."

Shooting Tallin a wary look, Maya moved back towards the carriage. "Your guards are wounded. That doesn't fill me with confidence right now."

Tallin ascended the steps behind Maya and sank back into the seat opposite her. "Oh, do not worry, the creatures you just had the misfortune to meet are the result of magic. Most of the owners of the manifestations are in my court. Although I have control of the woodland that does not mean there are not creatures out here stupid enough to challenge me every now and again. They are growing more confident especially now that rumours about my son, grandson and ancient artefacts are circulating."

"You told me you had control of the woodland. Did you lie to me? I know how you like to play games." Maya studied Tallin, waiting for a sign of deception.

Tallin's vehemence surprised Maya as he leant forwards and glared at her. "I have control of the woodland! I gift power sources to my court to keep them happy, but the chance to get hold of an endless source of power is always a temptation. Haydan is the most vulnerable. Your lack of bond keeps him weak." Condescension tugged at his expression as his brows furrowed. "You might want to think on that whilst you are here, chosen one, because so far, except for goading my son and grandson, you do not appear to be fulfilling any of your chosen one duties. You might find the goading entertaining, but you will not find it so funny if Haydan does end up kidnapped because of your failings. Guilt is not an enjoyable emotion to experience." Folding his arms, he hunkered down into his seat, glowering at her before pulling his hood up and turning away.

Maya chewed her bottom lip and dragged the throw around herself, hoping Tallin wouldn't notice her tears. His contemptuous words once again reminded her of her failings to protect Haydan, a man she was supposed to adore, not fight against with every breath she took. Never before had she felt so alone.

∻∻

Diego

Enjoying the view of the pretty blonde shreken female pinned beneath him rather more than he should be, Diego switched his attention and stared up the field towards Arianna. It intrigued him that she could wear the mask. The thought that if Arianna could wear the mask, then it might permit Maya to wear it too skittered across his mind. He heaved an inward sigh of relief that Maya hadn't put the mask on in the kitchen at Isaac's house. Faced with Maya wearing the mask, he would have felt the need to put her in her place and that would have been an interesting scrap for supremacy.

Arianna's smug look settled onto Haydan and she raised her eyebrows. Diego manoeuvred to get a better look at Haydan, who glared at Arianna with an expression on his face of quiet resignation mingled with anger, but then the controlling magic that Lavinia was using on his son would be taking its toll by now. Haydan would only be able to resist it for so long before succumbing.

Arianna sauntered down the field towards Diego,

playing her part, looking like the sassy, rebellious warrior that she was so good at being. The mask glinted every now and again, refracting light from its surface as she moved. When she got closer, her smile broadened. "So now I've got to deflect half of Tallin's army? That's not going to win you any points with the elven king. He doesn't like me as it is."

Diego bit back laughter. He was talking to Kaleshar more than Arianna by the sound of it, but the impudent response suited her too. "Tallin knows what I'm like. That's not really a concern right now. Get my mother to back off, please."

With a small huff, as though suggesting she couldn't be bothered, Arianna threw her hand out. Her grin broadened as glowing green energy leapt across the field and rose up in front of Lavinia. Diego turned to enjoy the view of Lavinia looking furious. Her hair blew in the breeze, her expression souring as she realised her son had just outmanoeuvred her.

"I think it's time you left and took your army with you. I'll catch you up when I'm ready, Mother." Diego waved, basking in the disdainful look his mother fixed on him.

The spirit released the lockdown on the planet and with a final glare of displeasure, Lavinia dropped her tornado around herself, Haydan and Sandau and vanished from sight, taking the army with her. Whilst she would probably have enjoyed forcing Diego to join her, her focus was on her weaker grandson, which had just served Diego well. Haydan was safer away from Storm Lands, and regardless of what waited for Haydan in the elven realm, he was more protected by Tallin than he would be by Diego.

Diego was already a figure of interest to the dark

gods; now Arianna was too. The further away Haydan was from him and Arianna the better. The dark gods needed to believe they were a storm rider family in conflict with each other for the plan to work. If they believed any of this to be a set-up, they wouldn't take the bait, and that was essential to Tallin's carefully laid plan.

Diego returned his attention to Arianna as he stood and pulled the woman beneath him to her feet. Teeam moved across to Diego and a group of riders and warriors took her and hustled her away. Without a leader, the team was weaker. Repercussions couldn't fall on a pack without its leader being present. Diego had probably just saved the pack leader's life.

Standing next to Diego, Arianna folded her arms. "What?" she asked, raising her shoulders in a manner that conveyed arrogance and displeasure.

"You know what. Take that off." Diego leant in, fixing Arianna with a hard stare. "Now, Arianna."

Diego focused on the nearest pack member, the male with the tracks shaved into his hair. "You need to take your pack and go before I have Storm Lands evict you. The lockdown is lifted until you leave, then it's reinstated. Get out of here, before I lose my patience with all of you too."

Next to Diego, Arianna moved her hand up to her face to capture the mask as it disengaged. When it had fully detached, she passed it across to Diego. He took his time in taking it from her extended hand. The shreken with the dark hair looked across, taking note of what transpired before he slid his gaze back to his pack and followed them towards the small portal where they had entered. Diego slipped Kaleshar into his inside pocket.

Once the shreken had all left the realm, Diego turned to Teeam. "You think that's going to work?"

Teeam was still staring at Arianna with a look on his face of rapt adoration. "Oh, I think Arianna put on a convincing show. Your main concern now is making sure that the dark gods don't find you anytime soon. If they find out about your carefully planned deception it will not be well received. The gods don't like being played."

Arianna continued to study Diego. He gave her a questioning look.

"That's why you've sent Sandau with Haydan, isn't it? Because Sandau knows who he's dealing with. You could have just told me that," Arianna said, raking her hand across the back of her neck in obvious irritation.

Diego leant in towards Arianna, relishing the way she shrank back ever so slightly from his proximity. "I need Haydan with the person who can keep him safest and yes, Arianna, right now that is Sandau. You should understand that and respect that. You and Haydan need a breather from each other as well, but as being with Sandau affords Haydan greater protection, I made that call. Besides, Haydan has always responded better when he feels secure. He's more confident when he's cushioned from danger. I'm not sure why he's so sensitive to it. Perhaps because you and Maya never reassure him on that front, he overcompensates, who knows?" He enjoyed watching her squirm as she appeared to consider her response. Her attention locked onto the floor by his feet.

"I apologise for my earlier challenge, but I meant what I said." Arianna raised her chin, defiance flaring in her eyes again. "Haydan does act defensively around me all the time. It knocks my confidence when he doesn't trust me to lead when it's appropriate and you compound that by kicking me to the side to replace me with Sandau when it suits."

Her whining was irritating. It was like trying to negotiate a peace treaty when the different sides wouldn't stop fighting. Diego wanted to prepare for leaving Storm Lands for a while. He had a number of things to do including tracking Rebekka down before he left. Lavinia had been in the realm for an hour or two. That was plenty of time for her to find Rebekka and stir things up for him and now he was babysitting Arianna too.

"Arianna, you're warrior. Get over it and grow the hell up." Diego gave Arianna a furious glare and strode off. "I'll find you later once you've assumed your responsibilities."

❧

𝒥allin

By the time his summer court came into view, as rocks appeared and the forest fell away, Tallin's mood had soured further. The portal still hadn't activated and he had just snapped at Maya. He hadn't meant to, but after her earlier challenge, he had felt the need to remind her of his displeasure at her lack of bond with Haydan. Maya moved forwards in her seat to peer out of the window. Her puffy eyes suggested she had been crying.

"I apologise for snapping. I am concerned for Haydan that is all." Tallin pushed shame at his behaviour aside and followed Maya's wide-eyed stare.

"You call this your summer court? It's a small city; no, it's more of a fortress," Maya said.

Tallin's summer court rose up from the centre of two fast-flowing rivers which wrapped around the edges of the huge walled construction, before plunging into two vast falls on either side. Accessible by two wide and heavily guarded bridges, his summer court was a grand show of power and opulence. If Maya thought the view across to the two falls was impressive, she would be equally impressed by the view from inside the court looking down over the town housed within the walls. The carriage pulled left and skirted the edge of the rivers at the head of the valley. Huge rock faces rose up on both sides, adding further protection. Maya continued to stare out of the window, before rubbing her eyes presumably in an attempt to hide her earlier distress.

"I am holding a masked ball in a couple of days' time. I want Diego and Haydan, when they arrive, to start getting to know more about this realm and meet some of my court. In the meantime, we have much to talk about, but once we are inside, yes?"

Maya scowled and nodded as she sank back into her seat.

"You have not brought your furry friends with you, I notice." Tallin couldn't detect the whirling dervishes at all. Last time they had accompanied her into the realm and helped her escape, but now there was no sign of them.

Maya shrugged, looking irked by his prying question. "They've been avoiding me since I reject Haydan so much. What does it matter anyway?"

Maya's belligerent tone was irritating. Tallin didn't appreciate being addressed like that. "It matters greatly,

Maya, because those small balls of fur, who are sacred to the gods might I add, are very particular about who they are friends with. They prefer the light to the dark, remember that." He fixed her with a cold look intended to convey his irritation. "Please stop addressing me in that aggressive tone. If you speak to Haydan like that I am not surprised he is upset at you."

Maya huffed, peering back out of the window again. "Haydan isn't upset at me. He understands, but since I'm his anyway, what does it matter? He gets his own way at some point regardless." She glared at Tallin. "I thought you would understand a little more how I feel."

Why would she think such a thing? Tallin had always adored Lavinia. He had argued with her and played games with her in his equivalent of Maya's teenage years, but he had always loved everything about Lavinia. Maya's resentment of Haydan seemed more deep-rooted. "You perhaps find being told off by another chosen one humiliating."

Maya's face flushed and she nodded, but didn't meet his eyes. "You're like me. The first time I met you, you conveyed respect and understanding of my predicament, but now you seem irritated by me, short on patience."

Tallin inhaled sharply and selected his next words carefully. "You were nine years old last time I met you. I treated you like an adult, not a young child in need of guidance. Perhaps I am wrong to expect maturity from a fifteen-year-old human. You display a worrying, aggressive hatred towards Haydan, who is my grandson. If I am to be completely truthful about this, I find that quite disturbing, as does Levi."

Maya turned away as though trying to ignore his penetrating eyes. She only gained respite from that when the portal activated and the familiar presence of Lavinia returned to his mind. Warmth flooded his thoughts, bathing him in delight and easing his bad mood. The soft thump in his chest reminded him that his storm rider was back and it thrilled him deep down to his soul, which thrummed in response.

You have them? Tallin had detected three life forms entering the realm. A quick check indicated two storm riders and a warrior. He knew one was Lavinia, the question was whether Diego or Haydan had returned.

I have the most important, Haydan, with Sandau. Diego is following on with Arianna once the trap has carefully been laid.

Tallin loved Diego and Haydan equally as did Lavinia. Her description of Haydan as the most important merely conveyed that he was the weaker of the two and therefore more of a priority. Sandau knew the dark gods. He knew their tricks and games. Haydan was safer with Sandau than with Arianna. Convincing Diego had taken some doing, but he had come around.

Are you following on in one of the carriages?

Yes, I need to make amends with Haydan. He is livid at being kidnapped. I will of course let him know your hand in this too so you can share his displeasure.

Tallin was certain Lavinia would, regardless of the fact that he was sitting with the other half of Haydan's soul. He needed Maya to understand her role in helping Haydan, because without her and Arianna's assistance, Haydan would never master the twelve kingdoms.

"You probably already know, but Haydan has just entered the realm."

Maya nodded her understanding. She would have felt Haydan enter the realm with the same sensations Tallin experienced.

"What do you know about your family tree?"

Tallin's question was met by a furrowed brow as Maya looked across at him as though baffled by his question. Her hair had dried. It was wavy when it dried naturally. He couldn't help wondering what trick she used to keep it straight normally.

"My father was storm rider. He died before I was born. I don't know anything about my grandparents. They gave my mother up for adoption when she was a baby. She doesn't even have a photograph of them, or names, and has no idea why they abandoned her." Maya's eyes filled with tears. "Why do you ask?"

"I am sorry about your father, Maya. That must have been agony for your mother. I am curious about you. You are different and I wonder if it is because of your bloodline. Levi mentioned you have wards on your property. She believes they are set by the gods. Any idea why?"

Maya shook her head. "No, but I love the way I find all of this out from you rather than Haydan or Arianna. No one tells me anything, you know. It's like I'm not important enough or something."

At Tallin's chuckle Maya glared at him.

"Why is that so funny?"

Her indignation made him laugh even more. She looked furious, her nose scrunched up.

"You are the point where Haydan's world begins and ends. He does not tell you because he is protecting you. Keeping information from you is his way of doing that. You might not like that, but it is the truth. The question is when we talk later, will you do the same for him?"

Maya appeared startled by his words. The fury dropped away from her eyes like water dousing fire. "Contrary to popular belief, I do adore Haydan. I would do anything for him and yes I would keep a secret to protect him." She paused as though about to add something else, before clearing her throat and staring down at her hands. "He's my entire world. He reminded me of that the other night when he reconnected our souls." Her eyes filled with unshed tears as she settled back in her seat. "My biggest fear is hurting him. That's why I avoid the subject of bonding. I'm scared that one day I will hurt him. I will hurt him to protect him. Can you understand that delightful contradiction, Tallin, fae king?"

It was possibly the strangest thing Tallin had ever heard. Would he hurt Lavinia to protect her? If it meant saving the soul he loved, he would do whatever it took and apparently Maya felt the same. "Yes, I can understand that. Are you in some kind of trouble?"

Maya's headshake seemed final. She angled her body away from him.

"If you ever need help, you only have to ask. If it involves protecting Haydan, I will also do whatever it takes to keep him safe, no questions asked."

Her smile was one of the saddest, most heart-wrenching little smiles he had ever seen. Now he understood why Haydan adored her; she was the most unique contradiction he had ever met and that required a special kind of love. The haunted look in her eyes would stay with him for a long time, but one thing was certain, he no longer doubted her loyalty to Haydan.

Entering Tallin's summer court via the bridge, the carriage swept around to the right and moved towards his residence. Tallin inhaled, his skin tingling as he crossed the threshold. His people often talked in terms of light and dark magic and the town was so full of light magic his mood always soared as they approached his home there.

The town was in darkness, except for the trees and walkways festooned with floating lights. The magic exuded by the summer court had always fascinated Tallin. It penetrated everything around the town, bringing the town alive in strange and wonderful ways. Glow bugs frequently landed on certain bushes and loitered there as though feeding from energy released by the foliage. Lynx often crept around at night, rummaging in plants and sniffing about specific trees as though drawn to them by some unseen power. By morning they had always vanished.

There were frequent sightings of shadowy figures wandering about at night too. Given that all the residents were accounted for, no one ever knew who the strange nocturnal visitors were. The figures were often said to have glowing eyes, so Tallin was fairly sure it was the gods drawn to the area, although he didn't know why. That was a contradiction, as according to the water book Theander had specifically drawn his attention to in the library, the gods didn't like the walled city. The magic it exuded disguised many things. It was rumoured to be full of traps and secret passageways which made it hard for the gods to safely navigate. As far as Tallin was concerned, the fact the gods didn't like the court made it a perfect location for the showdown that was coming, although he did need to check with Theander about the night-time visitor. He had never met him or her, which made it difficult to know who it was.

Once they arrived at his residence, Tallin descended the carriage steps and held out his hand to help Maya down. A quick glance towards where his guards stood confirmed his request for additional security had been actioned. His guards blended in, but there were a lot more of them. Seemingly oblivious, Maya trailed behind him as they ascended the huge sweep of steps up to the entrance. She looked awed by the entire experience. He paused to allow her a moment to take it all in. She spun around, peering up at the beautiful building carved out of white stone. The air was heavily scented by damp dew, fresh blooms of moonflowers, night-scented orchids and evening primrose, which filled his gardens. The front one was more relaxed in its style. The outdoor areas at the back consisted of formal landscaping and his favourite woodland section. He had chased Lavinia around those on a number of occasions; the memory made him smile.

Tallin showed Maya to her quarters. The huge, opulent bed in the centre of the room gained a gasp of approval from her as she launched herself at it, flipped onto her back and spread her arms and legs wide, moving them about like she was swimming. Closing his eyes, he fought back the urge to reprimand her for inappropriate behaviour. Something about her delighted giggle stopped him from spoiling her good mood. Lit from below, the bed looked like it was hovering in thin air, which seemed to fascinate her. She spent the next five minutes leaning over the edge, peeping underneath whilst waving her hand about. She had yet to discover the light shower in the corner of the room. That would be the subject of much speculation, especially when she worked out that the three rotating balls rose up as she approached as though inviting her in. The water mingling with light cascaded down around the edges and would make her think she was going to get wet again. He fought back the urge to giggle at her misunderstanding of the most fascinating part of his summer court: the transport system.

Tallin warned Maya to change into something more appropriate from the wardrobes before meeting for dinner, then returned to his own quarters to select his evening attire. He opted for a loose-fitting tunic and trousers. He sank into one of the seats by the window and waited, giving Maya a little more time. Knowing what Lavinia was like, it would take Maya a while to find something that fitted, was a suitable colour and pleased her enough for her to venture out of the bedroom in it. He stretched out and dozed off.

When he awoke, his attention was drawn to the glowing blue eyes in the corner of his room. Theander had returned and judging by the direction he approached from, he had already worked out the transport system that would undoubtedly fox Maya for days. Studying Theander's approach, Tallin narrowed his eyes. It was time for Theander to provide a few answers.

Chapter 9

Arianna

Watching Diego's back receding was irritating. Diego had allowed Arianna to make herself a huge target in the search for the mask and then left her to her own devices.

Teeam moved to her side, his amber eyes focused on her face. "I would suggest you stay close to Diego. What you just did was incredibly brave and when he stops worrying about Haydan and where Rebekka is, he will come to understand that."

Arianna turned her head. "You are suggesting I disobey a direct order from Diego?"

Mischief glinted in Teeam's eyes as he chuckled, the sound warm and inviting. "I am suggesting that you follow him, but keep your distance. Lavinia has been here. She will have found Rebekka and she will have stirred up trouble for Diego. Do you remember the soul Haydan found last time he visited Tallin?"

Arianna nodded. Haydan had apparently returned that to the sea. Diego never talked about it, but given that their people were reborn that meant little, and it hadn't been forgotten.

"That was Diego's chosen one's soul. Rebekka will not want Diego reuniting with her. She has got her hands on a powerful elder who is heir to the fae throne. She will not let Diego go easily. She loves him. Diego cares for Rebekka, but she is not his true love. That honour lies with his chosen one. Lavinia likes Diego as a free rider. Do you understand what I am indirectly saying?"

Arianna moved off, following Diego. "Yeah, you're saying to watch Diego's back because Lavinia and Rebekka might be scheming to permanently separate him from his chosen one. That sounds underhanded. I'm on it."

"Diego's chosen one's soul isn't back in the sea, even though Haydan says she is. I have checked. That means Haydan has some sort of protection policy in place with the gods. He is protecting the soul for his father, but I don't think Lavinia or Rebekka need to find out about that, do you? Keep her safe. Diego has lost her once; it will destroy him if he loses her again."

With a quick glance over her shoulder to meet Teeam's nod of confirmation, Arianna broke into a run. Diego moved fast when he needed to and he already had a head start.

Searching for Diego proved a challenge. Arianna was approaching the river and had almost given up when she heard a sharp sound. Brushing the nearby foliage aside, she found Diego with Rebekka. He was rubbing his jaw, and judging by his agitation, Rebekka had just slapped him. That was brave given who Diego was, but then he enjoyed a feisty relationship with her and thrived on the challenges she posed.

"You never told me and I had to hear it from her, Diego." Rebekka's honey-blonde hair fell in waves to her shoulders. She glared up at Diego, who seemed to be equally furious. "Don't even get me started on the shreken female you had pinned beneath you before on the field either. You looked like you enjoyed that little show of control." Rebekka huffed and continued to eye Diego. "I had to hear it from your mother, who hates me, that Haydan not only found the soul of your chosen one, but had the honour of bringing her back. No one told me, betrayed by my own family. Say something."

"My mother should have kept that to herself, but you know what she can be like. Anyway, it's none of your business. I'm not even sure how I feel about it myself, and don't blame Haydan. All our souls are sacred, hers even more so. I have to go to Tallin's realm. Come with me and we can talk about this."

Drawing herself up to make herself look even more dangerous, Rebekka bestowed a murderous look on Diego. "No, you go without me. It's not like you need me with you, is it?" She recoiled from him.

Diego hung his head. That was his exasperated pose and he appeared to be short on patience with Rebekka that evening.

"This is about our son. Haydan is in danger. I don't want to leave things like this with you." Diego reached for Rebekka's sleeve and tugged her closer.

Rebekka looked ready to burn anything in the vicinity if it would solve her current problems. Her eyes narrowed. "Oh, now you don't want to leave things unresolved? Go, Diego. Go and help our son in your parents' realm."

That sounded like a brave challenge of his parents' status, as though Rebekka was suggesting Haydan was perfectly safe and this was some sort of ruse from

Diego to off world for a while.

"And whilst you deflect with that excuse, consider that when you return, my snug won't be as welcoming. I've given you everything you asked for and more. I helped you get Haydan out of the depths with the girls and that needed a special kind of persuasion. You have strong heirs to make your parents proud, all borne by me, carrying both our bloodlines. If you would rather have your chosen one, by all means go and find her snug instead."

Diego reminded Arianna of a tomcat as he straightened up, raked a hand through his hair and cursed. Rebekka looked furious. The air around Arianna stirred as a rumble of thunder sounded in the distance and dark clouds started forming low in the east.

"The dark gods want Haydan for the mask. They want his loyalty. If they can't get that, they will likely try to kill him. This is no ruse. You should know better than to treat me like you do. I am protecting our son from a fate I never wanted for him, but one that he's destined for. You always knew this was a once in a cycle event, Rebekka. Are you trying to renegotiate our terms?"

Rebekka's face fell. Perhaps she had been unaware up until that point about the true danger that Haydan faced, or maybe his warning about their unique relationship being brief had hit home.

"You speak of my presence no longer being welcome in your snug, but reflect on this, you have a great honour bestowed on you this cycle," Diego said. "If you choose to push me away, then maybe you'll find my chosen one out of the depths sooner than you anticipated. Her arms were always welcoming." Diego paused for effect, letting his threat register. "I'm the fae's royal line. I can live a long life this cycle if I choose to, but you dishonour me with this misplaced outpouring of fury and manipulation. I have enough of that from my parents. I will not accept that from you too." Diego drew his shoulders back and peered down at Rebekka, who appeared to have lost some of her earlier ire. "Perhaps when I return, I will no longer want your snug any more. Perhaps you should reflect on that whilst I am gone." He folded his arms.

Haydan would be devastated if his parents separated. It seemed that Diego's feisty defence of Haydan, attack on Rebekka's behaviour and consequent dismissal had the desired effect on her.

Unshed tears shimmered in Rebekka's eyes. "I love you. You know that. Yet you remind me of our arrangement like it's a weapon to hurt me with. Lavinia didn't tell me about the danger Haydan is in."

"No, why would she when Tallin offers safety? And you should know better."

Rebekka moved in and placed her hand onto his arm as though seeking a sign of forgiveness. Diego's body remained rigid, like a regal statue chiselled in stone. Cold. Unforgiving.

"Don't lock me out, not now, not if Haydan's in danger." Rebekka leant in, brushing her cheek against Diego's. "I adore you. I can't help being jealous. I want you all to myself. I don't ever want to let you go. Can you blame me?"

Diego lowered his folded arms. Rebekka moved fluidly into his reluctant embrace. Wrapping her arms tight around his waist, she burrowed her head against his neck, almost forcing him to hold her. After a moment of hesitation Diego capitulated. He dragged her close and embraced her, lowering his head to bury his face in her hair. He raised his head a moment later and stared into the distance.

Arianna couldn't help but wonder if he was thinking about his son, or his chosen one. Clearly the issue of what happened on their last trip into the fae realm was still festering. Had Diego been to visit her in the sea? Did he already know Haydan was keeping the soul safe for him?

After a prolonged and intimate kiss, Rebekka turned and walked off. Diego waited until her back disappeared into the woodland before turning his intense green eyes on Arianna. "Did you enjoy the show? I asked you to wait until I found you. I take it Teeam intervened?" One of his eyebrows raised as he awaited her response.

Arianna lifted her shoulders then nodded. "Teeam said I should stay close to you. He's concerned about Lavinia and Rebekka and what they might be up to. They don't want you reuniting with your chosen one."

"Really? But Teeam will already know that my chosen one's soul isn't back in the main sea. Rebekka is probably checking on that right now, which means that the real focus of their attention will be on Haydan, because he knows where she is."

That seemed an odd declaration. "That doesn't bother you?" Arianna asked, surprised that didn't make Diego furious.

"He's keeping her safe for me. Well, he better had be. I'd rather she was safe from Rebekka and my mother; she has been traumatised enough in the fae realm. If Haydan has found a solution to that problem, then it's one less thing for me to worry about, and I have enough on my hands right now. Speaking of which, we need to go before Storm Lands locks down again. I need to work on distracting the gods and keeping them focused on us rather than Haydan. There's a problem on Atis that needs dealing with, so brace for battle. I've dealt with my main priority, let's go." Diego strode purposefully towards Arianna, coming to a halt in front of her. "Thank you, for what you did earlier. Making yourself a target to protect Haydan was brave."

"You're welcome. That's what I'm here for."

Diego appeared reassured by Arianna's mature response. She smiled and waited for Diego's storm cloud to drop around them. They had a diversion to create and that was going to take time. Keeping the dark gods away from Haydan for as long as possible had just become her sole focus.

సౌ

Tallin

Theander approached with slow, somewhat reluctant steps. Tallin remained seated and still, in no rush to unnerve his visitor with sudden movements. The setting he had chosen appeared to bother the god, who spent far more time looking around and assessing the periphery of the room than he had done in the library.

"Take a seat. You are perfectly safe right now." That meant Theander would have to move into the light and Tallin was curious to finally get a good look at the god who was Asanda's most favoured heir.

Theander dropped into the high-backed padded seat opposite Tallin with a dramatic flourish. "The magic that surrounds this area is stronger within these walls," he said.

His voice was rich and deep, although the hesitant statement bemused Tallin. The god continued scanning the room. His hair was styled in a casual manner. He clearly didn't share Tallin's penchant for flamboyance and elegance, preferring a more relaxed appearance, although he was handsome enough to carry off any look he chose.

Tallin nodded as his skin tingled from Theander's presence. "Yes, it is rather wonderful, isn't it? I need to show you around and introduce you to all the traps so you know how to avoid them."

Theander's eyes widened, his hands gripped the seat arms tighter and his fingers flexed in agitation.

Tallin leant in, fixing Theander with his most scandalised expression. "Well, if dark gods are coming, it is only appropriate that I give them a suitable welcome, isn't it?"

"You have traps here? It's no wonder my family hate the place." Theander glanced around before returning his attention to Tallin. "You need to introduce me to the traps now. You can trap dark gods here too?"

Tallin picked up a glass and offered one to Theander, who shook his head. He placed the glass down on the table and reached for the decanter, sniffing the contents to find his favourite bourbon. The strong, heady scent overwhelmed him as he poured the liquor. Theander wrinkled his nose as Tallin took a sip. It burned his throat on the way down before settling in his stomach and warming his insides. "I can. Would you like them once I have caught them? They will be quite furious when they discover why I chose this location, which you of course knew I would. You hate the place because it interferes with your own magical powers and you cannot detect danger in the same manner as you can normally. They will hate it because it is the opposite of their abilities. They will have to repel my energy all the time, which is exhausting for them, and they will sense it is riddled with traps and misdirection." He didn't wait for an answer. "I gather figures with glowing eyes have been seen here at night moving about outside. I do hope that was you."

Theander smirked then nodded, looking pleased with his accomplishment. "Yes, I would like them, and yes, that was me. I knew you would choose this location. I've been trying to acclimatise to it. It still sends all my senses into overdrive, it's overwhelming. You are holding a masked ball here in a couple of nights?"

"Indeed I am." Tallin couldn't hide his grin of pleasure. "Would you like an invite? My parties are always a delight and as guest of honour I would make sure you would want for nothing."

Theander grimaced. "I would be pleased to accept, but don't draw attention to my presence. I want to meet the two ladies in Haydan's life … discreetly. Have you figured out a way to get Maya to join in the adventure yet?"

Chuckling, Tallin threw his head against the back of the chair. "Oh, Maya is a curious little thing, you just have to push the right buttons. She nearly fell into my lap when trying to figure out the fae realm. I have prepared her for a serious discussion about Haydan and protecting him. I am taking her to dinner shortly, which will be the perfect opportunity."

Theander continued to look uneasy. He perched towards the edge of the chair, as if ready to spring free at the slightest provocation. "Good, they have to figure this out and soon. Is Haydan in this realm yet?"

Tallin nodded. "He is on his way with Lavinia and Sandau. Diego and Arianna are diverting his pursuers and buying us some time. I am not sure I can deal with your uncles alone. I can sense your power, but if they are on a par with Kai I am a little ... well, not out of my league as such, but they concern me."

Theander grinned, flashing a dazzling smile at Tallin. "I have that in hand." He glanced back towards the light shower in the corner of the room as two figures entered one after the other. The first one looked more like a long, furry creature as it melted into the shadows and darkness on the edge of the room. The second one, rougher looking with dark shadow across his jaw and top lip, moved with a swagger that suggested he commanded those around him and expected everyone to comply with his demands. A certain level of arrogance flowed from him as he moved. Surrounded by a dark cloak that swept around his body and fastened over his shoulder Kai wasn't quite as Tallin had expected. The strange-looking rodent carried the more worrying energy signature.

Kai's scowl fell away as he glanced around him, a small smile tugging the edge of his thin mouth upwards. "Well, this is interesting, Thee, but I'm not entirely sure I like this place yet."

Theander smirked and relaxed back into the chair. "Oh, you'll come around to it. Our host is full of surprises." He rewarded Tallin with a knowing grin and peered into the room behind Tallin's head, ominously adding, "As are we."

Tallin tensed at the sensation of being studied by a power so penetrating he felt like it was slowly analysing

every cell in his body. The energy behind him switched.
The air in the room rushed past him in a sudden blast.
His hair moved in the breeze and his bond tattoo
released an unexpected burst of magic at the thrill of
being near the most powerful god in existence, because
it was Asanda standing behind him. He could tell by
the awestruck look on Theander's face that he couldn't
quite believe his achievement either.

"So, Tallin, fae king and chosen one, aren't you a
lucky man this evening."

Asanda's voice sounded gravelly and authoritative.
If Theander oozed serene control, Kai radiated
arrogance and Tallin couldn't even put a label on the
aura that Asanda emitted. The god standing behind him
had the most distinctive energy signature he had ever
encountered.

Kai focused on the door, before moving off, hauling
the door wide open and surveying the corridor beyond
with a confidence that bordered on haughtiness. Tallin
hoped Maya hadn't taken to sneaking about in the
darkness out there. Kai was drawn to something, unless
he was being overly cautious because of the magic
around him interfering with his normal senses.

"So, may I stand and greet my guests?" Tallin
asked, leaning forwards to rest his elbows on his knees,
wondering if Asanda would consider it rude to keep his
back to him. Theander bit back a smirk as his mouth
twisted up and he shook his head.

"You will show all of us the traps set around this
castle, Tallin, fae king," Asanda said.

Asanda arched over the back of Tallin's chair, so
close there was a haze around Tallin, who straightened
up and swallowed uncomfortably. Did the god
really have to get so close? His presence was quite

suffocating.

"Of course, but I am surprised by your presence, My Lord. Forgive me, but last time you encountered Haydan, you were more hostile. I do not understand why you would help now."

Theander's eyes widened, possibly in alarm. "Haydan has talked about that?" Warning burned in his intense expression.

Tallin couldn't help releasing a sharp peal of laughter. "Goodness no. I have not seen Haydan since he left my realm for Acquorous last time. Diego mentioned Haydan is still licking his wounds from meeting Asanda. He assumes Haydan met Asanda given that the merest mention of him panics the boy. Haydan seems particularly affected by certain situations and has sensitive trigger points. Whatever occurred in your realm last time hit one of them."

A look passed between Theander and Asanda, confirming something had happened that no one was going to talk about. Kai drew Tallin's attention away as he released a soft snort of laughter from by the open door. "Don't be shy, My Lady, come and say hello." Kai peered into the darkness, looking like a charming but dangerous rake as he surveyed his quarry.

A scuffle in the corridor suggested whoever was there had tried to run. Kai tutted and threw a ball of energy from his hand, which slammed out into the hallway like a whip.

"If that is Maya, do not hurt her," Tallin said, rising from his seat so rapidly that Theander startled. That sensation assaulted Tallin again. A blast of air rushed out from behind him as though Asanda had switched back into whichever form he first entered the room in.

Kai slowly reeled in his catch, dragging a furious-looking Maya into the room. She had changed into a teal-coloured gown which showed off the soft curves of her bodice and her svelte waist before plunging to the floor in swaying folds of fabric. She had pinned her hair up leaving a few tendrils loose around her face and shoulders. Looking less like the hellcat on the loose in his carriage earlier and more like a demure young lady she glanced around the room, brushed her fingers over her flushed cheeks and glared indignantly at Kai.

"Tallin was taking his time, so I came looking for him," Maya said. "May I ask who you are?"

She was within arm's reach of Kai, one of the most enigmatic and secretive gods in existence and appeared oblivious to how dangerous he was. Kai assessed her, his intense stare sweeping over her body.

"Hi, I'm up here."

Maya shot Kai a sassy look and a sarcastic smile as his attention returned to her face. His expression remained blank, as though he was still deliberating his response to her. The glowing rope remained wrapped around her waist and Tallin couldn't shake the uncomfortable feeling that Kai enjoyed having his magic cocooned around a female form that wasn't his. When Kai tugged on the rope again Maya was forced to take another step closer. Her glove-clad hand flew out to brace herself against Kai's chest.

Thankfully Maya was wearing something which would lessen Haydan's fury. Perhaps she had done that deliberately after Tallin kissed her hand earlier to rile Haydan. That thought made him smile even as he inhaled a sharp breath and focused on Theander. The younger god leant forwards and peered around the edge of the high-backed chair he was sitting in. He also appeared fascinated by Maya.

If Maya had overheard any of their conversation she would know Tallin lied if he gave a false name for his guests. "Gentlemen, there is a lady in the room, can we behave with due decorum, please. Maya is my guest. Maya, say hello to Theander and Kai."

Maya had noticed Asanda standing behind Tallin. He couldn't very well introduce Asanda without it being obvious; the god had a very distinctive name. There was movement beside him as something dropped to the floor and Maya's focus moved to the side of the chair, close to the floor. How odd … unless Asanda had switched back into the form he arrived in. He could sense tension flowing from Theander and Kai as they both tracked Maya's stare to the same spot by Tallin's seat.

Maya lowered her hand from Kai's shoulder and turned towards Tallin. "What the devil are you doing with Pablo?" She dropped into a crouch and held her hand out to the small slinky creature that ran towards her from beneath Tallin's feet.

Theander's jaw lowered but no sound came out. The expression on Kai's face was one of rapt adoration as the energy from around Maya evaporated and she scooped Pablo up into her arms, stroking his furry head as though nothing out of the ordinary was occurring.

"Are we going to dinner or not?" Maya asked, sweeping her innocent gaze across the men as she dropped Pablo back onto the floor like a feline. "What are you all gawping at? I know I'm wearing a ridiculous dress but it was the best of the odd selection. I'm starving, please can we eat? Pablo's one of my pets. He must have followed me here. He knows how to sneak about, rather like Tallin."

Straightening up, Tallin strode across and extended

his arm to Maya. "Gentlemen, please join us, I am sure dinner will be fascinating." He walked out followed by Theander and Kai. Dinner with the gods in residence was a rare treat. His days grew stranger by the second, but he wasn't about to squander the fantastic opportunity that had just presented itself.

Chapter 10

Haydan

Lavinia only released the glowing ball of light by Haydan's head once they reached the faerie pools; by then he felt too lightheaded and daft to care. He lay on his back in the arrival area after they had moved through the portal to the fae realm, rocking about feeling giddy. A moment later Sandau dropped into the pod and lay beside him. Sandau's odd grey-coloured clouded irises glinted in the dark as though glowing. Haydan giggled, wondering when he would feel normal again and when everything would stop moving around him.

"When you sober up, you are going to throttle that woman, aren't you?" Sandau continued peering up at the ceiling in the darkness. "She deliberately made a show of kidnapping you. I mean, I know I goad you about not being bonded, but that's just banter. You are Diego's firstborn son and I owe that man my life. She should show you more respect, although you do realise that was all for show, don't you? Diego was probably in on it too. Deflecting attention from you keeps you safer for longer…"

Haydan inhaled a few times, trying to feel normal again before he spoke. "No one in my family is ever entirely truthful about anything. Why are your eyes glowing in the darkness? Only the gods have glowing eyes. Wait … are you a god?"

Silence returned. Sandau appeared to ignore the question. After a few minutes, he turned his head. "How do you think I know so much about the dark gods, Haydan? My mother was a dark god. I, on the other hand, saw the light, which I can thank my father for. Light into dark and dark into light. No one can hold both inside them. It's not possible."

Before Haydan could ask more, the opening widened and Lavinia stuck her head in through the gap. "Could you boys quit with whatever this is, a bromance perhaps, and get out, please. We have a long way to travel and Tallin is keen for us to reach his summer court." She moved off.

Haydan cringed at the term. Katherine used it with Isaac and Si all the time. Sandau sat and drew his knees up, wrapping his arms around them. "Bromance? A play on brothers and romance. That's an Earth phrase, I'm guessing. I have heard of your grandfather's summer court. It's legendary amongst the dark gods, mainly because they are intimidated by it and there usually isn't much that daunts them. It's labyrinthine, full of secret routes. In fact, it's a perfect location for Tallin to choose."

"That figures. Tallin and Lavinia love games." Animosity rippled through Haydan's tone as he sat up and peered up at the opening. "Tallin had better not be filling Maya's head with stories again. I had enough of that last time, and you're right, I am going to throttle my grandmother." He threw himself at the opening, aware of Sandau scrambling after him, probably concerned by his sudden and rather violent activity.

There were guards emerging from numerous other arrival cocoons around the portal. It looked as though each one arrived in their own pod and the number of pods varied, depending on how many were travelling. The space filled with the sound of voices and scuffling as the men ascended into the space and began packing up their weapons.

Haydan caught up with Lavinia by the carriages. Holding a fleecy throw out in her hand, she turned when Haydan grabbed her shoulder and disarmed him with a smile of delight.

"I have missed you very much, sweetheart. You look so handsome. Maya is going to be missing you terribly. Shall we get going?"

Lavinia tried to put the throw around Haydan's shoulders as though he was a child. "Don't you dare act like nothing's happened!" He pushed her arms away. "You've just made a spectacle of kidnapping me, making me look stupid in the process and now you can't even acknowledge that you're out of order, and that's before I get started on what happened last time I was in this realm." He staggered for a moment trying to orientate himself as his world rotated around him. The sensation made him feel weak and woozy. "You behaved despicably. Maya is my chosen one. You should know better than to interfere."

Lavinia rolled her eyes, reached into her pocket and held the purple shock of hair up in her hand. "You need to get back to Tallin."

Haydan already disliked the traitorous ball of purple fur, which was nothing but trouble.

Lavinia threw the creature up into the air and

released a quick blast of energy from her palm, which sent it shooting off into the distance. Apparently satisfied with her achievement, Lavinia refocused on Haydan. "You're still not bonded though, Haydan. She's still not protecting you. You choose women who let you down and I'm not one of them. Tallin sent me to protect you and I am doing just that."

"Maya's fifteen, on Earth that's too young to bond." Haydan raised his voice; he couldn't help it. Lavinia appeared oblivious to his fury. "And before you say it, Arianna is also too young to be free of my controls, so don't even try that. I'm not having her distracted, and Arianna is already being pursued by Sandau." He shot a withering look at Sandau who sauntered up from behind him and peered into the nearest carriage before ascending the steps and throwing himself back into the seat. "Maya will bond when she is ready. I'm prepared to wait if that's what she needs."

"If she truly loved you, you would already be protected." Lavinia's silvery-green eyes locked onto Haydan's. "She is scared of bonding with you. That's hardly normal. Is the thought of being bonded to you really so terrible? You are Tallin's heir. You are destined for greatness. You allow her rebellions and I'm at a loss as to why. Has Diego not raised you to be strong when you need to be? I have shown you many secrets on Storm Lands, shown you things that most storm riders don't know about, yet you still hide away from your destiny. I do wonder if you are afraid too."

"Oh, quit with the analysis." How typical for his grandmother to try and deflect things. "If I truly love her, then I'm prepared to wait. You know you and Tallin shouldn't be behaving like you are. It might be appropriate in this realm, but it's not in any other."

With a mutter of disapproval Haydan hauled himself up into the carriage opting for the side furthest away from Sandau as they waited for Lavinia, who appeared to be joining them.

One of the guards helped her up into the carriage and she bestowed a look of displeasure upon Haydan and Sandau as she took her seat. The guard retreated and closed the carriage door.

The inside was more modern than Haydan had expected, although the feeling of being cocooned by the carriage reminded him of home. He resisted the urge to smile at that as he glowered at Lavinia, who seemed to be unconcerned by his ire.

"We are taking the carriage because the summer court is difficult to reach from here with magic alone and we need to talk and resolve the issues that you clearly have with me. Tallin would like you to be in an amicable mood when you arrive at his court."

Lavinia appeared to be launching a charm offensive. She gave Haydan another delighted smile as she sank back into the soft grey seating.

This was Haydan's grandparents at their most manipulative. Lavinia's red hair cascaded over her shoulders as she tilted her head and raised an eyebrow as though daring him to speak first.

"Oh, right, Tallin expects me to be in an amicable mood, does he? You've just kidnapped me. Tallin has kidnapped Maya. He's touched her twice just to drive his point home since taking her."

Lavinia's nose twitched.

"Which you must have felt too."

Her jaw tensed; Lavinia knew about the contact and definitely didn't like it.

"I was coming into the realm anyway and you just

had to make a show of dragging me here, didn't you?"

Lavinia chuckled. "Yes, I did. Got their attention, didn't I? Made you appear weak. Haydan, understand something and quickly, please. Sandau let me into Storm Lands with the guards before it locked down although he did not know details. Tallin sent me as a show of strength. I kidnapped you to show the shreken your weakness. Arianna distracted them, drawing their attention fully from you to her when she put the mask on. Diego is now with her diverting their interest further away from you, to give you a fighting chance of working out a few things first. Maya is in the safest place she could possibly be right now." Lavinia glanced out of the window into the darkness, before returning her cool stare to Haydan. "Tallin has just protected your most treasured possession and you are now trapped here with her. Your father has even loaned you his warrior as added protection. If I was you, I would thank our maker and Tallin for the inconvenience and humiliation he has just inflicted on you, because it might just save your life and that of the two women closest to you."

Silence returned as Haydan mulled over her announcement. "Sandau and Diego were in on this, with Arianna?"

Sandau shrugged as he sank back into the seat looking unconcerned. "Your indignation made it appear more authentic. Don't expect an apology from me, it was Tallin and Diego's idea." He drew his leg up onto the seat beside him and wrapped his arms around it.

Haydan focused on the mist that blanketed the surrounding woodland. It crept between the trees like a shroud, slowly smothering everything in its path. A shiver slid down his neck as Lavinia leant forwards and peered out of the window. Her straightened back and tense eyes suggested something was bothering her.

"Stay away from the windows and don't stare off at anything lurking out in the woodland," Lavinia said.

A ripple of energy ricocheted past the carriage. Haydan's altera tingled as it absorbed a tiny amount of the freely offered power which slid into his body like a drug. When he turned to look back out of the window, he could see columns of light in the darkness of the woodland and cloaked figures gathered around the columns as though drawn to a source of interest.

"I said don't make eye contact."

One of the figures closest to them turned. Haydan couldn't help challenging it with a cold look. Lavinia reached out to yank on his jacket sleeve. Reluctantly, he returned his attention to her.

"Why not? I'm your grandson. I hardly think they're going to mess with me, are they?"

Lavinia's edgy laugh sent unease racing through Haydan's mind.

"Oh, you would be surprised at what the temptation of an endless source of power can do to my people. You are a lure, Haydan, and you are not bonded, therefore weak. Stay close to Sandau, myself and Tallin, at least until Arianna and Diego return that mask to you."

Haydan gave Lavinia a glare of disapproval. "Why do I feel like you're enjoying this?"

Lavinia's delighted, wicked grin confirmed he was correct. "I'm stuck in a carriage for the next few hours with two of the most interesting men I know. I'm enjoying this. I haven't seen you in years. We have a lot of catching up to do."

Haydan couldn't disagree with that assessment.

They did have a lot of things to catch up on. Hopefully by the time he reached Maya he would have overcome his annoyance with Tallin, but he doubted it. Still sore about Lavinia's deceit, he returned his attention to her and resigned himself to being trapped with her for the next few hours.

❧

Arianna

Diego's storm cloud dropped around Arianna as they left Storm Lands behind. His tornado reflected his power more when he stood within it too. It slammed down, wrapping her in an energy unlike anything she had felt before, then lifted, leaving her feeling bereft but tingly all over. If he was aware of the effect on her he didn't show it as he pushed her back against a tree trunk and pressed his finger to his lips. Being so close to him thrilled and overwhelmed her all at once. Her eyeline reached just below his shoulder, which pressed against her face as he angled himself to peer around the tree. Arianna glanced away into the surrounding trees, unable to deal with Diego's proximity. She suspected he had done that deliberately because Haydan was off world and couldn't intervene. His heady, masculine, spicy, fresh scent was stronger up close, although that conflicted with the pungent scent of burning that reached her. Something was on fire.

Men were talking nearby, their voices hushed. Creaking of stirrups and rattling of reins confirmed there was a group of men and horses gathered close by.

Diego sniffed the air and grimaced. "There is a warlord present."

Diego's soft, resonant voice sent a small shiver down Arianna's neck. His breath brushed her skin creating goosebumps where it touched her. "They are burning the nearby village, taking everyone useful as slaves, probably killing the rest. I need the warlord to see me and sense the power I wield before we leave. Two of our teams are approaching from the other side. Stay close to me and watch my back. I've got too much else going on to worry about who is sneaking up on me. Back to back, Arianna. You've done this in training, yes?"

Arianna nodded. Her throat felt tight and dry. "Yes. Does this mean you need to connect?" she asked, keeping her voice low. They sometimes connected with other riders temporarily in combat; it made for faster communication between them, which was critical in battle. Connecting telepathically used more energy if it wasn't between a storm rider and his own warrior; the temporary connection lessened that. In battle, they saved as much energy as they could and this was a workaround. It also meant if a rider was injured they could leave their warrior with another and return to Storm Lands.

Diego nodded and rearranged the cuffs on his jacket. Last time they had tried this, she had been overcome and had failed the training exercise. That had been a year ago. He was taking a risk trying it out now. Diego moved away, allowing her to turn and present him with her neck. She swept her braid aside and focused on the tree bark as Diego's altera slid against her neck, his hand cupping the back of her head. Awareness of a connection forming with him reached her. It felt as though he was prowling on the edge of their link, waiting for her consent. Taking a deep breath, Arianna slid her hands up and around his wrist, brushing her fingertips over his altera. It was the only time she had ever touched an altera when forming this type of connection with another rider. The fact it was Diego she was sharing the connection with sent a shiver of delight through her mind. His altera felt warm and inviting.

"Concentrate, Arianna, and stay alert."

Diego's warning refocused Arianna. "Of course, My Lord, back to back." She released her hold on his wrist and a moment later he pulled his altera away from her skin. She could sense the connection between them, his mind now linked to hers. She could only use the connection to communicate about the battle, anything more was considered an infringement of the privilege.

Arianna was about to fight with Diego as his warrior. The honour of such a significant moment wasn't lost on her as she reached for her weapon and focused on the gathered men. Somewhere in amongst them was a warlord and he might be small in stature but he would be dangerous, skilled in battle and devious.

If Haydan had been present, he would have told Arianna to pay attention. Her excitement melted away as she focused on protecting Diego. When she turned back around he was standing close behind her holding the mask in his palm.

"Are you ready for this? Because once I put this on, the warlord out there will know we are here."

Arianna nodded and held her breath as Diego slid the mask onto his face. His skin rippled as it made contact and bedded down into the surface. The nearby sounds silenced. Now it was time to prove herself.

❧

Maya

Maya's rich teal-coloured dress trailed behind her as she walked with Tallin down to the dining room. Quick glances behind her confirmed that Theander and Kai were following at a safe distance. She knew she was in the presence of gods because she recognised the unusual names. Theander didn't seem overly concerned by her staring. Kai tried to ignore her, but when his intense cobalt irises locked onto hers she sensed dislike from him. The narrowing of his eyes suggested he did not welcome her attention. Tallin gave her arm a gentle tug and his dark eyes settled onto her, warning burning in their depths. She refocused on their walk through the summer court.

The building was vast and full of huge corridors and walkways that led between different rooms. They descended a large sweeping staircase and walked down another hallway. How Maya would find her way back later she had no idea. Pablo ran ahead, pausing at regular intervals to wait for them to catch up. Every now and again they passed what looked like the three balls that hovered in the corner of her bedroom. Unlike the ones in her bedroom, those in the corridor didn't light up or have water cascading from them. The spheres rose up as they walked past, almost as though trying to anticipate if they were going to walk any closer, then lowered back down to the floor again. Maya couldn't stop watching them, taking the opportunity to shoot another furtive glance behind her at Kai.

Kai stepped forwards so he was alongside Maya. "Perhaps you would prefer my arm instead of Tallin's? Then you can admire me all you like, because I clearly fascinate you."

Tallin settled a steadying hand over Maya's, maybe sensing her apprehension and the tension in her body. She found herself staring up into Kai's glowing blue orbs, because they did glow in the darkness. The sight was hypnotic.

"Forgive me, but I am sure Maya does not mean anything with her curiosity. You are known as being reclusive. I think perhaps she is a little overawed by your presence. It is a form of flattery, My Lord."

Kai blinked. Maya took a shuddering breath in. He had for a moment or two deliberately held her helpless in his hypnotic gaze. Kai turned his head, releasing Maya from the intensity of his attentions. Her heart pounded in response. She had just been given a tiny hint of the power Kai held and its presence had enthralled her. He was a magnificent creature, but far more troubled than Theander appeared.

Kai's glowing orbs locked back onto Tallin. "I don't care for flattery and I don't like being stared at."

Theander moved ahead ignoring the stand-off. "Kai, this is what happens when you hide away from the world. You have a pretty lady ogling you and you act defensively. What is for dinner? I think we should eat with the lady present, then retire to discuss the more private matters we talked about earlier."

Theander seemed to know the route already. He didn't break his stride, thankfully diverting Kai from Maya as he did so. Tallin pulled on Maya's arm, urging her onward and breaking her focus on the fascinating, secretive god. Kai had detected her hiding in the corridor earlier when none of the others had. Listening in on their conversation had proved intriguing. His interruption had been most ill-timed. She wanted to know more and judging by Tallin's attempt at ignoring her questioning look, he was fully aware of that. She was hooked on finding out more and knowing Tallin, that was exactly what he intended to happen. Tallin shot her a sly glance and gave a tiny headshake indicating she should keep quiet as they followed Theander into the dining room.

"So, you have already assessed the layout of this building, I see," Tallin said, focusing on Theander. Leading Maya around to one of the seats, Tallin pulled the chair out for her.

Servants were surprisingly few in number, but then that was probably deliberate so that no one saw or could talk about the visitors. The table was laid with ornate plates adorned with the royal crest, fine, twisted silver cutlery and glasses. The centre was full of platters of food mingled with large stone urns. Flat on top, fireworks exploded above the urns with no discernible source. Maya couldn't help smiling at the sight. The room was vast with huge plush rugs that ran around the edge of the seating area. The floor beneath was wooden. Beautiful frescos filled the walls. Bold, sweeping, tribal-like patterns flowed through the designs, appearing as a type of sunken relief, reminding Maya of ancient Egyptian art. They changed every now and again, but she never witnessed it. In fact, when she stared at them for any length of time they remained the same, until she glanced back and a different picture was on display.

"So, gentlemen, do you wish to talk about the

reason for your visit, or should we keep that for when we are more private?" Tallin asked, as he gestured to seats for Theander and Kai across the table and took his own seat near to Maya, perhaps to reassure her.

Kai ignored the seat offered to him, instead vaulting onto the table and walking along it. Tallin's frozen face suggested he was perturbed by his guest's behaviour, but of course he was too polite to say anything. Kai stopped in front of Maya and glowered down at her, before using magic to move the nearest urn out of his way with a flick of his hand. He then proceeded to move along the table, rearranging the nearby urns with the same careless throw of his hand, before jumping back down and walking along the perimeter of the table. Kai moved like a predator sizing up its next meal; his intense stare scanned the perimeter of the room, then the table. Hopefully he wouldn't choose the seat immediately across from her – which of course he did.

Rewarding Maya with a challenging look, Kai swung himself into the seat directly in front of her and reached for the nearest flagon of wine. He didn't pour it into a glass but swigged directly from the bottle. Maya found herself more amused than scared by his challenges. Tallin's face was a picture; apparently swigging wine from the bottle wasn't considered etiquette in his realm either.

Theander opted for the seat opposite Tallin and slid into it without comment as though used to Kai's unbecoming behaviour. Maya was so busy staring at Kai and Theander that she gasped when Pablo glided along the table, wrapping himself around each urn as he advanced slowly down the length of it. He came to a halt close to her, sniffed at a nearby platter and pulled a couple of slices of ham across onto a nearby plate with his mouth. Whether Pablo and Kai meant to be rude or not, she found the display of manners from Theander amusing given the total disregard for etiquette displayed by the other two. She focused on Pablo.

"Would you like some potatoes, Pablo? There are some vegetables as well." She grabbed a nearby large serving spoon and began serving food for Pablo, who sat back on his haunches and watched as the plate of food grew in size.

Kai placed the flagon back on the table. "No, I think we should talk about the dark gods and the danger Haydan is in, because when my brother shows up, it will be too late to protect the boy from harm and Asanda and I have to right a few wrongs from our past. If that means we collect a few dark gods for our vault in the meantime, so be it."

Maya swallowed; her throat felt parched. She reached for a jug of water and poured some into a glass. Her hands shook, the realisation adding to her unease as everyone watched her. She gulped down some of the water and placed the glass back on the table. "Who is your brother? Why would he want to hurt Haydan?"

Kai swigged from the flagon again, before slamming it back down on the table. Maya startled at the sound, her eyes clashing with Kai's again. Trying to act casual, she started putting her own food out.

"My brother is a brutal beast. His name is Iskar and he wants the mask. He still wants the mask and its owner to pledge allegiance to him. Nothing has changed from last time. He's slowly piecing together what happened six years ago. Do you know what he'll do to your beloved storm rider if he doesn't declare loyalty to the dark gods and their cause?"

Maya shook her head, barely able to breathe. The food no longer held any interest for her.

"Well, let's put it this way, Haydan won't be declaring loyalty to them, I'll make sure of it and they will likely kill him for that."

Maya dropped the spoon she had been holding. It clattered onto the plate, startling Tallin, who reached for her hand again, placing his over hers to reassure her.

"Yes, well, it will not come to that will it, Kai? Because we will make sure that does not happen," Tallin said. He sounded confident enough, but his shaking hand resting over Maya's told her otherwise.

Chapter 11

Arianna

An arrow whistled past Arianna's head, landing in a nearby trunk with a soft thunk. Diego dropped his storm cloud around her, pulling her away with him. He opted to land them in the middle of the group attacking the nearby village. Fortunately, the raiders all retreated and a cry of "riders" went up from the midst of them. She resisted the urge to roll her eyes as she backed up against Diego. For some reason, the riders always drew more attention than the warriors. Warriors did more physical damage but were less flamboyant with their arrival; perhaps that was why.

The burning smell emanated from a thatched roof on a nearby hut. Searing heat hit Arianna along with the acrid stench of smouldering straw. The village was in chaos. The screams and shouts of the locals mingled with the cries of the people attacking. Two men nearby went down with a yell as a couple of balls of energy found their chests. Arianna had no idea if they were stunned or dead, but knowing Diego he wouldn't leave that to chance.

Arianna blocked then parried the swing of a short,

stocky woman who tried to catch her with her sword. The sword looked of too good a quality to be swung by such a clueless brute. She had clearly acquired it in an underhanded fashion. When Arianna fended off the attack, her lip curled and she took another swing at Arianna using more aggression. Sweat ran down her face as she again tried her luck. Arianna blocked the thrust and followed through with an elbow to her face, before smashing a knife-hand move to her neck, using the edge of her free palm to slam into the weakest spot she could find. The woman collapsed at her feet.

Duck!

The command from Diego dropped Arianna to her knees as a man swung a cudgel at Diego's head with so much force she glanced up to see his sweaty armpits pass overhead as momentum carried him around in a full circle. She grabbed the sword of the stocky woman from the ground, before thumping it into the back of the man who had just tried to decapitate Diego. It was a well-made blade, with a good balance between the handle and sword; it cut through the man's back and chest like butter. After a sharp cry of pain, he didn't make much sound as he went down to join the stocky one.

"Separate them!" The commanding voice of the warlord cut through the surrounding commotion.

Turn one-eighty!

On instinct Arianna spun so she ended up where Diego had been standing. He would be searching out the warlord. Another couple of figures dropped nearby as an explosion of magic slammed out from behind her. She scanned upwards in time to see outstretched arms and catch the confused-looking face of a hairy male as his body sailed overhead before he fell face first into the back of a group of people fighting some of the locals nearby. They all collapsed after the impact like a deck of cards as the momentum swept them off their feet. Diego didn't mess around and the locals made quick work of finishing off what Diego had started.

Another group had peeled off from the main swathe and were making straight for them, probably to carry out the planned separation. Arianna caught a glimpse of a bright, vibrant green light between the palms of the warlord. At full height he was a little higher than her waist, but that didn't make him any less deadly. He stood in the shadows of a large building set back from the fighting. *Green fire to my left, near the large hut.*

Turn ninety, clockwise. Blades high, low and at the ready.

That was Diego's warning to Arianna that another turn was imminent and she should have both her swords positioned for attack. The thrill of fighting was bringing her soul to life as it revelled in the raw fierceness of the moment. This was what she was designed for. This was her chance to prove herself to Diego. Failure wasn't an option. He would never let her near Haydan again if she didn't blaze a trail of devastation and assert herself. Like a battle cry, her soul thrummed in response as all her senses ignited.

ॐ◌ॐ

Haydan

"**D**o you remember when you were younger and we

went off exploring the ancient part of Storm Lands?"

Haydan mulled over the strange subject shift that Lavinia introduced as the carriage rumbled along. He couldn't see much out of the window. The forest sat in darkness, shrouded by mist and blanketed by an inky black sea of sparkling stars. Sandau had dozed off next to him. His heavy breathing proved an added irritation. Sandau possessed his father's ability to sleep anywhere. Haydan had never mastered that particular skill.

"I remember you forgot to tell me about the flecky beast that patrolled the area. My magic wasn't as strong as yours and because it was a female it charged at me."

Haydan had been young and unbonded. His magic hadn't worked very well in the more ancient part of Storm Lands. It was only his grandmother's quick thinking that saved him. She had panicked and thrown power at him. It had slammed into his stomach winding him as it dragged him away. He had felt the creature's tusks graze his leg as it careered past.

Haydan had come to in a huge underground cavern. His leg ached. Investigation indicated a gash where the creature had caught him. Fortunately, it had looked worse than it was. The gouge didn't go too deep into the skin tissue. He didn't like to think back on what he found in those caves, but he had been grateful Lavinia had the good sense to find Arianna and bring her to Storm Lands because without his grandmother's rapid reactions he might never have found his way back out.

"Why are you bringing that up? Diego went crazy when he found out. He wouldn't speak to you for months."

"That was a horrible feeling to not know where you where, or why I couldn't reach you. You always enjoyed our adventures together. I showed you things your father didn't approve of for a reason, Haydan."

"Which is?" This would be good. Lavinia was either going to be truthful with him or play him again. He didn't have the energy to argue with her.

"You are my grandson. You are my heir and the result of many of our souls loving each other. Diego has tried to raise you to be strong and brave, but you need to open up your mind more to new experiences. I adore you, sweetheart. I know I shouldn't have done what I did last time, but it was only out of concern for you. Tallin shares my concerns, you know. Of course, he won't say that directly, but he does. You made interesting choices in the sea. Of all the souls you could have chosen, you selected Maya and Arianna, teased them out of the depths, and when Diego entered the sea just after Rebekka, you finally rose from the abyss. Two storm riders entering the sea together to activate it is rare and you gained an elder and elven prince for a father as well, an added bonus you might say. I still don't think you fully realise how momentous that was."

"Go on, say what you have to say and set your next game in motion." Haydan leant back in the carriage and waited for Lavinia to continue.

Lavinia lowered her focus to Haydan's altera, then swept her attention back up to his face. "Haydan, you have taken control of the mask of the gods. The dark gods wanted it; they still want it. You, Maya and Arianna are all in danger unless you can figure out your next move. Incidentally you won't be able to communicate much with Maya at the moment. The summer court is more protected from magic use than any of Tallin's other residences."

"Did you know?"

"Know what?" Lavinia said.

"About Leylani harvesting our souls?"

"I was aware she was up to things she shouldn't have been, but proof of that was harder to come by."

"So, you knew. That's a yes?" Haydan wanted a straight answer from Lavinia. He could occasionally get her to be honest with him, but to do so he had to be direct with her.

Lavinia rolled her eyes. "Yes, Haydan, I knew. What's your point?"

"You knew, yet you didn't stop her." Haydan folded his arms. "That could have been any one of us."

"Do you really think so little of me? You think…" Tears welled up in Lavinia's eyes. She bit down on her bottom lip and didn't meet Haydan's challenging expression. "It's one thing to suspect something, quite another to confirm that suspicion, especially in this realm. You should know all about that."

Perhaps that was a dig about his last adventure in the realm and Tallin's game playing, but before Haydan could ask what Lavinia meant, she leant forwards and reached for his hand, wrapping warm fingers around his.

"You're fifteen now. How are you? How are the girls? I understand Arianna is showing great promise, but what about Maya? Is she showing any signs of coming around yet?"

Lavinia eyed him with curiosity, but her expectant expression masked something else, perhaps concern. Haydan sank back into the seat. "How old were you when you bonded with Tallin?"

"I don't remember. A similar age to you now, I think. Why?"

Knowing that didn't help Haydan feel any better. He shrugged. "I wondered how long Tallin made you wait." Even Tallin had granted Lavinia her full powers before Maya would grant him his. He had hoped Tallin had made Lavinia wait longer. Disapproval flowed from Lavinia, although she hadn't said anything. His senses prickled with awareness of her displeasure at his predicament.

"She will make you wait until she comes of age. You have three years left. Start mastering the mask, Haydan. If you don't, not only will it frustrate you, but you'll remain in danger. The mask has to work with you and the girls to figure this out to protect all of you." Lavinia stared off into the forest, falling silent as though she had said too much. A moment later she returned her attention to him. "Leylani will likely be at the summer court. Watch yourself around her. I'm certain she would like a powerful soul like yours captured for her own use."

"Leylani wouldn't dare—"

Lavinia's face an expression of utter fury, her hands clenched in her lap. "Leylani has a way of capturing our kind. I don't know how she does it, but I don't want you caught up in her games. Diego moves with Tallin's intimidating swagger, but you are, in her eyes, the weaker connection."

Condescension rippled through Haydan's mind. When he was younger, dealing with Lavinia had been much easier. Now he had to worry about every deception, every anomaly and every little tell she inadvertently gave to him. "I thought she was a friend of yours."

Lavinia's eyes narrowed. "Really? It can be hard to tell my friends from my acquaintances. Tallin is no different." Apparently satisfied with her response, she settled back into her seat. "Spending time with Tallin will be good for you and the girls."

Haydan pursed his lips, sank back into his seat and yawned as the evening caught up with him. He would be able to see Maya again soon. Hopefully she had behaved herself and hadn't landed herself in any trouble. He was going to have to focus on facing Tallin. A chosen one kidnapping another chosen one was unheard of, not to mention bold and extremely brave. It could not be left unchallenged. That was going to be an interesting showdown.

∂∞∂

Maya

"Why would Haydan be in danger?" Maya's question startled Theander. Perhaps he found her tone aggressive, but she didn't care.

Kai swigged from the flagon again. Above him on the frieze, three ball shapes in a triangular pattern kept appearing then moving about, reappearing on different parts of it. Maya found herself tracking the movement. When her gaze lowered Kai was watching her. Every time she looked away, then back, he maintained eye contact with her. Her face became heated under his scrutiny. Aggressive was definitely the word for the god directly across from her. When Maya met Kai's stare for the third time, he leant forwards.

"What are you, Maya? Friend or foe?"

Hostility flowed from him now and another emotion, one that she found harder to place, curiosity perhaps. His mesmerising blue eyes flared again, the aura proving as distracting as the first time.

For a few silent moments Maya was unable to break his hold. She finally managed with some effort to blink, overcoming the spell he held her under. She turned her attention to Theander. He didn't carry himself with the same intimidating swagger as Kai. "Are you going to answer my question? You've just told me Haydan is in danger. Tell me why. How can I help him and Arianna if you keep me ignorant?" she said.

Pablo unfolded himself from the bowl of fruit he had wrapped his long sinewy body around and straightened up. His fur bristled, making him look larger as though he had been possessed. "Leave Maya alone!"

Kai cocked his head to the side and sank back into his chair, releasing a rough, gravelly chuckle as he did so, leaving Maya with the odd impression that he still wanted an answer. His eyes lingered on her with a precision that was unsettling. She remained the focus of his attention. He was evidently waiting for his moment to strike.

Theander cleared his throat. "Maya, you should concentrate on me, not Kai."

A warning glare passed from him to Kai, as though he was silently communicating something that Maya didn't yet understand. Their secrets were annoying. She released a small growl of frustration, which gained her Pablo and Theander's attention. Had she surprised them, intrigued them, or did they regard her as a challenge? She had no idea, but their enigmatic responses were as fascinating as they were irritating. A cunning idea slipped into her mind, bringing a smile of delight to her face. Pablo's brows dropped into a scowl. She let the smile melt away and returned her attention to Theander. "I'm sorry, you're hard to read. Is there a library around here somewhere? Maybe that could help with deciphering your strange little mannerisms."

Theander's eyes widened again and Maya detected a flare of light in the azure depths. She had hit a nerve again, because even Theander was now silently communicating things to her that she had no hope of understanding.

"You tell me Haydan is in danger, yet no one will tell me how or why. Whatever it is, I'm assuming it's something pretty major for us all to be gathered like this, but you all remain silent about what's going on. You're as bad as storm riders with your secrets. Or is this because I'm female and you think in some misplaced act of male bravado you're protecting me?"

"I really need to know." Kai's eyes locked with Maya's again. In what felt like a heartbeat, he was up from his seat, standing on the table in front of her.

"Gentlemen, I don't really—"

Tallin's plea for calm didn't seem to register with any of the men. Captured in Kai's intense stare Maya was trapped. He held her rapt, the cool, inviting depths welcoming her. He moved closer and powers she had never felt before released and wrapped around her body, holding her still. Her own thoughts abandoned, she felt tiny and helpless as the predator in the room closed the gap and dropped into a crouch, lowering himself to her level.

Kai's right hand raised. His glowing fingertips released a flow of light into the room. Maya heard a small gasp, perhaps from Tallin. Then Kai's left hand raised. His left hand was darker; it didn't glow in the same manner. The light flowing from his right hand still held her rapt, but curiosity about the other hand overcame her and she risked a glance across. His left hand was black. Strands of darkness drew towards his left hand, sliding like mist towards his fingertips. It reminded her of a black hole, dragging energy towards it, distorting the air around it.

Maya stood and pushed her chair back. Kai was offering her something, giving her options, and her choice mattered greatly to him. Tallin, Theander and Pablo had all fallen silent but she sensed the expectation as they waited for her to choose. Kai moved his hands together so the tips of his thumbs almost touched.

Maya met Kai's cobalt eyes, which started glowing again. His hands framed them as though he was the devil himself offering her two options, one of which could be her undoing. He no longer intimidated her. He was the most fascinating creature she had ever met, if only because he understood the way her mind worked. One god, two options – the light and the dark. The only sound was her heavy breathing. Her own instinctive choice surprised her as she raised shaking fingertips up.

Chapter 12

Arianna

The blade that met Arianna's as she spun around sent a reverberation shuddering down her arm. The woman glaring at her looked as unforgiving as Arianna felt. With a growl of frustration, she landed a swift kick to the woman's stomach, sending her flying backwards. When the woman picked herself up, she bounded back across to her. Her blade clashed with Arianna's again. Arianna punched the side of the woman's head hard. She staggered and reached behind her back. Arianna stabbed forwards, disabling the woman's shoulder before she could grab the smaller blades she had anchored to her back. With a snarl of pain the woman backed away. The number one rule of battle was never to leave an injured opponent close by where they could surprise you with an unexpected attack. Her injured arm hanging loose at her side, the woman appeared to be weighing up her next move.

Arianna dropped down low. Spinning on her knee, she kicked the woman's feet from under her. As she plunged, Arianna released her second sword, which fell to the ground. She grabbed the small blade on her back, powering through with a swift downwards motion into the woman's chest.

Diego deflected the first ball of energy the warlord threw his way. Crouching down, he placed his hand on the ground, making it vibrate as he continued to challenge the warlord. Lightning released from the ground around Diego and Arianna.

The man might have been small in stature, but he didn't look concerned by the strange phenomenon at their feet; instead he seemed impressed. He reached into a cloth bag that hung around his neck and threw a small object towards Diego's feet. Diego sent a ripple of energy out through the ground, which deflected the object, spinning it into the air with so much force it moved like a bullet. The resultant explosion made Arianna's ears ring as she returned her smaller blade to her back and grabbed her fallen sword. An arc of light overhead indicated the presence of one of Kaleshar's shields, which bounced away whatever had been intended for Diego.

Behind them, a group of guards had regrouped and were edging closer. *Five guards approaching my side, Diego.*

I'm sure you can handle five men, Arianna.

Diego's response made Arianna smile. She *could* handle the men. Diego felt comfortable allowing her to take charge of that. An explosion of movement behind her indicated Diego was moving to defend himself from attack.

The first two guards slipped nearer, clearly waiting to see if Arianna would take the lead. She remained in her defensive stance, with her swords angled downwards. It gave the false impression that she would be slow to wield them, but she didn't always brandish her swords the way they did.

The first man inched forwards. After a quick scuffle, he cried out as Arianna sank her blade into his thigh and twisted. He wouldn't get up anytime soon. A swift kick to his head ensured he wouldn't surprise attack her either. The second one didn't see her coming as she dropped down, swung her leg and kicked his feet from underneath him. She slammed her blade into his shoulder, the one holding his weapon, and rounded on the remaining three. The third one lunged for her and they parried and blocked each other a few times before she managed to dislodge his sword from his hand with an upward sweep of her blade into the hilt of his weapon. He staggered backwards in surprise. Arianna thumped her swords into the ground, her fist into his cheek and, in a deft movement, wrapped her hands around his neck. Dragging him forwards, she planted a knee in his stomach, causing him to collapse. It would take him a few minutes to get his breath back.

The remaining two circled Arianna, moving out to opposite sides. One carried a set of nunchucks, the other an angled sword designed to inflict major injuries on anyone it came into contact with. A few minutes later and both men were injured and down on the ground bleeding out from injuries to their legs and torsos. She sank her blades into their chests making sure they wouldn't get back up. *I've dealt with the five men.* She straightened up, sensing Diego's amusement through their connection.

"Who are you and why are you interrupting my plans for this village?" the warlord asked.

"I'm Diego, storm rider elder, and you are not razing this village to the ground. My people won't allow it. Move on before I demonstrate why."

"Well, that isn't happening. You don't fight like the

rest. Why not?"

"Fighting like the rest would suggest I share similar characteristics to them, which I don't. I'm unique," Diego said.

"Hmm, aren't you just. I could use someone like you on my team. Name your price, because everyone has a price."

Either the warlord knew how storm riders worked and was being clever with Diego, or he was ignorant to their ways, but no storm rider would accept an offer of a bribe.

"I don't have a price, I'm not a mercenary. There are more of my people here awaiting my command. Move on, warlord, before I make you sorry."

The warlord scrutinised Diego. "Why is your face funny-looking? Have you found some sort of new toy, storm rider elder? I'd like to know more about that."

Arianna fought back a grin of amusement. The warlord had fallen right into Diego's trap. All it would take would be a few questions from him about masks and ways to boost magical abilities to the right people and the rumours would spread, drawing further attention away from Haydan. With shreken warriors and warlords talking about enhanced powers it was bound to lure the dark gods, exactly as intended.

Maya

"Lose the gloves, Maya."

"Haydan will know."

Maya hesitated; contact with Kai's skin would trip all of Haydan's warning systems. There was no understanding from Kai; defiance reflected back at her. He didn't care. He fully expected her to touch her bare fingertips to his and make her choice. She had no idea how she knew that, but she did.

Maya reluctantly peeled the gloves off and passed them to Tallin. She took a deep breath in, preparing for the wave of nausea from her connection with Haydan, and intertwined the fingers of both hands with Kai's. Locking her fingers down between his, she pressed her fingertips into the back of his hands; their palms met. She stared him down, delighting in the slight widening of his eyes as he acknowledged her direct and forceful challenge.

Kai's power hit Maya first like a tidal wave and was followed by overwhelming nausea from her connection to Haydan. She gritted her teeth as saliva flooded her mouth. She refused to back down or appear weak.

"Maya, let go," Tallin said.

"No."

She heard Tallin's sharp inhalation at her defiance. Movement off to Maya's side indicated Theander had slipped around to her side of the table. He stood within reach of both her and Kai, but didn't touch either of them. Theander's attention had locked onto Maya's hands, which now reflected the same colouring as Kai's, but her left hand had turned dark and her right hand glowed light. The contrast was intriguing. Her dark fingers were enveloped by his glowing ones and vice versa with her other hand. For a moment, she thought Kai had done something to her, but that made no sense. She had made her choice, light and dark. She had no idea what that choice meant.

"Maya, enough, release Kai's hands before he hurts you." Theander regarded Maya with his measured stare. If he was surprised by the turn of events he didn't show it.

Maya didn't want to let go. She didn't want to show Kai weakness. She ignored Theander and focused on Kai. The flow of his powers intensified. She had no idea why proving herself was important, but she wasn't ready to back down.

"Why doesn't Kai release me? Why don't you ask him that?" Maya asked. The nausea remained, swirling around her stomach.

"After you, Maya. Ladies first – you do look a little pale, are you sure you're alright?"

Kai feigned surprise as he studied Maya, clearly delighting in her obvious discomfort. A sheen of perspiration covered her brow as she tried to focus on anything other than feeling ill. Her hands felt like they had melded with his, but the silent fight for supremacy continued between them.

Kai increased the flow of power. Lowering his head, he moved his hands back out, dragging Maya's with his. His intense glowing eyes remained locked on hers. The contact with his hands was beginning to hurt.

"Maya, let go, this will not end well for you if you do not."

Was that Tallin or Theander? Maya could no longer distinguish between the two. Her face felt warm as the nausea returned.

"Maya, stop this immediately!" Tallin's fury rolled off his every word as he moved to Maya's other side. "If I was Haydan right now, I would be livid and rightly so."

The reminder of Haydan snapped Maya out of her

challenge with Kai. Blinking a few times, she lowered and bowed her head to him. Shame flared through her mind like wildfire. "I'm sorry, My Lord, forgive me. Help me protect Haydan. He's the most precious thing in the world to me and I would do anything for him."

The pain flowing in waves from Maya's hands intensified. Kai refused to release her from his grip. Tears spilt onto her cheeks as she tried to free herself. "Please, My Lord. I'm sorry. You're hurting me."

"Kai, enough," Theander said. "Maya has challenged you and is now apologising for overstepping the boundary."

"She is not on her knees."

Kai's quiet voice was laced with warning, granting Maya a glimpse of his unforgiving nature.

"When she kneels, I might think about releasing her."

All the fight left Maya's body. Heat and pain overwhelmed her as Kai continued to flood the room with his powers. Unsteady on her feet, her legs buckled and she slumped to the floor. With her arms now held by Kai above her head she felt vulnerable and weak.

"Now you have your answer, release her." It was Pablo's stern voice that finally granted Maya relief from the intensity of Kai's hold over her.

His power released and her arms dropped to her side like lead weights. Desolation overwhelmed her as tears coursed down her cheeks. Her stomach lurched and she inhaled a huge gulp of air, fighting back the urge to vomit. She had no idea what had just happened, but strangely the release from Kai's powers bothered her more than the fury from Haydan that roiled around her mind like a storm-ravaged ocean.

❧❦

ᚺaydan

Haydan bolted upright to find the carriage shrouded in darkness. Sandau was still sleeping. Lavinia too looked like she had nodded off. She was reclined in her seat like a regal goddess.

Nausea churned around Haydan's stomach. Reaching for the side of the carriage for support, he took a few deep breaths as he fought back the sensations overwhelming him. It wasn't the movement of the carriage that was making him feel ill, it was connected to Maya. He only reacted like that if she touched another male. The sensations intensified. He gritted his teeth and closed his eyes, willing her to stop whatever she was doing.

What are you doing, chosen one, and who are you doing it with?

That was a most intriguing question, because Alex wasn't in the realm and he would have been Haydan's first choice. The sensations assaulting him felt stronger than the last time Tallin briefly touched Maya. Well aware of how much it would upset Haydan, Tallin had deliberately kept his taunting contact to a minimum. This time it felt more challenging. Haydan had no idea why a more powerful being would want to touch Maya, but he didn't like it.

Maya didn't respond to Haydan's question. A wave of heat hit him. It was the most intense assault of power he had ever endured from their connection to each other. He lowered his head fighting back the nausea. Maya wouldn't be enjoying this either. It felt as though he was dying. He dropped his head into his hand and rested his arm on his knees as his vision swam.

Haydan jolted awake a moment later. The sensations from earlier had gone, although he still felt weak and disorientated as he raised his head from his lap. Tallin wouldn't let anything happen to Maya whilst she was in his care. He felt confident of that. Tallin held a strong sense of loyalty to his family and great respect for the storm rider hierarchy. He had demonstrated that when he deferred to Teeam the last time Haydan was in the realm. Tallin regarded Maya as his future family and regardless of Lavinia's meddling, he would protect her for Haydan.

Knowing that didn't help. Possessed by thoughts of terrible things happening to Maya whilst he was unable to help her, Haydan struggled to calm his raging mind and silence the unease that tugged at his conscience.

Lavinia and Sandau were still sleeping. Relieved, Haydan turned his head and peered out into the darkness of the surrounding forest. He didn't want them seeing him so weak and exposed. The woodland looked deserted, although his subconscious prickled with the awareness of being watched by something. The realisation left him feeling uneasy as he took in the bleak landscape. His mood remained grim as he sank back into his seat and let exhaustion wash over him. A growing sense of dread built within him, reminding him he was back in his grandfather's realm and vulnerable.

Chapter 13

Maya

Maya raised her head when she felt well enough to do so. The room swam around her. Kai sat in the seat opposite her with his foot up on the seat next to him and a piece of bread in his hand. He nonchalantly chewed a bit of it whilst watching her with a curious look on his face.

Tallin helped Maya back up, placing a concerned arm around her shoulder as he did so. The only reason she didn't feel ill at his contact appeared to be the gloves on his hands. "You never cease to amaze me. Are you quite recovered, young lady? I am not entirely sure challenging the second most powerful god in existence was wise, but you are still alive so I will take that as a good sign." Tallin tried moving her back to a nearby seat.

"What does that mean? The choice you just gave me?"

Kai ignored Maya. Reaching for a tumbler, he poured himself a glass of something that looked like a strong liquor. He swirled it around then took a sip.

Theander moved around the table towards Kai,

who slammed his glass down and stood, before glaring across at Maya with a look of total fury on his face. "Nobody ever challenges me like that. If you ever challenge me like that again, chosen one, I will kill you."

"She didn't understand what she was doing. Maya requires special handling. Let me talk to her. Not everyone is your enemy. We talked about you working on your communication skills more," Theander said. His arm raised in a calming move, which failed to register with Kai.

The men stared each other down.

Their stand-off appeared to alarm Tallin. He fidgeted around in constant agitation beside Maya. There was no sign of Pablo.

"Then get her out of here before I change my mind," Kai said.

"I require special handling? How dare you. That's out of order."

Kai and Theander both turned towards Maya at the same time, their eyes flaring as they did so. Tallin hustled her towards the door.

"Maya, you need to sit outside and calm down. You are in the presence of powerful gods and most of your actions are wholly inappropriate."

"But Haydan's in danger," Maya said.

Tallin led Maya to a velvet-covered seat in a recess in the corridor outside the room and forced her into it with a hand to her shoulder. "Do not leave here until I return and stay out of trouble in the meantime. I will explain later but I cannot just give you the answers you seek. It does not work like that. You have to earn them." He placed his hand against his forehead in obvious frustration at the challenges she had thrown his way that evening. "You said you do not know anything about your grandparents."

"I don't, I told you already. My mother was adopted as a baby."

"When you were a baby did Haydan give you a special gift? Something to entertain and amuse you as you grew up?"

The shift in topic seemed odd. Haydan had gifted her Maechi when she was a baby, it was her pet dragon, but he couldn't be referring to that. "He gifted me a toy dragon when I was born."

That appeared to draw Tallin's attention. Plumes of mist released from his neck, drifting around him as he assessed her. "Did he now? Tell me, did it start out as a dragon or as something else?"

Maya tried to remember what her mother had told her. "It changed a lot before settling on the dragon form. Why do you ask?"

Tallin's eyes tensed, suggesting there was some hidden significance in that information. "Did your mother get a similar gift from your father? Or was there something significant between them that was what you might call a private joke?"

"Mum always says feathers remind her of my father. He used to leave little piles of them around the house and hide gifts in them." Tallin's stare reminded Maya of a hawk. "Why, is that significant?"

It always felt as though Tallin was hiding fascinating secrets inside his head. His eyes glittered with mysteries.

"It might be something and nothing. I need to get back to our guests. Do you like to dance?" Tallin started waltzing around the hallway as though holding an imaginary figure in his arms. "Tomorrow I'll teach you before the ball. Stay here, yes?"

Maya nodded, resigning herself to a lengthy wait

as he turned and stalked off. He shut the dining room door behind him, closing off the room to anyone spying on them. She had no intention of trying to sneak a look at what was happening in there. Kai had sensed her earlier and she had already riled him far more than she should have.

Movement off to Maya's side drew her attention. The purple ball of fur from Tallin's pocket slid towards her out of the darkness from over by the three balls, which she was certain had just moved back to the ground. The pixie post slid along the hallway and around the corner. Without heeding Tallin's warning to stay put she followed.

ॐ

Haydan

Haydan awoke to find it was still dark outside. The trees receded as the road widened and the carriage turned left. To his right-hand side water cascaded down from his grandfather's summer court, which rose out of the side of the valley as a majestic citadel, looking dramatic and impressive whilst holding an air of mystery. For once, the presence of water proved reassuring. He didn't have a great track record around water. It surrounded the portal and had guided him into Acquorous when Kaleshar pulled him through the portal last time. Then the lagoon by Asanda had nearly drowned him. Having his snug flooded by whirling dervishes and almost being drowned when he was younger by one of the ancient ones probably didn't help either, but in Tallin's realm, water felt more protective and cosseting. The sight made him smile; it was typical Tallin. The building in front of him convinced him Tallin would be in his element.

Edging forwards in his seat, Haydan peered out, his sense of dread from earlier disappearing. He felt more optimistic now that he could see his grandfather's home. Maya was with Tallin. He wouldn't have long to wait before they were reunited.

Sandau slept on, curled up like a feline. Lavinia surveyed him and smiled. "He's a fascinating creature, isn't he? One of the greatest mysteries about your father, that Diego chose Sandau as his warrior. He's the only one of us who fully understands the gods and their ways. Your father has loaned you his greatest gift given your situation. Keep him close and use him wisely." Sitting back, she focused on the view out of the window. "This is Tallin's summer court and he will be incorrigible whilst here, so I have warned you. You struggle to deal with him when he's so flamboyant, but it's because of the nature of his court that he behaves like that. It's one of my favourite places in the realm for that precise reason."

The carriage turned towards the gates leading into the walled city, which felt ancient, as though it had been built before the surrounding forest grew up around it.

Sandau jolted awake and smiled as he stretched out. "You've never been here before, have you?" he said, shooting Haydan a curious look.

"No, I haven't. Are you going to share some of those secrets with me about this place, or are you going to hold out on me?" Haydan asked. Sandau would keep him hanging a little longer, he felt certain.

"Give me a chance and I'll go one better and show

you." Sandau smiled, his expression speculative as he stared out of the window. "The summer court is Tallin's favourite place because it's as mysterious as he is and as playgrounds go it's perfect. It's a massive warren of traps designed to catch any type of magic user, particularly those adept at dark magic. It drains their power too." Sandau returned his attention to Haydan. "So, why do you think Tallin chose this location, Haydan?"

Haydan tried to keep the hint of sarcasm from his tone as he fixed a withering look on Sandau. "Because he loves playing games and showing off?"

A sharp bark of laughter left Sandau's mouth. "No, Haydan, that's the wrong answer. Tallin is one of the most astute game-players going and if he's chosen this location, it's with good cause. Never underestimate your grandfather. When the dark gods come here looking for you, which at some point they will, he'll lead them a merry dance before they catch him. Once you understand the secrets of this place, you'll be able to as well." Sandau's brow furrowed. "Are Maya's furry friends here yet?"

Lavinia shrugged, apparently unconcerned by the absence of the whirling dervishes.

The carriage rumbled along the road into the city before the main citadel came into view. Sandau fidgeted next to Haydan, suggesting he wanted to be on the move. His growing impatience had the same effect on Haydan.

Lavinia's cool silvery-green eyes flitted between the two of them. "Sandau, what's wrong?"

Sandau's nose twitched. "I can smell something unusual. I assumed Tallin was careful about what he allowed into his court, but perhaps that was a mistake."

Lavinia's smile confirmed she approved of Sandau's astute observation. "Tallin knows what he allows into his court. If you smell something unusual, it's there because Tallin wants it there. You will wait for the carriage to stop, won't you?"

Sandau's raised eyebrow suggested that announcement intrigued him. "I'm warrior, My Lady. Don't tell me what to do." Leaning forwards, Sandau opened the carriage door and caught the attention of one of the guards, who brought a saddled horse alongside the carriage. Sandau stepped into the stirrups and gracefully mounted the beast before moving off.

Lavinia chuckled as she leant forwards and closed the carriage door. "Tallin is upset with you. Six years is too long, Haydan. He found you six years ago and you only return when you have no choice. Make some effort with him, please."

"Make some effort? He kidnapped Maya. Then he touched Maya deliberately, because he knew I would hate it. He tried to trap Diego and me here last time as well. I'm not sure I've forgiven him, so don't tell me to make some effort. He needs to make the effort with me."

The carriage came to a stop. "Haydan, wait, please."

Haydan reached for the door before Lavinia could stop him and flung it open. Descending from the carriage, Haydan gave one of the nearest guards who rushed towards him a glare. He had no intention of waiting for the guards to open the door for him and suffer the indignity of them helping him down from the carriage. Lavinia was on her own with that show of theatrics. He turned towards the summer court. A huge staircase rose in front of him. On either side there was a tall plinth. A statue of a wolf sat on one side and an eagle surveyed the steps and his approach from the other. Movement up at the top of the steps drew his attention. A woman sashayed down the steps towards him; her blonde hair glinted in the moonlight. Now he understood what Sandau had meant earlier when he mentioned an unusual smell. The breeze around him picked up, as though Tallin was warning him of impending danger. The woman in front of him reeked of the strong, pungent scent of witch.

The woman brazenly strode up to Haydan, her eyes raking over him as she did so. A lingering look at his wrist confirmed she knew who he was, or at least suspected he was a storm rider. When she drew level with him, she pouted at him. "Well, you're a handsome boy, or should that be prince?"

Haydan remained silent and she rewarded him with another sultry look as she puffed her chest out. He refused to lower his gaze, keeping it on hers.

"Yes, you look like a prince, the younger one if your lack of confidence around women is anything to go by. I'm sure your father, Diego, would be able to handle me."

Haydan drew himself up as heat flooded his face. The cheek of the woman drove him to fire off a feisty response. "I could handle you fine, sweetheart, I just choose not to. I have no interest in you and your witchy charms."

The glint in the woman's eyes changed from playful to flinty. "No, but you at least acknowledge that I have charms." The playfulness returned. "If you're this much fun, I can't wait to meet your father." The sound of a sword unsheathing behind her ensured she straightened up. "Oh, I'm disappointed, you've brought one of your lapdogs with you."

Sandau placed his sword against her neck as he stepped up from behind her. "I'm not Prince Haydan's lapdog. I'm someone else's warrior and you're treading all over my toes right now, witch, so back off."

Lavinia moved to Haydan's side. "I asked you to wait for a reason." Her gaze locked onto the woman's. "You're not supposed to use the main entrance."

Sandau moved his sword away as the woman eyed him over her shoulder and dropped into a curtsy. "No, My Queen. I apologise. With it being such a late hour, I assumed it wouldn't matter. I have just been attending to a couple of the king's injured men."

"Injured men? How were they injured?" Lavinia asked.

"Creatures hiding in the woodland challenged the king earlier. The guards got in the way." The woman's attention locked back on Haydan's right wrist. When he noticed, she immediately glanced away. "It is a great honour to meet your grandson, however."

"I'm not sure Tallin will believe you." Lavinia's forced smile suggested an unseen battle waged between the two women. "Haydan, meet Leylani," Lavinia said.

Chapter 14

Maya

Maya followed the pixie post down the corridor. He descended the stairs to the next level then led her down the corridor and through a set of huge double doors into a room that appeared to be a makeshift library. At one end moonlight cascaded in through the vast windows. Books lined one of the walls; the rest were bare, but her attention was drawn to the golden gates at the other end. Mist rushed out along the floor towards her, as though something was burning inside. It reminded her of the mist released from Tallin's bond tattoo creeping towards her with an awareness that made the hairs on her neck lift. Something caught the light from within the darkness behind the intricate metalwork, as though calling her. The gates glinted as she approached. Tallin's magic caused them to catch the light unnaturally and it looked as though he had a mirror on the other side. Moonlight from outside the building glistened on the surface of something reflective – water. As she drew closer, the gentle ebb and flow suggested a river or small loch had been hidden away. Hiding a water source in a book made no sense whatsoever. She fought back the urge to laugh at such an absurd notion. Tallin exuded magic, anything was possible in his realm, but she wanted a closer look at the water book, if she had found such a thing. She ran her fingertips over the metalwork of the gate, which felt warm to the touch. A quick pull confirmed the gate was locked. The brush of fur against her leg and movement by her ankles made her gasp. She glanced down into the eyes of a silvery wolf sitting at her feet. Baring its teeth at her, it growled and all its hackles raised.

An eagle perched on top of the gate. It ducked its head and tapped the metalwork with its beak, filling the room with a soft metallic noise. Maya didn't know if she was being warned about the book, or invited to find out more. Tallin had never been defensive or aggressive towards her, so perhaps it was a test. His wolf was closer to her than the eagle, which she felt certain was Lavinia's representative in the dark fae's realm.

"Hello, beautiful," Maya whispered to the wolf. Its fur continued to bristle. "You're Tallin's guardian, aren't you?" The growling stopped. "Tallin wants Haydan safe, but how can I keep him safe if no one will help me. Will you help me?" She dropped down onto her haunches and gazed at the creature. It was striking, with thick, bushy fur that looked soft to the touch. Its teeth disappeared as all the aggression vanished. She sank her hands into the fur at its neck and ruffled its ears. "See, you understand me. The eagle still isn't sure about me."

The eagle flapped its wings and turned its head away as though in disgust.

"Haydan is the most important person in the world to me and I know he is to you too. Even bonded I couldn't protect him. This is about the mask. I wouldn't ask if it wasn't important. I've seen the weird book with the water in it. You wanted me to notice it, so help me reach it."

The wolf remained silent. The eagle ignored Maya.

"Great, thanks, you were a lot of use. I'll remind you of that when the dark gods finally arrive."

With a small huff of displeasure and more than a little frustration, Maya returned her attention to the gate. There was no obvious sign of a lock, but the gate was firmly closed. The erratic tinging noise started up again. Maya glanced up to find the eagle peering down at her with something hanging on a chain from its beak. Closer inspection revealed an orb encased in an ornate metal cage. Extending her hand, she reached out and grabbed hold of it. The eagle released the chain and flew off into the darkness.

"Great, now what?"

The wolf remained by Maya's feet. "Do you know what this is, or what I'm supposed to do with it?"

The wolf bared its fangs again, reached a paw up and tried to knock the trinket from her hand.

"What are you doing?" Maya snatched her hand away. The growling continued. "You want me to drop this? On the floor?" The growling stopped. "Okay, I should be used to this sort of thing by now."

Maya dropped the ball at her feet. For a moment, nothing happened then the metal surround fizzed and the ball split into three. Panic snatched her breath away as the three balls rolled around her, shot into the air and the golden gates vanished from in front of her.

⤫

Haydan

"**Y**ou're Leylani? You're a witch. One that harvests souls."

Leylani's smirk dropped away as her expression changed to one of fury. "My mother was a witch, my father supposedly a shapeshifter, so I'm not sure what I am. I heal and care for the sick and injured. You would be wise to check facts before accusing me of harvesting souls, especially given that the royal line and their guardians have distinctive souls."

Sandau growled as Leylani met his eyes with a cunning sideways glance, before returning her attention to Haydan's right wrist. Haydan made a point of pulling his jacket sleeve over his altera. He had already tempered his powers as he entered the realm after recovering from Lavinia's magic spell, so was confident it wasn't his magic that drew Leylani's attention. She appeared fascinated by it, however. Her gaze brazenly slid back from Haydan's wrist to clash with his and her full lips curled upwards.

"I assume you'll all be attending the king's masquerade tomorrow night?" Leylani said. "I'm very excited about it, as is Magellan, especially given that the theme is 'where the wild things roam'." Her smile dropped away on mentioning her husband's name. "I gather you met Magellan last time you were here." Her smile returned. "Although it's fair to say his description didn't do you justice, My Prince. If you need anything whilst here, or if I can be of any assistance, please don't

hesitate to ask. Handsome princes should always be
well cared for. Speaking of which, where is your lady
hiding?" Leylani glanced back towards the carriage,
then at Haydan.

Her question proved as irritating as Leylani. Haydan
felt relieved that Maya wasn't there, however, as it
meant Leylani couldn't identify her. Agitation followed
rapidly. It surfaced like a violent tsunami because he
didn't know where Maya was and there was no sign of
Tallin either. Tallin's absence was surprising, given how
much Haydan expected his grandfather to want to see
him and Lavinia.

"Haydan's chosen one is with Tallin and she is our
guest in this realm. It goes without saying that all our
guests are accorded the same levels of respect as Tallin
and I enjoy," Lavinia said.

Leylani lowered into another curtsy. "Yes, My
Queen, of course."

Lavinia swept her arm into the crook of Haydan's,
forcing him to bend his arm and endure the walk up to
the next level with her in close contact. Haydan took
his grandmother's lead and started ascending the steps,
shooting Leylani a withering glare and sweeping past
her as he did so.

A figure moved in the darkness of a nearby bower.
Someone was lurking there, keeping an eye on things.
Haydan couldn't make out who it was.

Leylani bobbed into another low-level curtsy. As
they left her on the ground floor, what disconcerted
Haydan the most was the fact that her intense eyes
hadn't left his right wrist. The realisation left his soul
cold.

᷐᷐

Arianna

The warlord stretched his arms out, clenching and unclenching his hands. Irritation pulled at his features as he ruffled his hair and dropped his arms down to his side. "I want that thing on your face. Tell me what you want for it."

Standing side-on to Diego, Arianna could keep an eye on the warlord's army and the situation with Diego.

Diego shook his head, scattering dark inky strands of hair as he did so. "It's not for sale. I'm not bartering for it, and no, you can't have it. It's nothing to do with my home world either and I don't keep it there, so don't even think a raid on Storm Lands will gain you what you seek. Not everyone has a price."

The warlord's expression remained grim. He scrunched his face up, reminding Arianna of an angry child. Given that he couldn't bully or buy what he was after from Diego he would resort to other more underhanded tactics to get what he wanted.

"Yes, well usually they do. Okay, I can just kill you then. I'm sure prising that from your corpse will be easy enough," the warlord said.

Diego's laugh was cold. "True, but there's a further problem with that plan, one your brain won't even comprehend right now."

The warlord's face turned red, his vexed scowl so deep his forehead had vanished into his long, shaggy mane of hair. "Oh, and what could that possibly be,

Diego, storm rider elder?"

"You have to be worthy and–" Diego assessed the warlord with a cursory sweep of his hand "–you don't fall into that category. If you kill me, this adornment you are so keen to get your grubby little paws on will simply disappear. That's a bit of a problem for you."

A disparaging look slid across the warlord's face. "In that case we are not leaving until you give me that thing off your face and my army will continue to destroy this village. They owe my employer a large amount of taxes."

Diego folded his arms. "You would do better to tell your employer to ease off this village. How are they supposed to pay anything when they have no livelihood left? You've just burned everything to the ground."

The warlord seemed unconcerned. "Not my problem."

A sneer of disapproval confirmed Diego disagreed. "No, their suffering never is. Which means this is not my problem either."

Diego backed away, pushing Arianna along as he did so. She resisted and stumbled over the collapsed men near her feet. Diego walked away and did nothing to help the villagers. Everything about that felt wrong.

"What are you doing?" Arianna asked. She kept her voice low. Diego had to have a plan of some sort. He couldn't just leave.

Diego's intense green eyes communicated all sorts of cunning plans as he stopped moving once he reached a safe distance away.

The warlord followed Diego's movements. Satisfied Diego was leaving, he beckoned one of his men over, presumably to have Diego followed. The man he summoned to his side bore the insignia of a mage. The tiny continuous flow of magic symbol was visible just below his ear. The warlord whispered to the mage and focused back on Diego, before sweeping away towards the main village as though dismissing Diego and Arianna.

Diego lowered himself to the ground and pushed his hands into the dirt. The ground shuddered. He was using his elven powers. Arianna staggered and almost lost her balance. Arcs of dancing, crackling lightning reached up from the ground, moving away from Diego as though he had triggered a spectacular light show. Spinning back around, the warlord glared at Diego as he backed away from the nearest arc, which slammed into the ground by his feet.

The lightning arcs distracted the warlord from the small portal that sprang to life behind him. Taking another surprised step backwards, as another arc smashed into the ground by his feet, the warlord breached the portal boundary. He glanced backwards, probably wondering where his foot had gone and yelled out as he was dragged beyond their reach.

Diego's arm raised and a spark of light illuminated overhead. That was the signal for their people to enter the fray.

Arianna gasped as Diego pivoted towards her, grabbed her arm and landed his swirling tornado around them. The last thing she caught sight of before they left the realm behind was the mage, who folded his arms, looked impressed and said, "Run fast, storm rider. I'm right behind you."

Chapter 15

Maya

Maya spun around to find the golden gates behind her. She was inside the restricted part of the library. Her foot caught on something and instinctively she knelt down to pick up the orb that rested by her feet.

The wolf passed through the gate, coming to a stop close by. On the shelf, the water book caught the light. Maya grabbed hold of it. It was cold to the touch. She tilted it in fascination as water sloshed around the outside as though she had created a wave. Various keyholes rose up from the water then sank back down again.

"I'll bet Tallin has the key," she said. Shaking the book resulted in water splashing onto her feet. She slid it under her arm. The wolf cocked its head.

"I'm not stealing, I'm borrowing it. I intend to return it once I've figured out how to open it."

Maya reached for the orb, before conducting a final scan of the bookshelves. She couldn't read any of the titles. On the higher shelving a series of books caught her attention. She assumed they were a series, all the titles had a similar style of writing and the design on the spine was similar with rapidly moving clouds. Resting on the shelf in front of her was an unusual bronze-coloured pair of glasses, or perhaps they were binoculars; she couldn't tell. The arms on them suggested they could be worn like spectacles, but the arrangement of the lenses reminded her of eye-testing equipment.

The room remained quiet. Tallin would still be talking to his guests. A quick inspection wouldn't hurt. Maya picked them up and slid them onto her face, glancing around to discover a whole new hidden world unveiling itself.

Two tiny faeries sat on the upper shelves curiously watching Maya back. Their arms were folded and their legs hung over the edge of the shelf. A huge butterfly with feathers surrounding its colourful wings perched on a large volume with a flurry of vines and leaves growing out of its spine. Gasping, she removed the glasses to check. None of the new additions were visible to the naked eye.

The book titles sprang to life in front of Maya as she put the glasses back on. The series she had been so fascinated by introduced itself as the words 'hello, chosen one' slithered down the book spines as though it was some kind of elven billboard. Maya wondered if she was expected to respond. The spines cleared and new words were displayed. 'Would answering be such a bind?'

"Sorry, hello. Can you understand me?" Maya asked. She was certain she was talking to herself, but in Tallin's realm anything was possible.

'Heathen human. I understand you better than you me… '

Maya couldn't argue with that. A book spine communicating with her was something new. "Heathen is a bit harsh, but you're right. Talking books are a novelty to me, although the voice-activated thing works, I guess. What's your name?"

'No name. It's your mood I see. Pick whichever book takes your fancy.'

The elven billboard disappeared leaving Maya with another choice over which book from the series to pick. The titles that had been present on the book spines earlier had vanished. A soft trail of mist flooded out from the inside of the books. Curling around the spines, it slipped along the shelf. Maya surveyed the books, deciding to pick the only one that made any attempt to communicate with her. Its spine glowed from within, pulsing gently as its glow emanated out into the room. She dragged the volume from the shelf, put it with the water book and pocketed the glasses.

Now Maya would have to move fast. She had to hide her stash of books and return to the dining room before Tallin realised she was missing and had disobeyed his instructions to stay where he had left her.

Tallin

The guided tour of the various traps and routes through the summer court had gone without a hitch. Each trap was activated in a different way, so it was important to know the locations of them and how to escape and activate each one. The gods left shortly afterwards, although Tallin had no idea how they travelled from his realm to theirs because the portal still hadn't activated, meaning they definitely had other routes into the realm.

That left Tallin with an uncomfortable concern about where Diego was and when he would be joining them. Lavinia and Haydan, however, were back. Haydan would be livid about his daring kidnap of Maya and Lavinia's methods of his extraction from Storm Lands. The show of bravado had been necessary to gain the attention of anyone connected with the dark gods and make Haydan look weak. It was the only way to protect him.

Tallin left the dining room in a rush to reach Lavinia and Haydan. His agitation amplified when he realised Maya had disregarded his instructions to stay put. The seat where he had left her was empty. He silently cursed and fixed his cold glare on the small purple shock of hair that ran back towards him down by the skirting boards.

"Please tell me you took Maya to the library to help her find the weight of water volume? If not consider yourself dismissed."

The creature scowled up at Tallin, before placing its hands on its hips. The sassy gesture wasn't lost on him. He fought back the urge to smile.

"She found the weight of water and picked from the tome of moods," the creature declared.

"Did she now? That is intriguing. Which tome did she choose?"

The creature rewarded Tallin with another sassy look. "Pocket."

"No," Tallin said. The purple shock of hair wasn't manipulating him any further.

"Pocket, or no deal."

Tallin shot an unamused glare at the irritation. Nothing in his realm worked properly without playing games with him first. It did occasionally grow tiresome. "I can just find out myself then."

"Yeah, but I saw what happened. If you weren't connected to your wolf at the time you won't know about it."

The annoying ball of fur made a valid point. With a huff of disapproval Tallin patted his pocket and folded his arms as the pixie scrambled up his trouser leg and clambered into his pocket.

"She chose the tome of forgiveness. Oh, the eagle helped her get into the restricted section and she found the deciphering glasses and took them with her."

"Who left those out? I have not seen a pair of those in a long time and mine are locked away. Or at least I thought they were. I should check." He would investigate before meeting Haydan and Lavinia to satisfy his curiosity. "Where is Maya now?"

The pixie peered back out from Tallin's pocket. "She went back to her room to hide the items. All of this begs the question of what has she done to need forgiveness for?" The creature shrugged and disappeared inside Tallin's pocket.

"You do know I am going to ask you to go and find Maya and bring her to meet Haydan, yes?"

The small thump as Tallin's jacket grew lighter confirmed the pixie was being kept busy and left him with the uncomfortable thought that perhaps Maya hadn't yet committed the heinous crime that required the tome of forgiveness. Just the thought of that put his earlier meeting with Asanda and his family into perspective.

With a heavy sigh Tallin moved towards his office to check on the deciphering glasses, which were still safely hidden away in his drawer. His curiosity satisfied he walked to the summer court entrance, bracing himself for an excitable Lavinia and a long overdue meeting with his furious grandson.

৵৽

Diego

Diego liked surprising Arianna. She startled as he grabbed her arm and pulled her close. Her breath caught, her heartbeat hammered, yet she never seemed alarmed by him, rather like Maya – very like Maya. He felt like she enjoyed his little unexpected moments of catching her out. "Stay close, Arianna. Follow my lead and keep your wits about you. Mages can be unpredictable."

Arianna studied Diego, her expression speculative. "I know that feeling well enough." She grinned as he let go of her.

The tree canopy was high overhead; forest surrounded them. Wind brushed through the trees. Occasionally Diego could hear things dropping from the trees onto the ground. He had chosen an Earth location as his starting point. Rain thrummed against the nearby foliage. They would move through three other realms before returning to the portal into his father's realm. He was aiming for misdirection with his route beginning where it would ultimately end.

A crack of a tree branch nearby indicated that

Diego had a worthy opponent in the mage. Something arced towards Arianna. Diego let Kaleshar deal with that. A flick of Diego's hand sent whatever was destined for Arianna shooting off into the nearby woodland. He grabbed her arm and dropped another tornado around them. He could no longer linger.

Storm Lands was an obvious choice. Diego avoided that. He opted for two of the more uncomfortable realms next: Ortalis, otherwise known as the realm of portals, and Atis. He would have to move quickly in Ortalis as he didn't want to encounter the lord of Ortalis, also known as Valendri, whilst there. As adversaries went he topped Diego's list. Last time Diego met Valendri he had ended up imprisoned on Atis. Valendri had close links with Atis, which ensured Diego disliked him even more.

Diego raced through both realms, dragging Arianna with him. In each realm, Diego moved them to three different locations before leaving that realm behind and jumping to the next. The mage was close on his tail and nearly cornered them twice.

The last realm on Diego's list of those to visit was Touranga. That was one of his favourite realms and was home to a number of races including valerians. The royal family of Touranga were friends of Diego's and had assisted him on several occasions. Now he had to hope the queen would let his fleeting visit pass without incident. The queen considered it bad form to pass through her realm without at least saying hello and Diego was about to take a huge liberty in the hope of waylaying the mage.

Diego landed in the middle of the training ground. Touranga had a substantial training camp exclusively for mages. He ensured his tornado blasted the whole of the large field they arrived in. Nearby, various target boards, wielder stones and magical debris were scattered everywhere.

Arianna steadied herself and surveyed the immediate area, orientating herself. She noticed the surrounding fencing and the vast stone walls of a garrison. *You've picked Touranga?*

Diego fixed Arianna with a challenging look, mainly because she had just asked him a question that was none of her business via their telepathic link. "Yes, Arianna I have. Do you have a problem with that?"

"No, My Lord. Sorry." Arianna lowered her head. Spinning around, she conducted her security sweep of the area.

Diego could hear their arrival being announced through vibrations that travelled through the air. Three female mages with silver hair emerged from magical runes on the ground and stood on guard, with their right arms extended, ready to attack at a moment's notice. Arianna moved in front of Diego. She could do little to deflect a magical attack, but the gesture made him smile.

"Garrick, I need your help," Diego shouted. "It's I, Diego, storm rider elder. Forgive my lack of protocol. There's a powerful mage following me. I need him detained. Slow him down for me, but do not hurt him. Give me a head start. I will owe you and the queen a favour."

The woman who approached from a nearby rune on the ground seemed as fierce as the three who stood on guard. Her dark hair was full of braids and she bore markings on her face, runes that indicated her rank and status. Keilty Garrick was as breathtaking as Diego remembered. Her snarl melted into a huge grin as she recognised Diego.

"So, the wanderer returns. You break my heart every time you leave."

After Sasha, before Rebekka, Keilty had been a good friend of Diego's. Occasionally those lines had been blurred, but he had always held a soft spot for the woman in front of him. "Not now, Keilty. This cycle I'm more complicated than previous lifetimes. I can't stay long. Will you help me?"

"You promised me this cycle and a child, Diego, or have you forgotten that?" Keilty said. Her voice sounded wistful until her eyes locked onto Arianna and her expression hardened.

"I've not forgotten, Keil, no. Things grew problematic and I had to change my plans this time. You know I wouldn't make a decision like this lightly." Diego gave her a wary look, praying she would understand. "This is Arianna, my son's warrior."

"You have a son?"

Now Keilty looked bereft and the sight of her hurting cut deep. Diego had spent such a long time without Sasha that he did sometimes enjoy being in the company of other females. Keilty was fascinating, entertaining and a good friend. He had learnt a lot from her regarding Touranga mages and how the realm worked.

"What a handsome boy he must be. I'll bet he has his father's stunning eyes."

Diego could detect the sting in her tone. He winced; this was going to hurt. "I have four sons, five if I include Xav, and there are three girls."

Her head angled in a way that indicated he should have kept his mouth shut.

"Please, Keil, this mage will be here soon. I don't

have much time. My son needs me. I need your help. I don't have time to deal with him myself and I can't let him follow me where I'm going."

Keilty contemplated her options for a second then nodded as the mage chasing Diego materialised nearby. "This guy here?"

Diego nodded. Keilty gave a chuckle and turned towards the mage, who looked confused by his surroundings. The female mages on Touranga were formidable and only a brave mage would take on four of them. The mage didn't appear to realise his predicament as he focused back on Diego.

"Caught you again. You're not very good at this game, my friend."

"I don't have time for this," Diego said. "These ladies on the other hand do. I'm sure they'll keep you entertained." He focused his attention back onto Keilty. "Thank you. I will come and visit as soon as possible."

The silver-haired mages concentrated on the one chasing Diego. Strands of magic flooded out from their hands as Diego grabbed Arianna's arm and lowered his tornado around them both. His next destination was Earth and then a return to his father's realm, and Keilty and her team would give him the head start he needed. He removed Kaleshar from his face as he travelled.

Diego didn't expect to find a welcome party at the portal into Aveyamara as they reached the faerie pools on the Isle of Skye. The shreken warrior he walked straight into looked as surprised as he did. A quick scan indicated the portal was under heavy guard. Now they had a serious problem.

Chapter 16

Haydan

Tallin bounded down the steps as Leylani left. Mist drifted out from behind him as he moved giving Haydan the odd impression that, even though his countenance was unreadable, his grandfather was energised and delighted with the return of his family.

Lavinia gave Haydan's arm a gentle squeeze. "Play nice, Haydan. Tallin is upset that you choose not to visit him." She sniffed. "Actually, I am as well. I miss our little get-togethers."

Tallin's face melted into a warm smile as he moved in close to Lavinia and swept his arm around her. Resting his palm at the base of her back, he dragged her against him and brushed a not so gentle kiss against her mouth. Lavinia acquiesced before raising her palms to Tallin's chest when his kiss lingered longer than was appropriate.

Clearing his throat, Haydan glanced away, finding Tallin's display irritating, unnecessary and also a tiny bit heart-warming. His grandparents adored each other and had apparently sorted out whatever issues had arisen from Lavinia's absence in the realm when he was younger.

"When you have finished mauling each other, I would quite like my chosen one back so that we can leave." Haydan folded his arms and glowered at Tallin. "I have no intention of staying, not when you show so much disregard for proper etiquette and resort to such underhanded tactics to get your own way."

Lingering a moment longer with Lavinia, Tallin seemed to ignore Haydan completely. Lavinia tensed, the only sign that Haydan's belligerence was not well received. Tallin's adoring gaze hardened as it moved towards Haydan. He let go of his hold on Lavinia and took a bold step towards Haydan.

"Haydan. Grandson. It is so good of you to join us and this time you have managed to follow correct procedure when entering my realm. Maya has been my guest and we have been getting to know each other better. She is a fascinating and beautiful young lady. I am proud to call her family."

Tallin's brittle smile suggested he was suppressing his true feelings, although Haydan couldn't decide if that related to Maya or himself and his absence from Tallin's life.

"Okay, what's with the formality?" Haydan asked. Tallin was speaking to him as though he was a visiting dignitary, not his grandson. "This feels strange. You kidnapped Maya from her home. You took my chosen one without permission and dragged her into your realm. What are you playing at? Because in my realm this is not how you treat people. You understand that I am not staying and neither is Maya?"

Tallin glanced around as though ignoring Haydan.

"I'm talking to you." Haydan took a step forwards. "Are you not even going to apologise for your behaviour? What's more, you enabled Lavinia's kidnap of me. Do you have any idea how humiliating that was? Tallin?"

"Oh, I am sorry, you are addressing me?" Tallin's icy tone confirmed he was displeased. "If you are not going to grant me the respect and formal recognition I am due as your grandfather, then you will call me king and kneel." The ground at his feet crackled releasing static into the air around him, lending him a menacing edge. Tallin's frosty eyes rested on Haydan as the mist from around his neck stilled, giving the odd impression that he was awaiting Haydan's response.

"I understand you're angry at me for not returning to visit, but you didn't act in a welcoming manner last time I was here and I experienced the full extent of your power first-hand."

Tallin drew himself up, his expression livid. Opening his mouth as though to speak, he remained silent as Lavinia intervened and slipped her hand into his.

"You both need to work at this. Haydan is upset you resorted to underhanded tactics and you are upset he hasn't ventured back since last time. Take a deep breath, Tallin, and calm down. He's not being disrespectful on purpose. He's as angry at you as you are him, but for different reasons."

Tallin's hand closed around Lavinia's, his expression one of barely controlled restraint. His throat bobbed as he glared at Haydan before glancing away feigning disinterest. "I think you might find that plan somewhat disrupted, storm rider. Maya has been well cared for since she arrived. She dined with me earlier this evening, in fact."

At the mention of Maya, all his ire at Tallin

retreated. "So where is she then? I was expecting more of a welcoming party."

"Meaning you did not want to meet me tonight." Tallin's eyebrows rose into his hairline as his stare intensified.

Haydan wasn't sure if Tallin was making a statement or expected a response. Sandau strode up beside Haydan and bowed to Tallin.

"Your Majesty, it is an honour to be here. Once Haydan remembers his manners he will show a little more respect than he is currently. When you have a moment, I need to talk to you in private."

"Yes indeed." Tallin finally granted Haydan respite from his hostile look as his attention and a charming smile shifted to Sandau. "Thank you for your assistance with all of this. I trust Diego took my advice?"

Sandau nodded, his expression mysterious. "He did. He should join us soon with Arianna. He may not make it for the ball though."

Tallin's face relaxed into a warm smile. "I'm sure Diego will make a grand arrival in advance of my ball and set many tongues wagging. Anything that diverts everyone away from myself in my court is a welcome relief. Being the centre of attention all the time is exhausting. It is about time he shared the limelight."

Tallin settled another hard look onto Haydan as though silently suggesting Haydan disappointed him. "Shall we locate your chosen one, storm rider, and you can work on this ridiculous notion that you are leaving my realm anytime soon?"

"Suggesting what? That I'm once again your prisoner, trapped in your realm? You need to quit with that ridiculous notion as well, Tallin, because it will not end well for you. The mask won't let you trap me here."

Tallin's jaw tensed. Lavinia's hand tightened around his. Tallin suppressed the ire that flitted across his features before relaxing his face into a warm smile. "The mask that you do not have in your possession at the moment." Tallin drew himself up as indignation flared in his eyes. "Welcome to the twin realms of Aveyamara, the fae and elven kingdoms, as King Tallin's guests. I am always complimented on being a wonderful host and I do not intend to disappoint any of you." With a dramatic sweep of his arms towards the summer court, Tallin grinned as the sky filled with explosions of light and loud booms – fireworks.

Maya loved fireworks. Haydan hated them. His ears rang with the noise. Lavinia covered her ears with her hands and shook her head. Tallin acted like he was in his element. Great plumes of mist rolled off him now, suggesting the show energised him, or perhaps that he was controlling it with the release of his magic into the air.

Even Sandau watched Tallin as though he found him fascinating. He kept glancing across and studied the king with delight.

Despite his ire at Tallin, Haydan couldn't deny that the elven king possessed a fascinating combination of presence, warmth and intrigue. One thing was for sure, his time in the realm was once again going to be a valuable learning experience.

꙾

Arianna

Diego seemed preoccupied as they arrived near the portal and he walked out of his storm cloud and straight into the shreken warrior. The lapse in judgement was unlike him. Arianna dived forwards as Diego took a startled step backwards.

The element of surprise worked in Arianna's favour because the shreken warrior hadn't drawn his weapon. Her guard rose up, and she placed her fists in front of her face. She punched the warrior hard and blocked his returns. He looked livid at being attacked so unexpectedly.

Duck, Arianna. Let me deal with him. Get your blades ready. There are more over there.

Sidestepping, Arianna dropped to the ground, allowing Diego to reach over the top of her and tap his fingertips to the side of the shreken warrior's head. The warrior collapsed to the floor.

Arianna reached for her blades, opting for a shorter one from the sheath on her lower back, which she kept hidden behind her, and a longer blade from the sheath mounted between her shoulder blades. She barely had time to draw them before more shreken were upon her. She kicked the nearest one away with a powerful push to his stomach. He staggered backwards giving her time to deal with the others.

Diego sent out blasts of magic. The ground shuddered beneath Arianna's feet as each one released.

The shreken further back crouched down and started whispering to each other. Arianna didn't have time to worry about them as her longest blade met with the weapon of the nearest shreken. He was strong and skilled in sword fighting, but he didn't see her smaller blade, which swept around, catching his side. The warrior snarled at her and backed away in surprise.

Can you get your father's men to help?

I don't know. I've never tried this before. Provide me with cover.

Diego and Arianna were surrounded. Shreken were closing in from all sides, although the rough Scottish terrain gave them an advantage because the shreken further out had more ground to cover. Diego lowered himself to the ground, sinking his hand into the grass. Arianna stood over him, regularly scanning the area and spinning to watch the advancing shreken. She dealt with two more warriors including the one she had wounded with her blade before Diego stood and backed up against her.

"I've tried it, let's see if it works."

"And if it doesn't?" Arianna asked. "Please tell me you have a plan B."

A cold bark of laughter and a snap of energy released from Diego. The energy ball hit the nearest shreken, sending the woman flying backwards. "Plan B is we fight our way out. I didn't expect them to be here guarding this portal, but then perhaps this was always their plan."

Diego had been caught out by the shreken. Either they were a step ahead of him, or they were covering all eventualities. That proved a disconcerting realisation. Arianna was in charge of protecting Diego and she was beginning to feel the pressure of that responsibility.

Whatever happened, she would have to ensure he reached the portal regardless of her own safety.

I'm tiring. I can't keep this up forever, Arianna.

We just need to get to the portal.

No, they can't follow us into my father's realm. He will not tolerate their incursion, and he has enough to deal with, without me adding to his problems.

Drop, Diego. Stay low.

Another warrior launched at them from a nearby rocky outcrop. Arianna growled and flipped her blade into the air, catching the handle so it faced downwards. The shreken warrior swung her blade. Arianna ducked low and sprang out of her crouch to slash her longer blade into the woman's side and stab her neck with her shorter blade.

Arianna took another two shreken warriors out when she slipped into stealth mode and surprised them as they crept up on Diego.

A holler sounded off to the side. It sounded like a war cry and a warning shout from an attacking army. Arianna glanced up to find a multitude of fae warriors running down the grassy, rocky ground. She smiled in relief. Tallin wasn't leaving the protection of his son to chance.

Diego's call for help had worked. Diego backed up against Arianna and angled his head so his mouth was close to her ear. "We let the fae deal with the shreken. You need to conserve your energy because I've no idea what awaits us in my father's realm. You've done well today, Arianna."

A route towards the portal cleared. Arianna grabbed Diego's arm and pulled him towards the pool where the portal was hidden. "You need to move now."

Diego let Arianna take control of the situation

without intervention. The realisation delighted her as they rushed towards the pool. She paused just long enough for Diego to check the fae had dealt with the shreken. She instinctively knew he would want to do that before leaving for his father's realm. As the last shreken fell, Diego returned his attention to her and nodded his agreement.

Arianna let Diego dive into the water first, then followed close behind. The next part of their journey back to Tallin had begun.

Chapter 17

Haydan

The firework show came to a spectacular end. The loud booms as the display finished jarred Haydan's whole body. Maya emerged at the top of the steps and Tallin turned, his smile broadening as he caught sight of her.

"Here she is, looking lovely. I think you will find my realm agrees with her."

Lovely was an understatement. Haydan's breath caught as he watched Maya descend the steps. Bounding down them with the same enthusiasm as Tallin had done earlier, she came to a halt in front of Haydan with a huge grin on her face.

"Haydan, you took your time. I've got to show you my bed. It floats."

When Haydan didn't respond, Maya linked her arm through his and added, "By magic. This place is amazing. I've not had a chance to explore the gardens yet. There are these weird things in every room, like three balls. I've no idea what they do, but I'm sure when we figure it out it'll be brilliant. Tallin is going to teach me to waltz and there's a ball happening soon as well."

Maya paused for breath when she realised everyone was staring at her. She remained giddy and excitable until she noticed Lavinia and her smile faltered. "Lavinia."

Lavinia smiled and mischievously glanced at Haydan. "I brought you an indignant storm rider by way of apology for my behaviour last time. Good luck taming him, he's livid right now, although I'm sure you'll charm him into a better mood."

Maya's eyes widened when she caught sight of Sandau. "Hello, you're new. I'm Maya."

Sandau's smile glided up his face with all the stealth of a forest feline, followed rapidly by a smirk of delight. "Maya, it's an honour to finally meet the lady I've heard so much about. I'm Sandau."

Maya gasped. "You're the one who kissed Ari."

Haydan cringed at Maya's declaration. Now Sandau knew he had been gossiping about him.

Sandau shot Haydan a scandalous look but didn't skip a beat as he said, "I did, but then Haydan spoilt the party. He's no fun at all." He leant towards Maya conspiratorially. "But you on the other hand look like you have a great sense of humour."

"You're wearing a dress?" Haydan said by way of distraction. The dress fitted Maya's curves perfectly, cinching her waist in before plunging to the floor in folds of fabric. "It looks stunning on you, but is this some attempt to appease me for the bizarre sensation I felt earlier when you were in close contact with someone else?"

Tallin suffered a sudden coughing fit. Maya wouldn't look at Haydan. Her face flushed, and the flush spread to her chest as she met Tallin's eyes and some silent communication occurred between them.

"Nothing untoward happened. Tallin was the perfect host, although dinner was interesting and I've got to show you the library, come on." Maya pulled on Haydan's arm.

Haydan resisted, partly because he was flummoxed at Maya's excitement at being kidnapped by his grandfather, but also because he was annoyed at her lack of explanation for the strange incident when he had been in the carriage earlier.

"We are leaving, Maya, and you are coming with me."

Maya giggled, the sound soft and breathy, before a defiant glint surfaced in her eyes and she let go of Haydan's arm. "Well, I'm staying and Tallin agrees." For some bizarre reason her eyes locked onto Tallin's neckline. "Besides, you're safer here with me and you know it."

A small doorway hanging from a chain around Tallin's neck worked its way loose. Tallin glanced down as though aware of the movement. Haydan couldn't decide if it had slipped loose of its own accord, or if something else was going on. Knowing Tallin it was something else and Haydan wouldn't like whatever it was. He returned his attention to Maya.

"Safer here with you? What do you mean? You're defying me. You know I don't like that."

Maya drew herself up; her rebellious stare was charged with playfulness. "I'm not challenging you, darling." She batted her eyelids at him. "I'm suggesting you might want to reconsider. Besides, it wouldn't hurt to visit your grandparents for a few days. You haven't seen them for years, so spending some time here is long overdue. Tallin wants to get to know you better."

Tallin nodded his agreement. The doorway started

levitating and lifting up from his neck, angling itself towards Maya as though trying to reach her. Tallin discreetly grabbed hold of it and pushed it back into the folds of his top. What was that all about?

If Maya noticed she didn't say anything about it, although she did add, "Lavinia has no doubt missed you."

Haydan gained the distinct impression Maya was trying to distract him from the doorway, perhaps hoping he wouldn't notice the odd new development. He let the incident pass without comment, but it added fuel to his theory that Maya and Tallin were up to things.

Lavinia looked delighted by Maya's chosen one display of manipulation. She nodded enthusiastically and returned Tallin's knowing smile, as if to say 'I told you so.'

Maya raised her shoulders and extended her hands in a placating gesture, her smile dazzling. "Plus, the break would do us both the world of good. Where's the harm in that?" Gathering her skirts up, Maya walked away. She turned back a moment later as though waiting for Haydan to catch her up.

Tallin, Lavinia and Sandau all turned towards Haydan, awaiting his response. Clenching his hands into fists, he deliberated an answer. Maya was manipulating him. They all knew it. He couldn't and wouldn't leave without her. Forcing her to leave would ensure he incurred the wrath of pretty much everyone gathered with him. Quiet resignation seemed the most fitting response.

Haydan moved off, coming to a halt next to Tallin. "If you think I don't know you've played a hand in working this to your advantage, you're very much mistaken. I've also not forgiven you for kidnapping Maya."

Tallin, incorrigible as usual, met Haydan's scowl of displeasure with a cheeky grin. "I know, but in truth I do not care. You will forgive me at some point. I am persuasive and a visit here is long awaited. You are fully aware of that."

"I would like to join you when you talk to Sandau in private."

Tallin rocked on his heels and considered his response. "Ah, so suddenly I am of interest to you, just not in the way I want." He sniffed, his expression one of wounded pride. "I am not sure that you are mature enough to deal with that yet. If I change my mind I will notify you."

Movement by Tallin's feet indicated the purple shock of hair had returned. It clambered up his trouser leg as he stood motionless.

"Given your behaviour, isn't that a little hypocritical? Lavinia talked to me earlier. I'm aware of the situation."

Tallin's mouth twitched. "You are aware of the developments, yes, but there are other things to talk about and you are not ready for them." His intense chocolate-coloured eyes flitted to Maya, before returning to focus on Haydan.

There was no point arguing. Tallin didn't strike Haydan as the sort of man to respond well to an argument about maturity. "Very well, but if you think defying a request from a storm rider wise, game on." He didn't refer to Tallin's chosen one status, but his grandfather could read into his words and find his hidden meaning.

Tallin inhaled sharply in response, his glare hardening. "A brave statement from an *unbonded* storm rider, but game on, Haydan."

Haydan pulled away and followed Maya up the remaining flights of steps into the summer court. He could feel the victorious looks of his grandparents and Sandau burning into his back as he departed. Now he was safe in the knowledge that the games in Tallin's realm were only just beginning.

❦

7allin

Sandau remained a respectful distance behind Tallin as they returned to the interior of the summer court. Lavinia made her excuses and departed once inside. Tallin led the way through to his office space. Sinking into a high-backed chair, he waved a hand in the general direction of the other chair.

"Take a seat, Sandau. Diego has reached this realm. I have left a carriage for him, but being my son he may well find another route here, especially as the woodland is no longer safe. I need to discuss a few things with you." Resting his fingertips either side of his temple, he considered where to begin as Sandau landed in the seat provided. "What do you know about the magic that the gods use?"

"I don't understand the question. There are light or dark gods who use whichever magic is their true calling. You think Diego will risk using his powers to transport himself here faster?"

"Yes, but as I understand it, there are rules about that magic. If a god is dark then they are unable to use the light. It leaves them once they choose what they are." Tallin stretched his arms out and reclined in his seat. "I know Diego will use his powers. My son is here and he will want the realm to know about it. He needs to keep the attention on himself and off Haydan. The portal activated a few hours ago as well, although I have kept that to myself. I know nothing about the woman who entered this realm, except that she asked my guards about meeting with Haydan or Lavinia. Any ideas who that could be?"

A mysterious smile lit up Sandau's face as he nodded. "That will be Rebekka, following her men into this realm. She's protective of Diego. He's a rare prize from the sea."

That explained Lavinia's sudden disappearance. She no doubt intended to rendezvous with Rebekka. That meeting bothered Tallin, but he would permit Lavinia's games for now and find out from her later what was going on. "Indeed, he is."

Sandau's misty irises glinted in the light from the wall lamps, adding to his air of mystery. "The gods choose as they are born which form of magic they will embrace. Light and dark. Dark and light. Where one takes hold, the other takes flight."

Tallin had no idea how to pose his question without receiving a slew of queries in response. "Are there any exceptions to that rule? Any gods who can hold both at once?"

Sandau stilled, his expression unfathomable. "Not that I am aware of no, although–"

Tallin waited for Sandau's explanation. His neck tingled with anticipation. If what he suspected was true then the tangled web he was caught up in was becoming ever more complex.

Sandau leant forwards, resting his elbows onto his

knees. "There is a rumour, and it's but a whisper, that there is one god who holds both. It has never been confirmed so I have no idea if it's true. Why are you asking me about this?"

Tallin could hardly breathe. His heart pounded as he angled his body forwards, drawing in Sandau's attention. He suspected who it was, but he needed to hear it from Sandau first. "Which god?"

"Kai. That's why his relationship with Asanda has always been strained. He can control both forms of magic and Asanda hates that. He regards the dark magic as an abomination and a reminder of Kai's mother's treachery; at least that's what the whispers would suggest. No one has ever seen Kai practise both and he's one of the most elusive gods in existence. His closest allies are Asanda and Theander, who are also as secretive as they come. I will repeat my question. Why are you asking?"

"Yes, yes, I will get to that part. How does the use of light and dark magic display itself with the gods?"

"Their hands glow if they are using light magic. If they use dark magic it's the opposite. Their hands turn as black as obsidian."

Tallin's throat was dry as he swallowed hard. "Kai does hold both. I have witnessed it. He demonstrated it first-hand in my dining room over dinner not so long ago."

Apparently intrigued by the conversation, Sandau continued to study Tallin. "I always suspected as much." He reclined back in the seat with his arms hanging over the edges and one of his legs stuck out in front.

Tallin's words came out as barely a whisper. "So does Maya."

కిళ్ళ

ᴅiego

Diego rocked in the safety and darkness of the soft landing pad, which should have eased his mind; instead it filled with unease. Something was wrong. He could sense it with an uncanny awareness that had to connect to his fae abilities. Springing up, he clambered out and stuck his head into Arianna's arrival pod. "Hurry up, Arianna. No time to rest. Something is wrong here and I don't think lingering would be wise."

Arianna climbed out of her landing pod and stood as if waiting for Diego's instructions. Her silence surprised him, but she was gaining in confidence with every day and that reflected in her understanding of when to speak and when to defer.

"Stay close to me until I understand this unease that is racing through my mind."

Arianna followed Diego out of the arrival area and down the gravel path. A few of Tallin's guards stood close to the walkway exuding an air of alarm and wariness. Diego recognised the nearest man as the commander who greeted him the first time he entered Tallin's realm. Diego acknowledged him with a nod. "What's going on? I can tell something is amiss here."

The commander dipped his head in reply. "Prince Diego, there is unrest in the forest. Your father had it under control, but the perpetrators have grown in confidence." He looked uncertain, as though he had something else to add then focused on Arianna as she moved around to Diego's side.

"This is Arianna, Prince Haydan's warrior. What exactly does that mean?" Diego asked. The lack of information from the commander alarmed him. The man was hiding something and Diego knew he wouldn't like whatever it was.

"I'm not sure we can get you safely to the summer court," the commander said, appearing fearful of reprisal.

Diego could hear the commander's heartbeat pick up as the pungent scent of sweat reached him. His fury surfaced. He had travelled a long way to protect Haydan. He had to make the safety of Tallin's summer court. Being trapped near the portal wasn't an acceptable outcome. "What are my options then? I do have choices, I'm Tallin's son, so let's not pretend I'm easy to capture." Silence reflected back at him. "Answer me."

The commander looked thoughtful. "Well, there are rumoured to be triple halos hidden in the woodland, but I do not know where they are and only the royal line can activate them."

Grimacing, Diego shook his head. Tallin had mentioned triple halos to him when he summoned Diego to the realm with the purple pixie nightmare. He had discussed the summer court being full of the triple halos. Those in the woodland appeared to have escaped his attention. Diego uttered a silent curse. Knowing about them would have been useful.

The commander stepped in closer to Diego and Arianna and lowered his voice. "If you don't know the whereabouts of the triple halos, then the only other alternative is to make a run for it."

That was a choice Diego could live with. He studied

Arianna, wondering if she would be up for one final adventure before reaching Haydan. "So, we make a run for it. Arianna, what do you say to that?"

Arianna shrugged and a mischievous grin pulled at her mouth. "Agreed. Better that than hanging about here. I can't protect Haydan from here."

The commander nodded and focused on the woodland before beckoning them closer. "You either take a horse and race as far as you can down the path before using your abilities to get yourselves as close as you can to the summer court, or you forgo the horse and use your talents from the start." He seemed pensive, as though the whole idea of what he was suggesting concerned him. "I would go for the first option, as they may not expect your skills to manifest as they do and I gather you are quite gifted." The commander gave Diego a thoughtful, inquisitive look. "Once you use your powers, they will move fast and you will draw more of them. That's why I suggest the first option. You will get further."

"I thought my father kept those who invade the woodland in check by gifting them power?" Diego said, disconcerted by the thought that Tallin had lost control of the woodland in his own realm.

The commander smirked. "He usually does. I think this is part of his plan. The king rarely does things without an ulterior motive. You can't get captured though. That would be disastrous."

Tallin was drawing the magical manifestations towards the court, making himself the focus. The more Diego thought about it, the more it made perfect sense. Taking a deep breath in, he reminded himself of his unusual heritage. "I'm not easy prey and neither is Arianna. Don't underestimate me. I'm a hunter and I like games as much as my father."

At Diego's side, Arianna rocked on her heels as though gearing up to run.

"Is my horse here, the one I rode last time I was in the realm?" Diego asked. The answer would confirm to him whether this was also Tallin's plan.

The commander appeared puzzled. "Yes, the king did request that your horse was brought around to the portal. I was unsure why, since there are carriages as well, but the king was very specific about it. The beast is saddled up and waiting for you."

Diego grinned at Arianna, who also seemed to register the significance of that. She smiled and looked expectant.

"Take me to the horse. If there is anything else I need to know about, now would be a good time to tell me."

"Once you breach the treeline you are in the woodland and in their territory. Move fast and if you stare off with them, they see you as a challenge." The commander turned and led the way to where the horses were saddled.

The treeline was a distance away. Diego placed his hands onto the ground. He focused on the woodland, which was unnaturally quiet. His skin prickled with unease. He was being observed, his subconscious aware that he was being studied by creatures as intrigued by him as he was by them. He discharged a pulse of energy into the ground, sending it as far away as he could. The shudder of air that left the forest indicated the trick had worked. The creatures had followed the power source, but the trick once discovered would not do him any favours.

Diego turned, sprinting towards his steed. He

hauled himself into the saddle and reached down for Arianna's hand, pulling her up behind him. With a nod to the commander, Diego dug his heels into the flanks of his horse and galloped off, kicking up clouds of dust behind him.

Chapter 18

Maya

Haydan fell quiet as Maya dragged him back towards her room. She pulled him along corridors and up a flight of stairs before reaching her destination and flinging open the door to the large bedroom. She threw herself onto the bed. "Look at this, the bed floats. How cool is that?" She waved her hand about underneath the bed and grinned at him. "Tallin is protecting you, can't you see that?"

"Sure, I'm not happy about his tactics though, and you're learning from him." Haydan sank onto the bed beside Maya. He reminded her of a regal god as he surveyed her reactions. "Who touched you earlier? I have never been as ill through our connection as I was before. I want to know who it was."

She had no intention of telling him it was Kai. Haydan was currently in a calm mood, but that would all change if she mentioned dinner with the gods. "Tell me about your god friend. What's his name again?"

A sly look slid across Haydan's face. "Look, I'm relieved we aren't fighting right now, but I'm fully aware of the cute little game you just played with me in front of Tallin. Stop the game playing, chosen one." Haydan rubbed at his forehead. "And stop trying to divert attention by asking me about a friend of mine who happens to be a god. You have a way for Tallin to reach you. That's how he kidnapped you, so let's start with that. What happened when Tallin took you?"

Haydan seemed relaxed as he settled back on his arms and waited for Maya's response. She curled up and moved closer to his side. "Last time we entered this realm, Tallin gave me a charm, a hidden charm, so that he could reach me if he needed to. I was nine years old, and I was both a little scared and delighted by our secret, so I kept it. Not to deceive you as such, but because it was a special moment I shared with Tallin to protect you when the need arose." Maya kept her head down aware that if she made eye contact with Haydan, he would regard that as a hostile move. "When I flicked the charm with my finger three times it activated and Tallin landed in the swinging pods in our garden." She leant in towards Haydan, delighting in the way he conspiratorially lowered his head to meet hers. "I didn't know he could do that, did you?"

"No, I didn't know he could do that either. I'm glad you're safe, but I'm not happy at your deceit. Do that again and I will express my displeasure in a different way. I know you just manipulated me outside to get your own way." His voice lowered and danger brushed his words. "Do not do that again, chosen one. Is that clear?"

Maya nodded and stuck her bottom lip out, wondering how far she could push Haydan. "If you know about it happening, it's not really a secret, is it?"

He caught her chin, his fingertips warm against her face. "Stop manipulating me." Now he was angry.

The playful, reflective quality had left his eyes, which appeared cold and full of cunning. "Enough of the games, I should not have to ask you more than once."

"You like the games. I know you do. Your soul finds them intriguing." Maya retreated over to her pillows and gave Haydan her best disappointed look. "You've been here two minutes and you're raising your voice at me. I've missed you and you're being horrible to me." She sounded like a sulky child, but didn't care.

Inhaling sharply, Haydan raked his hand through his hair. "I've missed you, too, Maya, but I'm having one hell of a day being manipulated by everyone. I don't need to be adding you to the list." With a growl of displeasure, like an agitated beast disturbed from its comfort, he rose up and stalked off towards the door. "Goodnight, Maya. I'll see you in the morning. Don't get into any trouble whilst I'm sleeping." The door banged shut behind him as he left.

His rejection made her feel ill and ensured sleep wouldn't come easy that night. Left alone with her own dark thoughts, Maya's concentration shifted back to the books she had taken from the library. The words of the mood book stayed with her giving her the uncomfortable thought that she would betray Haydan but she didn't know how or when.

Maya cracked open a sleep-hazed eye and pulled the duvet up around her body as a cold chill brushed her shoulders. Awareness prickled her skin at the exact moment the fingertips on her right hand started glowing. She sat bolt upright, her eyes locking on the glowing blue ones across the room. "For the love of…"

For a moment nothing moved.

"Kai?"

The gaze vanished behind a leisurely blink before returning with more intensity as its owner nodded.

Maya's left hand was so dark she couldn't make it out in the darkness. Even when she held her right hand near it, it didn't reflect anything back. "Why are you creeping about? How long have you been in here watching me sleep? Why do my hands do that when you're near me? They don't do it any other time."

"Which question should I answer first? I could ask you the same thing. Why do your hands do that? I'm certain you control that, so you want us to know you are here. I'm listening."

"Are you always so evasive? I don't control it, you made it happen earlier. What have you done to me?"

Soft laughter reached Maya.

"Your naivety surprises me, or maybe you're just clever at the games. I've been watching you for about ten minutes. I could have killed you in any number of imaginative ways by now. Haydan's very trusting. I haven't consciously done anything. You responded to my proximity. Maybe you recognise the similarity that we share, or find me irresistible." Kai lowered his gaze to the floor. "It's in your bloodline, Maya."

That didn't sound good. Maya's throat felt dry when she swallowed. "What's in my bloodline? This light and dark business is?"

Kai nodded again and shifted his weight around as though agitated with her.

Realisation shuddered through Maya's mind, filling her with dread. "You're not suggesting that I'm related to you somehow, are you?" Kai's mention of bloodlines left her in a state of total panic. His silence ensured it amplified. "You're not my grandfather, are you?" Kai was too young to be her grandfather, but then maybe he didn't age like humans, Tallin and Lavinia didn't. The thought was too weird to contemplate. He would tell her not to be so stupid and to forget the whole idea, then she could stop panicking. The wall lamps flickered on, adding a soft glow to the room.

Kai blinked a few times. "No, Maya, I am not your grandfather."

Maya exhaled in relief, but her mind wouldn't let her leave the family tree trail alone. "Do you know who my grandfather is?"

"I suspect who it is, yes. He's never confirmed the existence of your mother though, not officially, so I'm not sure." Kai blinked again as an awkward silence descended. "She was most likely an accident."

Kai had found Maya in the middle of the night to tell her what exactly? The silence became irritating. "Great, thanks. That was a subtle kick to my gut. So, who is my suspected grandfather then?"

"I'm not discussing that."

"Why not? Are you for real? I want to know. You're in my room creeping about. You made my hands glow and do this weird black hole thing." Maya shook her left hand. The darkness bothered her more than the light. Maybe if she shook her left hand enough it would take the hint and leave her alone with the light. "You have no right to hide the truth from me. If you know who my family is, you should tell me."

"I am not discussing your grandfather or his curse. We do not talk about cursed things. They are cursed for a reason. I am not hiding anything."

"What curse? Am I cursed? Is this your fault? Did

you do something?"

Kai's glowing eyes narrowed as though he was in discomfort. "I. Am. Not. Talking. About. It."

Kai sounded irked although Maya had no idea why. That was the biggest contradiction she had ever heard. "Wow, you're a real charmer with zero conversational skills. You're also a liar and a hypocrite. You're hiding who my grandfather is, genius. Theander told you to work on your communication. That's some progress you've made. Do you dismiss everything you create in the same manner with so much finesse?"

"No, that all depends on whether my creation is cursed or not. You could find yourself cursed … it all comes down to whether you behave, or whether you're secretly a little turncoat at heart."

"Turncoat?" That was an unusual historical term to use. "How old are you? Why is he cursed?"

Soft laughter returned. "Move on, Maya."

With a huff, Maya turned away and pulled the duvet over her head. "I hate you. Go away."

Maya felt sudden movement in the air before strong arms wrapped around her body and she was dragged off the bed with the duvet around her. Her indignant squeal of surprise didn't gain her any respite. Kai deposited her onto the floor in a deft movement that ensured he didn't come into physical contact with her.

"You do not dismiss me from your bedchamber. On your feet now, child, before I decide to punish you for your insolence." His powers flooded the room again.

Kai stood within Maya's personal space, glowering down at her. The blue glow within his eyes pulsed and danced as though alive within him.

"No one else holds both. How do you do that? Is it a trick of some sort? Who are you? I command you to answer. Only when blessed will you answer the true call from another god," he said.

The hypnotic swirl of Kai's eyes overwhelmed Maya again. She felt herself pulled into his mesmerising gaze as words left her mouth that she had no control over. She looked up at him, well aware of his power and how insignificant she was to him. Being by his feet on the floor exacerbated that feeling. "Light to dark. Dark to light. Where both merge, both take flight. I am the light and I am the dark."

Standing on shaky legs, Maya glared up at Kai. "What did you just do to me? What do you want? Haydan won't like you being in here."

Kai took a step back from Maya, the move suggesting he was putting distance between them for a reason. Realisation struck her; this was his way of displaying respect, but it could also be wariness or fear.

"Were you blessed at birth, or is this a trick? Answer me." Kai's tone cut the air with an authority indicative of his status. He looked tense as he waited for her response.

"I have no idea what you're talking about. Are you even listening to me? Haydan—"

"Of course he won't like another male in your bedchamber," Kai said, his voice low and with an edge to it. "That would suggest the other male has a right to be in your bedroom. Effectively I created you, so I have a right to be here. Your right to be here is questionable." Kai moved towards the corner of the room where the three balls sat on the floor. "You on the other hand are an abomination. You should not exist because your grandfather should not exist."

Kai's words left Maya feeling cold. "You're entitled to be in my room because you're not my grandfather.

but you created me? I don't understand and Haydan will not agree with that."

"You will never discuss your cursed bloodline in anyone's presence. Is that clear?"

Kai's frosty command left Maya in no doubt she should take that on board and not refer to it again. "I don't know my bloodline and you're talking in riddles. Why am I not surprised by that."

"When my brother Iskar arrives with the dark gods you had better make sure he doesn't figure you out. If he does, I will kill you myself. Asanda will not have you influenced by the darkness."

Maya had no idea what Kai was talking about, but he didn't strike her as a god who made idle threats. "Iskar is your brother? I thought you didn't name the dark gods."

A harsh laugh cut the silence. "You have so much to learn. Grab the deciphering glasses. Where we're going you'll need them." Coming to a halt in front of the three balls, Kai folded his arms, appearing unamused.

Maya pulled the strange glasses out from underneath her pillow and followed Kai across the room. She left the water book hidden in the pillowcase. Kai didn't need to know she had taken that as well. The labyrinth that was Tallin's realm was growing more exciting by the minute and Kai gave the impression he was about to reveal something to her.

"Wait a minute, how do you know about the deciphering glasses?"

Kai chuckled. "I saw them on your bedside table when I scoped your room out earlier. You did not attempt to hide them. I gave them to Theander when he was an infant. Where did you find them?"

"In the library."

"It seems I am not the only one helping you out, child." The edge of his mouth curled upwards. "Time to go."

Reaching out a hand, Kai grabbed Maya's arm and hauled her towards the three balls, which glided up into the air and flared around them as they left her bedroom behind.

&

Diego

An angry shriek of annoyance emanated from the forest Diego and Arianna cleared the treeline and Diego dug his heels into the flank of his horse. The beast bolted along the road and onto a small track leading into the woodland. Arianna clung to Diego, her body in close proximity to his and her head nestled against his shoulder.

The shrieks grew louder and Diego detected movement in the woodland as the creatures hiding out there began to return and realise what he was up to. He hunkered down and spurred the horse onwards. The glowing, eerie figures reached the edges of the trees that lined the road. They moved quickly and fluidly, which added to their menacing appearance.

Once the odd magical manifestations cleared the gravel road Diego was on, he was officially in trouble, and he was going to find out if he was gifted enough to outsmart them. Arianna's fingers dug into his waist refocusing him on the task.

Diego startled as Arianna gasped and gripped his

waist harder. One of the creatures had cleared the trees and made its way out onto the path. It wasn't quick enough to catch them, but it was gaining on them. He lowered himself and urged the horse on. The breeze whipped at his ankles. Arianna yelped behind him and he knew the creatures were closing in. That wasn't a breeze around his legs, it was magic lashing at his feet and trying to dismount him. "A little longer, Arianna, just a little longer."

Arianna gripped Diego tighter, almost cuddling him as her arms wrapped around his waist. He could feel the movements of the creatures as they snatched at him trying to get a grip on him. Just as one got a firm hold of his leg he dropped his storm cloud around them both.

Using as much force as he could, Diego left the horse behind and landed himself and Arianna in woodland with the summer court in front of them. If they made it to the drawbridge they were safe.

"Run, Arianna!" Diego roared the words at Arianna, grabbing her arm and dragging her forwards. She kept pace with him as they ran through the woodland and down onto the road that led to the summer court. The path snaked as it made its way to the bridge and Diego risked a glance back. He could hear the creatures advancing through the woodland, searching them out. They were still a reasonable distance away, but at some point soon they would find him and Arianna. He didn't like how quickly the magical creations could move. They were stealthy but fluid in their movements and the main emotion Diego had picked up on during his fleeting contact with them had been a sly, malignant cunning that turned his flesh cold. He raced ahead trying not to think about the things hunting him. Magic abilities manifesting like theirs did wasn't natural. He couldn't understand how his father had permitted it in the first place. He would have to speak to Tallin about it at some point.

Arianna pointed as a light glided up into the sky from the trees and dived towards them, before dropping back down into the darkness of the forest. Diego shuddered and focused on the run to the drawbridge, which was in sight.

Magic whipped at Diego's feet again. He heard the cries from behind him of creatures so close to him he couldn't bear to turn around. He could feel how close they were and that was more than enough. Arianna made it just ahead of him, although she didn't appear to realise she had cleared safely as she continued running across the drawbridge.

Magic tightened around Diego's legs. The howls of their pursuers were now so close his ears hurt and it sent a shudder through his body. He didn't slow down. Every time they tried to grab him he used brute force to break free. He reached the drawbridge as one last tug at his legs almost toppled him over. He grabbed onto the drawbridge handrail and dragged himself into the safety of his father's court. His body shook as he acknowledged how close to being captured they had come. A quick look back indicated how near the creatures had ventured. They halted right on the edge of the drawbridge entrance, their eyes glowing. Diego glared down the nearest one. "You had better have a good hiding place, because when I find your elven or fae masters in my father's court I will rip you apart."

Diego didn't like the creatures. Hiding any sort of magical ability was wrong. Hopefully he wouldn't have to get as close to them again. The most sinister thing about the creatures staring back was the slow, amused laughter that reached him. They weren't scared; in fact, they were emboldened by what had just happened. The realisation set Diego on edge.

∽◦∾

♄aydan

Haydan returned to his own room after his conversation with Maya, still bemused by her change of heart about Tallin kidnapping her. Normally she rebelled against anything and everything that restricted her, but then perhaps Tallin embraced her rebellion and encouraged it. The fae king was infuriating, but strangely tuned in to how they all ticked. He had given Haydan a room close to Maya's, probably well aware that Haydan wouldn't want to be far away from her.

Assessing his room and studying the strange sculpture in the corner for longer than he should have, Haydan landed on the bed. The lights hidden in the sconces dimmed, as though recognising he was growing drowsy. The vast space above his bed bothered him. In his snug he had control of his surroundings, but not in Tallin's realm. His room housed two of the ball sculptures, one in the corner behind the door and the other near the bathroom, if he could call it that. It was more like a bathing suite than a bathroom, with a huge sunken bath in the centre.

The summer court was as vast as it was beautifully sculpted and minimalist, with high, sweeping, vaulted rooms and wide corridors. Haydan's gaze settled on the sculpture again. Sandau had mentioned the transport system. Haydan had assumed he was talking about hidden walkways and corridors, but the trio of orbs kept drawing him towards them. Dismissing it he closed his eyes.

It felt like moments later when Haydan detected movement in his room. He had nodded off. Cracking open an eye, he watched the figure creeping closer.

"I could have just killed you, storm rider."

Sandau – Haydan sat up. "How did you get in here? What's going on?"

"Diego and Arianna have just arrived."

His father was back. Haydan couldn't hide his smile of delight. "He's here? Thank goodness for that. Are they okay?"

"They are unharmed, but the forest is in revolt. They just made it."

That didn't sound good. "What do you mean?"

"I mean that the more powerful amongst Tallin's court are flexing their muscles. There are gifted descendants of the elves and fae in this realm and they are growing restless."

"I thought Tallin had control of the woodland?"

"He does most of the time, but now rumours of his family have reached the court and they are emboldened. They crave power and unless Tallin deals with them and soon, he will have a mutiny on his hands and you, Maya, Diego, Arianna and me are all of interest to them."

"Great, and my day goes from bad to worse. So, does this mean the ball is cancelled? Maya will be disappointed if it is and I was looking forward to dancing with her."

Sandau exploded into laughter. "Are you kidding

me? No. This is Tallin you're talking about. The magic in this place has been stirring for hours. Tallin is going to put on a show they will never forget. The theme is 'where the wild things roam' and they are definitely going to be roaming for the next few nights. I encountered some of them on the way here. Walk with me." Sandau headed to the door. "I would take you the quicker route, but I need to talk to you. I have some questions for you."

"Okay." Haydan moved towards the door. "Ask away."

Sandau reached for the flat panel on the door that acted as a door handle. He touched his fingertips to it, then held the door as it opened with a soft click, and turned back towards Haydan. "What do you know about Maya's family tree?"

"Not much to be honest. Katherine was with Lucas, her storm rider, until he died protecting her and Maya from his ranada. Katherine barely escaped with her life. She was pregnant with Maya at the time, a few months along, but I'm certain the ranada knew. Why are you asking about that?"

An ancient curse left every storm rider with a ranada. Believed to be created in the storm rider's image at the time of the storm rider's birth, the creatures were the antithesis of storm riders and lacked a soul. Before a storm rider turned twenty-one, they fought their ranada. If they didn't fight by their twenty-first birthday the ranada had access to Storm Lands. Consequently, they always fought. Few of them made it, hence their numbers dwindled. No one knew where the curse originated from, or why it had been created to haunt their lives.

Sandau nodded his understanding and opened the

door. "So, you know nothing about her grandparents, great-grandparents, that sort of thing? Anything unusual about Katherine that makes her different somehow…"

Haydan shook his head. "No, sorry. Well, now you mention it—"

Sandau came to a halt. "Since you have suggested something, you should probably fill me in."

"Kat goes to pieces when she sees a feather, which I've always found a bit odd. And she adores Isaac. He's human and is Arianna's father, but he's hard to read. Mind you, so is Si. Si is Maya's adopted uncle and a good friend of the family. Maya's surrounded by unreadable males."

"Or Katherine is…"

"Yeah, or Katherine is. Why are you asking this?" Haydan asked.

"Curiosity. Why do you not trust Arianna? You left the sea with two females and yet you play games with both of them. I come back to this time and time again with you. Why? Is it about them … or is it about you?"

They had descended to the next floor and moved along the wide, airy corridor in silence as Haydan mulled over his response. Sandau had succeeded in making him feel uncomfortable and he had no idea why. Sandau remained silent. Turning, Sandau raised his index finger to his lips and pointed towards a nearby door.

They crept past in silence, pausing so that Haydan could catch a glimpse of who was inside. Lavinia was sitting in the drawing room talking to someone in a high-backed chair who had their back to the door.

"So, Diego invited you to join him, did he? Tallin will not give you the help that you seek. This is not something he will get involved in, not when it concerns our souls," Lavinia said. She didn't appear to be on friendly terms with whoever was sitting with her. "Haydan will not help you either. Not because he doesn't love you, but because it is not for you to decide. The decision rests with Diego."

Haydan's heartbeat picked up as his palms became clammy. The only person Lavinia could be talking to was his mother. Haydan had hidden the soul of Diego's chosen one where she could not reach it and the only logical conclusion he could arrive at was that his mother had found out about the soul and come to the fae realm searching for it.

Chapter 19

Maya

The room Maya found herself in was as vast as the main summer court, but was full of ornately carved pillars that vanished into a roof space that she could not see. As Kai moved her away from the three balls they lowered back to the floor.

"The balls are a transport system? Where are we?"

Kai rolled his eyes, perhaps at all her questions. "We are in the bowels of the summer court. The triple halo is one of the oldest forms of transportation ever created. They are not merely balls." Condescension rippled through his tone and his expression grew scornful as turned and walked deeper into the hall.

Not wishing to be left alone, Maya followed Kai. He moved with a confidence born of his unique abilities, as though nothing and no one could ever touch him. It lent him a sinister, cold quality which sent a chill scuttling down Maya's neck. She had never encountered anyone so devoid of emotion before. He was the most bewildering, aloof contradiction she had ever met.

"All the triple halos have a secret. Some move you to unexpected locations. Some give you a gift once you have used them. You have to talk to some of them and others throw up strange mysteries. If two people travel together in the one in your bedchamber they end up here. It doesn't do that if you travel alone, which leads me to wonder why Tallin gifted you the bedchamber with such a secret hidden within it." Coming to an abrupt halt, Kai surveyed the space. "I wonder also what secrets your mother holds. Is she like you, a creature of both light and dark, or is she all light or all dark?"

Another chill shuddered down Maya's neck. It had never occurred to her he would target her mother next. "Leave my mother alone."

Kai pursed his lips. "Ooh, feisty. You do realise I will have to find out. You carry her bloodline and that is where the secret to who you truly are lies."

"Stay away from my mother and my family. They are nothing to do with this." He wasn't messing with her family. "I mean that," she added, to make it crystal clear to him.

Kai turned towards Maya, his expression inscrutable. "I will be the judge of that. Besides, it's time I introduced myself, don't you think?"

That was a definite challenge from him, one Maya would never win. Perhaps a conciliatory tone would work in her favour better. "I think you should stay away. Please, Kai. My mother's a typical chosen one and you will terrify her, you're all … alpha male."

If his smirk was anything to go by, Kai seemed pleased by her warning.

"Chosen ones are designed to like alphas. Maybe that is why she likes Isaac so much…"

Maya tensed her hands into fists as Kai's gaze slid back to her.

"Leave Daddy out of it too. Isaac's human. He's no match for you and you know it. Let them be. They're happy in their little bubble."

"He's not your daddy, little girl." As though disgusted by her term of endearment for Isaac, Kai walked away, moving deeper into the cavernous space. The scale of the vault didn't seem to concern him. "He's an invader, a bold one at that. You underestimate your mother. She's far more capable than you give her credit for, or maybe that's just what she wants you to think."

"Do you have to be so vulgar? Isaac raises me as though he's my father and I adore him. I know he's not my biological father." Maya was part awed part overwhelmed by her surroundings. "So, what is this underground room then?"

"It's so much more than an underground room. Put the deciphering glasses on and you will see what I do," Kai said.

Maya put the glasses on, expecting to find a few creatures wandering about. Nothing prepared her for the sight that confronted her.

Haydan

Movement to Haydan's side caught his eye. A large leopard padded past with its head down. A long plume of feathers trailed along the floor behind it. Sandau tracked the creature with the same curious expression as Haydan. Rolling his eyes, Sandau moved off, before flicking his head to indicate Haydan should follow him. They walked to the entrance hall to find Diego and Arianna talking to Tallin. Arianna was giddy and wild-eyed. Diego seemed fired-up as he cast a quick glance up at Sandau, then turned his attention to Haydan.

"Ah, there you are." Diego waited for Haydan to descend the staircase into the vast hallway before striding towards him and hugging him, finishing with a thump on his back. "You made it okay, I see, and have been settling in. How is Maya?"

"She's fine. Apparently being abducted by Tallin agrees with her."

Diego cocked his head to the side and grinned. "Your little firecracker finally toeing the line? Somehow I find that hard to believe. I suspect it's more that Maya's learning how to smooth your feathers down when she has ruffled them." He shot a mischievous look at Tallin, who nodded his agreement. "We need to talk," Diego said. His attention flitted between Haydan and Tallin. "In private with no prying ears."

Haydan nodded his understanding. The discussion was inevitable. He could sense the unease flowing between Tallin and Diego from their tense body language and penetrating looks.

Arianna moved to stand in front of Haydan and lowered her head. All the tension shifted to the two of them as he waited for her to speak. Even Sandau focused on the pair, his eyes burning into Haydan as he appeared to wait for the outcome.

"I would lay down my life to protect you. I apologise for acting disrespectfully to you in the snug before we left," Arianna said. She raised her head, her eyes defiantly locking with his. "In future though, you will defer to me when it's necessary to do so."

"Then stop challenging me, Arianna, and I will find it much easier to defer to you when required." After a momentary pause Haydan added, "I accept your apology, warrior."

Arianna went to stand by Sandau, waiting for Tallin, Diego and Haydan to walk ahead before following.

Tallin walked them through to a room which was full of large cream cocoons hanging from chains anchored high up in the roof space. The nearest one opened up at the front as he approached, revealing a large padded dark area inside. Butterflies with huge ornate wings hung from the interior. They flew out as Tallin approached and landed on top of the other cocoons.

In response to everyone staring, Tallin turned back with a mischievous look on his face. "The theme for tomorrow's masked ball is 'where the wild things roam' and it would not be a masked ball without wild things wandering about now, would it? I have activated them, so they will continue to spring up all over the place. Do not worry, they are harmless."

Sandau moved towards one.

"Do not touch them. It interferes with the magic and creates a few hiccups with the process." Tallin turned and stepped into the pod, before beckoning for everyone else to join him.

Haydan focused on Arianna. "I would like you to go and check on Maya. I want to believe she has behaved herself and gone to bed, but I would like the reassurance of knowing she's safe."

Arianna nodded and moved off as Haydan climbed into the pod. Crossing his legs, he seated himself across from Diego and next to Tallin.

Sandau placed himself at the entrance with his feet

hanging over the edge a safe distance away. He had a knack for making himself look relaxed, when really he was gauging every corner of the room, making a note of entry and exit points and where any attacks would come from.

Diego reached into his jacket pocket before withdrawing the mask slowly from the folds. It caught the light that emanated from within the walls of the cocoon as he held it out, giving the odd impression that Kaleshar was rather pleased with himself.

Tallin studied the object as though transfixed. Mist poured from his neck, floating out towards the mask as though magnetically drawn to it. A light thrumming indicated the air around the mask was vibrating. It blocked the advance of the mist, which bounced against an invisible barrier before withdrawing to Tallin, suggesting the incident had annoyed the king.

Tallin lowered his head. "Perhaps we got off to a bad start last time. Kaleshar, I would like to formally welcome you to the twin realms of Aveyamara."

The surface of the mask rippled and glowed. Tallin extended his hand out, palm facing upwards. He moved it beneath Diego's hand. "Let go, Diego. You can return him to Haydan in a minute. I am not going to interfere in that."

Haydan nodded his agreement and Diego withdrew his hand. The mask levitated over Tallin's hand before a flood of green mist released from the back of it.

"What secrets do you hold within?" Tallin raised the mask up and studied the gap between his hand and the back of the mask before returning it to where he first held it. Mist discharged from the back of his neck, twining with the green mist emitted from Kaleshar. The mists never merged as they assessed each other.

Tallin leant forwards, his face inches from the surface of the mask. *"Kiti apparitaire forno cache profonicalle."*

Sections of the mask separated out and levitated. Rising up from the surface, they floated above the main part of the mask.

"What did you just do?" Haydan asked, hardly able to breathe. He had never seen anyone do whatever Tallin had just achieved.

Tallin smirked, clearly pleased with himself. "Every magical object houses secrets. You just have to understand how to unlock them and speak the ancient language to draw them out. This is Kaleshar's secret. This is Kaleshar coming out of his shell so to speak. Now he's a little more enhanced. Once you master the twelve realms his power will amplify." Tallin appeared fascinated as he continued to study the mask. "Is it heavy? What is it like to wear it? Is it not strange, to share yourself with it?"

Diego fixed Tallin with a hard look as though he found Tallin's curiosity intriguing. Tallin had just unlocked the mask, but expressed more interest in wearing it than he did his achievement.

"It's lightweight, almost like a layer of gossamer on your skin, and I don't share myself with it when I wear it, I'm almost at one with it, as though it's part of me. It only accesses from my mind what I choose to share. I have no idea what the experience is like for Haydan."

Was that a sly dig at his unbonded status? Haydan ignored it. "Much the same, except it can still overwhelm me." He grabbed the mask from Tallin's hand and admired the flickering, levitating surface for a moment. "You can stop showing off now." The surface returned to its usual appearance, the levels settling back down again as the green mist extricated itself from Tallin's white mist and shrank back into the mask. "So, you enjoyed your little jaunt with my father, did you?" The surface roiled in response, like liquid metal. "And now you're letting Tallin under your skin, little traitor." Shooting Tallin a challenging stare, Haydan dropped the mask into his inner jacket pocket, well aware of Tallin's eyes tracking his every move.

Haydan's anger from earlier resurfaced, as he glared across at his father. "You permitted Lavinia to kidnap me from Storm Lands so you could play your little game with the shreken earlier. Sandau helped her and he would only do that under your authority."

Diego pursed his lips and shifted his shoulders back, straightening himself up. "You still push the mysteries away and pretend they don't exist. You can't deny them forever. Haydan, I allowed Sandau to liaise with Tallin and arranged the earlier incident, yes. I did so to protect you, which was the ultimate goal of all of us, your grandparents included. I separated you from Arianna so you were here with Sandau as well. Sandau knows the ways of the gods much more than I do. Even though he does not share much of that with us, I trust him without question. By now I'm guessing Lavinia has filled you in on the potential dangers you face. No doubt you played those down because you're still annoyed with her." Diego's expression was challenging; he didn't wait for a response as he continued, "Lavinia adores you. Despite her games last time, she was trying to protect you. She was misguided, yes, but this realm is all about games. Once you understand that, things here fall into place much more. Tallin has been warned about the dark gods and their growing awareness of the mask surfacing. He kidnapped Maya for that very reason, to incentivise you to come into his realm to retrieve her. You are safer here than on Storm Lands. You were coming here anyway, I just ensured with Tallin that you had a reason to do so."

Haydan couldn't keep the incredulity out of his voice as he turned to Tallin, who as usual looked full of mischief. "How does Tallin know all this? He's isolated here, cut off from the universe and you're telling me he has been warned about the dark gods?"

"Oh, I have a reliable source." The edge of Tallin's mouth twitched. "It is amazing just how much information I can acquire being *cut off* from the universe."

Haydan couldn't decide if Tallin was annoyed by his put-down or not. He gave little away behind his expressionless façade, but his cold tone suggested his dislike of Haydan's dismissal.

"In fact, I often find that the universe has a funny way of coming to me. I had an interesting chat with Maya on the way here. She does adore you. Sometimes hurting the ones we love is the only way to safeguard them. I would do anything to protect those I love, as would she."

Haydan glared in exasperation at Tallin, who looked his usual unapologetic self. "Do you always talk in riddles?"

"You are too close to this to understand. I think you are going to require the help of Maya and Arianna to achieve what you need to. I believe they are the key to this. Haydan–" Tallin leant in conspiratorially "–with Kaleshar, you need to start mastering realms. There are two here and Storm Lands will give you a third. I cannot just tell you, or show you, what to do. You must earn the right with Kaleshar to master the realms first."

"Earn the right … what the hell are you talking about? Why does no one here give me a straight answer to anything?" Haydan said. He could no longer hide his irritation at his grandfather.

Arianna burst into the room and rushed across to the pod. From her face alone Haydan could tell that she wasn't happy about something. Standing, he rushed to meet her and pulled her to the side out of earshot of Sandau, who remained perched on the edge of the hanging pod.

"I don't want to alarm you, but Maya isn't in her bedroom. Also, I have just caught sight of Rebekka with Lavinia. She's hunting for the soul you found last time you were here. What are you going to do?"

"Why did you not tell me this telepathically the moment you found out? I know my mother is here, but that will have to wait."

"Diego hasn't released me from the earlier temporary connection that we formed and I didn't want to use the energy to reach you, in case I placed you in danger."

That was a surprisingly mature response. Haydan turned back towards the men and raised his voice. "I have to find Maya, she's not in her room. Diego, release Arianna back to me, please."

The edge of Diego's mouth lifted, suggesting the news about Maya irritated him. "She's doing a good job of smoothing your feathers then. Chosen ones toe the line in public, but in secret–" he pursed his lips and inhaled loudly through his teeth "–you can't trust any one of them. Your mother's no different in that respect."

Before Haydan could ask his father why he had just mentioned Rebekka, Arianna tugged his arm.

"I've got to go. I'll come and find you once we've found Maya. I'm sure you'll still be talking whilst I'm gone."

Tallin issued a curt nod. Diego gave Haydan a look suggesting he was correct, before adding, "As always, I'm sure this will be interesting. You have Arianna back. Keep her in check."

The summer court was vast and a search would take hours. Where could Maya have gone? No doubt she had found some sort of trouble, or it had located her. Haydan rushed after Arianna wondering how he was going to find his missing chosen one.

Chapter 20

Maya

Overhead a riot of foliage climbed down from the roof space. In certain places, creeping plants wrapped around the pillars, reaching almost to the floor. Tiny birds darted about, their wings thrumming as they moved. Landing on the pillars, they scurried about. In the middle of the space a stone spiral rose out of the ground. Water started cascading over the stone from the top. Maya could hear the water splashing, yet when she removed the deciphering glasses, she couldn't hear anything or see the plants or creatures.

"Wow, so you can see all of the other stuff without wearing these?" Maya raised the glasses back up and chuckled. "This is fantastic. What is this place?"

"Well, there is a question. I know what this place is, but it is not up to me to tell you, and the fact that your room connects to it would suggest what?"

"That Tallin's leaving a trail of breadcrumbs for us to follow."

Kai's sphinx-like smirk suggested he found her answer amusing. "It's more for you to follow. Tallin is a clever man. If you discover the secrets of this realm as well, then he has you caught in his web, along with Haydan. He's giving you a puzzle to figure out and allowing you to have some fun as you discover how to solve it."

"Why can't I see this without the deciphering glasses?

"Your abilities will develop over time."

"Do you know how to unlock books that have covers full of water and lots of locks floating around inside?"

Kai shook his head in an exasperated manner. "I do, yes, but as I have already told you, I am unable to answer the question. If I do that, when you open it, the contents will hide from you because you are not worthy of them. I am more interested in the other book you acquired, the one on your bedside cabinet upstairs. The forgiveness book from the tome of moods is an interesting choice." He settled his cold blue eyes onto her and continued. "Is there something you need forgiveness for?"

"I don't know what you're talking about. What about the doorway around Tallin's neck – the one that has a tiny creature inside? He indicated it's a doorway to a realm, I think he mentioned the fae realm, but how do I access it?"

Kai took a step closer, his face blank and unreadable. "Did Asanda bless you when you were born?"

"What does that matter? How and why would Asanda bless me? What about the doorway?"

"Why are you asking me these questions? If you want to find out more then follow your curiosity, just do not expect Tallin to be pleased when you do. Asanda would have blessed you at birth and he would have done so in the knowledge that you descend from my bloodline."

Maya's body felt chilled to the core at his announcement. "If you claim you created me, but you're not my grandfather, then you must be a more distant relation. I must descend from you somehow to be able to do this." Maya held up her hands. "You're my great-grandfather, aren't you?"

"That is the more likely scenario, yes. Your grandfather hid you from me, but Asanda was not fooled by the sleight of hand and regardless of that fact, Theander found you by accident through Haydan. Asanda despises evolution, so consider yourself on his watch list."

The realisation that Maya was standing in the presence of her great-grandfather, who looked around thirty years old, was more disturbing than a cursed grandfather. Her cursed grandfather sounded cool. Kai was terrifying, overwhelming and no doubt controlling. He displayed no warmth towards her grandfather and currently gave the impression that he was disinterested in her too. His threats added to her alarm and she was alone with him. Her words came out as a whisper. "Are you going to kill me now?"

"No. That's the least of your concerns. You should be more worried about who your great-great-grandfather is."

"So, what should I call you then, seeing as we're related?"

"You call me Kai, or Lord God Kai. So where are the whirling dervishes? They seem to have abandoned you. That's not a good sign. You're letting the darkness claim you. You have to maintain balance."

"I still don't know what you're talking about."

Kai scowled. He was ill-tempered, which was his main mood most of the time. "I know you are a sharp little thing, so stop playing games." His voice was gruff, his displeasure evident. "The dervishes like the light. Get them back and whilst you are at it, stop giving Haydan such a hard time. That is the darkness taking over." He moved to stand beside Maya. "I need to get you back."

Apparently, he wasn't keen on talking either. It seemed as though Maya had overstayed her welcome and was now being returned to her room. She fought back the urge to challenge him. Kai appeared to find her intriguing and that would work in her favour if she didn't annoy him.

Haydan

"**S**o, you had fun on your little adventure with my father and Kaleshar?" Haydan asked, striding into the corridor. He allowed Arianna to lead the way back to Maya's room.

Arianna didn't falter as she rushed ahead. "I enjoyed being allowed to protect your father, yes. He lets me lead when I need to. I would have preferred to be protecting you though, although I understand you were safer with Sandau."

The response from Arianna seemed surprisingly mature. The time with Diego appeared to have done her confidence good.

"Have you spoken to Lavinia? How are things?"

Arianna said.

"She's trying to make amends in her own way. I have no idea about Tallin, but he has just officially welcomed us here, so we will see. Did the diversion work then?" Haydan asked.

"Diego thinks so. I met a real-life warlord. They are as short in stature as we have been told, although the weapons they use are something else." Arianna came to a halt at the top of the staircase up to the next floor. "The forest is out of bounds right now. Diego and I were attacked by creatures hiding in the woodland, well, manifestations of magic from the court or whatever the hell they are. They rushed us just after we arrived. Diego used his magic to get us as close as he could to here and we made a run for it. Tallin has a real problem out there right now."

"I'm sure Tallin has that all under control, Arianna. He likes his games and he didn't give the impression earlier of being bothered by the situation. I'm certain if Tallin has a problem in this realm, he deals with it swiftly."

Maya's room remained empty. Soft lighting illuminated the space from somewhere overhead as they arrived. There was no sign of her as they entered and Arianna conducted another quick search. Haydan sank down onto the bed as Arianna moved around the room.

Where are you, Maya?

Lying back on the bed, Haydan ran his hands over the bedding. The sheets felt cool to his touch. He couldn't sense Maya at all and given their close connection, the realisation was frustrating.

"Storm alive, where could she have got to? I'm certain if she was in trouble I would sense it." Haydan pushed his powers out seeking the merest hint of

Maya's whereabouts.

"Whoa!"

Haydan's eyes snapped open at the declaration from Arianna. "What's wrong?" He flipped onto his side and stared across at her primed for the merest hint of danger.

Arianna was staring at the back of the bed beside Haydan's head.

"No, do that again, whatever you just did. You made the pillow glow. What is that?"

Haydan repeated the process and the pillow lit up. He grabbed the pillow and reached inside, dragging a puddle of water onto his lap. Closer inspection revealed the strangest-looking book he had ever seen. Shaking it splashed cold water onto his legs. Gripped in his hands, the book, if that was what it was, glowed even brighter and locks surfaced.

Arianna looked as stunned as Haydan felt. "What is that? There's another book over there as well." She tilted her head towards a large floating pebble that doubled up as a bedside table.

Placing the water book down on the bed, Haydan reached across to grab the other book from the bedside table. The water book stopped glowing as soon as he put it down. When he picked it up again it glowed, allowing him to read the spine of the other book in the ambient light, which said 'forgiveness'.

"What is Maya doing with a book on forgiveness?"

Arianna's expression was perplexed. "What do you mean a book on forgiveness? Can you read that?" She pointed at the book that Haydan was clutching in his hand.

"It says 'forgiveness'." Haydan could quite clearly read the words on the spine. When he opened it, the inside was full of empty pages. In confusion, he stared up at Arianna. "I must be able to read it because of my elven and fae heritage."

"Well, I can't read a word of what's on the spine," Arianna said, leaning across the bed to study the book in more detail. "If you can't read the inside, storm rider, then maybe it isn't meant for you."

"In that case, it would appear that it's meant for me," Maya said.

Maya stood across the room in front of the trio of balls sculpture. She seemed to be unharmed. Her hair hung in loose waves and the dishevelled appearance made her look even more inviting than usual. Relief flooded Haydan's mind as she moved closer and pulled the book from his hand, before sliding some odd-looking glasses onto her face and staring down at it. She opened the book to the first page and began reading from it.

"The Book of Forgiveness is now open for business. Whatever the crime, Maya, you will do the time. Penance works a treat, why don't you take a seat. Amends can only be made when you are no longer afraid." Maya removed the glasses. Tears brimmed in her eyes as she glanced back up and inhaled a deep breath. "And you wonder why I push you away? I'm a freak, don't you see? Some things just aren't meant to be. I'm an aberration from the sea."

Maya was speaking in the same rhyming manner as the book, which struck Haydan as odd and indicated her disturbed state of mind. She finished the strange announcement off with a flourish as she snapped the book shut.

"I should not be here. That's what he told me."

"What who told you? Maya, is this Tallin upsetting

you?" Haydan had never seen Maya look so desolate before. Tears flowed down her face, adding to his sense of misery. He had no idea how to console her. Throwing the water book onto the bed so that it splashed water everywhere, he took a step towards her.

Maya retreated from him, drawing her arms up and shaking her head. "No, no, no, I can't be near you right now. It's nothing to do with Tallin. I can't even talk to you about this, but I've just met my great-grandfather and he's as messed up as I am."

Arianna moved in towards Maya and wrapped her arms around her to console her. Maya hugged Arianna close and began sobbing.

Haydan's concern was replaced by utter fury, which swept through his mind like wildfire. Before Arianna had any opportunity to realise what he was doing and try to stop him, he turned and made for the door. Tallin knew what was going on and he was going to get some answers.

Diego

Tallin lay back on the padded floor and splayed his arms out. "Maya is quite fascinating. Her father used to leave feathers for her mother, before he passed away. Does that not strike you as a little odd?"

"No, all storm riders leave gifts for their chosen one. Perhaps Kat likes feathers for some reason, or it's a private joke between two people who love each other."

Tallin interlinked his fingers across his chest and

shook his head. "Oh, I think it was more than that." He extended his hand out and a wolf moved into the room. Sandau tensed. "This is Astaria. He is my eyes and ears when I am unable to see – a guardian of sorts." The wolf moved towards Tallin's extended hand, gliding past Sandau, who watched its progress with the intensity of a hawk. "The eagle, Astrix, is Lavinia's guardian."

"What did you do to the mask earlier?"

"Well, that has to be discovered. I activated the enhancement. That does not mean I know what the enhancement is." Tallin ruffled the wolf's fur and ears. Sitting up, he scrutinised the creature. "I think we need to make some additions before tomorrow evening, don't we?" He rubbed the wolf's ears and the fur extended. He ran his hand along its body and the silvery fur darkened to a steel colour punctuated by darker circles of black fur. Gradually those colours changed into a rich green backdrop with purple patches. Tallin smiled and ruffled the ears again. By the time he finished, the long fur on the ears matched the strange new colour scheme; one ear was green, the other purple. Tallin fashioned the fur into a point so the ears looked otherworldly. "Tomorrow night you shall be Harlequin." Tallin grinned, looking pleased with himself. "Watch Leylani, she is up to things." He planted a kiss on the wolf's head and turned to Diego as Astaria sauntered off. "I think Maya descends from the angels."

"Rubbish." Diego spoke before considering the announcement. "Everyone knows that the angels plummet from grace and lose their wings if they fall in love. I doubt Lucas would have taken pleasure in reminding Kat of that."

Tallin glanced across at Sandau's tensed back. "What does Sandau think to that, I wonder. Cursed things don't tend to follow the rules and I've met the cursed thing, so I know he exists."

Sandau turned his head towards Tallin, his ghosted irises glowing faintly in the ambient light. "That sounds like an interesting story to tell, but that's a family tree you should stay well away from. You think Maya's mother descends from Dark Angel?" Sandau moved his attention to Diego. "Does Katherine have wings?"

"No, she doesn't, so there you go, that's a ridiculous suggestion," Diego said.

Tallin surveyed both of them before stretching his arms out behind him and leaning back. His outrageous expression suggested that he was about to land a bombshell. "Well, if it is so ridiculous please explain to me why Maya's hands glow like Kai's, one light and one dark and why she challenged him in front of me at dinner last night. It was quite an impressive challenge, too, might I add. I thought he was going to tear her apart in front of me, but he seems rather fascinated with her as well."

Diego couldn't formulate a response. If Maya was part light and dark, she was capable of cruelty and that news did not please him. Sandau remained mute. The silence was broken by pounding feet and Haydan charging back into the room looking furious.

"What the hell have you done to Maya? Every time she comes near you, you stir her up. She's claiming to have met her great-grandfather. She's very upset about it and that's before I get onto the water book and the Book of Forgiveness."

Tallin settled a smug grin on Diego, before smiling at Haydan triumphantly. "Haydan, we need to talk."

Chapter 21

Lavinia

Finding Rebekka waiting in her room earlier had been unexpected. She had looked furious as she stared off with Lavinia and waited for her to take a seat. Entering Tallin's realm was brave, but also foolish. Tallin had no time for anyone else's game playing aside from his own, or Lavinia's.

"Rebekka, this is a surprise. Does Diego know you have arrived?"

"No, not yet, although he did invite me to join him. I came straight to you. I know better than to interfere in whatever Diego is up to. His chosen one's soul is not back in the sea. Do you know where she is?"

"You've come all this way to ask me that?" Lavinia leant forwards, rewarding Rebekka with a hard glare. "You must really love him. Take my advice and leave this well alone. Even if I knew where she was, which I do not, this is not something you should be getting involved with."

Rebekka smoothed her honey-blonde hair down before shifting in her seat. "No, you would prefer that I stayed out of it most probably. You don't like me, you never have. Somehow I doubt any woman has ever measured up to your ideal partner for Diego."

The woman was deluded if she thought hiding Diego's chosen one a wise move. "Diego will live a long life. He has you at his side. He seems happy with that. If he wanted his chosen one back we would not be having this conversation, he would have already reclaimed her."

"You think so?" Rebekka regarded Lavinia with a suspicious look. "And perhaps that is why he is here. I would simply be removing the option. Do you want him tied to another chosen one? Somehow I think not."

Rebekka was stepping into dangerous territory with this; even Lavinia knew trying to remove Diego's chosen one was a ridiculous notion. "If you keep pushing this situation, Rebekka, you will find yourself with more than a furious Diego on your hands. Tallin will not take sides in this. We have a ball tomorrow night. Stay for that, then I can see you returned to the portal. It's up to you whether you speak to Diego about it."

"I don't understand you, Lavinia. I asked you about Diego's time here and you were elusive about it. Then you mentioned that woman who has been capturing our souls. Diego has always been vague about his chosen one's soul and what happened to her. You knew I would pursue this. I have to know if he found her. I also came to meet Tallin. One day Diego will be king and I'm his queen. I thought it time I met all of his family."

Everyone always thought Lavinia was plotting things. The realisation made her smile. "I wanted you introduced to the realm. Remind Diego of what he has at his side and he has no need to return to her. I will get you your introduction, but you must leave the soul alone and do not speak of it to Tallin. This is one game he will not tolerate. Whether Diego chooses to be with her or not, his chosen one is sacred."

A flash of purple hair in the corner of the room, behind Rebekka, caught Lavinia's eye. Choosing to ignore her visitor, she settled back into her seat.

Lavinia wanted to know where the soul was hidden as much as Rebekka, partly out of curiosity and also out of a belief that greater powers were at work. Someone was helping Diego, because the missing soul was still not back in the main sea. Lavinia had checked when she was on Storm Lands.

❧

Isaac

The metal on the staircase reverberated as someone pounded up the stairs then Si dived onto the mezzanine. He acknowledged Isaac's presence with a cold smile.

"Kat's away with the baby, the rest of your brood is holed up at my mother's house and you're not even going to come over for a drink and say hello. I'm suitably disgusted." Si was clutching a bottle in his hand, which he made a poor attempt at hiding behind his back.

Isaac moved the report he was reading off his lap and placed it onto the sofa beside him. "Yeah, so disgusted, in fact, that you drove all the way over here and brought a bottle of something interesting with you."

Si's glare melted into one of his most rakish grins. "Okay, you've got me." He threw himself on the leather sofa across from Isaac, landed the bottle on the floor and pushed his white linen shirtsleeves up his arms.

"I hate to piss on your chips, mate, but I was planning an early night. I've got a meeting first thing tomorrow, and Kat didn't go, she wasn't feeling well. She has a migraine starting."

Si pursed his lips and leant forwards, placing his elbows on his denim-clad knees as he cocked his head to the side. "You're the boss, change the appointment. I need to talk to you." He picked the bottle up and studied Isaac sharply. "This helps."

Isaac was intrigued. Si had been preoccupied for the last few months. He had never been able to figure out what was bothering him. At first, he thought Si was having marital troubles, but he still seemed to adore his wife and both were happy, so Isaac ruled that out. Eve, Si's mother, didn't know what was wrong either, although Isaac wondered if she was being entirely truthful.

"Okay, but only if you're going to tell me what's bugging you. You've been acting weird for months. Is your business okay? Are you having problems with the practice or something?"

Si shook his head. "Nah, mate. Well, aside from a few awkward customers. I design stunning properties, but I always get a few difficult clients who change the brief without telling me and then whinge." His face bore an aggrieved expression, before he settled back onto the seat. "It gets sorted. I'm not comfortable in my own skin right now. It's kind of hard to explain." He studied the back of his hand for a minute as though something about it disturbed him.

"Is this to do with you trying to find your dad?"

A strange thumping noise emanated from outside. It sounded as though someone was pounding on one of the bins.

"Did you bring the aggravation home?" Isaac asked. He assumed Haydan and the girls were back. Haydan had taken the girls to visit his grandparents; at least that was the story Isaac had been told. It seemed odd for them to have arrived back so soon.

Si shook his head, before scraping his hand through his dark blond hair. "Nah, it's probably cats, or a fox."

The noise continued for a minute or two before things fell quiet. The silence stretched out. It bothered Isaac far more than the noise had. "I'm going to check. That doesn't sound right to me."

One by one the spotlights overhead winked out. Isaac met Si's wide-eyed stare as they were plunged into total darkness.

Haydan

"**M**aya has the Book of Forgiveness?" Diego seemed fascinated as he waited for Haydan to take a seat next to Tallin. "What is the Book of Forgiveness?"

"It's from the tome of moods collection. It offers the reader a choice and the mood most relevant to the reader activates. It seems Maya has done, or will do, something that requires forgiveness from my people, or Haydan … or both." Tallin locked his curious stare onto Haydan. "Any idea what it could be?"

"No, none. Don't deflect this. She claims he told her she should not be here, that she's an aberration from the sea. I'll not have her spoken to like that. Who is her great-grandfather?" Haydan said.

"Haydan, have you ever considered the fact that Maya came from the depths with Arianna and there might be more in play here than you can see? You trust her but you do not look concerned by the Book of Forgiveness," Tallin said.

Diego's attention flitted between Haydan and Tallin. He looked as enthralled as Tallin did at Haydan's response. Diego cleared his throat. "Whilst the water book sounds fascinating, the Book of Forgiveness concerns me far more. I will not stand back and watch Maya hurt you without getting involved."

Haydan was dealing with two men who didn't understand the intricacies of coping with a chosen one and warrior who were strong-willed and independent. Occasionally he wondered why himself, then one of the girls would do something to remind him why he had chosen them in the sea. Maya would gift him an unexpected hug or Arianna would surprise him with a moment of maturity and defer to him. "Who is her great-grandfather?"

Diego ruffled his hair and met Tallin's mischievous stare. "Tell him, Tallin, or I will. If Maya is who you think she is, then it's time he knew your suspicions. You don't look fazed by all of this either."

Tallin shook his head, his curls bouncing around. "No, I trust Maya. Tomorrow I am teaching her to dance and I should get to know Arianna a little. I am, however, more interested in the newly enhanced mask. Have you figured out what the enhancement is yet?"

Tallin was not dodging the question, not this time.

"Who is Maya's great-grandfather? Answer me now, or so help me…"

Looking a little perturbed at Haydan's aggressiveness, Tallin sighed. "It is possible that her great-grandfather is Kai. I am not one for gossip, but there was a rumour that Kai fell in love with and consequently stole one of his father's angels. Such things are forbidden. In turn they created a child, a boy who they hid away. They did not hide him well enough. In fury at Kai's daring actions, Asanda cursed the child, turning him into a fallen dark angel. I have met Lawson, so I know he exists. If he created a child, perhaps a daughter, it makes sense that he would hide the child for fear of Asanda cursing her as well. Perhaps he did not hide her well enough either."

"You think that's why Maya's mother doesn't know who her birth parents are? Her parents are this cursed angel and a mystery female?" Haydan considered the new twist. "Well, I guess that explains why Asanda turned up when Maya was born."

The silence as both men focused on Haydan made him inwardly smile. "Did I forget to mention that to you?" It was rare to see a stunned-looking Diego. "It must have slipped my mind. He blessed Maya though, he didn't curse her. Perhaps Asanda's had a change of heart."

The purple shock of hair ran across the pad towards Tallin's hand. Settling a withering look on the creature, Tallin lifted his hand out of its way. Unperturbed, the creature clambered up his jacket, using the buttons as a climbing frame. Once by his ear, it whispered something to Tallin that Haydan couldn't hear, then slipped down his jacket and into the pocket.

Tallin tried to ignore the interruption. He couldn't,

however, ignore the sudden movement in his pocket, which started violently leaping around. Rolling his eyes, Tallin muttered under his breath, then snapped, "What is it now, Aaushk?"

Reappearing, the purple shock of hair hauled something out of Tallin's pocket. The creature looked disgusted as it flung the offending item across the padded floor.

In the darkness the object that had been discarded glowed before rising up and floating a couple of inches off the floor. Small and curved with clearly defined, raised edges and a relief effect across the surface, it looked like a piece of Kaleshar. That was not possible. Kaleshar was in his pocket. Haydan patted the pocket. Kaleshar was still safe inside.

Tallin shot a disparaging glance at the item and tensed, before straightening up. "Well, look what we have here. Haydan, where is the mask?"

"In my pocket." He patted the pocket again to make sure. "It's still in my pocket."

"Diego, check your pocket."

Diego checked his outside pockets and found nothing, then reached into his inner pocket. Frowning, he withdrew his hand, holding another piece of Kaleshar aloft so they could all study it. The piece Diego held was a perfect mirror of Tallin's. Tallin flipped his piece around in his fingers with a skill and dexterity Haydan had seen croupiers use at gaming tables.

"Haydan, where is Kaleshar?"

Haydan reached his shaking hand down into the folds of his jacket and withdrew Kaleshar. The pieces Tallin and Diego held were a perfect match to the upper outside sections of the mask. They remained visible on the mask, but had become more opaque and the sections now pulsed at the edges as though signifying that parts of the mask had disengaged. The middle forehead section also glowed as did the bottom two pieces.

Diego tried to return his piece to the mask. The mask resisted, deflecting his attempts. Tallin continued flipping the piece between his fingers, before holding it up in front of him.

"Gentlemen, I think we have discovered Kaleshar's secret. Go on then, your audience awaits. Finish your party trick," Tallin said.

The piece Tallin was holding transformed into an exact replica of the main mask. He gave a little cry of delight.

Chapter 22

Isaac

The inky blackness was suffocating. The garage had roof lights but there was too much cloud cover to allow Isaac to see much.

"Isaac."

"Si."

"Last time I checked, a fox couldn't cause a power outage and except for the movies, power cuts don't happen like that."

Isaac's nerves already frazzled, Si's clever observations didn't help. "I don't think that's a fox, and will you shut up."

"You think that's Haydan yanking our chain?"

Haydan had pulled a few tricks on Isaac and Si when he was younger, but this didn't feel like a Haydan game. "Doubtful, Si. He hates you, but we've worked through our differences." Isaac fumbled for his phone, which was somewhere on the seat beside him. Cursing, he knocked the report he had been reading onto the floor.

"I can hear something coming up the stairs." Si sniggered. "Isaac, I'm scared. Will you hold my hand?"

"Will you shut up, you idiot? I'm trying to find my

phone." Isaac's hand caught something that felt cool and metallic.

"There's a slinky black thing just reached the top of the stairs. I know these sort of things are normal around here, but I'm hiding behind you if it attacks."

The screen sprang to life and Isaac found the torch app. "That's Pablo, you total fruitcake. Hi, Pablo, what's out there?"

The light of Isaac's phone reflected eerily off Pablo's eyes as the strange rodent glided across the mezzanine floor towards him. When Isaac blinded Pablo with the torch the weasel-like rodent reared up, folded its middle set of arms across its front as though annoyed and covered its eyes with the other set. Pablo had a strange way of communicating totally different messages with his two sets of arms.

"The dark gods have found you. The wards placed on this property are keeping them at bay for now, but you can't go beyond the boundary or they will get you. Isaac, you need to lead them away from here."

"How could you see Pablo in the dark?" Isaac asked Si. "I mean, it's pitch black in here and I can't see my hand in front of my face."

"Maybe that's something else I can thank my father for," Si said. He kept a close eye on Pablo as though expecting the creature to turn at any moment.

"Hmm." That was a lie; Isaac could see right through Si's attempt at deflection. "Given that I'm not gifted with Haydan's abilities, how am I going to lead them away from here? Why can't you do it anyway? I'd like to live to see my youngest's first birthday."

"Says the man who's fascinated by all of the weird things that happen around here," Si said, eyeing Isaac suspiciously.

Si and Pablo both focused on something by Isaac's hand. Glancing down, Isaac found a small sculptured piece of metal sitting on the sofa beside him. Surrounded by two Y-shaped pieces of metal, the centre of the object rose up from the surface, like a shield. A tiny stud protruded in the middle, reminding Isaac of a button, the sort of button you never wanted to press unless there was an emergency.

Si reached towards the object, which moved closer to Isaac. "Well, it's not meant for me, that much is clear."

Isaac stared at Pablo, who shrugged and waved one of his upper arms at Isaac as though suggesting he get on with it. His middle arms remained folded across his chest implying that being in the garage that evening irked him for some reason. Isaac picked the object up and placed it onto his palm, where it levitated.

Pablo didn't seem concerned by its appearance, which bolstered Isaac's confidence. He extended his index finger towards the button, which pulsed as though inviting or daring him to press it. Isaac had never been one to walk away from a dare and he wasn't about to start now. Taking a deep breath, he touched his finger to it.

Arianna

It took a while to calm Maya. Eventually, she removed her arms from around Arianna's neck, sniffed a few times, wiped her eyes on her sleeve and sank down onto the bed.

"Where do you suppose Haydan's gone? He's going to be furious. I haven't seen him in days and when he arrives this happens," Maya said.

"He's worried about you. You were upset. You can't blame him for being annoyed. You're his entire world."

"Yeah, well maybe I shouldn't be."

A gasp escaped before Arianna could stop herself. "Did you really just say that? It's the here and now that matters, not the past. I know how much you adore that guy, so don't you dare disrespect him. I understand you're hurting and whoever you met earlier said some nasty things to you, but that doesn't mean you should deflect that onto Haydan. It's not his fault. Your battles with him are so pointless."

Maya released a huff of air through her nose. "You would say that. He's your entire world, too, except without the attraction part."

"Yeah, that privilege is all yours, Maya, don't forget that. I protect him and you love him, or you're supposed to, when you're not suffering from a manufacturing defect."

Maya shot Arianna a sneer of disapproval. "As if I could forget. I have everyone to remind me and thanks for that – manufacturing defect? I'm not perfect, Ari, and I've already had Diego try to reset the defect, not that it worked out too well for him."

"In Haydan's eyes you are perfect. Please stop with this. I would lay down my life for him, but the way he watches you when he thinks no one is looking? Well, I hope that one day I can find someone to look at me in such a way."

Maya turned away and stared across at the Book of Forgiveness. "Sometimes I think your role is the better one. You don't have the messy attraction part to deal with."

"The messy attraction part – and by that you mean the part where your soul is connected to the storm rider that you love?" Maya had a permanent conflict over this issue and it still festered and had done ever since she moved into her teens. Katherine insisted it was a phase; that Maya would figure out her feelings for Haydan in her own way, but at fifteen, that still hadn't happened.

"Look, until you bond, where is the harm in keeping Haydan happy? He puts up with a lot of grief from you and you pile it on. He's fed up with it. I'm fed up with it. You are capable of so much more than constantly antagonising him."

Maya glared up at Arianna, her expression so fierce it made Arianna hesitate.

"You have no idea what I am capable of."

Sighing, Arianna focused on the polished floor at her feet. The summer court had to have been created by magic; it was too perfect and pristine to have been man-made. "Oh please, you think the scary act works on me? Grow up, Maya, and whilst you're at it, consider how lonely you will be without Haydan around. When he has had enough of your petulant mood swings, with any luck he'll decide to leave you to stew for a while. Then you'll know what it feels like to be alone, without your best friend beside you. After your mother's experience, you should understand that better than anyone."

"How dare you? Get out," Maya shouted.

"Oh, that's right, push me away too."

Perhaps Arianna shouldn't have mentioned Katherine, but Maya was off on one of her dramatic episodes again.

"Get out of my room now."

Arianna ran her tongue around the back of her teeth and suppressed the anger building inside her. "Are we really doing this right now? I can't leave you, not until Haydan gets back. He'll discipline me if I leave your side and I'm not taking a punishment that should be yours."

Maya ran her hand through her hair and huffed. "What's it like – when Haydan disciplines you?"

It was a mortifying experience and Arianna hated it as much now as she had the first time it happened. "I hate it. It's like when I argue with Daddy and say mean things to him. At the time, I'm so angry and I lash out, but afterwards I feel bad. It doesn't hurt me, but I feel all that shame in one huge blast and I hate the other riders knowing that I've displeased Haydan. It's like being publicly outed for being disobedient." It was, however, also strangely addictive and satisfying on a deep level as well. There were times when she wanted and needed the reminder to behave herself. She had no idea why and had no intention of telling Maya that.

A naughty smile twisted Maya's mouth up. "You kissed Sandau. Was it any good?"

This was an interesting conversation shift, but Maya had now met Sandau, so the question was inevitable. Maybe Arianna could distract Maya further and persuade her to talk about something else instead of the usual dramatics about Haydan. "It was very good, yes, until Haydan spoilt it, that is. Where did you find the books?"

Maya gave the impression she was delighted by Arianna's revelation. "They kind of found me … in the library."

"I'm sorry for reminding you about your dad. That

was out of order. I protect Haydan. You love him. I need you to work with me on this one and I hope you're going to tell me what's happened since Tallin kidnapped you, because you're not going to believe what I've been up to with Diego. The woodland isn't safe either, we were attacked."

Maya looked pensive and Arianna silently counted down from five to one. By the time she reached one, Maya had caved in and patted the bed next to her. Aside from the situation with Haydan, Arianna could ease Maya out of most of her moods and where Maya was concerned, information was power. That little arrangement worked both ways.

Chapter 23

Isaac

Isaac cracked an eye open and peeked out. The object levitating in his hand had transformed into a mask, one very similar to the one haunting his sleep. The part Isaac had found next to him on the sofa manifested as a solid object. The rest of the mask was opaque but magnificent as it floated in front of him. Green mist rolled in gentle plumes from the back of it.

Si moved in closer to get a better view. "Okay, that's a pretty cool party trick. What the hell is that?"

Pablo seemed disinterested. "That's the mask of the gods. It looks like Tallin has figured out its secret feature. Every magical artefact has one. Given that this is the object that the dark gods on the other side of the barrier are looking for, I think it a wise idea to make sure they have sight of it before you leave. I can give you a safe route to follow, one that will lead you somewhere secure, but you have to move quickly. If you dawdle they will find you much quicker and I'm certain that will not end well for either of you."

"I've got to get Kat and the baby."

Si settled one of his mischievous looks on Isaac. "I

thought you had a meeting to be at?"

Isaac leant in conspiratorially, but Si appeared uncomfortable under his intense scrutiny. He glanced away and fidgeted.

"Stuff the meeting. Angel and the baby are way more important and this is the first time I've had a dark god chasing me. In the event that I don't make it, you have permission to tell me I should have hidden under my duvet and pretended this wasn't happening."

Si chuckled as the strange banging noise resumed and everyone turned in the direction of the sound.

"I assume the other children are with Eve," Isaac said, praying they were safe and not something else he needed to worry about.

"The kids are with Mum. You don't need to worry about them right now."

Pablo swivelled his head back and looked up at Isaac. "There are a lot more dark gods than just one, Isaac. Get Katherine and the baby and follow the route. Do not deviate."

"So, they can't get through the wards protecting this place?" Si asked, looking fascinated.

Pablo shook his head. "No, but somehow they know you are here. That is why they cut the power. Maybe the mask draws them in. Act oblivious until you have Katherine and the baby, then make your move. The first portal will be on the driveway waiting for you. Once you leave here, you are fair game and I cannot protect you without drawing attention to myself, which I would rather not."

"I want some of these wards on my place. I always knew you got the better plot," Si said, giving Isaac a charismatic grin. "So why don't we just set up camp here? I mean, if they can't get in … then…"

Pablo rolled his eyes. "You want to wait here and never leave ever again? Good luck with that. They will wait for as long as it takes to capture either you or someone connected to you. You have no choice. They will only leave here if what they seek–" he indicated the mask clutched in Isaac's hands "–leaves first."

Standing, Isaac pressed the button on the mask. It transitioned seamlessly back into the small piece. He slipped it into his pocket and followed Si across the mezzanine. Pablo descended the stairs with them, but disappeared into the shadows as they reached the bottom of the steps. The banging noises outside continued until Si opened the garage door and peered out. The silence was so acute the hairs on Isaac's neck stood up. Isaac shoved Si out of the way. "I've got an air rifle somewhere. That should take care of the noisy wildlife, and if I can find the instruction book I'll fire the generator up."

Isaac opened the front door to find Katherine halfway down the stairs with the torch out. She shone it in Isaac's face and blinded him as Si followed him in and slammed the door. The noise resumed with more force than earlier.

"You'll wake the baby. And what is that banging?"

"Least of our problems right now. I know you're not feeling great, but there are dark gods on the boundary of our property. Get the baby, we need to go."

Katherine returned a few minutes later with the baby strapped to her front. That was one of the many things Isaac loved about his wife: she didn't hang around for an explanation when it involved something out of the ordinary.

"How are we getting out of here?"

"Pablo is helping us. He's set up a safe route to follow, but we need to be quick, so put your running shoes on." Isaac pulled the piece of the mask out of his pocket and pressed the button. The mask sprang to life in his hand.

Katherine gasped as she studied it. "What happens if you put that on?" she asked.

"I don't know. I'm hoping I don't have to, but if it comes to the point where you or the baby are in danger, I'll find out and send you the memo."

"Er, what about me? How come I get left out of this?" Si asked, feigning disappointment.

"Ha, ha," Katherine said, ignoring Si. "I love you, but this is not the time for messing around, Isaac. Haydan has mentioned a mask in passing recently. Something to do with his time in the fae realm and his mischievous grandparents. He was a bit coy about it. I got the impression he didn't want to talk about it much, but he did say that we might be in danger."

"And you kept that to yourself because?"

Katherine shrugged. "Need-to-know basis and you had enough on your plate with work." She pushed ahead of Si and opened the door as the noise stopped again.

The gravel beneath their feet crunched as they moved beyond the protection of the porch. The silence proved overwhelming. Isaac's skin prickled with awareness as he stared into the gloom, trying to make out the figures that he knew were lurking there. He could feel eyes boring into him as they moved out into the open.

Hidden behind Isaac's back, the mask felt heavy and warm. As soon as he revealed what he was hiding, the creatures on the other side of the wards would regard him as the target. Moonlight illuminated the driveway and Isaac caught his first glimpse of the dark gods. They were standing behind his bin store and looked as though they were made of darkness itself. The moonlight didn't illuminate them; the light didn't penetrate them. As to how many had gathered it was hard to tell. Two or three, perhaps more. He didn't stare at them for long; instead he focused on the portal that opened up on the driveway. The surface reflected the moonlight and shimmered like the surface of a loch.

Katherine walked up to it and peered in as Si moved to her side and swept his arm around her shoulder. Isaac strode up behind them and glanced over his shoulder towards the bins. He deliberately left the mask behind him, aware they would see it. Spinning around, he brought the mask to his front and it illuminated in the darkness, announcing itself to the gathered crowd.

He could hear creatures whispering amongst themselves. *He has the mask. It's here. Tell Iskar.* Isaac had no idea who Iskar was and he had no intention of hanging around to find out.

"Oh, you want this, do you?" Isaac held up the mask and suppressed a shudder at the strange noises from the other side of the boundary. One of the figures released an excited shriek. Another hissed, the sound so sinister a chill slithered down his neck. "You'll have to catch me first. Good luck with that."

The boundary erupted into a cacophony of bangs as the gathered audience began slamming their hands against the invisible divide. That explained the unusual noise. The idea of being protected by a few wards on his property seemed ridiculous to Isaac, but he could see the barrier glowing red around their hands on every impact. Whatever had been set to guard his home, he had never been more pleased to have the invisible protection as he was in that moment.

He rushed after Katherine and Si, not wanting to be left behind with the gathered mob of hostile dark gods who now no doubt regarded him as the devil incarnate. The feeling was mutual.

❧

Maya

Arianna led the way down to the room where the men were gathered. Maya had persuaded her to take her to find Haydan. It was Tallin Maya wanted to speak to, but she had no intention of telling Arianna that. Tallin felt like a suitable confidant and mentor in the strange new reality she was navigating.

Finding the men talking in a huge levitating dark cocoon was amusing. Maya gave Sandau a flirtatious look as she slipped past him. A quick glance behind her confirmed that Arianna's cheeks had turned a charming shade of pink. She fidgeted as Maya left her to join the others.

Tallin gave Maya an enchanting grin as she entered the cocoon. He lazed back, with one arm folded beneath him as he lounged on his side.

"Ah, there you are. I suspected you might come to find us at some point this evening. Are you quite alright? Haydan mentioned you were upset earlier."

"I'm fine now. Although Haydan disappeared before I had a chance to calm down."

Haydan was sitting cross-legged across from Diego;

his hard stare was reproachful. It would be even more accusatory when he discovered what she was really up to.

"I can't sleep and Arianna wouldn't leave until Haydan came back, so I asked her to bring me here. You said you would teach me how to waltz. I was hoping we could do that now."

Haydan rested his elbows onto his knees and leant forwards. "What's going on? I know you're up to something on account of the fact that you take dance classes and already know how to move that body of yours without any help from Tallin."

Maya sniffed, moving her gaze on to Diego, who watched her with the intensity of a hawk.

"Maybe I should teach Maya how to waltz instead." Warning rippled through Diego's rough tone as he continued to assess her.

Tallin's sly smile told Maya he knew what she was up to and that he was ahead of her. He patted the floor beside him and waited for her to step over Haydan and Diego. Haydan caught her ankle on the way past. His warm fingertips slipped underneath the bottom of her pyjama leg, before caressing her skin in a manner that was both teasing and a subtle warning.

"Chosen one, I know you're up to no good, so why don't you answer my question."

Heat flooded Maya's face. It was rare for Haydan to touch her anyway, so in the company of others it felt strangely intimate. "I don't have to answer your question. Tallin promised he would teach me how to waltz, that's it."

The chain around Tallin's neck worked free of the shirt he was wearing and the tiny gateway slid into view. It hung there tormenting Maya as though challenging her to reach for it. Haydan released a huff of air that told her he was unamused. Diego made a tsk noise at her defiance.

Haydan's attention followed Maya's as she kicked free of his grip and lunged at Tallin with her hand out. Her fingers wrapped around the locket as the tiny paw shot out to meet her. The pod was left behind in a blur of swirling movement.

Tallin muttered a curse under his breath followed by, "Well, it is about time, young lady." He stood and brushed himself down, before turning towards the approaching creature. "Haydan is going to be livid after that little stunt and Diego, well, you are a long way off being in his good books as well." The edge of Tallin's lips curled upwards. "Maybe that is why you need the Book of Forgiveness."

Given the size of the paw that had tried to reach Maya through the gateway, the creature was bigger than she had expected. Instead of hands it had paws and it moved much like a human, walking on its hind legs. It was difficult to tell if the creature was male or female, not that Maya concerned herself with that because it was beautiful-looking with a delicate face, a long, thick mane of grey-and-aqua-coloured hair and beautiful scale-like markings across its temple, cheeks and nose.

"You are the one who has been drawing my attention." The creature furrowed its brow. "You are not fae." It lowered its head in greeting to Tallin. "Tallin, fae king, you know the rules. Only those of fae or elven blood are allowed across the ley line into the fae realm."

Tallin glanced around and sniffed. "I know that, but in this room that does not matter. Maya is my grandson's partner. One day you will have to let her beyond the ley line. You invited her here. I would go as far as to say you tempted her here on a number of occasions knowing the outcome of that."

"Yes, well that time is not today. Your grandson is an altogether different matter. He is able to walk this realm in the same way as you and your son."

"How does the owner of the mask of the gods master this realm?" Maya asked. The question was bold, but time was running out. Haydan hadn't mastered any of the realms and although she had found the crypt beneath her bedroom with Kai's help she was no closer to figuring out how to claim any of the realms.

The creature locked its mysterious, grey-flecked eyes onto Maya and took a confident step closer to her. It now seemed bigger and more imposing.

Tallin's eyes widened in alarm. "I am sorry. Maya can be quite direct. I know that is not your way, but Haydan, my grandson, is in danger."

"Yes, he is. If he doesn't master both of the twin realms soon, he'll be in great danger and so will Arianna and I; she's Haydan's warrior."

The creature's attention flitted between Maya and Tallin. "So, you do not want this realm as yours?" Its eyes narrowed as its gaze returned to Maya.

"Don't be absurd. This is about Haydan. I'm not going to lose him, not now. We've come too far for that."

"What a strange thing to say, Maya." Tallin stared across at her, his expression inscrutable. "Given your strange bloodline you are capable of great beauty and also great cruelty. I am under no illusions about your games with Haydan. There is something else going on with you, I just for the life of me cannot figure out what it is. Furthermore, when I do, I hope you do the right thing and do not disappoint me. You have not seen what I am capable of when I am furious about something. If you hurt Haydan, I mean really hurt him, I will tear you apart."

Tears stung Maya's eyes as she gave Tallin what she hoped was a reassuring stare. "We've already discussed this. I thought we had reached an understanding. I adore Haydan. I will do whatever it takes to protect him."

"Yet you are a contradiction. At times fierce, at other times, submissive, and occasionally you are something else altogether. A mystery surrounded in layers of intrigue, wrapped in a surprise. When you bond, that is when I will see the real you, isn't it? Haydan is the royal bloodline. You hurt him, you hurt me and Diego. Consider this your only warning. If I do not like the surprise, I will make my feelings very clear."

That felt like a number of statements rather than questions. Maya fought back her tears and focused on her primary goal as she returned her attention to the creature. "I need your help to protect Tallin's heir. Will you help me?"

"If I deem him worthy I will show him how to master this realm, but he needs the keystone to complete the task."

The creature glanced down at Tallin's hand, then back to Maya, before reaching around its neck and removing a chain with a key hanging from it, which it passed to Maya.

"What's this?" Maya asked.

"Something you may find useful at some point soon. The keystones release one at a time. You must go back now."

Maya nodded and let Tallin take her arm. He bowed

theatrically to the creature and stepped away, the world around his neck dissolving as he did so.

∂∞∂

ϩaydan

Tallin returned Maya to the same place they had been before she dived for him. Standing to the side, Haydan glared at her, deliberating how to respond to her latest game. Maya was taking a moment to recover from their sudden shift in location and reorientating herself. He was grateful for the moment of reprieve to marshal his own confused thoughts. Tallin moved off as the lighting in the room began pulsing red. Sandau and Arianna drew their weapons and took up guard positions nearby.

Shouting, which sounded like Tallin's guards, could be heard further off in the summer court. Tallin turned back. "We have unexpected intruders. Stay here until I tell you it's safe."

Apparently unable to bring himself to look at Maya, Diego silently communicated his disapproval with a murderous look directed at Haydan. He swept out of the padded space and into the room with his usual finesse. Sandau moved into the corridor, leaving Arianna on the perimeter of the room.

Maya grasped Haydan's nearest hand with warm fingers. She brushed her other hand up into his hair and pulled his head towards her, planting a firm kiss on his mouth. Catching him by surprise, the move shocked and thrilled him in equal measures. She looked mischievous as she pulled away and calmed her erratic breathing, leaving her hand buried in his hair.

"I know you're furious at me right now, but that was all for you. You have to master some of the realms with Kaleshar before the dark gods arrive. Each realm has to be unlocked with a portal stone. This is a twin realm, meaning there are two of them here. We are standing in one of them and now I know where the fae realm is."

"It's in the locket around Tallin's neck."

"Exactly. I think I've found the cavern in this realm as well. I can reach it via my bedroom. I'm not sure about the portal stones, but I might have the key to one of them around my neck–" she showed him the key hanging from the chain that the strange creature had just given her "–and the other I suspect Tallin is wearing on his finger. That odd ring that he wears is a portal stone, I'm sure of it."

Interestingly she fumbled with another odd-looking necklace at the same time, one that looked like a small cage of some sort. "You could have just told me that." Haydan slid the fingertips of his free hand around the base of Maya's throat. Her pulse throbbed, the regular beat a reminder of his own pulse calming with his proximity to her. He moved closer, sensing her apprehension mingled with delight. "I'm not going to hurt you," he whispered close to her ear. This was one of their reconnecting techniques and a way for a storm rider and chosen one to regain their equilibrium. "I just need the reassurance of your soul. Your neck is the closest I can get right now. I sense your soul fluttering in response." He tilted her chin, the swirling underside of his altera pressing against her jugular. This was all he needed to know. If she allowed this, he had his answer and he would feel comfortable releasing her and allowing her games to continue.

Maya relaxed. Her hands slid up and wrapped around his wrist. The contact between her skin and his altera shocked him. She had never done that before. It signified acceptance, understanding and unconditional love. His soul surfaced inside his altera, anchoring his wrist against the base of her throat. Instinctively, he nuzzled his face against her neck and inhaled. Her soul thrummed in response, the vibrations washing over him like a drug. Her hands locked over the top of his altera and they held each other like that for a few moments. Adoration was the only emotion he could identify. No deception. No betrayal.

The moment passed and Haydan knew he would have to release Maya. Much as he was enjoying it, he couldn't stay like that. It served as a reminder of what he could have and would have at some point in the future, but not yet. His soul retreated back into his altera and he sighed in frustration and resignation. He kept his tone teasing. "You like playing games with me. You like the pull of attraction, followed by the sting of rejection." He had punctuated his words with hostility before he realised what he was doing. "I never know where I am with you. I don't like where you are going with these games. Are you truly mine, or is this some elaborate ruse before you break my heart? I have just suffered another earbashing from my father, after you disappeared with Tallin, over your behaviour. In front of Tallin it's embarrassing for both of us. Is there anything else you would like to offload whilst you're feeling talkative … any other announcements you would like to share?"

Maya's bottom lip quivered and her eyes brimmed with unshed tears. Would she share the secret about her great-grandfather with him, or was that something else she was hiding away? Her silence confirmed it was not something she planned on divulging.

That cut deeper than Haydan expected. She didn't want to, or chose not to, share the truth with him. He inhaled, fighting back the desolation and sense of betrayal that flooded his mind at the realisation.

"I need you to do something for me, beautiful." Haydan battled to keep his tone level, although Maya's tensed body told him she knew he was suppressing raw emotions. "You won't like it, but I need you to do something for me, just this once and whilst we are here. Can you bring yourself to do something I ask?"

"Yes." Maya blinked as though trying to clear the tears, before rewarding Haydan with a forlorn look. "I will try. I don't mean to anger you–"

"But you still do so, knowing how much it upsets me. Behave in front of my family. Can you do that for me? Or shall I chalk this up as yet another lie you are hiding deep inside where you think I can't find it, or won't know about it? I know your soul. I know every intimate and hidden part of it. Don't think for a moment that I am playing a game I don't like the sound of here. Maybe it's the elven and fae blood that thrums in my veins and delights in your games, I don't know, but I've known since I brought you out of the sea that you're different, special and breathtakingly beautiful in body and soul. You shouldn't be able to hide things from me and despite your best intentions, you are attempting to bury things."

"I adore you, Haydan–"

Not enough to tell him the truth it appeared. "Yet you won't bond and gift me our most intimate connection. The lack of bond leaves me weak. You are designed to please me, yet you fight me at every turn. Kaleshar is convenient for you. He lets you off the hook for a while, but if you think I have forgotten about our lack of bond, think again."

"Please don't do this, not now. I have enough to deal with at the moment."

"Like not telling me the truth?"

Haydan's fingertips settled at the base of Maya's throat again, seeking her pulse points below her jaw as he tried to calm the angry beast stirring within. The persistent throb beneath his fingers soothed the flood of irritation, allowing him to bring his own heartbeat back into time with hers. Maya remained still, perhaps recognising that pushing him away was unwise given his current mood and need for reassurance. She stared up at him as though mesmerised.

"What do you mean? I don't know what you're talking about."

"You're lying to me and I know you are." The tensing of his hand was a swift way of letting her experience how angry he was.

Maya exhaled then stood up on her tiptoes to plant a gentle kiss on his mouth. "I'm protecting you," she whispered, nuzzling in against his neck. "Trust me and I will never fail you."

Arianna rushed up beside them. "We've got unexpected guests."

Haydan let go of Maya's neck and turned to glare at Arianna. "Hopefully not dark gods?"

"No, not dark gods. There's a secret route back to Sandau's room I can use. Is everything okay?" Her attention switched between the two of them. "Everything seems to have grown very tense in the last few minutes."

Haydan released a snort of disgust. "Not really, Ari. Maya has a problem with telling me the truth. Keep a watchful eye on her. Now, let's go, you're both coming with me."

"Tallin ordered us to stay here or in our quarters. He was quite clear about that," Arianna said in a sharp tone.

Uncomfortable silence descended as Haydan eyed his warrior and waited for her to correct herself.

"I'm not speaking out of turn. This is his realm and you're annoyed at Maya. It's clouding your judgement, but if you want to disregard Tallin's instructions and take another public route, that's your prerogative and I will of course support that."

Maya looked as devastated at his behaviour as Haydan felt at hers. Ignoring her, he turned and stalked off. He hated her games, yet he was destined to play them. They were intriguing, fascinating but unhealthy. Somehow the most disturbing realisation of all was the fact that he knew that and somewhere deep down inside a tiny part of him always had.

Chapter 24

Isaac

Katherine moved surprisingly fast given that she was carrying the baby. Even Si seemed to have mastered the knack for quickly and easily finding the next portal.

"It's this way, Isaac, move!" Si shouted as he rushed along with Katherine.

Isaac ran after them, clutching the odd mask in his hand. They made it through the first realm without a hitch. It was much like Earth, except the far-off buildings were medieval in appearance and like large castles. He could see huge winged creatures in the distance and resisted the urge to start shouting about dragons to Katherine and Si. They were not on a sightseeing mission.

A sprint along a cobbled path led them down a hillside and to the next portal hidden in amongst trees.

The next realm involved an even shorter sprint down a field of long grass. The portal was hiding at the bottom. Something moved off to Isaac's side. A glance confirmed a swirl of dark cloud had dropped into the field next to him. It rippled with light. He didn't pause to acknowledge the rider who knelt nearby, but he recognised Teeam. Teeam raised a hand, presumably to hold back his people from attacking, which could only mean that Isaac was running for his life on Storm Lands. The realisation made Isaac chuckle as he barrelled after Si and Katherine, who hadn't slowed. Teeam would quickly work out what was happening and would understand their invasion of his realm. If there were consequences, Isaac would deal with those later.

"We're on Storm Lands."

Katherine didn't slow down and if she wasn't slowing, Isaac wasn't. The portal at the bottom of the Storm Lands field landed them into an isolated realm. Surrounded on four sides by sea they had arrived on top of a large, flat expanse of weather-battered island. A stone structure reared up in front of them. It reminded him of Stonehenge, with vast slabs of rock that rose up as though they had grown there. To the side he could see two other smaller islands.

Si scanned the main island, his attention flitting in every direction. He focused on the stone structure as something screeched to the side of them and a figure strode onto one of the nearby smaller islands.

The creature unveiled itself and turned its head. It was as black as midnight. A dark god. Isaac could tell from its colouring when it arrived and the way it moved. Once the figure had fully materialised, its appearance was more like a human, the dark form perhaps a way in which the dark gods travelled.

"It's this way. Shift yourself!" Si shouted again.

Isaac focused on the route to the portal. A thump nearby indicated the dark god had moved himself across to their island. He rushed towards Isaac with a menacing look on his face. Ahead Katherine had reached the portal. Si followed her through. Isaac had two options and getting caught wasn't one of them. He put his head down and urged his legs to move faster as he dived towards the portal.

He only just made it. The portal closed in behind him and he heard a muttered curse from the dark god as Isaac slipped from his grasp.

He found himself in a dark space.

Katherine cried out from up front. "We're trapped."

Isaac moved forwards and reached for the ornate metal gate before rattling it. Si ran his hand through his hair and banged the metal in frustration as he caught his breath.

Footfalls, shouts and the sound of metal clanging on the various floors rang in the distance. The lighting changed to red and around the gates it pulsed as though announcing them to the realm they had just reached. Katherine stepped back against Isaac, away from the gates, as guards rushed into the room. The men were shouting to find the king.

Katherine studied the nearest guard. "I have a child with me. We mean you no harm. What is the king called? Is it Tallin?"

The guard spun towards Katherine and bashed his weapon against the gate as silence settled over the room and a figure strode in. He moved with all the swagger of royalty. He came to a halt not far from the other side of the gates and scrutinised them, his intense, dark eyes sweeping over each of them before resting on Katherine.

"Are you Tallin? King Tallin? Your partner is Lavinia?" Katherine asked.

Mist flowed from his hair creating the odd impression that he was in some way possessed. "I am

King Tallin and you are?"

"Oh, thank the gods. I'm Katherine, Maya's mother. You have my girls here and Haydan. This is Isaac, my husband, and Si. He's a family friend."

A sly smile nudged the edge of Tallin's mouth up as he appeared to relax a little. Isaac's daughter stretched a tiny hand out and cooed at the king.

"Well, well, well and what an angel you are," Tallin said, turning to Katherine. "You brought your unreadable males as well. How delightful." Tallin raised an eyebrow as he reached for the gate and pulled it open.

"Welcome to the twin realms of Aveyamara." Tallin offered Katherine his arm, choosing to ignore Isaac and Si and turning his back to them. He held out a finger and the baby grabbed hold of it before trying to eat it. Tallin chuckled softly. "What a wonderful little person you are. You must come and see Maya and Arianna and tell me all about what brings you here. Diego will join us."

Tallin moved off, propelling Katherine along with him, leaving Isaac with a sense of delight at seeing the girls, mingled with dread. Tallin had singled out his wife for special treatment and Isaac didn't like the way he looked at her, or his child either. Behind his back he pressed the button on the mask and slid the smaller piece into his pocket as Diego came into view.

Katherine was Isaac's angel and his alone. There was no way he was going to be outsmarted by Tallin. Haydan had indirectly warned him about Tallin's games with a few comments he had made and it would be a cold day in hell before Isaac allowed himself to be outwitted by an elf, even if he was a king.

༂∘ཉ

ᚻaydan

Haydan moved down the corridor without waiting for the girls, who trailed behind him. He could forgive Arianna because she was trying to protect him, but irrational irritation at Maya's behaviour festered. She was still young, only fifteen. She was around Tallin, and his world was full of intrigue and misdirection. Her behaviour indicated she was settling in and finding her feet, but the discomfort around his soul remained, heightening his agitation.

The wall sconces were dimly lit, perhaps reflecting his mood as he stalked the route back to his room. His footsteps echoed off the tiled floors, the reflective quality of the surfaces adding to his disquiet. Tallin had told him to stay where he left him and he was ignoring that warning, but with Arianna close by and Diego also on the loose in the court, his fears were lessened, and he refused to bow to Tallin and take orders like a servant of the crown. He would probably face a dressing-down from both of them for ignoring a direct order from the king. He huffed and hunkered down as he reached the steps up to the bedrooms.

He was well ahead of the girls now. Arianna started running, giving chase to try and close the gap that had opened up. He ascended the stairs, his bedroom and destination in sight.

Something flickered off to his side, a sudden movement in the shadows that indicated somebody was hiding there. Coming to a halt, he turned as a shadowy figure darted at him from out of the darkness. It moved too quickly for him to register what it was or try to defend himself using his magic. A leg connected with his stomach, winding him as he doubled over, and a hard object, possibly a fist or elbow, made contact with his temple. The floor came up to meet him as his altera arm was swung up and around his back. His stomach roiled as fingertips brushed his altera and he realised too late his mistake. He had separated himself from Arianna. His warrior was now too far away to defend him from the assault.

"Master will be pleased. You do have a physical soul, a special one as well. Diversions serve us well. His most treasured possession left unguarded, silly Tallin." The voice addressing Haydan was female. She sounded soft and breathy as though she had exerted herself in carrying out her daring capture. Haydan let the warning reach Arianna via their connection as he struggled to free himself.

Something made impact with Haydan's head and he slumped onto the cold floor as his consciousness started fading and darkness rushed in around the edges of his vision.

A shout from nearby sounded like Arianna. His arm released as the woman holding him muttered under her breath and said, "Don't go anywhere, sweetheart, I'll be right back for your soul."

❧

*A*rianna

*H*aydan. Arianna darted ahead of Maya, barging her aside and launching her into one of the nearby triple halos to get her to safety as she plunged into the darkened corridor. Haydan was already on the floor with his arm twisted behind his back. The woman who had dared to attack him stood over him looking jubilant.

"Not on my watch, lady," Arianna said to herself, before shouting, "Intruders! Unbonded prince down."

The woman cursed, said something to Haydan and knocked him out with a blow to the head with what looked like a nunchuck. She glared into the darkness as Arianna slid into stealth mode and rushed towards her.

Arianna dropped out of her stealth mode close to the woman, lunged low and slammed a punch into her stomach. The woman sailed down the corridor on her behind, before spinning herself around and springing back up. She didn't have the same reflexes as Arianna; if she did, she would have pre-empted her attack.

Throwing herself at the woman, Arianna landed with a thump and ducked as the nunchucks were swung at her head. Springing back up, she darted forwards, punching the woman twice in the head before spinning and sweeping her legs from underneath her. The assailant cried out as she landed on the hard tiled floor and tried to grab Arianna's hair. Arianna blocked her arm with a quick swipe of her own and launched another punch, flinging the woman back onto the floor. Her head made a sickening thump as she impacted the tiles. Standing, Arianna kept her fists up ready for attack as she stepped across and glared down at the collapsed, inert figure. Further down the corridor the main lights activated and guards rushed forwards to grab the woman who had attacked. She looked no older than Arianna. On her forehead, a mark surfaced from beneath, like a rune. It glowed for a few seconds then vanished.

Sandau moved out of the shadows with Maya at his side. He held her wrist tight in his, suggesting Maya hadn't arrived in Sandau's room in the best of humours. It had been the safest place to send her. Sandau's room was his stronghold. He had set up various runes when he arrived so he would know if anyone entered his private quarters unannounced. They had agreed it was the safest place to deposit any of their party who was in trouble, and Sandau would understand that Maya's arrival meant something serious had just happened.

Arianna turned away as Maya knelt at Haydan's side and shook his shoulders. "Haydan? Wake up. I'm sorry. If anything happens to you I'll never forgive myself."

Haydan groaned and raised a shaky hand to rub his head where the woman had hit him.

"Are you okay?" Maya peered at Haydan, appearing so concerned Arianna wondered how she could ever bear to push him away. Yet she did so frequently, without any regard for how much it hurt him.

"I think so. Storm fire, she came out of nowhere."

Haydan stopped talking as Maya launched herself at him. Flinging her arms around his body, she held him as though her life depended on him.

Sandau met Arianna's stare, smiled at her and

nodded his approval. "Now you understand your role. You are at your finest when you do what you are designed to do without overthinking it."

Tallin swept into view further down the corridor. He made his way towards them as the guards hauled the woman to her feet. "What just happened? I told you all to stay put. Are you incapable of doing anything I ask of you? Are Haydan and Maya okay?"

"They're both fine." Arianna waved a hand in their direction; not that she could see much of Haydan; only his dark hair was visible by Maya's shoulder. He appeared to be enjoying Maya's attentiveness as she continued to hold him close, refusing to relinquish her grip.

"She tried to kidnap Haydan. She wanted his soul for her master. She said her master would be pleased. She wasn't working alone, that's for sure. Oh, and there was a mark on her forehead, a red rune that vanished after she hit her head on the floor. What was that?"

Behind Tallin more people arrived. Arianna recognised Diego, Katherine, Isaac and Si. The sight of her father sent her emotions soaring. Isaac's tense expression melted into a mischievous grin when he realised she was okay.

Diego moved around Tallin, but remained as a barrier between Arianna's family and Tallin. Arianna wondered at the significance but dismissed it as coincidental.

Tallin strode up to the woman and glared at her as huge plumes of mist rose up around him and drifted towards the woman's face. She grimaced and tried to back away. With the guards holding her she couldn't go anywhere.

"Who is your master, Lyra?"

"You know her?" Arianna found that surprising.

"She is one of my less experienced healers."

Lyra burst out laughing. "I won't tell you and neither will my master. He'll kill me first."

Tallin growled and refocused on her. The mist wrapped around her face. Convulsions rippled through the woman's body at the contact. Tallin's scowl deepened and he pulled back from her. "Find Lavinia. Find her now."

"Why do you need Lavinia?" Diego asked, moving closer.

"The use of runes is powerful magic. If I try to force my will on her to get what I want from her, he will kill her. I am hoping Lavinia's magic might fool him."

"Who will?" Diego asked.

Tallin moved his attention to the guards holding her. "Does my magic mark her body anywhere?"

The guards checked Lyra's arms and inspected her body for any markings before shaking their head.

"There have been rumours of powerful mages amongst my court for years. My advisors and consorts hide certain abilities from me, probably because I prefer to have the powerful ones on my side and visible as part of my army. The hidden ones store their powers and set them loose in the woodland. They remain linked at all times. Every now and again they challenge me. Their strength and numbers are growing. They have been emboldened by the arrival of Diego and Haydan. They think I am distracted and that they can weaken my control of the realm by trying to hurt those close to me."

"The figures in the woodland the night I arrived," Maya said. She turned to face Tallin, letting go of

Haydan as she did so.

Tallin nodded. "The energy I threw out that looked like coloured powder will have marked them with my magic. Perhaps they did not appreciate my trick to find them. I have been gifting them power for years. My way of keeping them happy, but they never are. They want more and more. It appears that perhaps I have been a fool to expect to maintain the balance. They have been construing my need to pacify them as a weakness. Tomorrow night I will set that record straight once and for all." He returned his focus to the woman. "I need answers from you, young lady."

Her body trembled and the tremors grew stronger.

Tallin's nose wrinkled. "And of course Lavinia picks a time like this to block me from telepathic contact," Tallin said more to himself than to anyone gathered. Another rune surfaced on her forehead, a purple one. It spread across her skin like a fire clawing its way along a route already carved out.

"Lavinia!" Tallin shouted.

Lavinia rushed forwards as the woman's body convulsed and her eyes rolled into her head. A moment later her lifeless body slumped forwards. The purple rune faded as they all stared at her.

Tallin clenched his fists as Lavinia reached his side and surveyed the gathered crowd. "I'm here. What is it?"

"You are too late, my love. It seems the most vicious of our hidden court mages would rather kill an innocent than be named in my presence. No more pacifying my court. Tomorrow night I am going to make them regret their trickery." Tallin lowered the woman's eyelids and bowed his head for a moment.

"Take her away," Tallin said to the nearest guard.

"Make sure she receives a proper burial and her family are informed of what has happened here tonight. It was not their daughter's fault. She stood no chance against a mage as powerful as this one."

"She's dead?" Maya asked, looking shocked.

"Yes. I cannot stop a death rune forming once a mage has activated it."

"As long as you don't lose sight of who is truly important in all of this." Diego's voice cut the air like a knife. Tallin turned towards him. "You brought Haydan and Maya into this. You protect them ahead of everyone else. I will protect the rest of Maya and Arianna's family. You have managed to trap us all here, somewhere between your feuding court and dark gods. This is not a good strategy."

Tallin inhaled a deep breath as Lavinia slipped an arm around his waist and cuddled in against him. "That all depends on whether this was the plan from the start."

On that cryptic note Tallin turned to Maya and Haydan, pulling Lavinia with him. "Katherine has arrived with her unreadable males in tow. Diego will take you all to your rooms and I will have extra guards on duty tonight. No doubt the warriors will make their own arrangements to protect their storm riders. The triple halos will not transport you beyond any of our bedrooms. I suggest everyone gets some sleep. We all need to rest. Tomorrow is showtime."

Chapter 25

Diego

The hallway was shrouded in silence as Diego walked back to his room. Hunger gnawed at his stomach. Hoping to find a snack of some sort, he entered the dining room. Plates of nuts and fruit perched on the sideboard. There were jugs of water and glasses stacked up. He picked up a glass, poured water and crunched on some nuts, before selecting some grapes. Throwing them into the air, he captured the first few in his mouth. The fourth one was snatched from mid-air in front of his face by a sudden blur of purple hair – Aaushk. That brought a smile to his face.

"That's a liberty, stealing from a prince. I'll bet you don't get away with behaviour like that around my father."

Aaushk crouched under the sideboard. The strange little creature clutched the grape, studying Diego with a wary expression.

"You wouldn't dare steal from Tallin, but you'll steal from me, is that it?" Diego deliberated what to do next. Aaushk hadn't eaten the grape, but held it like a prized possession.

"Well, go on then, seeing as you've mauled it, you may as well eat it."

Aaushk shoved the grape into his mouth, making strange little satisfied noises. His table manners were lacking; grape juice dribbled down his chin.

Diego crouched down. "You enjoyed that. Why don't you just take what you want from the table? Are you not allowed to take food or something?"

Aaushk shook his head. Diego held out another grape. Aaushk grabbed it and retreated under the sideboard with it, once again waiting expectantly as though for permission to eat.

"It's yours, eat it. You spy for my father. I'd like you to spy for me. One day, I will be king. It wouldn't hurt to show me the same respect you show him."

Aaushk paused; his mouth was wide open, but not touching the grape. The grape lowered back down and the strange little creature gave Diego a disgruntled look as though Diego had just disappointed him.

"You don't like that idea? Tallin doesn't have to know. We could keep it between us. I'll feed you, you filter information through to me about what my father is up to." This was a good idea. Tallin did this sort of thing all the time. In his realm, this was normal behaviour, nothing out of the ordinary. Diego could play this game as well as, if not better than, his father. "On Storm Lands, you can have food whenever you like."

Aaushk devoured the grape and wiped the back of his hand across his mouth. "You think you feed me, so that makes me loyal to you?"

Diego grimaced and deliberated how to respond. Being direct was probably unwise, but he couldn't lie. He opted for caution as he said, "No, I know you're loyal to my father. I'm just asking you to share some things with me sometimes about what he's up to. Occasionally, I could use the help and a bit of assistance. I keep you in food, you keep me informed about a few things that I'm unaware of."

"Or I could just tell Tallin. You're not the first to try this game, you know. Courtiers do this all the time because they want me to spy on the king for them. I, of course, agree to their request, but then I also tell the king. You're no different. I'm disappointed. The only way you get my loyalty is if you outsmart me. You don't have the power of the realm at your fingertips, so that's never going to happen, and after Tallin I am wise to your games."

Now the creature looked devious and cunning as it appeared to assess Diego's reaction.

"You didn't want to leave me the last time I handed you over to Tallin. Or is that part of your game with me? Pretend you want to stay so I think you're easy to manipulate? That would be about right for my father. I'll bet he wants me to try and outwit you, just so he can enjoy some entertainment."

Aaushk folded his arms. "You want my loyalty, you've got to catch me."

"Oh, right, that's your attempt at a challenge, is it? The only way I get your loyalty is to prove I'm more cunning than the master game-player himself?"

Aushk raised his eyebrows. "Good luck, storm rider."

Diego launched himself across the floor. Aaushk ran with a speed that suggested he was possessed. Diego almost captured a leg, but just missed and smashed into the sideboard at the same time, sending glasses crashing to the floor. The noise would wake half the castle and his father would already know why.

⮞⭒⮜

Haydan

Haydan cracked an eye open, observing Maya as she slipped back into the bedroom clutching a tray of food. She crept across to the bed. Peering down at him, she rewarded him with a warm smile as he met her gaze.

A dull ache had settled across the back of Haydan's head from where he had been hit the night before. Wincing, he sat up, stretched and waited for Maya to slide the tray onto his lap. "Breakfast in bed from my lovely chosen one. This is a real treat. It's a shame we can't wake up like this more often."

Maya sat down next to Haydan. "That would be difficult given that you never stay over any more unless you're injured. Apparently when you're injured, you're fair game."

Maya's demeanour suggested she was in a playful mood. Haydan matched it. "Then bond with me and I can stay over whenever you like."

A bob of Maya's throat was all that indicated her uncertainty over the topic Haydan had just directly addressed. She lowered her attention to the tray. "I found the breakfast room further up the corridor. Tallin has had this whole section shut down so no one can go anywhere. He's furious you ignored his request not to budge. Mum arrived last night with Isaac and Si. Diego has warned her about Tallin's focus on the baby. If he asks questions about how many other children there are in the family we are under strict instructions not to talk about it."

"Why? Tallin now knows there is more than just you regardless of what anyone tells him and it was an order he gave, not a request. Yes, I will have to apologise. No doubt Diego will be livid as well."

Maya rewarded Haydan with a dismissive shrug. "Probably, but you were mad at me, so how guilty do I now feel for contributing? Diego thinks there's a problem here with low birth rates and since I'm from a big family, it's safe to assume Tallin will find that fascinating. He's worried Tallin will kidnap the kids. They're a new bloodline."

Haydan snorted before he could stop himself. "Really? I love the way you tell me that, as though it's the most normal thing in the world. In any case, I'm sure Tallin has enough on his plate at the moment without worrying about your siblings." His laughter died away. His head throbbed and the cut at the back of his head was stinging. "I don't want you feeling guilty for last night. I have no one to blame but myself. I didn't listen to Arianna either."

A grin nudged the edge of Maya's mouth upwards. "He's crafty though and he's able to tempt what he wants out of people very easily. Reminds me of someone, can't think who." Her grin broadened before dropping away. "The dark gods turned up at the house last night. They tried to capture my family. They're getting close. Diego and Arianna tried to distract them before they joined us, but that was only going to buy you some time. You have to start mastering the realms with Kaleshar."

"I know. I will. You need to show me this chamber you've found."

Maya acknowledged Haydan with a nod just as

Arianna sauntered across from the corner of the room where the triple halo sat.

"And someone needs to introduce me to the unique transport system," Haydan said.

Arianna smiled at Haydan. "How's your head?"

"It's sore but I'll live."

Sitting next to Maya, Arianna grabbed a piece of toast off the tray. "Sandau needs to show you the transport system and he can do that once Tallin releases the lockdown. I bumped into him in the corridor before. Tallin wants us all to have breakfast then we have to sort out outfits for tonight. The team who have designed them are in later. After that he will release the lockdown, but the court will be busy today with preparations for tonight. Oh, and Tallin wants to teach Maya to waltz." Arianna fished something out of her pocket and held it out to Maya. "Gloves. You should wear them, or Haydan will be seeing his breakfast again sooner than he expected."

Maya grabbed the gloves. "May I go?"

Her submissiveness that morning did not escape Haydan's notice. She never asked his permission to do anything any more and he never expected her to. He considered the question for a moment then nodded. Maya rushed off as though welcoming the release from his presence, or as if in a hurry to be somewhere else. The realisation once again irritated him. It seemed that morning's respite was only temporary.

తళ్ళు

ന്വaya

Maya knocked on Tallin's door and bounced from foot to foot as she waited. It opened a moment later and Lavinia surveyed her, before stepping back to let her in. The sight before her felt surreal. Tallin was surrounded by a group of men who were a mix of elves and fae. He stood half-dressed with his bare chest on show as they deliberated what he should wear. Far from being concerned by Maya's presence, Tallin gave her a charming smile.

"Good morning to you."

Every time the men moved away, mist flooded from Tallin's neck in great swathes. It retreated to Tallin whenever they moved closer. The strange doorway hung from his neck, nestled against a light smattering of dark chest hair.

Maya's stare clashed with Lavinia's. She waved Maya away as she went to pick up her drink from the sideboard. "You can admire the view and suffer the consequences with Haydan later." The statement sounded hostile, but Lavinia leant back against the unit and returned Tallin's smouldering look before refocusing on Maya and smiling. "This I am used to. He does this every morning. Then he has his hair done. He is worse than me and I have been dressed for an hour."

Tallin grinned. "Yes, and I am sure you will make a point of getting your own back tonight, when you keep me waiting, my sweet."

"You can count on it, Tal. I have a rather fabulous outfit planned for tonight as well. You'll need Balcarres distracting and I think I can manage that."

The gathered dressmakers had decided on a crisp white shirt with coloured edging on the collar and cuffs and matching buttons. They slipped the garments onto Tallin as he stood like a mannequin waiting for them to finish their primping. Before they touched the buttons down the front, Tallin said, "Leave that, this is Levi's favourite job." The men moved away and began discussions over which waistcoat Tallin should wear, perusing a selection laid out on the huge floating bed.

Lavinia placed the glass down and swept across the room. As she fastened the buttons Tallin watched Maya over the top of her head. "So, I promised to teach you to waltz." That look, the mysterious one that always set Maya on edge, burned in his intense stare again.

"You did, but I have a proposal for you."

Tallin pursed his lips and studied Lavinia with a scandalous look on his face as she finished fastening his buttons. Lavinia pulled on the hem and stepped back to admire her efforts.

"A counter-offer, how interesting. Are you in a bargaining position? I am not sure you are. Bonded to Haydan, you might have more sway. Your family seem nice. How many brothers and sisters do you have? Lavinia has been a little vague as to numbers, but I gather there are a few siblings not here yet." He straightened up and rearranged his cuffs as the dressmakers held out a luxurious petrol-blue waistcoat. With a nod of approval from Tallin they swooped in for the next stage in dressing the king.

Lavinia moved to Maya's side. There was an undercurrent of unease between Tallin and Lavinia now. Maya couldn't put her finger on it, but something had displeased Tallin and Lavinia appeared tense.

"Well, tell the king what your counter-offer is. Tallin will be busy today with preparations for tonight. Time is of the essence."

The men had finished dressing the king. They brushed down his clothing and stepped back, before gathering up the discarded items from the bed.

"I would like you to teach me to waltz and I would like to borrow the ring you wear, that green one. Just for tonight. I need it for Haydan."

Tallin slid his fingers over the top of the ring and his expression hardened, his shoulders drawing back. "Absolutely not. You need to learn to waltz. The ring you are asking to borrow is not leaving the hands of the royal line. Are you the royal line, Maya?"

"No, not exactly, but—"

"Well, there you go. No, you may not borrow it."

Tallin stated the word 'borrow' in a cold tone, suggesting Maya's use of it had offended him somehow.

"Why are you asking about my family? My siblings aren't your concern. I need you to help me and so far, you seem reluctant to do so. Or is that just me?"

A bark of laughter left Tallin's mouth. "Ironic, coming from a reluctant chosen one, no?" His eyebrow raised as he fixed a scornful look on Maya. "I am more subtle in my assistance than you can possibly imagine." His attention flitted to Lavinia, who drew herself up. "You found the library without a problem, did you not?"

"Stop glaring at me like that, Tal. I can handle Balcarres and, Maya, elves do not borrow things. It's regarded as the equivalent of stealing."

"It is not your handling of Balcarres that bothers

me. It is his handling of you that I dislike and what is more, he knows it." Tallin sniffed and brushed Lavinia's hand away as she tried to fasten the waistcoat buttons. "Leave it, Levi, enough fussing."

Tallin was jealous of Balcarres, whoever he was. That was the undercurrent between the two of them. The men all bowed and rushed out of the room, closing the door behind them. Tallin returned his cold glare to Maya. "So, waltzing. Aaushk, play some music, please. Can you dance, Maya? Do you have a sense of rhythm?"

"I love dancing. I do dance classes: modern, contemporary, ballet, and I really want to do belly dancing. I thought that all chosen ones danced for their storm riders. Do you not dance for Lavinia?"

Lavinia choked on her drink. Tallin bit back a smirk. "No, I dance when my court requires it. It is a formality, nothing more. Angels have a great sense of rhythm though. I would wager your mother can also move herself to a rhythm when required. I am sure Haydan finds your dancing enchanting. Is he alright after last night? Lyra's brazen attack will have been a shock."

Maya nodded. "He's okay. Well, he's started pressuring me about bonding again, but his head is okay. He stayed in my room last night so I could keep an eye on him."

"That is unwise," Tallin said. He looked unimpressed by her announcement.

"He might have passed out. I wanted to be sure he was okay."

"Admirable, but you are sending mixed messages. You cannot give with one hand and take with the other. Last night Haydan was given a taster of what is coming his way. You offer him comfort when he needs it, then push him away, and you wonder why he is confused and angry at you?" Tallin's eyes narrowed. "Because he is confused and angry. No wonder when you treat him like you do."

Beautiful, haunting flute music began playing. Tallin stepped forwards and held out his hand, capturing Maya's hand in his as he pulled her closer and slid his other hand around her waist. Unsure where to look, Maya lowered her gaze to his chest. Tallin made a tsk noise. "Maya, waltzing is all about meeting your partner's eyes when required. Confidence and awareness are key. The male always leads."

Tallin cocked his head to the side as though waiting for Maya to challenge him; instead she smiled sweetly and met his steady stare. "Okay, you lead, King Tallin."

"You step in threes and count as you do so, in your head obviously." Tallin moved off.

Maya messed up her first two steps and ended up being stood on.

Tallin scowled at her, then huffed. "Again. Count one, two, three."

After another couple of false starts Maya got the hang of it.

Tallin moved in a poised, self-assured manner which thrilled her. She hoped Haydan would dance with her that evening, or maybe Diego.

"Have your little furry friends returned yet?" Tallin fixed her with a curious look as they moved. "You could do with tempting them back sometime soon and preferably before tonight."

"You want the whirling dervishes here? That's unlikely. They have abandoned me recently."

There was a knock at the door. Tallin chuckled as

he directed them back the way they had just come. Lavinia's attention hadn't left him since he took hold of Maya's hand, however, which amused her.

"Let me give you a small piece of advice if I may." He didn't wait for an answer as he swept her around and explained. "This is how you move around a corner. Whirling dervishes do not like dark magic. They thrive in the light. Let the light in, Maya, and you will find that you have your furry accomplices back." He raised an eyebrow as Lavinia tapped his shoulder. "Yes, my sweet."

"Your hairdresser is here, my darling, and I do hope you are going to dance with me tonight. It's etiquette to dance at least once with your queen. We need to discuss who is lying low in your court as well. There are a number of courtiers unaccounted for and if they were marked by your magic in the woodland, I need to know the details."

"Yes, my sweet. You are always one for spoiling the moment with something more serious and yes, I know it is important." Tallin's eyes twinkled in delight as he released Maya, fixed a smouldering, heated stare on Lavinia and hauled her towards him, before waltzing Lavinia around in circles. "How is this, my love? I have not lost my rhythm."

Lavinia squealed and giggled in response, composing herself before transferring her hostile stare onto the woman who was styling Tallin's hair. The platinum blonde faerie loitering near the door looked alarmed. It was no wonder. Maya was aware of the tensions that sparked between Tallin and Lavinia, adoration and jealousy part of the powerful emotions that simmered between the two of them. Regardless of appearances Tallin and Lavinia were a strong and united front at all times. The realisation made Maya smile and reminded her to go and speak to Isaac, Katherine and Si. Thanking Tallin, Maya left the hairdresser to her fate and opened the huge, ornately engraved door to go in search of her family.

Chapter 26

Haydan

After Haydan finished his breakfast, Arianna went to find Sandau, leaving him alone with his wild thoughts, Tallin greeting Maya half-dressed being the least of them. He took comfort in the fact that Lavinia was there, keeping an eye on his errant chosen one. The dark gods were coming, maybe not that evening, but they would come soon. Rebellions were breaking out in Tallin's court and Maya's entire family was now caught up in it all. With Kaleshar's assistance he was going to have to start mastering realms and the more he considered it, the more he felt as though that moved him further away from Maya.

He glanced up as someone approached from near the door. He expected to find Katherine or Isaac; instead he met his mother's intense grey-and-blue-flecked gaze.

"Mother, I didn't officially know you were here."

"No, I came in quietly. I wanted to talk to you in private."

"Does Diego know you're here?"

Rebekka shook her head. "Not yet. He will not be

pleased to see me. We will be introduced tonight, to the court, which will make it harder for your father to hide me."

Rebekka smoothed down her honey-blonde hair and pushed her hands down into the pockets on her slim-fit trousers. She appeared uneasy and in Haydan's experience that didn't bode well.

"Have you been fighting with Diego?"

"What a ridiculous question. You're the cause of it. Are you proud of yourself? I think secretly you must be."

Women never said what they meant.

"I don't know what you're talking about. Perhaps you could be a little more specific."

Rebekka's laugh was cold and mocking. "Your temerity is unbelievable. Last time you were here, I think you found something. It did not belong to you. It was supposedly returned to the sea. I went to check and it's not there. You didn't tell me." Her body tensed and her mouth turned down at the edges as fury distorted her features. "You chose to protect your father's fallen chosen one ahead of telling your own mother."

How could his mother know all of this…? Unless… "Lavinia told you, didn't she? Before she found me on Storm Lands, she came to tell you. Why would she do that? You have never got on with Lavinia. She's trying to drive you and Diego apart with this."

Rebekka folded her arms and glared at Haydan. "No, she didn't tell me any of it. I figured it out from her spurious comments and digs and you've just confirmed my suspicions."

Haydan grimaced and inwardly groaned at falling right into her carefully laid trap.

"Perhaps she is scheming with Tallin to get Diego

away from both of us. She has never wanted him tied to any woman. I may not be able to force Diego's hand, but I'm going to make it as difficult as I can for him to reject me."

"Tallin will not like this. Our souls are sacred and you are violating that. I didn't tell you because I didn't want to hurt you and because it's up to Diego to make his own decision. He is with you right now. He adores you. His decision is not made. He will live a long life. Let him make the choice. If you don't, you will push him away anyway by not respecting that."

"If she's gone he's mine. Where is she? What did you do with her?" Rebekka asked.

Pulled in two different directions, Haydan debated what to do. "I can't tell you that. I won't tell you that. It's not fair of you to put me in that position."

"Not fair? I'll tell you what's not fair, you coming out of the sea for Diego, but not me. That's not fair. Why are you so loyal to him? Does he have some kind of hold over you? You've always been his favourite son, the one who can do no wrong. Did your god friend help you? What's his name?"

"Theander. Mother … I came out of the sea for two storm riders, not because of any favouritism on my part. I didn't know until you entered with Diego that you were together. I don't want to fall out with you over this."

"Then tell me where she is."

"No."

"Then we're done here. I will find her and when I do–"

"You'll do what, Mother? Violating a soul is horrific. When Diego finds out he'll have to punish you. Don't do that to him."

His mother had managed to achieve what no other storm rider had, yet she still wasn't happy. Diego would go crazy if he heard Rebekka's plans.

"I want her gone. I will not share him." Rebekka's eyes welled with unshed tears as she slipped back out of his room, leaving Haydan wondering if he had imagined the entire event. Ironically, and in spite of her declaration, it appeared Rebekka had always shared Diego with his chosen one.

Arianna approached from the triple halo. Behind her a number of frogs crept up the wall in Maya's room. Haydan ignored them. Given that evening's theme there would be more than a few frogs to worry about.

"We've got to go and try on our outfits, then Sandau will show you how the transport system works. Tallin should be releasing the lockdown shortly."

Sandau appeared a moment later. He smirked at Haydan as he sauntered across to him. "I need to show you both how the traps work as well. When the dark gods land, the traps will be invaluable. Tallin has promised any captured dark gods to Theander."

Arianna didn't mention Haydan's mother's visit. If she had overheard any of their conversation, or seen Rebekka leave, she was wisely keeping it to herself. A look passed between Arianna and Sandau, one that made Haydan wonder whether they already knew. Even if they did, guarding Haydan and Diego was their primary concern anyway.

His nerves already frayed, Haydan nodded and remained quiet. If Rebekka caught up with Theander, that would be an interesting meeting. Hopefully she would keep her visit low-key. She would calm down at some point, but if Diego found out what she was up to, he would be furious and that concerned Haydan more.

His parents didn't often argue but when they did their fighting was epic.

ᒍsaac

Isaac left the safety of the bedroom and moved out into the corridor with Si and Katherine, who was holding the baby.

"Well, I'll give Diego his due, this is impressive by anyone's standard, but I never had him or Haydan down as princes," Si said. He skirted around a triple halo, pursed his lips and folded his arms when the balls raised into the air. "The levitating sculptures are a nice touch. I could do with a few of these for home."

"I don't think they're sculptures," Katherine said. She moved off down the corridor. "Don't mess with things that you don't understand, especially not around here. The fae are tricky, at least that's what Lucas told me. If you poke your nose in where it's not invited, you get into trouble. Tallin and Diego do not strike me as the sort of men you want to cross."

"Yeah, well I don't like Tallin calling you angel and maybe he doesn't want to cross me," Isaac said. He made sure he sounded more formidable than he felt.

Arianna stalked out of Maya's room. In full-on warrior mode she scanned the corridor and checked the location of all the triple halos in rapid succession before returning her attention to the group. Haydan walked into the corridor with a tall man at his side whom Isaac didn't recognise. The stranger was a solid chunk of male. He moved with the authority of a tomcat and the tenacity of a military man as he swept forwards and settled an arrogant look on Isaac that made him want to immediately return hostilities. It was rare to see such a large man carrying so much muscle, but there was no doubt that the formidable man standing at Haydan's side could handle himself.

Arianna glanced at the stranger, nodded as silent communication passed between the two of them and moved towards Isaac, Katherine and Si. That was Sandau, the warrior who had kissed Arianna. Isaac could tell, and the man continued staring at him as if proud of his achievement. The challenge wasn't lost on him.

Arianna's face relaxed into a warm smile and she rushed towards them and hugged them one at a time. "It's so great to have you guys here. I'm never allowed to share this stuff with you, but now you're here, so I can, without fear of reprimand from you know who."

Behind her Haydan rolled his eyes as he walked across. "Good morning, everyone. Have you been told you can leave your room?"

"No," Isaac said. "I didn't realise I was chained to my room and the door was open. Si wants to know what the three floating ball sculptures are all about, whereas I'm more interested in why Tallin is so taken with Kat and whether Sandau is going to try and kiss my daughter again." Sandau's startled gaze locked with Isaac's. "You are Sandau, aren't you?"

Sandau nodded, his face the epitome of haughtiness. "I'm sure what Arianna does on Storm Lands is none of your business, unreadable human, and I don't remember her complaining."

Arianna's cheeks flushed. "You caught me by

surprise."

Isaac bristled; he couldn't help it. Sandau just looked so smug and pleased with himself. "She's fifteen years old."

"It was a kiss," Sandau said, sounding bored.

Katherine brushed a hand against Isaac's elbow and smiled at Sandau. "Hello, Sandau. It's a pleasure to meet you." She turned to Isaac. "It was a kiss, nothing more. How old were you when you first kissed a girl?"

Thrown under a bus by his own wife. Katherine continued to smile at Isaac innocently. She had done that on purpose and was about to work her charms on Sandau as well.

"How old were you, Isaac?"

"I was–"

"Yes?" Katherine's expression remained innocent. She already knew the answer.

Everyone gathered turned to Isaac. Now he had no choice but to answer. If he didn't Katherine would and then he would look weak. "I was fourteen," he finally responded.

Katherine beamed at Sandau, then Arianna. "There you go, Isaac was fourteen, so he can't talk. Do you honestly think Arianna is going to end up with a human male? This is the world your daughter walks in." She cast a sideways glance at Isaac as she moved her focus to Haydan and Sandau. "Picking a fight with a warrior is hardly a wise move, my darling. You're more of a lover than a fighter and I should know."

Next to Isaac, Si snickered. "I'm saying nothing, my friend. Suffice to say that I think your lovely wife just saved you from a pummelling."

Sandau seemed amused although he didn't say anything. He lowered his head, grinned and winked at Arianna, who blushed, focused on Katherine and mouthed a 'thank you' to her.

"Haydan, how is your head this morning?" Katherine asked. "Is Maya okay? I saw her briefly last night and after all the excitement I knew you would need some time alone." She rocked the baby as she waited for Haydan's response.

Haydan smiled as though finding Katherine's diversion amusing. "I have a sore head, but I'll survive. Maya is talking to Tallin. He's teaching her to waltz or some such nonsense. It seems you've had your own adventure."

"Yes, definitely. Dark gods are scary and Isaac got closer than he would have liked to one. Luckily, he outran him. Tallin is fascinating, isn't he?" The baby squealed in her arms and Katherine turned to see what had caught the child's attention. A brightly coloured lizard ran up the wall nearby and blew a raspberry at the gathering. The baby gurgled and cooed in response.

Haydan's eyes widened although his surprise seemed misplaced. He leant in towards Katherine and fixed Isaac with a wary look. "Fascinating or not, Tallin's world is full of games. His magical creatures are entertaining your daughter and watching her. He seems taken with the baby and there aren't many of those in this realm. Keep him away from the child."

Katherine tried to laugh off Haydan's cautious tone. He didn't smile in response, but remained sombre.

"I'm serious, Kat. He won't hurt her, but curiosity from Tallin is not a good thing. Maya is already ensnared in his games."

Katherine's expression became more solemn as she realised the warning in Haydan's words. Shrinking back towards Isaac, she wrapped her arm around his waist.

"Have you been invited to the ball?" Haydan asked.

Si shook his head. "No, I'm sure the invitation is in the post though, right?" He smiled at Sandau. "I'm Si by the way. I'm a good friend of Kat and Isaac."

Sandau dragged his attention from Arianna and turned his calculating gaze onto Si. The men stared each other down and for a moment, Isaac felt as though silent communication passed between them as well. Sandau blinked rapidly, tilted his head and his shoulders drew back. He assessed Si with an up and down sweep before angling his body away. The move from Sandau seemed submissive and Isaac couldn't help thinking that Si had given the big man something to think about. When Sandau's focus returned to Si, shrewdness ticked away in his mysterious and somewhat creepy ghosted eyes. The thought of Arianna falling in love with a man like Sandau proved the most disturbing part of the journey so far, yet as everyone aside from Sandau left the corridor no one else appeared to have noticed the odd stand-off between the two men.

Chapter 27

Maya

A small purple shock of hair darted past Maya's foot as she pulled the door to Tallin's bedroom closed. It made its way into the corridor and ran along the recess at the bottom of the wall where the strip lights were located. Maya couldn't help wondering what trouble Tallin was causing now.

Standing opposite Sandau in the corridor, Diego crouched down as though fastening his shoelaces, even though he didn't have any. Out of the corner of his eye his gaze tracked the small purple shock of hair as it rushed along. Riveted by the strange display, Maya bit her bottom lip and slipped back into the shadows.

Diego placed his sword back into the recess. He had mounted the sword in a sheath on his belt and as he crouched, it ended up gliding along the floor into the cavity. The move was done in a subtle manner, but was deliberate. Maya had never seen any of the riders wear swords on their belts either, which made it even more conspicuous. Diego made a point of sliding his right hand around the sword hilt.

The purple shock of hair reached the sword and

tried to dart around it. Diego flicked the sword out, catapulting the poor creature into the corridor. It shrieked then rolled with the force of the momentum.

Sandau, who had been tracking everything, lunged forwards and stamped his foot down hard. Maya gasped and clamped her hand over her mouth. Had they just squashed the poor creature to death? Her heart pounded as she stared in utter shock at Diego's cruelty.

Diego moved in and reached down. Sandau had stomped on the creature's long hair to hold it down; the pixie itself was fine, if a little indignant. A moment later Diego held the purple shock of hair in his fist. He peered at the pixie post with a menacing look on his face as it hung in front of him and fought like a wounded animal.

"Look what I've captured. So, there you are, my father's little pixie post who he treats with contempt. Do you like that? Being treated like an insignificant little pest? I can do better. Sandau can do better." Diego hauled the creature closer. "I even have biscuits in my pocket."

The indignant creature hauled itself up to Diego's finger and bit it. He dropped it and both men dived about in the corridor trying to capture the purple shock of hair as it leapt about. It ran up Diego's leg, jumped across to Sandau, then ran up into Sandau's hair. If nothing else, it reaffirmed Maya's belief that even Diego had the odd catastrophe.

A light cough distracted them all. Arianna stepped out of a nearby room, pulled the door to behind her and gave the men a bemused look. "Aaushk, are they being mean to you?"

The shock of purple jumped off Sandau's back

and ran across to Arianna, who crouched and offered the creature her pocket. Glaring at Diego, the creature clambered inside.

Arianna straightened up. "It seems I'm a step ahead of you for once. Aaushk is rather partial to crisps. He likes bread as well. If you need his help with something come and talk to me. I'm sure we can sort something out."

Issuing a small grin of delight, Arianna checked her pocket. She glanced down at something in her fingers that Maya couldn't see, then she turned and disappeared back into the room she had been in, leaving them alone in the corridor. Diego and Sandau brushed themselves down.

"If anyone asks, that never happened," Diego said. "Clearly, capture also means to keep hold of the little pest for longer than five seconds."

Sandau nodded. "Agreed. I don't even know what you're talking about."

"Don't worry, boys. I won't say a word." Walking out of the shadows, Maya couldn't hide her grin of amusement as she wandered back to her room. "If you see Haydan, can you tell him I'm looking for him, please."

The expression on both their faces was priceless.

Haydan

Haydan led Maya's family through to the room set up so that everyone could select outfits for that evening.

The room was a riot of colour. Costumes hung everywhere. The table in the centre was a sea of masks. The sight amused him. Si disappeared between racks of clothing with Katherine and the baby. Arianna stood on guard by the door, which was ajar. Sandau remained in the corridor.

Isaac appeared to find the table fascinating. He ran his hands over a few of the masks, focusing on a wolf and a feline-like mask. His hand slid down into his denim-clad pocket as though checking on something before his eyes raised to meet Haydan's and darted back to the table.

"So, this is your grandfather's realm. It's pretty intriguing, but I'm not sure about it." Isaac moved closer and lowered his voice. "I assume you will keep Sandau away from Arianna."

"I can't promise that. I'll continue to intervene if Sandau tries it on. He's warrior. It's good for Arianna to be around Sandau at the moment. We could all learn a lot from him. He's highly respected, especially by my father. They have history together and I'm sure that's an earned respect, not a mark of formality. What's that in your pocket, Isaac?"

"Nothing." Isaac returned to perusing the table.

"Don't dismiss me, human. I asked a question, therefore I expect an answer."

Reluctance flowed from Isaac as he kept his focus on the masks. Interestingly, he no longer took offence at being called a human. "I received a strange gift, that's all. It looks nothing like these though." He flicked his hand over the table display.

"It wouldn't be a piece of this by any chance, would it?" Haydan reached into his pocket and pulled out Kaleshar. Isaac slid his hand back into his pocket and held out the top section of Kaleshar, the one with the small button in the centre. Isaac registered that the piece he was holding matched the mask, and in one fluid motion he pressed the button, unlocking the mask in his possession.

There were subtle differences. On Kaleshar the section that Isaac had was a more opaque colour indicating it had partially disengaged from the mask. The two pieces that Diego and Tallin were holding were the same. However, the mask Isaac possessed was mostly opaque, aside from the piece he had, which looked like a more solid part of the mask. He pressed the button again and returned the piece to his pocket.

"That's a neat trick and now I'm intrigued as to why you have a piece of my mask in your pocket."

"Your mask, huh?" Isaac smirked then said, "I don't know, but he seems to like it in there. He's not as sure about Si. Is that why the dark gods are looking for you? Are you in some kind of trouble?"

"Potentially big trouble. Maya's helping me. At least I think that's what she's doing. You're in even more danger here than you were back home. I'm sorry for involving you and the family in this."

Isaac pulled a face that suggested he wasn't concerned by that news. "We're family, or will be family. We look out for each other. What happens if I put the mask on? Can I take it off again? Is it powerful?"

It felt like a good time to fill Isaac in. Katherine and Si were laughing and messing around with various garments, oblivious to their conversation. Haydan moved alongside Isaac, pretending to peruse the masks with him.

"I wear the mask and share control with him. He's called Kaleshar. He's a god, or was a god. He will disengage from your face when you ask him to. Possession is only with consent. If you wear him and the dark gods see you, they will be after you, so be warned. Tallin and Diego have a piece of him too. Tallin did something that unlocked him. Apparently, all magical artefacts have a secret and this is Kaleshar's."

Isaac settled a bemused look on Haydan, as though he was intrigued by or evaluating him. "Well, that's not confusing for anyone now, is it? The dark gods will come here at some point. If this mask can separate itself out, then perhaps that's all part of the plan. It appears to have picked its players, now the games will unfold." Isaac lowered his voice. "You look to be missing a further two pieces, the little triangles from the bottom."

That seemed to be a statement, rather than a question. It also confirmed that despite Isaac being unreadable, the man did not miss any detail, no matter how small. Haydan nodded and stifled a smirk. "So, who do you think has the extra pieces, Isaac?"

Isaac moved off as Si rushed around the end of the nearest display clutching an outfit that would not look out of place at a carnival. He was laughing so hard that he could not speak for the tears pouring down his face.

"I'd put my money on the awkward females you surround yourself with. Get them to check their pockets later."

"Not Sandau then?"

Isaac laughed and shook his head. "No, he doesn't strike me as a man who needs much assistance. Me? I'm not proud, I'll take all the help I can get." Isaac walked up to Haydan and rested a hand on his shoulder as he leant in. Even in the fae realm Isaac smelt of his usual strong masculine aftershave. "I will help you in any way I can. Just promise me you will help me keep Kat and the baby safe. I know the girls are already in good hands."

"Thank you, Isaac."

Isaac backed away and turned towards Si. "It's this one you want to watch though, Mr silent stand-off with Sandau." Isaac laughed as he studied Si and flicked a sly look from beneath his lowered eyelids at Haydan as though conveying caution to him. Something about Si and Sandau had caused fresh wariness to surface in the unreadable human.

Si wiped his face and held out his hands in a pacifying gesture towards Isaac. "What are you talking about? You've got to see these outfits, they all do weird things."

Haydan had no idea what Isaac was talking about, but was grateful for his keen observations. There was hidden meaning in them and he often shared them, unlike his father. Diego kept his thoughts to himself, or only shared when he felt it pertinent to do so.

Frowning, Haydan wondered where Diego was that morning. Isaac wandered down the nearest aisle with Si. Haydan turned and moved to the door. He tapped Arianna's elbow on the way past. "Check your pockets for a small triangular piece of Kaleshar. If you find one, let me know. Oh, and have you seen Diego?"

Arianna's smirk suggested something had amused her. "Diego's just outside with Sandau. I think Maya is about as well. I have got a piece of Kaleshar in my pocket. I've just found it and haven't had a chance to tell you."

"Good, I want a word with her," Haydan said. "Sandau can watch the family for a bit. You're with me. What's so funny?"

"Oh, err the pixie post was about. I don't think Diego likes him very much."

Haydan had no interest that morning in the purple shock of hair that was akin to Tallin's pet. Without responding any further he stalked off in search of his errant chosen one.

৯৯৯

Jallin

Tallin seated himself as the faerie set out her equipment and turned to face him. "Add my usual plaits and royal statement pieces for now. I have something different planned for tonight."

Lavinia's gaze bore into Tallin. He tried to ignore her, but that as usual proved difficult. He huffed as the faerie leant in and started working on his hair. She had opted to start at the front, leaving him with an uncomfortable view of her chest. Lavinia looked fit to explode with rage. "My sweet, this is very awkward, not just for myself but for this lovely lady as well. Perhaps you would be so kind as to go and find Haydan and Isaac. I would like to talk to them. You can leave the door open. I am not up to anything I should not be."

Lavinia made a point of stalking off and flinging the door wide open. She disappeared and returned a few moments later with Haydan in tow. He seemed unimpressed at the imposition. In fact, indignant was a better description.

"Good morning, Tallin," Haydan said.

Lavinia regarded Tallin with a warning glare. "I

accosted Haydan in the corridor. Play nice. I'm going to find Isaac." Giving Haydan a grin of delight on her way past, Lavinia headed back out of the room leaving them alone.

Haydan's folded arms suggested a new level of challenge. The silence proved unbearable. Tallin suddenly felt lost for words but finally managed, "How is your head this morning?"

Haydan rolled his eyes and huffed. "Let's not do the pleasantries. I apologise for ignoring your instruction to stay in the room last night. I have a better set of questions for you. What is Leylani doing in your court? Given what happened last time I was here, she should have been locked up, not taunting me on the steps outside when I arrived. Where is Magellan? He seems to have disappeared and he's supposed to be Lavinia's ally. When did you meet Lawson, this Dark Angel you were on about? You need to tell me about that and the water book that Maya has. Let's talk on that subject as well."

Tallin placed a hand on the faerie's waist and nudged her out of his way so he could see Haydan better. She gasped and stepped aside so fast he almost asked her if she was all right.

"Has Sandau shown you the secret of the triple halos yet?"

"Why do you never answer the question asked?" Haydan scratched his head and glared at Tallin. "He's showing me the triple halo feature when you remove the lockdown on this part of the court. Along with the traps."

Tallin had never been one for answering direct questions. After a moment, he responded. "The water book will reveal its secrets soon. You might be ready to accept the mysteries hidden within it now."

Haydan tapped his foot, a warning to Tallin to stop diverting him.

"I met Lawson many years ago before Diego was even born. The details are not important right now. I have my eyes on all of my court. Leylani is a powerful healer but I am not sure what she is up to and I do not know where Magellan is. He is supposed to be on a trip. I am sure he will turn up."

"Well, that's funny because I think Magellan was in the darkness at the bottom of the stairs waiting for Leylani when I arrived," Haydan said.

Tallin's eyes narrowed. "You are sure of that?" The information seemed pertinent. If Magellan was hiding then there was a reason for that.

Haydan nodded and shifted his weight to his other foot.

"Maya's scared about bonding with you."

"Scared? Don't be ridiculous." Haydan's scowl darkened before there was a flicker of hesitation and he straightened up. "Why would she be scared? The bond isn't something to be afraid of."

"This is pure speculation, but I do not believe Maya has not bonded with you yet by choice. I think there is something unseen going on and when you bond, that is when you will start to see who she truly is. I can't shake the feeling that when you see the true Maya, you will have to choose whether or not you accept the real her. The outcome of that choice will have far-reaching consequences."

Haydan's face had paled. His wary stare swept over Tallin, then he drew up the nearest chair and sat down. "What makes you say that?"

"She is the light and the dark. She is capable of so

much love and affection, yet she also has a darkness within her. A darkness that yearns for release. Every now and again you find yourself on the receiving end of that."

"But why? I don't understand."

Tallin yelped as the faerie styling his hair prodded him with a pin she was using to fix his hair. "Do that again and I shall have you whipped, young lady."

"I'm sorry, My Lord. My hand slipped. I would never do such a thing deliberately."

"Hmm, I should think not. I know you are listening. I suggest you stop. Mind you, I will be wiping your memory of this morning in any case, so you will not remember." Tallin returned his attention to Haydan. "It is in her makeup. To win her approval you have to love all of her. Can you do that? Even when it gets ugly and she pushes you away?"

"Yes."

"You are quite sure?" Tallin waited for confirmation that Haydan was fully committed to Maya.

"I am."

"Why did you decide to leave the sea with Maya? You chose to surface when Diego and your mother entered the sea as I understand it. What made you choose them? I am not judging you, I am simply asking why."

Haydan's throat bobbed as he leant forwards and fixed a wary stare on Tallin. "According to my mother, I only surfaced when she entered the sea with Diego. I ignored her when she entered the sea alone, even though I would have had the same parentage either way. I left the sanctuary of the sea for two storm riders, one of whom I knew to be powerful and an elder. Diego's power is distinctive and hard to overlook."

Tallin raised his hand and waved away the woman doing his hair. "Wait outside, I need a moment." When she had gone, Tallin mirrored Haydan's pose and leant in. "Tell me, did you follow the power, or was there coercion involved?"

Haydan's face paled further. "Coercion? Why would you ask such a thing?"

"So, you followed the power? You chose to leave the sea on your own?" Tallin rearranged himself back in the seat and observed the fallout of his carefully placed words. Haydan looked thrown by the question. "Diego is powerful, but power means certain things can be swayed in a certain manner. I am just curious as to why you surfaced with rare souls for Diego. It seems … convenient for someone. He provides a generous amount of protection and reassurance, but there is a darker side to that."

Haydan appeared forlorn as he raised his head and nestled the lower half of his face in his hands and whispered, "I don't remember. I think I followed the power." His attention locked onto the ring on Tallin's finger, before returning to study Tallin's face.

Tallin smiled and slid the ring off before passing it across to Haydan. "Try it on. You may borrow it. You may find it more useful than I." Before Haydan could respond, he added, "I expect it to be returned when you are done. It turns a ruby colour in the presence of dark gods."

"Thank you." Haydan slipped the ring on and studied it before lowering his hands and resting his elbows on his knees.

Tallin squeezed Haydan's shoulder, moving right in so he spoke close to Haydan's ear. "I adore both you and Diego, is that clear? Diego adores you as well. I am not suggesting anything untoward when I ask this. Given what Levi remembers from the sea, you should recall more than you do. There are secrets hidden and either you or the girls hold them because someone is up to something. Lavinia and I are always here to listen without judgement. I need you to understand that."

Haydan nodded and lowered his head as Isaac cleared his throat from near the door then smiled awkwardly. Tallin looked up.

"The door was open. There's a tearful young lady outside. Is Haydan okay? I didn't mean to intrude. I can come back."

"Get Maya to start sharing what she has found with you," Tallin said. He turned his attention to Isaac and gave him a dazzling smile. "No there is no need, Isaac. Come and take a seat. I need to ask you for a favour as well. Just let me deal with my hairdresser. I told her I was going to wipe her memory of this morning. She has heard too much. That is probably why she is upset."

Tallin closed the door behind him, leaving Haydan and Isaac alone. They had an interesting dynamic and Tallin was curious about that. In fact, he was curious about both of Katherine's unreadable males, because Isaac and Si held secrets.

Chapter 28

Haydan

T he silence as Tallin left and the door closed with a soft thunk felt overwhelming. Isaac sat without saying anything for a moment. "Well, I don't know about you, but things have got really interesting around me since last night. That looked like a cosy chat you were having with Tallin."

"Yes. You overheard that?" Haydan asked.

"I got the gist. What are the trio of balls all about?"

"I think they might be a transport system. Sandau has promised to show me later."

Isaac straightened up and scowled. "I don't like Sandau. The man is bold and confident."

It was inevitable that Isaac would regard Sandau with a certain amount of hostility. Haydan fought back a smirk. "Isaac, when the dark gods come, Sandau is well versed in their ways. He's been coaching Arianna. I think my father has played a hand in that too. They think I'm oblivious, but they are both sworn to protect storm riders and Sandau has a soft spot for Arianna. If that weakness keeps her alive and indirectly me and Maya, is that such a bad thing?"

Isaac appeared to mull over that piece of news. "No, in fact, now you've put it like that, it puts a totally different perspective on it," Isaac said. "I take it Arianna proved herself last night."

Haydan nodded and rubbed the back of his head, which still felt tender. "She did. It's not her abilities that I doubt, she grows stronger every day, it's the fact she challenges me at every turn."

Isaac grinned, apparently finding that announcement amusing. "She's my daughter, of course she challenges. She operates like I do. Look, I meant what I said before. An odd look passed between Sandau and Si when they met in the corridor, as though they were weighing each other up. Then Sandau kind of backed off. Maybe I imagined it, but it felt weird. Also, the piece of the mask in my pocket avoided going to Si."

"I'm a firm believer in following your gut instinct. If you think something is off then it probably is. The harder question is whether it's worth worrying about. I'm not sure it is right now. You and Si are both unreadable. Sandau is also a little unusual. I'll keep an eye on Si if it helps."

"You have enough on your plate right now. Don't worry about it." Isaac's expectant expression became conspiratorial as he leant in. "It looks likely the dark gods will find this place at some point tonight. I get the distinct impression Tallin is expecting them. All the guards and everyone around here is twitchy." Isaac ruffled his hair. "I assume you have figured out Tallin's game plan for tonight already."

Frowning, Haydan shook his head. "No, not really. Should I have?"

Isaac's face melted into a mischievous grin. "Oh,

come on, you're supposed to be the smart one. It's obvious, isn't it? Your mask can make duplicates of itself and choose its game-players. There are those weird ball sculptures everywhere that lock down, and are some kind of transport system. This place appears to be riddled with them."

Haydan nodded, finding Isaac's rapid evaluation of the situation fascinating. "Apparently they are, yes."

"Tonight is a masked ball. This place will be heaving with Tallin's court hidden behind masks and Tallin's magic is creating wild things. Somewhere in the midst of all this the dark gods are going to arrive. I'm not up on my god magic, but dark and light gods suggests one attracts or repels the other. Is Tallin's magic dark or light magic? I mean, I know he's not a god, right, but his magic must use one end of the spectrum or the other, so which is it?" Isaac jubilantly straightened up, the glint in his eyes confirming he found Tallin fascinating. "This is a Tallin game of epic proportions. There are numerous copies of your mask around. The dark gods won't know who the real mask bearer is, will they? If Tallin and Diego have a piece of your mask too … tonight is going to be very interesting."

That piece of news was the most sensible thing Haydan had heard in a long time. He blinked a few times, trying to work out how Isaac could see something that was so clear now, but that he had completely missed.

Isaac grinned, looking delighted with himself. "You're too focused on Maya to have worked out the big picture. A word of advice, my friend, stop focusing on Maya and watch the subtle nuances around you. Tallin has carefully choreographed everything to protect you tonight. I'm not a betting man, more of a calculated risk kind of guy, but I'll bet he's left us talking deliberately as well. I can see what he is up to." Isaac's intense gaze flitted to Haydan's hand. "That's an unusual ring. I haven't seen you wearing that before."

Haydan fiddled with the metal band. "No, Tallin has just given it to me. It turns ruby in the presence of dark gods."

Isaac seemed to be delighted with himself, reminding Haydan of Arianna when she was in one of her giddy moods.

"What a coincidence. You might need that later." Isaac looked like a man comfortable in his own skin and confident in his astute assessments.

"I didn't think you would like Tallin."

Isaac looked uncertain. "I can admire the man and have a healthy respect for him. He strikes me as a man who likes his own way and isn't afraid to manipulate to get what he wants." Isaac's smirk returned. "He reminds me of someone, can't think who – speak of the devil."

Tallin swept back into the room and strode across to where they were sitting. Resting his hands on the back of their chairs, Tallin leant in. "You should not speak about devils, Isaac, you never know when they might be listening."

Isaac's unwavering stare homed in on Tallin as Haydan stood. "I was just explaining to Haydan that it's possible to admire someone and to also have a healthy respect for them."

Tallin returned Isaac's stare. For once he didn't respond, but he appeared fascinated and his gaze didn't leave Isaac as he moved around to the seat Haydan had vacated. "I will see you later, Haydan," Tallin said with a cold air of finality.

The dismissal would annoy Haydan for the rest of the day. Grimacing, he turned and stalked off.

Evidently Tallin had been desperate to talk to Isaac alone and Haydan didn't like being dismissed in the manner that he had. He swept past Lavinia talking to Diego in the corridor as he returned from Tallin's room. Both of them acknowledged him on the way past then returned to their discussion. No doubt they were catching up, or cooking up a plan. After their conversation in Tallin's room, Haydan felt disinterested in their scheming. He wanted to find Maya and begin mastering the realms. Sandau needed to show him the triple halos.

Arianna was standing on guard outside Maya's door, which meant Sandau was with Katherine and Si. Haydan considered Isaac's suggestion of Si holding secrets and dismissed it as rubbish. Si didn't like Haydan, finding the odd things that happened around Maya freakish. Isaac found them more fascinating, but Si couldn't accept the strangeness, although the uneasy feeling remained with him that Isaac thought something was off about the way Si and Sandau had greeted each other.

Haydan didn't bother knocking when he reached Maya's room. Maya had nothing to hide from him anyway. A quick search followed and he located her out on the balcony, leaning against the chunky stone balustrades. Standing with her back to him, she straightened up as he approached. He slipped his hands onto her waist and flexed his fingertips, surprised to find that she allowed the intrusion to pass without comment. She had changed and was wearing a floaty gown that wrapped around her like a toga and cinched in at her waist. Goosebumps lifted on the skin at the base of her neck as he moved closer.

"Is this a trap, or are you playing nicely at the moment?"

Maya angled her head to the side and eyed Haydan from beneath lowered lashes. "I'm playing nicely. Make the most of it, you know it won't last."

"I know, but whilst we're here, I like this. I like being able to talk to you. It breaks my heart when you won't even talk to me. Have you calmed down after last night? Are you going to tell me what happened?" Haydan moved in closer, pressing his front against Maya's back. "You're not an aberration. You're beautiful and unique. If your great-grandfather can't see that then it's his loss."

Maya rested the side of her forehead against Haydan's and they stood in silence with the breeze blowing against them. Her room looked over the back of the summer court. The view of the walled gardens below was spectacular. He could see two ornate mazes, nestled between two wide, flat rivers that fed into various water features and ponds spread across the grounds of the summer court. Beyond the walls the sound of the fast-flowing rivers reached him. Woodland filled the end of the gardens and the middle section was full of long, swaying grasses. The effect was mesmerising.

Something stirred in the grasses. In fact, the more Haydan focused on the grass, the more he became convinced something was moving through it towards the castle.

Maya followed Haydan's stare. "The whirling dervishes are back. They're back for you, because you keep me in the light. I don't deserve you. I know I don't," she said.

Haydan slipped his arms around Maya's waist and held her close. "Stop talking like this. I adore you, every inch of you, whatever mood you're in … although it's much easier to handle you when you're in one of your more relaxed, playful moods."

"I can't talk about my great-grandfather. He threatened to kill me and he meant it."

Haydan wanted to stay wrapped around Maya all day, but knew he couldn't. "Okay, you can tell me when you feel ready. I need you to show me this secret chamber."

Maya slid warm hands against Haydan's. Her fingertips found the ring on his index finger. She gasped and pulled his hand out to study it. "Tallin gifted you the ring. I think it's a keystone. Have you got Kaleshar on you?"

Haydan nodded and buried his face in Maya's hair. "It's on loan and yeah, I've got Kaleshar. I think he's quite happy pressed against your back right now. I have to say, I'm enjoying our cuddle this morning too."

Maya looked exasperated. Releasing her arm from over his, she grabbed his hand. He felt bereft at the loss of her body heat, which he had been enjoying rather more than he should have. The contact with her warm fingers provided a small amount of consolation. She pulled him back into her room. He had no choice but to reluctantly follow her as she made for the triple halo in the corner.

❧

Arianna

Arianna focused on the floor in front of her as she stood on guard outside Maya's room waiting for Aaushk to return from his spying mission. Something about the way in which Sandau and Si had greeted each other had been bothering her since they met earlier on. She had occasionally heard mention of a fifth elder being hidden somewhere and that made her suspicious of anything out of the ordinary. Diego had always regarded her father and Si with a certain amount of suspicion. They were both unreadable to storm riders, which was unusual as storm riders were adept at reading everyone they met.

Diego and Lavinia were talking close by. Mostly Lavinia filled Diego in on the preparations for the evening. Each appeared to be wary of the other as they maintained their distance and kept their tone formal. Arianna waited for that to lapse, because at some point it would.

"What happened last night? Have you spoken to Haydan and apologised for humiliating him on Storm Lands, Mother?" Diego asked.

"I have, but I've not apologised. Will you stop being so formal. I protected your future from Tallin when I left before you were born. I gave birth to you. I deserve a little respect for the sacrifices I made for you, do I not?"

Diego lowered his head and held up his arm,

permitting Lavinia to step towards him. She swept in mirroring his stance, allowing him to plant a kiss on her forehead.

When Lavinia pulled away, a smile of delight lit up her features. A moment later her delight melted away as she became more serious. "Haydan's still furious at me for last time he came into this realm. Everything I do is to protect my family and this realm is very different to Storm Lands and Earth." Lavinia sniffed and fixed a haughty look on Diego. "You need to spend more time here. You need to get to know your father more than you do and understand his ways." She took a step closer and twisted her hands together as though something concerned her. "Haydan met Leylani the night he arrived. She knows he's here. She couldn't drag her eyes away from his altera. I don't know what she's up to, but she is up to something."

Diego nodded his understanding. "She's here in the summer court because…?"

"She's a good healer. She has helped Tallin's men on a number of occasions when they were injured. If Tallin is distracted tonight … well … just keep an eye on Haydan, please. Tallin has marked those of his court who are plotting against him. They can't hide the damage his magic will have done to their skin and only he can undo that. There will be those tonight who are injured and angry. They are dangerous. It's likely one of those courtiers who tried to force that poor girl to kidnap Haydan last night."

Diego fidgeted, his expression unamused. "Have you warned Arianna about this?" He glanced across at Arianna, acknowledging that she was standing close by with a nod.

The gesture pleased Arianna. Diego was beginning

to show her the respect she was entitled to as Haydan's designated guardian.

Lavinia looked less impressed. "Not directly, but I know she's listening."

Diego reached for Lavinia's arm and dragged her further from Arianna's earshot, although she still caught most of it. "Why are you so competitive with other women? Any fool can see that Tallin is besotted with you … don't deny it. I know you better than you think, Mother. Jealousy is part of the games that you play with Father. You don't like women around me and you don't like Haydan's choice of females either. Why not?"

Lavinia refused to meet Diego's eyes. He reached for her jaw, capturing it and forcing her to meet his stare of disapproval. "Answer me."

Diego's head cocked to the side, with a look on his face that Arianna always regarded as Diego's irritated expression. He remained silent, leaving an uncomfortable void.

Staring Diego down for a moment, Lavinia blinked and her eyes filled with tears. "Rebekka has her subtle ways of manipulating you. She's here in this realm to present herself as your future queen tonight. Makes it harder for you to break off your arrangement with her doesn't it, the more she ties herself to you?"

"What about Haydan's females?" Diego released Lavinia's jaw.

Lavinia rubbed her face, suggesting Diego had hurt her. "Arianna challenges him, and Maya, well, Maya is afraid to bond. Something isn't right about their dynamics. Something is off kilter."

"I invited Rebekka to join me here. There's no manipulation involved. Well, if I exclude the fact that she told me she wasn't interested in coming here, there isn't. I suspected she would come. Let her maintain her secrecy for now. I don't have time for her games." Diego moved over to the window and braced his forearm against the wall, with his palm against his temple.

"So, she had a change of heart. Do you not wonder why?"

Diego's back faced Arianna. He stared out of the window for a moment as though lost in his own thoughts. "She loves me. She would do anything for me. Why does everything with you have an ulterior motive?"

Lavinia slid a sneaky sideways glance at Diego. "If I was where she is now and you were Tallin, I would do anything and I mean *anything* to keep him." Her expression was one of admiration. "You were the only glitch in that plan and since you are half of both of us and I love you as much as him, I permitted the temporary deviation to protect you. Now Tallin understands that, he has managed to forgive me. If roles were reversed and you were where Rebekka is now, what would you do?"

Diego lowered his head. "Whatever it took to keep her. I am Rebekka's for this cycle. That's where our agreement ends."

"So, what happens next cycle?"

His movements agitated, Diego rubbed at his forehead. "That's a long way off."

"You haven't answered the question, Diego." Lavinia's tone had switched to a teasing, soothing one, the sort a mother uses when cajoling truths from a reluctant child.

Diego ran his hand up into his hair and bowed his head. His answer came out as a broken whisper. "I miss Sasha. I think of her every day. I've never told anyone that before. She had the same steely, fierce determination that Haydan's women have. I knew where I was with her. I always feel that Rebekka sees me as more of a trophy, or a game, than an equal."

Lavinia stepped up to Diego, wrapped an arm around his neck and stood in silence for a few minutes with his head buried by her shoulder. Diego wrapped his arm around Lavinia's waist. The intimate moment between mother and son surprised Arianna. They were much closer than they appeared.

"She's not safe with me. I couldn't protect her last time," Diego said. He sounded distraught and his words came out as an anguished whimper. He released Lavinia's waist but remained close to her. "You don't like any of them. I know you don't."

Lavinia closed her eyes and pressed her face into the hair on top of Diego's head, comforting him in a way Arianna had never seen before. "Sweetheart, I want you happy, but your choice of partner is yours and yours alone. I will not have you manipulated by anyone."

"With the exception of you." Taking a moment to compose himself, Diego turned away and ran his fingertips over his cheeks.

Lavinia slid her arm against Diego's shoulder and moved in closer, her triumph obvious as she stared up at him. "Rebekka thinks like we do because she is storm rider. Never forget that. She is not submissive. She won't let you just walk away without a fight."

"What are you getting at with this, Mother?" Diego sounded tired.

Lavinia rested her head against Diego's shoulder and sighed. "You have a right to know. Rebekka is trying to find out where your chosen one's soul is hidden. I don't know what she will do with it if she finds it, but I don't think it will end well for Sasha if she does."

Arianna lowered her head and contemplated the news. Lavinia had just confirmed what Diego probably already feared. That would not make the betrayal any easier for him to bear.

"You told Rebekka, didn't you, Mother, about the soul that was lost in this realm?"

"No, I did not. Rebekka found me and began asking awkward questions about what happened last time you came here. She feels you have been distant since. She raised the question over your chosen one. I said I wasn't talking about that and it became heated from there. Anything she claims to know is purely her own speculation."

"Where is she staying?"

"I have a private suite adjoining my room, she is staying there."

Aaushk ran back down the corridor, keeping close to the wall. Tallin moved out of the shadows near his room and surveyed Lavinia and Diego, before his attention flitted to Aaushk. The purple shock of hair took a moment to realise Tallin was there. Aaushk's focus had been Arianna, until he realised Tallin was present.

Arianna inwardly heaved a sigh of relief as Aaushk peeled away from the wall and ran towards Tallin. The creature clambered up his trouser leg as he stood there and disappeared into his jacket pocket.

Arianna's problem now was that she still wasn't sure about Aaushk. Bribing him with goodies didn't guarantee his loyalty, it gave him access to more information that he or Tallin could use to manipulate her if they chose to.

Tallin's sly look convinced her she was part of his games already. His focus moved from her to Diego and Lavinia.

He coughed lightly, drawing Lavinia back to him. "Is everything alright, my love?"

Arianna suppressed a grin. Tallin really meant that he knew Lavinia was touching another male and whether it was his son or not, he was aware of it. Without a doubt Tallin was as protective of Lavinia as she was of him.

"I have been talking to Isaac. You should both come and join us. There are a few things I need to run through for tonight."

Lavinia and Diego walked across to Tallin's room. Tallin's attention remained on his family until they had wandered past, then his focus shifted to Arianna and he joined her.

Arianna turned her head as Tallin leant in so his face was close to hers. Mist released from his neck and tickled her face. Uneasy at his proximity, Arianna turned her face away.

"Aaushk is mine, Arianna. The wolf is also mine. Stop playing my games by trying to befriend creatures that you should not." Tallin turned his head so his breath brushed her neck. His closeness felt overwhelming. "When Leylani comes for Haydan, let her take him. I need her to feel confident in her kidnap."

"What?" Arianna's head snapped around to meet Tallin's intimidating glare. He was inches from her face and seemed totally unconcerned by the inappropriateness. She swallowed and lowered her focus to his chest. Staring into Tallin's eyes from such close proximity was embarrassing.

"I want Leylani's master. Someone is pulling strings and it is not Leylani. The ring Haydan is wearing turns a ruby colour if the dark gods are nearby. Worry about dark gods more than Leylani, Arianna. Do you understand me?"

Arianna could hear the smile in Tallin's voice as he waited for her response. She nodded, anticipating his move away. He took his time in doing so.

A thump resonated through the summer court and it felt as though the building shuddered. The nearest triple halo illuminated. Tallin straightened up and smiled. A purple light blasted along the light strip recessed in the bottom of the wall. The triple halo shimmered, and the lighting within it turned a vivid purple colour before switching back to its normal appearance. Tallin didn't look concerned by the incident, which disconcerted Arianna as much as Tallin himself.

"What was that? Should I be worried by it? Are we under attack?"

Tallin's smile oozed mystery. "No, I think we are on schedule. Remember what I said. I am relying on you to trust me. I may not fight for Haydan as you do, but I will guard my grandson with whatever it takes. Do we understand each other?"

Arianna raised her head. Tallin now stood a safer distance away. He hadn't moved far, but enough to ease her discomfort. "We understand each other, My Lord."

Tallin's grin of delight was disarming. "Good. See you later." He stalked off, like a predator eyeing up prey, his movements stealthy and fluid.

Despite his moments of alarming behaviour, Arianna couldn't help liking Tallin. Charming but cunning and skilled in the art of persuasion, he reminded her a lot of her father. Movement in her pocket drew her attention to Aaushk. Tallin had just returned him to her. She burst out laughing.

Chapter 29

Haydan

T he balls shot into the air as Maya dragged Haydan into the triple halo. The cascade of water that surrounded him didn't touch him as he passed through it. The device reminded him of the home Theander occupied on the mountainside of Acquorous. The lift that took him down to the lower level where the other sea was kept bore distinct similarities to that. Perhaps Theander had had a more modern version fitted.

The surroundings changed as Haydan reorientated himself. The cavernous hall he found himself in was similar to the one Lavinia landed him in when the flecky beast attacked him. That had been a number of years ago, but he had never forgotten the abandoned hall. Occasionally he dreamt about it, as though it had imprinted itself permanently into his mind where he could never escape it.

Maya reached into her pocket and pulled out some strange-looking glasses, which she moved up to her face. She shuffled in closer and Haydan burst out laughing.

"Okay, what are those things? And stop peering at me like that." Haydan raised his hands up and feigned pushing Maya away.

Maya gave Haydan a lopsided grin and folded her arms. "What are you talking about? These are the latest fashion accessory, I'll have you know. I'm going to manufacture them and make a fortune. Can you see the waterfall and the plants?"

"Yes, Maya, I can."

Maya's face fell. "Oh, I thought you would need the glasses like I do."

She sounded so disappointed at the news that Haydan almost backtracked and pretended he couldn't see them either. The hall he was standing in seemed more alive than the one on Storm Lands, but perhaps the hall back home had been deactivated by Storm Lands to conserve energy. A couple of tiny birds darted past, their wings thrumming as they moved.

Maya reached for Haydan's hand and pulled him along. He held back and she spun towards him with a puzzled expression on her face. "What's wrong?"

Haydan's fear and uncertainty melted away as Maya pulled off the strange glasses and moved closer. Sweeping her arms around his waist, she peered up at him.

"Maya, if I am about to master the first of the realms, I need to know if you will be by my side." Haydan swallowed hard as he searched for the right words to make her understand what he was getting at. "I'm not talking about bonding." He brushed a hand against her cheek and slid his fingertips against her jaw, cupping her face as he studied her. "If I master any of the realms, I'm walking a long and lonely path. I can't do that by myself. Every king needs a queen by his side as his strength and support. Tallin has Lavinia. Diego still misses his chosen one, even now. If I do this, I need to know I can count on you and since you currently have no wish to bond, I don't know where I stand with you."

A flicker of hesitation pulled at Maya's features as she lowered her eyes to Haydan's chest. "Don't put me in this position." Her bottom lip quivered as though she was fighting to maintain control of her emotions. "I have the Book of Forgiveness from Tallin's library. It drew my attention. Thing is, I don't know why I would need you to forgive me, or what I'm going to do that's going to need your forgiveness. I can't guarantee—"

"Let me ask you a simple question. Do you love me?"

"Yes."

There was no hesitation from her.

"If you have the Book of Forgiveness, does that not suggest you can be forgiven?" Haydan asked.

"Yes, but—"

"So, whatever you do, I will be able to forgive you at some point. I think you need to stop worrying about the book. If you give me your word that you will be by my side, no matter what happens, I will take that. But if you can't—" Haydan inhaled a shaky breath. That was what worried him.

Maya appeared to consider her answer as tears brimmed in her eyes. "I'm scared I'm going to hurt you to protect you. I know that sounds crazy. I have a darkness within me, Haydan, and sometimes I have to let that darkness run free. How can you love that part of me when it's so ugly?"

Haydan tilted his head forwards, resting his forehead against Maya's. "I love you even when you push me away. It's part of who you are. I will never try and change that. I know that sounds contradictory, because I do try and influence you sometimes as part of our games, but I always give you the space you need to be who you are. You will always find your way back to me. I get that."

Maya closed her eyes and nodded her understanding. The tears subsided when she opened them again, her eyes now conveying a steely determination. "I'll be by your side. I'll find a way to make it happen."

Haydan placed a soft kiss on Maya's forehead and moved away, letting her lead him up to the platform at the far end of the hall. Sliding Kaleshar onto his face, Haydan took hold of Maya's hand. His grip was tight.

Maya winced. "Ease up, that hurts," she said.

"Sorry, I'm nervous."

Maya came to a halt as she reached the bottom of the stone steps. "Hey, you're scared. I understand that. I'm here with you. You're not on your own."

Haydan attempted a weak smile.

"You're bound to feel uncertain. This is the first realm. This is where it all begins. I won't leave you."

Maya's smile delighted him. She brought his hand up to her face and kissed the back of it.

"Fear means you have two options right now. Flee everything and run, or face everything and rise." Her smile grew more teasing. "You don't strike me as the kind of guy who goes for the first option. If you did, I wouldn't be here now and Arianna wouldn't be on guard outside our room."

Maya had made a valid point. Haydan returned her grin. "Yeah, I would have to agree with you there. I go looking for trouble. It takes a special kind of storm rider to handle you."

Maya burst out laughing and pulled Haydan up the steps. At the top, there was an obsidian throne. Wide feet, reminding him of tree roots, anchored it to the ground. The surrounding platform was empty. None of the foliage or wildlife had ventured onto it, as though afraid to enter an area not designated for them. The realisation that nothing living was growing there added to his discomfort. He would have to do something about that if he was going to spend any time in the hall.

"What happens now?" Haydan asked.

Maya looked surprised by Haydan's question. "I have no idea. You need a keystone to master the realm. I think that ring might be one."

The ring on Haydan's finger looked ancient but it didn't strike him as a portal stone. The roughly hewn stone rose up like a tiny jagged mountain. The bottom part anchored to the base as though hacked off from a larger slab of stone. He ran his hand over the back of the throne, wary of it but resigned to the fact that he would have to sit in it at some point. It felt warm to the touch. He had expected it to feel cold. He braced his other hand against the back and stretched out his arms, lowering his head as he willed himself to feel confident enough to take that step into the unknown.

Maya appeared fixated by something on the platform and that drew Haydan's attention. He released his grip and glanced back up. She pointed at the throne.

"Do that again. Touch it. Run your hand along the back of it."

Haydan repeated what he had done with one hand.

Maya shook her head. "No, it's not that, you did something else. Put your other hand on it. It glowed a bit."

The ring looked different, as though more of the

crystal had pushed up from the base. Haydan placed his other hand, the one displaying Tallin's ring, onto the throne. More of the ring rose up from the base as the stone pulsed with light.

"So that's your secret," Haydan said, speaking more to himself than Maya. He glanced back up in surprise at his achievement.

Maya remained focused on the throne and hadn't noticed the ring. Haydan had been too distracted to observe that the arms had changed from smooth, glossy surfaces to rough-textured ones which sparkled. A chasm, which was the right size for the stone now protruding from the ring, appeared on one of the arms.

Maya grinned in delight. "I think I'm your lucky charm, because I would say this is a result."

"It's only a result when I take control of the realm."

Maya seemed fascinated and rather like a small child with a new plaything. "So, do it. Lay claim. The dark gods need to know you mean business."

Haydan seated himself on the throne and settled his hand onto the rough-textured arm. The stone in the ring continued to glide up until a large shard of the jagged crystal hovered and slowly rotated above the base. He grabbed hold of it, fixed a searching look on Maya and held the keystone over the slot that looked perfectly designed to hold it.

"Promise me you will find a way."

"I promise. I will find a way. I love you."

There was no hesitation from Maya. Haydan could take her at her word and she would not fail him. It would drive him crazy to be left alone without her and with so much responsibility on his shoulders. If she did fail him he didn't want to dwell on the fallout. He had to consider the possibility and accept the creeping realisation that if she did betray him it would feel even more bitter because of her innocent deception.

Haydan placed the stone into the allocated space. The green hue turned a vibrant purple and light travelled out from the stone in a huge wave that swept through the ground. The obsidian throne lightened and illuminated. He placed his shaking hand down onto the rough arm of the throne and a wave of energy released in a sudden surge as he did so. Now he knew how it felt to be addicted to something. The rush would stay with him for a long time. Even Kaleshar appeared to find the moment one of pure ecstasy although he didn't say that. It was a feeling that he got, a moment of clarity that Kaleshar was enjoying the moment as much as he was.

"Well, what do you think? What does it feel like?" Maya stared up at Haydan with her mouth hanging open as though she found the development fascinating.

"Whooo!" Haydan waited to feel normal again, unable to put into words how he felt. "That was such a buzz. Where's the next realm?" No longer able to contain his emotions he burst out laughing.

Maya's expression changed from one of fascination to wariness as she folded her arms.

Haydan beckoned Maya over. She moved close enough for him to grab her. He swept an arm around her waist and dragged her onto his lap. Maya shrieked in surprise.

"Seriously, beautiful, any idea how I get to the next realm?" Haydan whispered, delighting in the way Maya grinned, studied him uncertainly and ducked her head down, feigning shyness, before shaking her head.

"No, although don't forget I was given this." Maya reached inside her top, fumbled around trying to hide the necklace with the cage hanging from it and pulled out a chain with an ornate key hanging off the end of it. "Maybe this is a clue." She pulled the chain over her head and passed it to Haydan.

Haydan took it from Maya's hand and glanced down at the throne. The right arm now contained a keyhole. "I think I might have found the lock that fits this key." He pointed at the new addition and slid the key into the hole. It fitted perfectly. A red stone rose up from the front of the arm and stopped once the whole of the stone had been unveiled – the next keystone.

Grabbing hold of the red stone, Haydan intended to drop it into his inside pocket so that Kaleshar could keep it safe for him. Maya stopped him. She pointed at the base where the green stone sat. A smooth section appeared next to it.

"This is a twin realm," Maya said, reminding Haydan of the connection between the two realms. "The creature at the entrance to the fae realm said it would show you how to claim that realm, but maybe you can claim it from here. That space looks like it's meant for that keystone."

Haydan trailed a fingertip over the smooth surface of the recess in the base, which did suggest it was intended for the red stone. In a worst-case scenario, nothing would happen and he would have to repeat Maya's trip into the realm around Tallin's neck to complete the acquisition of the second realm. He brushed his thumb against the red stone and made his decision. The sensation of claiming another realm was too much of a lure to ignore it and every realm mattered.

The red and green stones shimmered as the colouring from each one flooded into the throne, merging with it and each other. Haydan felt the thrill of laying claim again. It slammed through his body with so much force that he gasped, closed his eyes and gripped the arms of the throne tighter. Kaleshar basked in the moment, gliding through his mind in a state of total ecstasy. Haydan waited until the moment had passed before opening his eyes. He slipped his hand underneath the green stone, which slid back into the ring. Once it had settled back into the base it looked exactly as it had done earlier. He pocketed the red stone, dropping it into the hidden inside compartment where Kaleshar resided. He grinned at Maya. "Time to go find the next realm. Have you figured out that water book yet?"

Sighing, Maya shook her head and fiddled with the unusual glasses clutched in her hand. "It's covered in locks. How am I supposed to know which is the right one? And I still don't know where the key is."

"Tallin passed this ring to me earlier." Haydan wiggled his fingers. "He's trying to tell you something with all these little clues. Maybe you don't need a physical key to unlock that book. He was desperate to show you how to waltz earlier. Follow his hint."

Maya squealed in delight, planted a kiss on Haydan's mouth and dived for the triple halo, dragging him with her.

She was breathless by the time they got back to her room. Grabbing the book from under her pillow, she chewed her bottom lip as she studied it.

"Try it. What's the worst thing that can happen? If it doesn't work, at least you know," said Haydan.

Maya gripped the book to her front and retraced her waltz from earlier. She gasped as the lake from the cover drained into a central plug hidden within the cover. A gurgling noise confirmed the book had emptied. She turned towards Haydan with a broad smile on her face, holding out the book. A vibrant blue portal stone sat on the bottom of the lake bed.

Haydan picked it up and angled it for a better look. Each portal stone had variations at the base. The green stone from the ring was quite jagged. The red stone was smooth. The blue one was a mix of smooth and jagged edges and the side that would connect with the base looked like a small mountain range. Haydan ran his thumb over the edge. "This is the portal stone for Storm Lands."

"How do you know that?"

Haydan's mouth was so dry he struggled to say the words. "I've seen the throne where it fits. I found it with Lavinia when I was a child."

Haydan remembered the ornately carved pillars that reached up out of sight and the floor that illuminated around him. In protecting him from the flecky beast, Lavinia had landed him in the darkest, creepiest and most obscure location he had ever seen. Black as midnight it had reminded him of a possessed snug. It had taken him a few moments of staring at the floor to realise it was space he was gazing at. Beneath his feet a galaxy had displayed itself. The more he fixated on it, the more it seemed to sway about as though guiding him through a route of the heavens. Back then he had no idea where he was and he knew Lavinia would be worried about him.

He had walked deeper into the cave, partly because curiosity got the better of him, but also because he sought a way back out. The cave deepened and widened revealing balconies and walkways overhead. The further in he walked, the more uneasy he had become. It was long abandoned but it felt as though he had intruded into a part of their ancestors' past that should have been left alone. Three banners had unfurled above him, dropping down at regular intervals as though welcoming him. The markings on each were ancient symbols and runes. The Hall of the Forgotten he could make out; the last set of runes he struggled to read. He had followed the unfurling banners, walking deeper into the underground hall before coming to a halt when he saw the route ahead of him.

At the end of the hall, stone steps had climbed up towards a platform. An obsidian seat was all Haydan could see at the top. Even thinking back to his last visit sent a shudder down his spine. The back of the throne arched and twisted up into what looked like arms that reached up into the air as though seeking something beyond his sight. The nearest one stretched towards him slowly as though beckoning him, or trying to lure him.

Had Lavinia known back then of his fate? Even Arianna when she arrived had insisted that after Haydan's leg healed he go back and explore further. Haydan had refused. Arianna had told him she was going back to take a look around. He had no wish to investigate further. The incident had terrified him more than he was prepared to admit, the isolated, dark space something he never wanted to return to. Even now he understood that hall better, his heart quailed at the thought of going back. He didn't want to claim Storm Lands; it felt wrong to do so, yet he would have to.

None of that mattered without Maya at his side.

"I love you." Haydan wrapped his arms around Maya, dragging her into a hug. He didn't want to release her. He could sense her soul as he tightened his arms around her body and nestled his altera in the space between her shoulder blades. "We could be like this all the time. It would be so perfect. Just you and me. Our two souls together as we should be."

Maya tensed in Haydan's arms before pushing him away with a look of total panic on her face. Initially he resisted. He wanted to see what she would do. Her panic increased along with her struggle for freedom.

"No. Let me go."

Haydan's delight melted away as he reluctantly released his arms from around Maya. "Every time I think you're beginning to understand this you step away from me and I'm left wondering what's going on. I don't understand it." Desolate, he took a step back from her and wondered if she would ever bond willingly.

Haydan's frustration with Maya turned to panic as the ring on his finger flitted between ruby red and its usual green colour once. That meant only one thing – dark gods.

Isaac returned to the room where Katherine and Si were choosing their outfits. He passed Arianna on guard outside Maya's room on his way there. Sandau was standing just inside the door as he entered. Isaac found it interesting that he hadn't opted to stand in the corridor like Arianna. Si walked away as he arrived, adding to his earlier suspicions.

"Interesting chat with Tallin?" Sandau asked. A knowing look on his face suggested he was hiding something.

Isaac wanted to ask Sandau what was going on between him and Si, but the strange warrior was unlikely to talk. Si had made himself scarce, as though trying to avoid any inevitable awkward questions from Isaac.

"Yes, very. Interesting chat with Si?" Isaac countered.

Sandau's eyes twitched, then he chuckled and moved back into the corridor. "I'll be on guard outside," he said, closing the door behind him flamboyantly.

Si excused himself to return to his room and Isaac walked over to Katherine. He wrapped his arms around her and snuggled in against her back, nuzzling his face against the soft skin at the base of her neck. Lingering, he added a few feathery kisses there, enjoying the way her breath caught in response. Their daughter was asleep in the papoose strapped to Katherine's front. The rest of their children were safe with Si's mother. "So, Sandau and Si?" Isaac asked.

"Really weird. They were assessing each other. Then Sandau spoke to Si. I couldn't hear much of it, aside from Sandau mentioning whether Si would answer the call or something to that effect. I didn't catch Si's response. Then they separated and spent the rest of the time keeping a close eye on each other. You could have cut the atmosphere with a knife after that though. Si was on his way back across to Sandau when you interrupted. Sandau has weird eyes but I don't know about his background or what he was talking about." Her body relaxed back against Isaac's. "Anyway, changing the subject entirely, you were a while with

Tallin."

"Yeah, I was. I respect him, but I don't trust him. Keep that in mind, angel," Isaac said.

Katherine dipped her head and reached for Isaac's arm, wrapping warm fingers around his bicep. "I'm not sure I entirely trust Si either. Keep that in mind, too, Isaac. Whatever secret Si is hiding, he's keeping it hidden away for a reason."

Isaac nodded his understanding and reluctantly released his arms from around her. Si had been acting oddly for a while. He had been a friend of Katherine's for a number of years. She had lived with Si, his sister and mother after she ran away from her adoptive family's home when she was sixteen, so the whole of their conversation felt strange and disloyal.

"Si's been making noises about trying to find his father. Maybe it's just connected to that. I feel like he wants to talk about it, but he's holding back for some reason," Isaac said.

A flurry of activity erupted in the hallway as pounding feet hammered on the tiled floor. Isaac followed Katherine as they rushed out into the hallway to find out what the commotion was.

Haydan's voice reverberated off the tiled floors as he said, "Tallin! The ring turned red."

Diego

"How many times did it turn red?" Tallin asked. His body tensed and his focus locked onto Haydan with the sharpness of a predator stalking prey.

Pacing in the corridor in front of Haydan, Tallin reminded Diego of a tightly coiled spring. Arianna and Maya stood close by. Isaac and Katherine had entered the hallway from a nearby room and they moved closer. Everyone looked alarmed.

"Maybe once," Haydan said.

"You are sure?" Tallin snapped, drawing his shoulders up in a manner that made him look dangerous.

"Yes, it flitted red once. I'm sure," Haydan said.

"Is it still red?"

"No, it's returned to its normal colour."

"Anything else you want to tell me?" Tallin's tone was hostile. He studied Haydan with one of his unreadable expressions.

Haydan glanced around at everyone who had congregated, then at Diego and finally at Tallin. He looked uncertain. "Kaleshar just took control of the first of the twelve kingdoms. Well, the first two."

"Was that what the purple light and shock wave indicated?" Arianna asked.

Tallin nodded, tutted and scowled at Haydan. "Who took control of the first two kingdoms, Haydan?"

"Kaleshar—"

"No. I have not helped Kaleshar take control of anything. Has that mask addled your brain?" Tallin's eyes glittered with fury as he glared at Haydan, who appeared to have missed his faux pas.

Silent communication occurred as Haydan scowled and considered his answer for a moment. "I have taken control of two of the twelve kingdoms."

Tallin's eyes narrowed. "That is the better answer. Did you find another keystone?"

"I've found the third, yes, with Maya's help."

Tallin's sphinx-like expression remained. A twitch of his mouth suggested the news had pleased him. "Well done. She figured out how to unlock the water book then – finally."

"Are the dark gods here because I've claimed the first realm, or is it coincidence?" Haydan asked.

Tension vibrated off Haydan's lean frame as he paced, a mixture of uncertainty and perhaps a hint of fear emanating from him. To the best of Diego's knowledge, his son had never encountered the dark gods before, although no doubt Theander would have shared a few more unsavoury details to heighten his concerns.

"I do not know." Tallin turned away from the gathering. Guards began running down the corridor. "We have intruders, possibly one dark god. Search the court in teams, working outwards. If you find any trespassers I want to know."

Sandau stretched out his arms. He appeared unconcerned by the incident. "One or more suggests an advance party coming in to check the area ahead of the chief party arriving. This is not the main event. All hell will break loose when that happens. Dark gods are not known for being subtle and whoever it was, they may have already left."

Tallin dipped his head to indicate understanding, then returned his attention to the guards. "I have briefed you on how to deal with them if you encounter them," he said.

The guards nodded and returned down the corridor the way they had arrived. Tallin turned back. "Haydan, I would suggest you stay close to Sandau and I. If the ring turns red again, or stays red, you get to either one of us as fast as you can. Is that clear?"

Haydan lowered his head, looking resigned to his fate. Tallin shot a disarming smile at everyone. "So, have you all picked outfits for tonight? If you have not found a mask you like, my team are in later and they can sort you out with something suitable."

Diego found his father's ability to switch from master game-player to playful host amusing, although his concern for Haydan remained. The gods had found them quicker than he had hoped and had even hunted down Isaac and the rest of Maya's family.

"I thought the only way into this realm was through the portal," Diego said. "You know when the portal activates. Kat, Isaac and Si, however, managed to reach the library here in the building and they were nowhere near the portal. How did that come about?"

Tallin's shoulders tensed as though he didn't want to answer Diego's question.

"There are other routes into this realm, Tallin. Start sharing the information," Diego said. His father needed to explain the other routes to everyone. The thought of dark gods walking out of the triple halos whenever they felt like it disturbed him greatly.

Tallin pondered his answer for a moment. "There is a more powerful triple halo in Maya's room. It only works from here. It will take you to the woodland near the portal that brought you here. I do not know how Kat, Isaac and Si reached here. I can only assume there are more powerful halos that the gods can use and manipulate. Maybe you should ask them who helped them to get here."

"Pablo did," Isaac said. "He gave us the route into the library."

"There you go then. Pablo is helping," Tallin said.

Tallin's response annoyed Diego. He always felt that Tallin was hiding secrets.

Maya jumped around from one foot to the other. Diego settled his attention on her. "Something to add, Maya?"

"It's just a thought, but in the dining room there are friezes on the walls and they are full of triple halos."

Soft laughter from Sandau and a nod of agreement indicated that Maya had figured out the hidden entrance. "Well done, Maya," Sandau said. "I suspect that is how the light gods enter, though, not the dark gods. The artwork exudes light magic suggesting it is their portal in. Tallin, are there other friezes concealed in the court?"

Tallin's smile widened. "That's a fascinating suggestion. I'll make sure the guards are increased around that room, and yes, there is another room in one of the quieter parts of the court where there are more pieces of our ancient artwork. I will have that room guarded as well."

A nearby door slid closed silently. Diego caught the movement out of the corner of his eye. Someone was eavesdropping. Sandau moved to Diego's side and reassuringly patted his shoulder. He appeared to have missed the intrusion.

"Haydan's in the safest place he can be right now and he has mastered the first two realms. When the dark god incursion has been investigated, I will show him the triple halo routes."

Diego nodded and steeled himself for the coming battle. Tallin was playing dangerous games and Diego and Sandau had to be ready for any eventuality.

Chapter 30

Lavinia

Rebekka had spent quite a bit of time loitering in the shadows. She turned and slid the door to. Perhaps she had been listening in on Tallin's conversation in the hallway with their guests. "I would like to go to the dining room for some lunch."

Lavinia felt certain Rebekka was doing that deliberately to annoy her, but then she had been restricted to the suite for a while and was no doubt growing bored of her surroundings. Nodding, Lavinia made her way across the room to the triple halo that dropped them into the hallway near the dining room. Fed up with entertaining her daughter-in-law, Lavinia hoped for respite soon. Maybe Rebekka would spend the night with Diego and give her some breathing space.

In the dining room, Rebekka made a big fuss of finding a seat with a view of the friezes mounted on the wall. Lavinia inhaled and fought back the irritation that swelled within her as the woman fussed and moved seats about until she was happy with the layout.

Reminding herself to behave like a gracious host,

she slipped into the nearest seat and gave Rebekka a brittle smile. "Better now?"

Rebekka nodded her agreement, reached for a sweetbread and began filling her plate with food. She remained transfixed by the wall frieze.

Lavinia cast a cursory glance over the unusual wall art. It had never been her favourite piece, but as with most things in the summer court, she had little say in how it was decorated. She reached for a teapot, hoping to find her favourite herbal tea rather than some of the elven infusions that Tallin enjoyed. The first teapot smelt suspiciously of one of Tallin's mint and liquorice concoctions. She turned her nose up and reached for the next one, which smelt more like breakfast tea.

Movement to her side and a shift in the air of the room indicated one of the servants had returned. "Please could you bring me the milk?" She poured the tea into a nearby cup and pulled it closer to sniff it. The servant hadn't moved. She waved a dismissive hand at him. "It's over on the side in the white jug. I take it you're new? Tell the kitchen I like the herbal-infused teas, not Tallin's odd combinations."

A tanned, muscled arm reached out and landed the jug Lavinia had requested in front of her. How unusual for a servant to be so heavy-handed when serving her and showing flesh, especially on such well-toned and strong arms. Tallin would not allow such a thing in his court. She followed the arm as it withdrew. Elven and fae males were generally slimmer and not as well built as this one was.

"Will that be all, My Lady?"

The resonant, masculine voice sounded mocking and was laced with a hint of amusement. A shiver passed down Lavinia's neck as she tracked the arm back to its owner. He had penetrating cerulean eyes and a handsome face. Stubble grazed his jaw. His hair was short and light brown, which only added to his rugged good looks. In response to Lavinia openly staring he gave a lazy grin. It was a smouldering, dangerous smile that warned her to watch herself. She swallowed and cleared her throat, trying to compose herself before speaking. "You're not one of our servants."

His smirk dropped away. "No, I am most definitely not one of your servants, My Lady."

Behind the handsome man pretending to be a servant, one of the triple halos in the frieze disengaged and dropped to the floor, before shooting up into the air. Another man appeared beneath it. He moved with a more formidable swagger, had darker hair hidden underneath a bandana tied around his head and looked fiercer than the first male, who stood within arm's reach of Lavinia. His expression scornful, the second man swept the room with his intense, searching eyes.

"What are we waiting for?"

His tone fierce and commanding, he sounded like the more formidable of the two and he glared at Lavinia with a look that sent her heartbeat stuttering. A subtle scent of chocolate reached her.

"Who are you and what are you doing in Tallin's dining room?"

"Tallin's dining room?" The second male gave Lavinia a condescending, hard look. "That—" he pointed at the frieze "—was there long before this was Tallin's dining room. So really, we should be asking you what you're doing in our dining room."

"You're gods." They smelt like gods and they were arrogant enough to be gods.

The second man sneered at her. "Well done, My

Lady." He stared off with the first man. "Why are you humouring this one?"

The first male drew in a deep breath. "Kai, we spoke about you working on your manners. Generally, people are in a better humour when you address them in a polite fashion."

Kai grumbled in disapproval. "It's definitely here. I've got places to be." He threw something onto the ground which scattered into three spheres. The balls rolled around him and Kai vanished from the room.

A flurry of activity in the corridor a moment later suggested that Kai's place to be hadn't quite worked according to his plan. Lavinia suppressed a smirk at the realisation.

Recognising the mobile triple halo, she had gifted Maya one very similar, Lavinia smiled at the remaining male. "You're Theander." She focused her attention on Rebekka. "Is that why you wanted lunch in this room? Did you know about this?"

Rebekka stood and made her way around the table to Theander's side. "My Lord, I was hoping to catch up with you. I would like to talk to you." She dropped down onto a knee as Theander turned.

Theander's expression was scornful as he surveyed Rebekka. "Oh? And why would you want to speak to me?"

"I need your help."

Theander's gaze slid back to Lavinia. "Do you now? If I find out that someone has been sharing things with you that they should not have, there will be repercussions."

Lavinia was not taking the fall for something she had not done. She mimicked Rebekka, by dropping onto a knee. "I apologise for addressing you so rudely before. I did not realise I stood in your presence, My Lord. Please forgive my lack of manners. I've told her nothing. Rebekka has been figuring certain things out, no doubt from her goading of Diego and Haydan."

Theander's expression remained sullen as he returned his attention to Rebekka. "Speak. Make it quick. I also have places to be."

Rebekka didn't initially meet his eyes as she wrung her hands together. "Is it true you have Diego's chosen one's soul hidden on Acquorous?"

Lavinia cringed. Directly asking the gods anything was never a wise move and Theander would immediately switch into his defensive mode where nothing would penetrate him emotionally.

The silence from Theander stretched out. Lavinia risked a glance upwards. His shoulders had drawn up and his head had lowered.

"I have lots of things on Acquorous and none of them are your business," he snapped.

Rebekka looked uncertain. She swallowed and fidgeted. "No, but Diego's chosen one's soul sort of is my business. Maybe you would be kind enough to tell me whether you have taken her from him. Or are you keeping her safe for him?"

Theander's eyes narrowed. "The distinction matters because?"

Rebekka appeared livid as she took a deep breath in. "I need to know the answer because Diego won't talk about it. He shuts me down every time I try to get an answer from him."

Theander leant forwards. "A word of advice, if I may." He didn't wait for Rebekka's response as he continued. "If Diego will not talk about it, you would be wise to take that as an understanding that he has not reached a decision about her … yet." Theander drew himself back, broadening his shoulders, which made him look even more intimidating. "The relationship between storm rider and chosen one is sacred. Bear in mind that if this is a test of your loyalty, you have just spectacularly failed it."

Rebekka seemed to consider Theander's response for a moment. "Failed it? If I didn't speak to you about it, that would suggest I do not care and I do care very much about Diego. Tell me, My Lord, have you ever been in love?"

Theander's expression changed to one of annoyance as a tiny crease appeared across his brow. His head tilted forwards and he moved into a more relaxed stance. "I once made that mistake. I will never do so again. What. Is. Your. Point?"

"I will not share the man I love with a ghost of the past and I *am* sharing him. He hasn't been the same since he last entered this realm. He's distant with me. You could make her go away and I wouldn't have to worry about her any more."

Theander glared at Rebekka from beneath a lowered brow. Menace oozed off him as he stared her down. His hands slid behind his back and wrapped around the handles of the blades he carried fastened into a leather carrier.

Rebekka dropped her head and sniffed. She looked forlorn and lost. "I know you regard what Diego and I share as an odd anomaly, but I would do anything to protect him."

Theander's hands flexed as he tightened his grip on the blades. In a moment Lavinia was going to watch him murder the mother of her grandchildren. She closed her eyes and debated what Diego would have her do in this situation. "My Lord, it's not my place to interfere—"

"Then don't." Theander's hands stilled on the blades, but he waited, allowing Lavinia to finish.

"This is a decision that Diego should be permitted to make. He broke with tradition when he left the sea with Rebekka, but as one of our elders he is capable of taking responsibility for his own actions, as are all of us. Rebekka is speaking out of turn, but would you be so quick to judge if she was a chosen one defending her partner, or if she was with child?" Lavinia left the question unanswered, wondering if Theander would notice the odd energy signature that Rebekka released. Lavinia had only noticed it a couple of times, but Rebekka was definitely with child.

Theander flexed his fingers again, but appeared to loosen his grip on the blades as though conflicted.

Rebekka looked like she was gaining in confidence, but she couldn't see Theander's hands from where she was crouched. Lavinia could and there was a definite battle going on within Theander about what to do.

"Exactly. My defence of Diego is no different to that of a chosen one—storm rider relationship, is it? So, why should I have to suffer this, knowing I'm second choice to her all the time?"

Lavinia wished that Rebekka would keep her mouth shut. The gods maintained a respectful relationship between their race and storm riders, but that could so easily change.

"Please, My Lord, Diego has suffered enough from the loss of his chosen one. I would respectfully ask that you allow him to decide his own future."

Theander ignored Lavinia and focused on Rebekka. "You knew when you left the sea with Diego what the lie of the land was. Every storm rider has a chosen one. Where is yours? I don't hear Diego asking where he is, demanding that I make him disappear. Perhaps that is a sign of his maturity and his worthiness as elder … maybe he made a poor choice in you…" Theander's hands flexed around the knives again.

"My Lord, Haydan and Diego would be heartbroken if…" Lavinia tailed off, praying that Theander valued his friendship with Haydan enough to back off.

It was interesting that at the mention of Haydan, Theander seemed to remember who Rebekka was, or perhaps he had noticed her odd energy signature. He lowered his hands, leaving the blades untouched.

"Like I have already said, there are many things on Acquorous that are nothing to do with you. Diego will choose who he wants as his mate. Given your behaviour, I would be surprised if it's you, although that may change when he finds out about the secret you're carrying."

He had noticed the fluctuation in Rebekka's aura. Lavinia inwardly sighed at the realisation.

Theander stalked off towards the door, leaving a victorious-looking Rebekka in front of Lavinia. She wisely waited until Theander left the room and pulled the door to. "So, Haydan *was* involved in this. I can work on him."

Lavinia's ire surfaced at Rebekka's stupidity. "Theander will tell Haydan about this. Haydan can't help you. He will not jeopardise his friendship with Theander for you. Their friendship spans numerous cycles; your relationship with Haydan does not enjoy that familiarity. You should have left this alone. Diego will not thank you for it and neither do I. All it will take is a word from Haydan or Theander to Diego and he will end what you have; he is already on the brink." If Rebekka truly loved Diego, she would back away from this as quickly as possible. "Leave this issue with Diego alone. I do not wish to see him hurt any more than he already has been. Respect that." She allowed that announcement to sink in then added, "Does he know about the baby?"

"No, not yet. Keep it to yourself, please." After studying Lavinia for a few moments, looking tearful, Rebekka swept out of the room. Lavinia closed her eyes and released a sigh of relief. The gods didn't reach for weapons unless provoked, so Theander clearly didn't like the unusual relationship between Diego and Rebekka. It was just a matter of time before Haydan found out about Rebekka's treachery and the question that preyed on Lavinia's mind was what he would do when he found out. She opened her eyes and caught a flash of something purple leaving the room. She cursed under her breath; now Tallin knew too.

❧

Tallin

Pounding feet on the tiled floors alerted Tallin to his guards returning. The lead guard stopped close by and dipped her head. "My Lord, we've found the intruder. He's near the dining room."

Tallin rushed after her, intrigued to know who had entered his realm unannounced. If they had entered with malicious intent, then he couldn't fathom why they had allowed themselves to be captured so easily.

Rounding the corner by the dining room he was horrified to find Kai surrounded on all sides by his guards. Kai looked like an irate, bristling hellcat. His guards were ready to attack Kai the moment he made a wrong move; their weapons were drawn and the tension was palpable.

"King Tallin, you need to get your lapdogs under control and fast before I rip them to pieces."

Tallin inhaled a shaky breath. "Stand down. It is fine, this is not who we are looking for."

His guards sheathed their weapons and the stand-off eased. Tallin inwardly released a sigh of relief. "You are dismissed. Patrol the rest of the court and stay alert."

Kai cocked his head to the side and raised an eyebrow as the guards left. "Who are you looking for?"

"Haydan's ring activated once."

"Which ring? Storm riders do not wear trinkets." Kai's tone suggested Tallin answer him and quickly.

"The Arvellan stone."

That announcement silenced Kai. He mulled the news over for a few moments. "Theander returned that item to you. How unexpected."

"Why?" That came out sharper than Tallin intended. He should hold his tongue in front of Kai. "It turned red. Was that you?"

Kai's lip curled into a snarl. "Of course it was me, you fool. I can't hide what I am from that trinket and it clearly lets nothing slip its attention. Even the half of me that is dark. It activates ahead of my arrival."

Maintaining his calm demeanour, Tallin waited for further elaboration from Kai, wondering if he would divulge why he found the return of the Arvellan stone to Tallin interesting. Nothing appeared forthcoming.

Tallin sniffed and decided to ignore the slight. "Apologies, I did not know. Theander did not notify me that it also announced your presence. He could have warned me."

Kai's snicker of laughter set the hairs on Tallin's neck on edge. "Theander knows better than to tell anyone the information about my heritage that you are party to. He returned a gift to you. That indicates trust. That's not a feeling I can relate to. I don't trust anyone." Intense silence settled over proceedings. "You are, in fact, just the person I was looking for."

Tallin's heart fluttered in response. He had a funny feeling he knew exactly what Kai wanted to talk to him about. "That is wonderful news. Let us move to my private office where we can talk undisturbed." He forced a smile across his face and quelled the unease rising in his chest.

Kai followed at a distance as they walked along the corridor and down into the private sections of the court away from the main thoroughfares. Tallin threw the office door open and entered ahead of Kai. "Do come in and take a seat." He indicated an available chair and waited.

The office was warm and cosy. The soft scent from the floral display on Tallin's desk mingled with the smell of oiled wood and leather from the chairs and the pine branches placed along the top of the large fireplace.

Kai hesitated on the boundary of the office, partway between the two spaces. His eyes homed in on the area of the wall where Tallin's safe was buried and that was when Tallin knew beyond a shadow of a doubt that Kai wanted his possession back and that it could communicate with its owner.

"I know it's here, Tallin. The first time, there was

just a whisper from it, but now I can hear it screaming inside my head as it seeks return to its true master." Kai inhaled as though in pain and stepped over the boundary into the office, permitting Tallin to close the door. "If I find out you played a hand in it being stolen, however—"

Laughter bubbled up inside Tallin at the absurdity of the suggestion and the subtle but aggressive threat from Kai. "I don't think I was a prince, or king, when this item was taken. I was a chosen one, and that's assuming my soul even existed whenever this item was snatched. I think it was long before my time and no, I did not take it, but I was loaned it in a time of need, by someone with wings the colour of ebony but edged in a vibrant purple and red."

Kai's expression softened and for the first time ever, Tallin witnessed a flutter of emotion in his face.

"That's new. As a child, his wings were always jet black, but I don't think he stole it from me. Theft has never been his style. When did he leave it here?"

"Many years ago, before I became king. The blade will confirm that." Dark Angel had always warned Tallin that the blade would find a way back to its owner. Now he knew who the owner was. It was no wonder Lawson had been so skittish about it back when they first met. There was clearly history between the two of them. Moments later Kai shuttered any hint of feeling away again behind his expressionless façade.

Tallin couldn't resist saying, "Lawson, he's your son, isn't he?"

Kai inhaled harshly and straightened up. "That is none of your business, King Tallin."

"Does Theander know he has an older brother? Does Lawson know he has a younger brother? It would help to know so I can safely navigate the politics of it all."

Kai's jaw tensed. "I assume Lawson intentionally left it with you, knowing I would refind it at some stage. That's surprising given that he has avoided any contact with me for a very long time. Unless he's sending me a less than subtle message. He has always regarded me as the devil himself. I want Devil's Curse back now, Tallin."

Without any further questions Tallin moved to the safe and started lifting his protective charms to retrieve the item. Kai had named the blade. That confirmed it. Devil's Curse had found its owner.

Maya

The afternoon was quieter and less eventful than the morning. Haydan went with Sandau to investigate the transport system, leaving Maya alone with the drained water book. She sat on the bed, crossed her legs and opened it up at the first page.

Asanda was the only remaining old god. The rest had retreated, which meant nothing to Maya, but they either chose to leave human form and retire into objects, rather like Kaleshar and the mask, or moved on to their place of sanctuary on Acquorous, known only as the realm of the ancestors. The gods searched ceaselessly for the perfect race. It was unclear from the book exactly what the perfect race meant and how the gods created races, but it appeared they could do so if they wished. Storm riders were named as one of the more respected races, but whether that meant they fell into the classification of being perfect, Maya didn't know.

The ability to create life meant the gods had to then take responsibility for that life and sometimes that didn't go according to plan. Evolution of a species was a recurring theme within the book. The gods feared evolution because of the problems it brought. There were a number of pages about races with the ability to possess another body. The gods had created certain laws around the creation of new life as a result, hence possession could not be forced. Certain realms enjoyed special protection and privileges to safeguard their futures. The information proved fascinating.

There was a section about the light and dark gods' abilities. Maya ran her hands over the pages, drawing in a breath as she absorbed the information. This she needed to understand better, but it would not make for comfortable reading. The darkest magic thrived on misery, suffering, pain and death. Light magic was more playful and fun. Light and dark magic could attract or repel each other; there was no clear-cut rule about that. The book made no reference to gods being able to hold both forms of magic, which added to her unease.

There was a section about chosen ones. Maya snickered at the term. "What about abominations with manufacturing defects, do you cover those?"

There were references to various individuals within that section, some of whom had striking names, such as the fifth elder, the changeling, and the king of twelve kingdoms. There were also a huge number of prophecies hidden in something called the Pool of Sorrows, which sounded intriguing.

Maya focused on the king of twelve kingdoms, ignoring all the other information, which she could return to when time permitted. Every time she concentrated on a particular section, the information contained within dropped into focus. The section relevant to Haydan was brief. It confirmed that the mask of the gods would select one worthy of its power to rule the twelve kingdoms and that the person chosen was honourable and had never held a desire for power. "Yeah, that's Haydan alright," Maya said. The twelve kingdoms were named. At last she had a steer on the scale of the universe and the realms involved. Further into the book, she found maps for each realm, showing the location of each of the obsidian throne rooms. None of the realms were named on the maps, which were hard to read. The drawings gave her little to go off to orientate herself.

The secret routes into the realms had their own section and were not easy to follow or locate either and the keystones had their own chapter as well. They were identified by colour, but Maya could not read the names of the realms that corresponded to the relevant keystones. She flitted through that section, annoyed at the scant information being offered and reached the part about mystical artefacts. She flicked through that portion, her irritation growing, and turned the page to find a chapter bearing the title of Cursed Things.

A harsh bark of laughter left Maya's mouth. "Ssshh," she whispered. "We don't talk about cursed things." She glanced up to find an amused Kai watching her from over by the triple halo. She hadn't heard him enter the room and had no idea how long he had been studying her for. Her heart thudded in response.

Kai had opted for a red, orange and yellow

feathered shirt. The feathers congregated in patches around the collar, along the shoulders and down the back. Some of the feathers on the shoulder had a ruffled appearance. The short sleeves bulged around his biceps and showed off the tattoo of flames on his arm, which looked as though it was alive. The flames leapt and danced around in a manner that Maya found mesmerising. Stubble covered his jaw and his eyes were such a piercing blue that she felt certain he would be easy to identify once he wore his mask. The intensity in his gaze was unmistakeable.

Maya cleared her throat. "Hi there, I wasn't expecting to see you today."

Kai made a noise that sounded like agreement and moved across to the bed. Maya feigned nonchalance although his proximity was as unsettling as the last time she saw him. He never made any effort to make her feel comfortable around him and she wondered if that was deliberate.

"No, clearly not. Do you always talk to yourself?" Kai scanned the room as he reached a distance from Maya that seemed to please him.

Kai was closer than Maya would have liked. She grinned and shook her head. "No, only when I'm frustrated."

Kai continued to focus his attention on the balcony area rather than Maya. "Someone tipped Tallin off about our entry point into the realm. I have just had to fight off a pack of angry elven guards."

Maya suppressed a laugh as she wondered who had been more surprised, Kai or the guards. The thought of Kai finding himself outsmarted and surrounded by Tallin's men was highly amusing.

His irritation obvious, Kai brushed his shoulder

down, flattening the unruly feathers.

"I will speak to Tallin about that, but right now I have other priorities." Turning his attention to what Maya was doing, Kai added, "If you used the deciphering glasses you would find the information much easier to read."

Emboldened by Kai's continued presence, Maya scooted across the bed, moving nearer to him. A wall of energy pushed her back as she got closer and he moved off towards the window before she could try again. The rejection was unexpected. She battled to hide her disappointment. "I would rather you told me about the cursed things, but you won't talk about them, so what's the point?" Abandoning the book on the bed, she dropped onto her front and propped her face up with the palm of her hand.

Kai paced by the balcony a safer distance away. "I am not comfortable talking about your grandfather."

"Why? Because he hurt you, or did you hurt him? Are you angry at him? Did you curse him?"

Kai's head snapped up. He turned and his brows furrowed, which added to his air of menace as he glowered across at her. "Did I curse him?" Kai spat the words out as though even uttering them disgusted him. "He was a child, an innocent! My only crime was not protecting him." His nostrils flared in irritation. "No – make that my only crime was creating him." His tone softened and for the first time a hint of emotion rippled through his voice as he ruffled his hair. "I should never have done that. I will never know peace because of it."

Unsure if she should move, Maya forced herself to stay still, letting Kai continue.

"I ought not to have come. I knew you would start

prying. You may hold the light and the dark like I do, but you will never understand me." Kai turned and moved towards the triple halo.

He was leaving. Maya had to say something to stop him. "I'm sorry for prying. I was just trying to understand you better by finding your pain points. I'm new to all of this. It was rude of me. Please forgive me."

Kai came to an abrupt halt. Close to the bed again, he turned and flopped down onto the mattress near to where Maya lay. The bouncing motion as the mattress settled reassured her that he hadn't abandoned her, but she would have to be careful about the subjects that she raised with him.

"If you don't want to talk about it, you don't have to. I can't force you to discuss it and I don't mind the company. You must get lonely, being the only one of your kind." That wasn't the case any more. Maya studied the metallic-looking sheet beneath her and wondered if pointing that fact out to Kai would be wise. Her hands flared, adopting the strange new colouring that activated in his presence. "I can only get my left hand to darken and my right hand to glow when you're close by. Why don't they do that at other times?"

Dropping back onto his elbows, Kai stretched out, placing his hands down onto the sheet. "Immaturity? Lack of training or skill? Refusal to bond? Maybe you're broken and this is just an echo of your heritage. Your guess is as good as mine. You are an aberration. Everything you do is unusual."

Maya pressed her thumbs together and once again wondered at the significance of her hand colouring. "Thank you for sharing your assessment. Now I feel even more of a freak."

"You're welcome."

Kai appeared to have missed the sarcasm Maya had directed at him.

"Get used to it. My father will never accept a creature that does not know what it is." Kai looked down at his own hands. The colouring flickered, rising up from the depths then sinking back into his skin again. "As a child I hoped the light could chase the dark away, but it does not work like that. The darkness never leaves." He stared off across the room, lost in his own thoughts.

"I don't understand. You're not with the dark gods, so your father can't have rejected you." Maya slipped her dark left hand across the sheet towards Kai's glowing fingers. She stopped a safe distance away.

"No, I was the son who was the least broken of the two." Kai's face distorted and his mouth turned down. "All my father has taught me is to not love anything. Everything I get close to gets ruined … corrupted … tainted."

Maya fought back tears. Blinking, she tried to clear her vision as she struggled to find the right words. Kai didn't strike her as a man who wanted or needed comfort.

"What about Theander?"

Kai whipped his hand away from Maya's and clenched it into a fist. "He's my recompense and the one thing I managed to get right." He breathed rapidly through his nose as he stood. "Even then, his creation was an act of rebellion." With a heavy sigh, he turned back. "I will see you at the ball. Stay out of trouble in the meantime."

⊰⊱

Haydan

Music from the band reverberated throughout the summer court. The unusual melody was both beautiful and stirring. Waiting for Maya in the corridor, Haydan fidgeted. He leant against the windowsill and looked out, letting lightning crackle around his fingers. The sound and build-up of static in the air around him provided a tiny amount of solace. Tallin and Diego would tell him off if they caught him, but the court was full of Tallin's magic and he used such a small amount that it would not be easy to detect.

The ring had remained a greenish colour all day, but Haydan still felt on edge and uncertain. By late morning, when Tallin lifted the lockdown, Sandau had shown him the triple halo routes. He had memorised them all. Each one took different paths across the court and they all behaved and activated differently. Every one of them housed a trap of some sort. One in the upper corridor was voice activated and to use it Haydan had to shout out his own name and as much as he knew about whoever was after him and needed trapping. In a reading room on the upper corridor there was a treacherous drop onto spikes for anyone who fell into the trap, which was also voice activated.

Arianna stood a safe distance away on the periphery of Haydan's vision. Her outfit was covered in fur and feathers. Dark stripes adorned her face and her mask complemented her choice of clothing. She had braided her hair into lots of tight plaits.

Haydan's outfit was that of a wolf pup. Tallin had insisted he look the part of a young prince, which meant adopting the wolf; apparently there was a connection between the royal line and the creature. In truth, he quite liked the styling and the overall effect was striking. His mask wrapped around his head and furry ears stuck out from the top. The sections around his eyes were decorated with elaborate layers of fur.

Kaleshar lurked beneath.

He had decided to wear the mask in case of need, that and it was impossible to wear Kaleshar over the top of the fur, so it was a better fit underneath.

The door to Isaac and Katherine's room opened and they walked into the corridor. Katherine's outfit was a vibrant affair, with brightly coloured feathers across the bodice and train. Isaac's outfit was more toned down and he had opted for scales, which shimmered across his face. His hair had been slicked back and, along with his neck, was covered in a layer of intricate leathery scales. For once Isaac kept his distance from Katherine as he held the door to their room open and let her walk ahead.

There was something about the way Isaac moved that bothered Haydan. His gaze followed Isaac as he walked off. A quick shove at Haydan's elbow drew his attention away. He glanced down to find another elbow against his and tracked slowly upwards to find sapphire eyes staring back at him. Buried in amongst a sea of wriggling blue, yellow and silver worms, the eyes twinkled with mirth. Haydan reminded himself that one of the many reasons why he disliked Si was the man's ability to be irritating.

Si pursed his lips. "So, I'm the king of the wriggling things tonight and I'm on my own. How do I acquire a date around here?" He stepped back. "Hey, check this out." He turned and straightened out his arms. His shoulders sprang to life as various creatures began to move and dance about. Tendrils of a creeping plant glided down Si's arms. "It's weird, but kind of cool once you're used to it." Spinning back around, Si grinned in delight at Haydan. "So, I need a companion for the evening. I mean I know I'm married but I'm not going to be a third wheel, everyone else is in a cosy couple, I'm feeling left out."

Wondering if Si was being serious, Haydan stared at him, unsure how to find him a date at such short notice. "I'm assuming you mean a companion for friendship, not romance?"

Si tutted and rolled his eyes in exasperation. "Obviously."

Arianna interrupted as she walked across. "Hey, Si, you can stay with me, but be prepared for lots of eyeballing from that man there." Arianna pointed at Sandau, who stood in the shadows with his attention focused on Si.

Si chuckled and raised his hands up. "I'm Arianna's uncle, well, adopted uncle. I'm not the one who has a problem with you kissing Arianna, my friend."

Si nudged Haydan's elbow again. If he didn't stop with that, Haydan was going to land his fist in Si's face.

"That's his issue." Si grinned in amusement, apparently unaware of, or unconcerned by, how annoying he was being.

They were distracted as the door to Tallin's suite opened and the king strode into the corridor. He turned back and bowed to Lavinia, who swept out of the room behind him. "You look beautiful, my sweet."

Tallin appeared to be using more magic than he

did usually. It distorted the air around him like a heat haze. Haydan considered the anomaly. Maybe that was normal when an event was being held in the court. Lavinia leant in and whispered something to Tallin, who tensed at her proximity. When she pulled back from the king, the unusual irregularity that pulled at the air had gone. How strange.

Tallin wore the more updated version of the wolf outfit. His ears were fluffy and striped. His cape resembled a wolf draped around his body, with its head resting on his shoulder. Lavinia's dress was a beautiful, vibrant blue with a plunging back and a train that looked as though it had been engulfed in a sea of matching feather boas. Closer inspection revealed creatures hiding within the feathers. As Lavinia moved off the creatures began to dart on and off the train as though playing. A weasel, a few mice and a couple of tree foxes clung to her skirt before chasing each other about.

Haydan was intrigued to know what Maya would be wearing. Whatever it was she would be stunning. Thankfully, Si had moved off down the corridor to talk to Arianna and Sandau, leaving him alone. He turned back to the window and stared out. The sun set over the rear of the court transforming the sky into beautiful shades of pink, yellow and orange. Dark clouds were settling in from the east. He suppressed a shiver of anxiety.

Si's wolf whistle drew Haydan's attention back to the hallway. Maya ventured out of her room. The wait had been well worth it. Her hair was straightened, the ends a vivid red. She was wearing a black bodice fastened over one shoulder, leaving the other bare, and the skirt and train looked like a mass of white fluffy clouds. No doubt there would be some sort of trick hidden within the garment. Crisp white feathers adorned her eyes so the top part of her face was covered. For a moment Haydan couldn't speak.

"You scrub up well," Si said. He fixed a bawdy grin on Haydan. "Grab your coat, I think you've pulled, mate." Chuckling, Si turned back to the others.

"Well? What do you think?" Maya chewed her bottom lip.

That reminded Haydan of the last time he had kissed her, in the lounge at her house. He had enjoyed that kiss. It was one of a few she had granted him so far and he looked forward to the next one, although he preferred the thought of kissing her once bonded. Only then would he be free of his father's awareness of their intimacy. The reminder made him cringe and inhale sharply. "I think you look breathtaking and rather like a princess should," he said, distracting himself from the topic Maya hated most of all.

Maya clutched gloves in her hand as though unsure if she should wear them. The charm bracelet on her wrist captured the light, but Haydan's attention was once again drawn to another slim chain, around her neck, which contained the odd cage with something inside that he could not make out.

"I'll keep those safe. You can have them back if you end up being subjected to dancing with the rest of my grandfather's court." Haydan pocketed the gloves and held out his hand, delighted to find that Maya slipped her hand into his without complaint. Her fingers were warm. He locked his fingers between hers and smiled as he pulled her hand up to his mouth and planted a gentle, lingering kiss on the back of it. "Showtime, beautiful."

Haydan glanced back out of the windows as they walked down the corridor together. The sky had darkened and grey clouds still drifted in from the east, making their way stealthily across the sky. His overall mood sombre, he tried not to dwell on that evening's events. There was a good chance of a storm arriving and for once Haydan dreaded it, especially if the bad weather brought dark gods flooding into the castle.

Chapter 31

Arianna

Arianna followed Haydan at a reasonable distance. She never enjoyed protecting him when he was in a sea of other people. She often joined him in the clubs on Earth, but that was easier to manage as he was surrounded by innocent revellers. In this realm it made the task of guarding him that much harder.

Sandau had just given Arianna some pointers as she stood with Si. She should stay alert and at a distance when there was more space around Haydan. If people closed in on him, she was permitted to move closer. Mages, as she already knew, were identified by markings on their neck, just below their ear, and usually needed more space to activate their magic. In Tallin's realm, they pushed magic out from their hands, but of course there was always the danger of a concealed weapon that could be grabbed. In the event of an incident, she should get Haydan and Maya to the nearest triple halo and move them away from the danger. Haydan would know if dark gods were nearby because of the ring on his finger giving him advance warning.

Arianna prepared for the assault on her hearing as they descended the stairs and the sounds from the gathering intensified. Haydan and Maya would arrive first. Diego would follow with Rebekka, and the king and Lavinia would arrive last.

Haydan swept ahead, with Maya's hand gripped in his. It was nice to see that they could on occasion act like a normal couple. Arianna doubted it would last for long. There were still over two years to go before Maya made the decision to bond and that would be a tense time for all of them, her especially as she had responsibility for Haydan's safety.

Haydan paused before reaching the last staircase down into the grand hall and turned to Maya. Leaning in, he whispered something to her. Whatever it was it made Maya laugh in delight. Haydan pulled Maya to the top of the staircase and held up their hands as though they were announcing themselves.

The gasp that went up from the gathered crowd surprised her. There were a lot of people waiting in the hall. A burst of applause erupted as the court welcomed the new wolf and his partner. Arianna followed Haydan and Maya slowly down the staircase, keeping her distance. The hall was a riot of colour, sound and movement. Soft music played. Glasses and goblets chinked. Her senses overwhelmed, it took a moment to realise that the first ball in Tallin's realm was going to be her biggest challenge to date.

Haydan took his time, maybe enjoying having Maya at his side, or more likely trying to delay walking into the massive throng of Tallin's court. Despite his trips into crowded clubs, he had told Arianna that he still found large groups of people a challenge. Storm riders didn't like being in close proximity to anyone other than their chosen one and the noise would be bothering Haydan's sensitive hearing.

The applause had tailed off by the time Haydan and Maya reached the floor, but they remained the centre of attention. Haydan moved through the gathering saying hello to the various courtiers who crossed his path, intrigue and fascination burning in the eyes of those desperate to speak to the young prince and princess.

Relief flowed through Arianna when Diego moved to the top of the stairs. His wolf outfit was distinctive and his presence immediately drew attention away from Haydan. She continued to sweep her gaze around the gathered courtiers. A couple nearby remained focused on Haydan regardless of Diego. The woman kept glancing down at Haydan's right wrist and Arianna could not shake the uncomfortable feeling that she was in the presence of the infamous Leylani. And she was paying far too much attention to the prince and his altera for her liking.

ᴅiego

The incessant chattering and laughter grated on Diego's ears. He would have to entertain his father's guests for most of the evening and Tallin expected him to begin to show more than a passing interest in the intricacies of his court. Diego had waited as long as he could before acknowledging that he would have to join the party ahead of his parents, and Sandau had made a point of knocking on his door to remind him before it was too late.

Sandau waited a polite distance away. His height meant he would be easy to find in the event of chaos breaking out, which if the dark gods arrived that evening, Diego would be grateful for.

Stopping at the top of the stairs, Diego scanned the room below. There were creatures and animals everywhere, crawling about on tables, wandering about on the floor. A number of butterflies and winged creatures fluttered about. Hummingbirds darted past alighting on trees and foliage that sprouted out of crevices, walls and various urns.

Isaac and Katherine were already there. Katherine was easy to detect as she had the baby with her and that gained them a lot of attention. Isaac stayed at Katherine's side looking bemused by the entire event. Two bulky males in garish costumes loitered close by. Diego tried not to stare, but it was hard not to in a room full of so many odd outfits, and the men stood out. He couldn't place why, but they did.

Si was mingling with a few of the more gregarious guests and appeared to be enjoying himself. Haydan and Maya were no doubt grateful for the respite from all the attention. For once they presented a united front, which was more than could be said for him and Rebekka, who would show herself at some point soon.

Taking a deep breath, Diego moved to the top of the stairs in full view of the guests. A figure dressed in red slid to his side. That answered his question. He didn't turn. He extended his hand out inviting Rebekka to take his – because it was Rebekka. Her scent as she moved in close was intoxicating. The folds of silk that made up her gown looked as beautiful as she would. She slipped her fingers into his and he closed his hand around hers, tightening his grip to warn her that her game that evening was not well received. He urged his anger back down deep inside and raised her hand to his lips. Kissing the back of it, he finally permitted himself a glance across at her.

Rebekka was beautiful. Her honey-blonde hair cascaded in ringlets past her shoulders. That was done deliberately because Diego liked her hair like that. She had worn red, his favourite colour on her. Orange and yellow intermingling, the halterneck dress fitted her in all the right places, pushing her ample cleavage up, before plunging into a long train that flowed behind her. She had chosen that style of outfit to ensure Diego's attention remained on her all night. Given the number of pretty things wandering about his father's court he couldn't blame her, but if she thought he was interested in any women in Tallin's court, other than her, she was mistaken. The outward display of her need to keep his attention, however, made him smile. Rebekka was often insecure about him. Considering the nature of their relationship and the size of their family, that frequently surprised him, but then maybe her desire to hold his interest that evening wasn't about other women in the court. No – it was about Sasha. Once again, his heart ached with longing and he closed his eyes momentarily, fighting back the emotions that surfaced.

Opening his eyes and narrowing them, Diego gave Rebekka a look that conveyed his annoyance at her power games without a word being uttered.

Rebekka appeared wary but rewarded Diego with a charming, if formal smile. It was an evening of decorum and playfulness in front of the guests. They would be polite all night. Later, unless the dark gods sabotaged the event, they would argue, before making up behind closed doors. He plastered a smile across his face and turned away from her, back to the adoring masses in his father's court. That evening's playtime was only just getting warmed up.

ᴴaydan

Haydan could sense tension between Diego and Rebekka as they descended the stairs together. His father looked ill at ease, his mother uncomfortable, which given that she didn't like crowds either made sense. A couple of times she winced and said something to Diego, who had a tight grip on her hand, without moving her mouth. It was too noisy for Haydan to hear what Rebekka was saying, so he couldn't make out the exact nature of the undercurrent between them, but something was festering. He could sympathise with the decibel levels. He himself struggled to deal with so many people in close proximity and the noise was overwhelming. In the clubs on Earth, he had learnt to tune out the noise using magic. Once he adjusted to the bass reverberating through his body he could manage it better, but he could not do that now, not given the dangers of using his powers in the court.

Arianna met Haydan's eye and flicked a sly glance off to her side. They had agreed she should keep her distance and act like the other guests so as not to draw attention to her presence. In the event that he got into trouble, he would be grateful for that. The silent communication from her alerted him and his eyes swept the nearby crowd. He caught the back of a male disappearing into the throng and a flash of blonde hair as his companion, at his side, melded with the other guests – Leylani.

Haydan glanced back. Arianna scowled and shook her head. He had scanned the crowd too late to catch her hidden message, but he had caught the general gist of it.

Someone in a green dress with a tree frog mask on darted down the stairs and a murmur went up from the crowd that Tallin was on his way. The room tensed; of course, the king and queen arriving at their own ball would be well received by those in the court. Haydan mulled this over, aware that his expectations and what was playing out in front of him were quite different. Tallin had given the impression that there were those in his court trying to oust him, but then it would only take a few powerful, bold mages to conspire against the king for him to be unsettled. The majority of his court appeared to adore the king, however.

Tallin arrived with Lavinia a moment later. He stood at the top of the stairs with Lavinia's hand held aloft, clearly enjoying the adulation of the court. Everyone whooped and hollered and applause erupted. Behind Tallin more creatures poured into the room and a wolf with purple and black ears swept past the king and descended the stairs before disappearing into the crowd. A sharp elbow from Maya to Haydan's ribs reminded him that he was supposed to be showing his appreciation for the king as well.

"You should be clapping, darling."

Haydan began applauding, resigned to the fact that he would have to join the first dance with Maya as well.

Granted, that part he would enjoy. However, he was more interested in finding out what Leylani was up to and that plan would have to go on hold now the main guests of honour had arrived.

Tallin took his time reaching the bottom of the staircase. He bounded down a few steps, waited for Lavinia to catch him up, then bounced down a few more. At the bottom Lavinia swept around Tallin and curtsied, before giving him an adoring glance and straightening up.

Haydan watched Isaac, who had a murderous expression on his face as he studied Tallin. Everyone was behaving very oddly this evening.

"Good evening, Prince Haydan."

The resonant, low voice addressing Haydan was male and familiar. He tried to place it, his mind racing to catch up with the new information.

"Don't turn and make a fuss, just acknowledge that I have once again crept up on you without your knowledge. Oh, and call me Thee in the presence of others at your peril. I'm not really here by the way."

Theander. The male at Haydan's side brushed past and walked ahead, before casting a look back over his shoulder at Haydan and grinning. Those azure eyes were unmistakeable behind his colourful mask. Haydan chuckled and returned his attention to Maya, reassured by the presence of his friend, even though Theander was clearly there for a reason.

Fortunately, Maya had missed the whole incident. She was too busy staring at a woman nearby who had all her hair piled up on top of her head and a litter of tiny kittens crawling about in it.

Tallin and Lavinia moved through the crowd to the dance floor, collecting Diego, Rebekka, Haydan and Maya on their way past. Maya moved in close to Haydan and he forgot about Isaac, Theander, small cats and dark gods as she pulled him onto the dance floor, turned to face him and took a step back. The lights had dimmed. This was where the ladies showed off their outfits. It was always the highlight of the evening.

Maya's skirts lit up, the explosion of light so bright Haydan had to blink a few times. Tiny hummingbirds released from the folds and darted off around the room. The light settled down and she turned, sweeping her skirts around as she did so. The effect was stunning; the bodice remained dark, but sparkled with stars, and the skirts were like brightly lit clouds.

Rebekka's dress released butterflies that matched the colour of her dress into the air. Lavinia's train unfurled and the creatures that had been hiding within her skirts lit up.

Another round of applause erupted and Haydan pulled Maya into his arms, spinning her around as the music grew louder and the dancing began. Maya relaxed against him, nestling into him and pressing her forehead into the spot she liked at the base of his neck.

A moment later Maya tensed against Haydan and looked across at someone standing nearby with an ornate, vibrant-coloured mask on and an outfit covered in feathers. She excused herself as the music finished and moved off into the crowd as though in pursuit of the man who had been standing close by watching them.

From the look of the flames around the top of his arm it was Kai. The question Haydan wanted answering was why Maya was sneaking off in search of the most secretive god in existence without telling him.

Chapter 32

Arianna

Haydan followed Maya as she moved off into the crowds. Arianna wasn't losing sight of him as well as Maya. She tailed him, keeping a safe distance. The room had emptied a little since earlier. No doubt the crowds had dispersed into other parts of the court after the main guests of honour arrived. Clearly agitated, Haydan scanned the court as he sought Maya out. It appeared she had managed to give him the slip. That would annoy Haydan, particularly because of the tense situation that evening. Reaching the bottom of the stairs, he ascended to the top level where it was quieter, presumably so he would gain a good vantage point. Once at the top, he stilled and his gaze cruised over the hall. He was evidently searching out his errant partner.

Halfway up the grand staircase, Arianna turned and surveyed the hall. A strange-coloured wolf slid past her, brushing against her leg as it did so. She gasped and watched it make its way up the stairs. The colouring amused her; the wolf was purple and green with long furry ears to match, Tallin had definitely had fun with the magical elements of the evening. Viewing the room from that height gave a better perspective. Katherine was with Si. Tallin and Lavinia were talking with a small group nearby. Well, Tallin was allowing Lavinia to hold court with the gathering. She was basking in all the attention, as usual. Diego was dancing with Rebekka, so Sandau would be lurking somewhere down that end of the room as well.

Isaac slipped past, met Arianna's eye and dipped his head without stopping. It was unusual that her father didn't say hello. She quickly dismissed it. She was working and he knew better than to interfere in that. He disappeared at the top of the stairs into a nearby corridor.

Haydan remained at the top of the stairs. Something had captured his attention on the staircase. Arianna caught a glimpse of blonde hair as the woman who had been staring at Haydan's altera earlier glided past. Her distinctive outfit was a toned-down, earthy colour with patches of a see-through material in strategic places, down the back and in a V shape at the front. The train was edged in ermine and strange little rodents ran in a continuous circuit around it. Their eyes glinted, giving her the unsettling feeling that the creatures were a type of lookout team. Arianna averted her gaze, but kept Haydan in the corner of her eye. She was certain that was Leylani. Inevitably he would follow the woman, likely landing himself in trouble.

Leylani reached the top of the stairs and turned down the corridor, moving away from Haydan. That woman was up to something. The more Arianna watched her, the more her skin prickled with apprehension and if she had got hold of Maya…

Haydan was in his grandfather's court. He knew

Arianna was close at hand; a furtive look at her confirmed that.

Tallin had warned Arianna earlier to allow Haydan to be taken. Her mind roiled with unease at that thought.

Apparently done considering his own safety, Haydan moved off from the top of the stairs trailing Leylani at a safe distance into the darkness.

Arianna hesitated for a second then followed. She would move closer and make sure this was the moment when Leylani was going to strike. She had to be certain and Tallin was oblivious to the entire event taking place; he was too preoccupied with his guests and Lavinia. She cast a quick glance at the king. He was still basking in the attention of his court – how typical.

The wall lamps resembled antlers, with a sweep of tiny lights around each one, and the corridor darkened as Arianna followed Haydan further into it. The lighting was probably intended to discourage guests from wandering, or designed to provide privacy for those wanting to conduct secret liaisons, or daring kidnaps.

Unable to draw on his magic as frequently, Haydan seemed wary, pausing every now and again to scan the corridor. Arianna dropped back into the shadows, melting into the darkness as she slipped into her stealth mode.

Recesses appeared as they moved deeper. Each one was like a large fireplace and home to a triple halo. They were discreet, but they were definitely there. Arianna tried to remember where each halo went, although she didn't recall the halos being there when she checked the court earlier with Sandau.

Something moved in the darkness close to Arianna and she spun towards a figure who advanced with the same grace as she did, although he was bigger and more solid than her. Sandau backed her up against the nearest wall and placed his arm up by her head, caging her between him and the wall. He grinned down at her. His mask only hid his eyes, but his intent was clear.

"I've been waiting for this opportunity all night, Arianna," Sandau whispered. "Make this convincing."

Sandau's mouth captured Arianna's. Their masks clashed and she squirmed against him, torn between fighting him off to get to Haydan and taking a moment to enjoy the taste of him. Her eyes flew open. Why had he asked her to be convincing? She caught movement in the entrance to the corridor as two figures swept down the hallway behind them. It was only once the figures passed them without comment that she realised Sandau's game.

One of the figures who was guarding the area snickered and spoke to someone hidden in the darkness. "The hallway's clear, apart from a couple of lovebirds, but they're a bit ... preoccupied."

"His warrior's not about then?"

"It doesn't look that way, no. He must have lost her in the crowds."

The figures moved off towards the darkened end of the hallway where Haydan had gone. Now Arianna understood what was happening. A door clicked shut and Sandau transferred his attention from her to the unusual activity further down the corridor, his ghosted eyes glowing softly in the darkness as he kept watch.

Isaac approached and came to a halt on Arianna's other side. Judging by the plumes of mist releasing from his neck, the man in the leathery scales wasn't Isaac.

It was Tallin.

She admired him even more for the clever deception. Despite telling Arianna to allow Haydan to be taken, the king did not look amused by what had just taken place.

࿓

Maya

Haydan smelt divine and being cuddled against him as they danced made Maya feel settled and loved. She opened her eyes and caught sight of the brightly coloured plumage on Kai's shoulder. The glint in his intense cobalt eyes conveyed his utter fury at her subtle message, which only he would understand, the black and white of her outfit perhaps interpreted as a dig at her light and dark heritage. He had just received the message loud and clear and she was in trouble. Not only that, but her fingertips sprang to life at his proximity. She slid her hand into Haydan's jacket pocket and discreetly pulled the gloves free. The first dance finished and as the floor filled with Tallin's courtiers she brushed a kiss against Haydan's cheek, excused herself and moved into the crowd. Following Kai, she slipped her gloves onto shaking hands.

Kai led her out of the ballroom and into an adjoining room that was full of hanging pods. Maya recognised it from the other evening when she had thrown herself at Tallin and incurred the wrath of Haydan and Diego. She had totally lost her bearings. He moved to the back of the room, to an empty pod, and gestured for her to climb in. The music and incessant noise of people talking and laughing didn't reach the inside of the cocoon. Maya smiled as she remembered the other evening and the feel of Haydan's fingertips on her ankle as he had issued his warning to her to behave.

Kai stepped barefoot into the pod beside Maya and sank to the ground as the pod closed. "Well, that was nice and subtle." He sounded irked, but his expression remained blank. He must have worked out she had no idea what he meant as he added, "The light-up dress routine … how to announce yourself to the universe."

"It looks like clouds, lit up by the sunlight from above. It was meant for Haydan, a subtle way of telling him I'm his wild thing and I like to roam. The bodice reminds me of the sea." She feigned innocence as she smiled across at Kai. "Why have you brought me here?"

"This is the most private part of the castle. These pods keep many secrets." Kai grinned as though remembering something he had no intention of sharing with Maya. "You need to be here where she can't find you."

Maya did not like the sound of that. "Who do you mean? Where who can't find me?"

Kai smirked at her. "Have you heard mention of a woman called Leylani? She is someone of interest to the king because she is rumoured to be capable of taking souls and using them for her own gain. Tallin is letting her take Haydan. He told me earlier today after he returned a long-lost possession to me. She will also be after you because your soul links to Haydan's and I am not having you taken hostage by anyone."

This was some sort of sick joke. "Are you serious? Why on earth would Tallin let her take his own grandson? You're here, she's not going to mess with you."

Kai shook his head. "I am not getting involved. This is Tallin's party. It is his mess to sort out. He is allowing Haydan to be taken so he can find out who is trying to oust him. This woman may not be working alone."

Maya had heard enough. "No, that is not happening." She moved to the exit, shuffling on her bottom as she tried to rearrange her skirts so she could work out how to stand up. Kai sprang up from the floor with alarming agility and blocked her route.

Maya's world roiled around her, all the colour drained from her vision and a cold shudder shot through her body from her neck. She gasped and wrapped her arms around her knees, drawing herself up into the foetal position. "What's just happened? Don't let them take Haydan. Please, Kai. I'll beg if you need me to." Tears sprang to her eyes as she battled to stay awake and focused.

Kai studied her reaction in fascination as though it was the strangest thing he had ever seen.

The last words Maya heard from Kai as she was on the brink of passing out were, "Breathe, Maya. Haydan will be fine. You just have to deal with this minor glitch tonight." His scowl deepened as he added, "Your connection with him must be very strong. You can sense that he has been taken. I did not expect that—"

Maya's vision swam as darkness swept in and claimed her.

༄༅

ᕼaydan

Leylani appeared unaware of Haydan's presence as he slipped after her. He cast a quick glance back down the corridor behind him. He couldn't see her, but Arianna would have his back, she always did, and she had been on the stairs not far off when he surveyed the court.

The corridor was as majestic as the rest of the court with its vast sections of sweeping, smooth stone. The ceiling was so high overhead Haydan couldn't see it in the dark. Leylani came to a halt at a door further up the hallway. He dropped back into the shadows by one of the recessed archways anticipating that she would search the corridor, which she did a moment later.

Haydan took a minute to consider his options. Leylani could have captured Maya already. The thought of her held hostage was unbearable.

This is probably unwise, Haydan.

Kaleshar did not often communicate with Haydan telepathically. He wore the mask more than he had at first, which had appeased Kaleshar's need for that type of contact. His intervention seemed well timed and another reminder that Haydan should not be sneaking about in the darkness chasing a woman who was mysterious, sinister and most definitely up to things she should not be.

It probably is, but she could have Maya.

That is doubtful. You are her more likely target and you are in out of your depth, unless I help you.

Which of course you will.

Yes, but that all depends on who is helping her. Even Tallin is wary of his hidden mages. Do keep that in mind.

I have you and Arianna, it'll be fine. Tallin is not far off.

Okay, but I have warned you.

There was still no sign of Arianna, although when Haydan checked again it looked like she had just entered the hallway from the stairs. Reassured by her presence, he moved to the door and listened for any sound within the room. It was quiet. He reached for the ornate silver handle and pushed the door open.

Haydan entered what appeared to be an empty reading room. A large fireplace occupied the end wall and the room was full of comfy seating and large bubbles of some sort. On Earth Maya had a beanbag, but he doubted the ones in this room were filled with styrofoam balls. It was more likely that they were filled with water, or magic; either was possible.

A disturbance in the air drew Haydan's attention to the side and two figures unveiled themselves. One dropped in from behind him and something cold slithered around his altera. He cried out in surprise. It felt as though a ton weight had just anchored itself to his altera arm and he was forced to drop to the floor. That was when shock set in. His altera no longer worked. He couldn't draw any power from it and Maya had been cut off from him. Coldness slipped down his arm to the core of his body with so much force it snatched his breath away. His body convulsed, his vision swam. This eventuality he had not allowed for.

Demented demons. What the…?

Even Kaleshar seemed stunned by the development, or perhaps more importantly the effect on Haydan. Haydan struggled to breathe. Every time he inhaled, ice shards caught in his throat. His eyes filled with tears as he struggled to free himself but to no avail. Two guards unveiled themselves; they had hidden near the fireplace. They moved to either side of it and stood with their heads bowed and their hands on their weapons. A moment later one of them walked off to guard the door.

A soft, breathy giggle of delight issued from the darkness behind Haydan. "Oh, I think someone has been caught out and he's strong too, master, full of fight and a soul with the body still intact. I've never held one like this before."

Leylani straddled Haydan's lap. The sensation of her form against his was drowned out by all the other odd sensations assaulting his body. He had no idea what they had just done to him, but it was as bad as the incident in the carriage. In fact, this was worse, because he had no control of his own body any more and nausea overwhelmed him.

Arianna would arrive soon; it would be fine.

"Get off me." Haydan could barely get the words out. The scent of Leylani was overpowering. He felt like he would never rid himself of it.

Leylani peered at Haydan and thrust herself down harder onto his lap. The floor hurt his ankles and her weight pressed down on his thighs, but that was the least of his concerns.

Kaleshar, do something. Haydan didn't know if Kaleshar would even hear him, but it was better than nothing.

I warned you. I want to know who her master is. Don't you? I'm intrigued and you brought us here. He's just over there. I vote we find out.

Haydan released a growl of displeasure as Leylani

pushed her body up against his, squashing her hands and breasts against him. Nausea swirled up from his stomach and Haydan turned his head away from hers. She responded by sliding her hands up to his head and grabbing handfuls of his hair. Pain stabbed at his skull as she forced his head around to meet hers. She tutted at him and pouted. "See, this is how it's going to work from now on, darling. You're mine. All. Mine. When we get your warrior and chosen one, they are all mine too. You do as you're told or this happens." The coldness around his wrist intensified and Haydan cried out again. He didn't like whatever was anchored around his altera, although he would enjoy wrapping it around Leylani's neck once he was free of her control.

Movement to Haydan's side indicated Leylani's master had ventured closer. Magellan dropped into view.

"You? Tallin is going to kill you." Where was Arianna? She was supposed to protect him and she wasn't doing a very good job of that right now.

Magellan chuckled. "There are a few things wrong with that declaration, Prince Haydan. One, as second in line to the throne, you are not in a position to be threatening me. Two, Tallin is oblivious right now to what is going on here, and three, he has to catch me to do me any harm and I have been a step ahead of Tallin for years."

Leylani had worked a hand underneath Haydan's top. She slid her fingers over his chest, delighting in his obvious discomfort as he tried to pull away and another growl of fury released from his throat.

"Where is this mask hidden? I want that item. Search him," Magellan said.

Leylani almost purred as she fixed a sultry look

on Haydan and began searching him with slow, gentle sweeps of his body. It felt like an eternity before she finally announced, "He doesn't have it on him. Should I double-check?"

Haydan wanted to strangle the woman who currently sat on his lap. That would give him some small satisfaction for the liberty she had just taken. No one touched him, no one but Maya. Leylani had just violated that and now he felt sullied by her. The only solace he took from the experience was that he still had clothes on.

Magellan dropped back into a crouch beside Haydan. "See, the trick with Tallin is to let him think he has the upper hand, and I have always been careful to play the dithering, bookish, weak Magellan, whilst concealing who I truly am. Your arrival and that of your father merely meant I could move my plans forward, and you are very much part of my plans. Oh, and just to be clear about this, Leylani is mine … aren't you, darling? My wife and my slave, all in one." He straightened up.

A look of distaste passed across Leylani's face, one that suggested her allegiance was given begrudgingly. Haydan made a note of that; perhaps he could use that to his advantage.

"*You* killed that girl."

Magellan grinned and lowered himself back down. "I did. Did you notice how rattled Tallin was by that? Death runes are hard to form and make work properly, but I managed it. Tallin thinks the woodland can still be controlled. He is so wrong, and now I can make his life and Lavinia's even more miserable."

Leylani continued to run her hands over Haydan's chest. He turned his attention to her. "Do you know something, Magellan? I think your wife quite likes my lap. She certainly seems to be enjoying abusing my body."

Standing, Magellan swung his hand. A loud crack sounded and Haydan gasped as Leylani was swept off his lap by the force of the impact. She whimpered and cowered on the floor at Haydan's side with her hand pressed to her cheek. Haydan had heard of abusive relationships, but he had never before witnessed such violence and brutality. Magellan was a monster.

"Your fate and that of Leylani are intertwined. Play that game with me, Haydan, and she will suffer the consequences along with you. I don't think your storm rider morals will allow such a thing, do you?" Magellan disappeared from view again. "I want the warrior and his chosen one found. Go and look for them."

The distraction as Magellan talked to the guard provided an opportunity and Haydan decided to try using his other abilities. Perhaps he could gain the upper hand with an unexpected attack on Magellan. Mages needed space and time to work their magic; it wasn't as instantaneous as his. He slid his free hand onto the ground and released a surge of energy that pulsed out into the room. Leylani and the remaining guard collapsed to the floor.

Magellan let out an angry, guttural sound and strode across to Haydan. "Don't even attempt that game with me. You are unbonded and rarely visit this realm. I can crush you whenever I choose to, remember that." He drew his hand back.

The sharp sound of Magellan's hand meeting with Haydan's face shattered the silence. The sting of pain brought tears to his eyes and a metallic taste flooded his mouth. Leaning forwards, he spat blood onto the ground, which caught Magellan's foot.

"Consider this your only warning. Do that again and it will be my foot that meets with your face. Given that you're quite handsome, you might want to stop with that." Magellan grabbed a handful of his hair and forced his head back. "Do you understand me, Prince Haydan? When I have that mask off you, you'll be even weaker. Where is it? Are you wearing it?"

"Why are you doing this?" Haydan asked. Anything that distracted Magellan from trying to wrench the mask from his face had to be a good thing. Kaleshar brushed his mind.

Have you had enough yet? Magellan wants me. After that you're Leylani's toy.

Stay out of it until I find out more.

Kaleshar withdrew from Haydan's mind slowly, as though unsure about his instructions.

Magellan's mouth drew into a thin line. "I hate your people. When you infiltrated the royal line that was too much to bear. All that corruption, making its way into the elven then the fae realm. You want to know why I hate your people so much, so I'll tell you. It makes little difference anyway. My previous wife became very ill and I could not help her. I begged one of your kind to take her soul and grant her eternal life, but he would not do that for me. I had to watch her suffer and die knowing that was the end for her. She died too young. His. Name. Was. Diego."

Magellan let the announcement sink in. "He doesn't remember me. Presumably you don't hang on to all your memories of each life you live. Apparently, I wasn't important enough for that and even if he does vaguely recognise me, he would never suspect me of this after last time we met. He thinks I'm a coward.

Your people are cruel and selfish. You are not having this realm and you are not taking the rest of the kingdoms as yours. I will not allow it."

Magellan grabbed a handful of Haydan's hair and dragged his head around, studying his face as he did so. Haydan's scalp burned. It felt as though Magellan was going to tear his hair out. Satisfied that his theory was correct, Magellan slid his fingertips around the edge of Kaleshar as he tried prising it from Haydan's face.

A sharp energy released and Magellan hissed and withdrew his hand. He shook his fingers and released Haydan's hair, flinging Haydan away from him as he did so. "I think I'll be setting a death rune on you very soon, Prince Haydan. You need to understand that even princes fall, and Tallin can't always save you."

Magellan crouched nearby checking on Leylani and his guard. Leylani moaned and started to sit up. With his head near the floor, Haydan stared across at the dark eyes watching him from underneath one of the nearby seats. The wolf that hid beneath had lowered itself and settled its face onto its paws. It watched everything intently. Haydan remembered something about the wolf being Tallin's guardian in the realm. He had been a fool to enter that room alone. Now he had to hope that Tallin was ahead of Magellan rather than the other way around. If he wasn't Haydan was in real trouble.

Chapter 33

Arianna

It was a clever move by Tallin to swap his identity with Isaac. It had even fooled Arianna. Tallin and Isaac were similar heights, which explained how they had carried off the trick so effectively. The mist releasing from Tallin brushed against Arianna's cheeks as he stood at her side with a murderous expression on his face.

"How many guards?" Tallin asked.

"Four out here, two in the room," Sandau whispered.

"Not for much longer," Tallin said. "This is Magellan's doing. I'm going to kill him. Act like you're having a good time, Arianna. Walk with us. Play along."

Tallin slid his arm around Arianna's waist and pulled her into the hallway. Sandau kept a grip of her waist from his side. Tallin stumbled and staggered around, making a play of being drunk. He made a convincing job of nearly pulling them into the far wall, then leant forwards and rushed them down the hallway closer to the guards.

Two of the four guards standing nearby in the

shadows sniggered at their antics. A fifth one walked out from the room and said, "I've got to go and find the loose ends."

"We'll watch the end by the staircase then." Two of the guards peeled away and began walking down the corridor away from the room leaving the other two guards on silent sentry duty by the door.

The lone guard headed back down the hallway to the stairs. That left one guard in the room.

Sandau pushed his face into Arianna's hair and inhaled. "You smell like … like … fine wine."

Tallin giggled as they drew closer. "I think … she smells like the pashq…" pausing for a moment he frowned, closed his eyes and appeared to concentrate hard on getting his words out "…like the pasqua fruit."

Apparently unconcerned, the guards watched as they made their way past. One of them said, "You should take your party somewhere more private."

Tallin let go of Arianna and swayed, peering at the nearest guard as though he had only just noticed him. "Good ideea. I shecond thaa." He saluted the guard and made his way past. Sandau released Arianna's waist. She dived at the nearest one and made quick work of silencing him with her blade. By the time she turned back, Tallin and Sandau had each grabbed a guard. Tallin hit his over the head with the hilt of a small blade. Further away Sandau snapped his guard's neck. Two bodies collapsed to the floor. They hauled the fallen guards across the ground and disposed of them in the nearest triple halos, which sprang to life.

Further up the corridor it looked like Diego and Rebekka had just silenced the remaining two guards. Diego stared into the darkness and nodded to Tallin.

A loud crack echoed from the room. Arianna

reached for the door release. Tallin grabbed Arianna's arm, shaking his head before tapping his temple by his eye. She had no idea what he was communicating, but it appeared to be something to do with sight. The waiting was unbearable. She could hear a muffled voice which sounded like Haydan and another male voice that she didn't recognise. Whoever it was, he sounded angry.

Sandau met Tallin's curious expression, dipped his head then moved off to the triple halo and waited. Tallin dropped to the floor, then pulled on Arianna's arm indicating she should do the same. He pressed his hand to the tiled surface. The corridor began glowing as cracks and fissures sprang to life in the walls. She could smell a hint of burning and knew Tallin was gearing up to fight.

The unidentified male who Tallin had named as Magellan said, "On your feet, boy. It's time to go." There was a scuffling sound and Arianna gathered Haydan was being dragged across the floor. She could hear him protesting at his treatment.

A look passed between Tallin and Sandau. The warrior stepped into the nearest triple halo, drawing his weapon as he did so. At the same time, Tallin reached for the door and waved his free hand in invitation to Arianna before throwing it open and vanishing from her sight.

Arianna dived into the room keeping low. Rolling, she came to a halt behind one of the seats and peered around it. Magellan glared across at her and grabbed Haydan's arm, shoving him towards the triple halo in the corner of the room. "Oh, look who it is, your little protector. Too late, warrior."

Haydan stumbled and half fell, half staggered into the triple halo, which didn't work as intended. He remained within it looking as confused as Arianna felt. His right arm appeared to be anchored to the floor and he struggled to lift it.

Magellan scanned the room, his attention focusing on Leylani and the guard, who was stirring. "Deal with the warrior." He clicked his fingers and another guard appeared nearby.

Arianna silently cursed, reached for her smaller knives and darted at the first guard, who ducked around the nearest chair. He grabbed for his weapons. She ran at the chair, slamming her body forwards to topple it onto him before he pulled his blades free. He wasn't fast enough to avoid the downwards swipe. Arianna made sure he wouldn't get back up and was already spinning towards the next guard with her knives out and at the ready.

The second guard struck Arianna as more of a brawler than a fighter. She edged forwards and every time she did, he moved back as though unsure of her. Swinging a fist at her head, he tried to sweep his other fist around and catch her jaw. Arianna dropped her upper body away from his attack and kicked hard and fast for his head. He went down with the momentum and she pounced on him with her blades out making quick work of silencing him for good. She spun around to find Leylani watching her uncertainly. Leylani didn't have weapons out. Arianna holstered one knife but kept the other out.

Tallin arrived in the room from a triple halo on the other side, drawing Magellan's attention away from Arianna and Haydan. "Magellan, what a nasty surprise you are. How's the rash? Is it itchy yet?"

Magellan sneered at Tallin, looking equally formidable. "I was going to channel Haydan's magic

to fix it. I'm growing used to the burning sensation."
Magellan's lips moved as though talking to himself
and his hand slid into the folds of his jacket, perhaps
seeking out a weapon.

Tallin stamped his foot and mist erupted in great
swathes from his neck. It filled the room, wrapping
around the walls and slithering across the floor in all
directions. It reminded Arianna of dry ice as it churned
out, enveloping the space around Tallin and making
him look terrifying. Part of the mist drifted steadily
towards Magellan. "Keep your hands where I can see
them, and enough of your magic and tricks. You have
deceived me for years. You think because I gift you
power that makes me weak?"

A rumble shuddered through the room. Magellan
lowered his hand and glanced upwards as chunks of
ceiling masonry began raining down on him. The mist
Tallin released wrapped around Magellan's legs. He
kicked it away, but it kept returning, each time more
insistently.

"You think your trick in the woods was wise, Tallin?
I will not be branded by you, like some kind of slave or
prisoner. There are others as powerful as I am that hate
you just as much as I do."

Sandau appeared next to Haydan, sliding up from
below as the reason for the new halos in the hallway
became clear. By the look of it they were special routes
into certain rooms within the court, no doubt part of
Tallin's game playing. Sandau grabbed Haydan's arm
and hauled him out of the halo.

"They will also be dealt with. Perhaps I will
indenture those you involved in this. Being slave
to my court might make them rethink their foolish
behaviour." Tallin took a step closer to Magellan,

who stood his ground. "Warriors, keep Haydan away from the triple halo in the corner of this room, do you understand me? Even if it activates, if you reach Haydan before he leaves you can keep him here."

Arianna nodded and moved around the room, keeping a close eye on Leylani.

Magellan grimaced and turned his attention to Sandau, who had crouched side-on to study the issue with Haydan's altera. The snap of Magellan's hand was quick, but that didn't seem to faze Sandau. His hand shot out and the magic that arced towards him disintegrated as it hit an invisible barrier around him and Haydan. He gave Magellan a withering look, his eyes glowing in the darkness.

The incident appeared to unnerve Magellan, who clenched his hand and swung his attention back to Tallin. The muttering began again. Tallin shook his head and the mist swirled around Magellan before smothering him.

Isaac and Lavinia were mingling and socialising. Lavinia burst out laughing and leant in to talk to the pretend king. Isaac was acting the part in a convincing way. Tallin had warned Isaac to keep chatter to a minimum as the more he used Tallin's magic the more it depleted and he would eventually stop sounding like Tallin. The ruse seemed to be working and Isaac looked to be enjoying his game. The man had a natural talent for being the centre of attention.

Rebecca stood at Diego's side as they circulated after dancing. She had angled herself so her arm was wrapped under his and around his back. It was a protective, possessive stance and he smiled as she snuggled in against him. "I know your game, Rebekka. We will talk about it later."

Raising her head, Rebekka rewarded Diego with a forlorn look. "I'm pregnant. It happened when the storms hit."

Another baby; Diego was indeed blessed this cycle in so many ways. When the storms hit, occasionally surprise babies were created. It was a great honour for it to happen to them. "That's wonderful news, Bekka, but stop the games. Stop chasing things that are not your concern. You know exactly what I'm talking about."

Diego kissed Rebekka's forehead. For all her protectiveness, she was what he needed this cycle, but he could not see beyond this lifetime. It would be a while before he returned to the sea; perhaps that would give him some perspective.

Rebekka moved her mouth close to Diego's ear. "I had to know for sure. The baby's the only reason Theander didn't kill me when I asked him directly if he has your chosen one safe. Well, that and Lavinia mentioned Haydan. Why do you never ask about my chosen one?"

"Theander is here?" Storm fall, was his partner crazy? Something tugged at Diego's leg distracting him: the pixie post clambering up his leg and body.

Reaching his shoulder, the creature moved towards his ear. "You should make your way to the upper level," it said.

Diego was reduced to taking orders from a pixie. The only reason he didn't snap at his father's pet was the fact that it was probably to do with Haydan and he should act on it. He pressed his face against Rebekka's hair and said, "We need to get to the top of the stairs. Something is going on. Haydan might be in trouble."

Rebekka moved off, but kept tight hold of Diego's hand and pulled him behind her. She had the same protective instincts as a chosen one did and any mention of harm coming to one of her children activated them.

They reached the top of the stairs and Rebekka snuggled in against Diego, wrapping her arms around his waist as he pushed her into the darkened corridor. Two guards walked towards them in the darkness. He knew they were guards, even though they wore costumes, because they carried weapons discreetly on their back. Tallin and Sandau had just killed two other guards. Diego could see them dragging fallen figures across to the halos. Arianna had taken out a third.

The guards passed them without a second glance. Diego moved fluidly with Rebekka to take both guards down before they were caught. The only sound was the thump as their bodies hit the floor. Diego glanced into the darkness and nodded to Tallin, who walked off.

They dragged the two guards to the nearest halo and Rebekka turned towards Diego, looking flushed from the exertion. "Is Haydan going to be alright? Tallin has this in hand?"

"Yes." Diego pulled Rebekka back out to the top of the stairs to act as lookout. Standing behind her with his arm around her waist, he waited by the balustrades. "Tallin has this and Arianna and Sandau are there." He wanted to be with Tallin but his father's instructions had been clear. When Tallin sent word, he should keep watch on the stairs. There was still the dark god issue to deal with and they could arrive anytime.

Scanning the room, Diego realised something was wrong. Her dress lit up and was distinctive but she was nowhere to be seen, so where the hell was Maya?

Haydan

On his knees by the triple halo, Haydan tried to work out what Leylani had done to his altera. It was surrounded by a molten gold liquid that he could not move. He tried remaining calm, but panic kept ripping apart his thought processes, sending his heartbeat thrumming and his mind into overdrive. What if it couldn't be removed? What if he was stuck like that? He would never be able to bond with Maya.

Sandau placed a calming hand on Haydan's shoulder and dropped down to his side with a serious but relaxed expression on his face. Magellan threw something towards them. Haydan didn't have time to and couldn't react to it. Sandau raised his hand, deflected the magic, growled and glared at Magellan. He let his eyes glow for a moment in warning to the mage, who seemed to take the hint and returned his attention to Tallin.

"It will take time to remove this."

Haydan's breathing was short and shallow. "But it can be removed?"

"By those with the right skills, yes. Do not worry."

Relief flooding his mind, Haydan's heartbeat calmed

from its frantic thrumming. "Thank the gods. I thought
… well." He didn't want to appear weak in front of
Sandau.

Sandau tightened his grip on Haydan's shoulder and
gave him a reassuring smile. "I understand."

Tallin and Magellan were trying to tear each
other apart. The mist Tallin released wasn't working.
It engulfed Magellan for a minute, then Magellan
deflected it, pushing it back to a safe distance. Tallin
swooped low and a pulse of magic ricocheted off the
tiled floor towards Magellan, flinging him backwards
into the wall behind him with a sickening thump. More
of the ceiling masonry fell, bouncing around Haydan as
it landed.

Sandau grabbed Haydan and moved him back
towards the triple halo. It was not the location Haydan
wanted to be after Tallin's warning earlier but they had
no choice. From what he could remember the triple
halo in the corner of the room had a trap contained
within it and if activated with a particular word, Haydan
couldn't remember what that word was, it meant certain
death. Tallin controlled the triple halos but given that
he was using all his energy to fight Magellan, he was not
going to be controlling or concentrating on the halos.

Magellan managed to fling Tallin backwards into
the other wall. Tallin looked even more venomous as
he picked himself up, wiped blood from his mouth
and returned fire. A huge chunk of masonry plunged
towards Magellan. Somehow he managed to slow it
down long enough to move from underneath it before
it smashed into the floor. The room shook from the
impact.

To the side of Haydan, Arianna kept her attention
on Magellan. She edged closer around the chair.

Magellan was so focused on Tallin that he didn't notice her. Arianna's hand slid back around to grab the other blade and she spun both blades so they were gripped in her fists, facing downwards.

"Why do you hate me so much, Magellan? How exactly have I offended you? Are you jealous that I am king?" Wild and untamed, Tallin glared across at Magellan, the mist snapping around him like whips.

"I could just about tolerate you, then I met your son, and what better way to hurt you both than to capture and torment the one person–" Magellan flicked his hand dismissively at Haydan "–you would do anything to protect. Your precious grandson, Diego's precious heir … and I will torment him, Tallin. I'll torment him knowing you and Diego are in a hell of your own making. You will know what it's like to lose someone you care about, like I did. Kesha died whilst pregnant. I lost a wife and a child that day. Your people did not consider her soul, or his, worthy of saving."

"It does not work like that. We do not take souls. They have to be freely given and be worthy." Tallin's scowl deepened. "You targeted Diego and I, why?"

"Diego refused her soul and you bask in the joy of having offspring like him, and before you ask, going after Diego was too easy. I wanted to watch him suffer. Maybe I'll just kill the boy instead. The only reason I didn't snatch him last time was because of that damned mask making an appearance. I had no idea what I was up against."

"So why did you let that other soul go?" Haydan demanded.

Magellan's laugh sent a chill through Haydan's body. "I didn't. I had no intention of releasing any of your souls back to you. She let it go." He glared at Leylani, who cowered in the corner. "But even that worked in my favour. Its damage should be done by now. I broke her, then I put her back together again and made her more beautiful in the process. Now she answers to no one. She has no ties to anyone, no storm rider, no warrior. She's free."

Haydan could barely breathe as he figured out what this news meant for Diego, unless Magellan didn't know Sasha was Diego's chosen one.

"I assume Diego will thank me when he figures it out. Consider it payback for what he did to me. A soul for a soul. At least Sasha's soul has survived."

That answered that question. Magellan sneered at Haydan as Arianna jumped. She moved so fast that Haydan only saw a blur. Sinking her blades into Magellan's shoulders, Arianna let momentum drag them downwards, raking huge, gaping wounds in his back as they both went down.

Arianna stood and wiped her blades down as Magellan shuddered. His body twitched, spasms rippled down his arms and he just managed to slide his fingertips back into the folds of his jacket.

"Stop him!"

Tallin's shout startled everyone. A small glass ball rolled out from inside Magellan's jacket. He wrapped his fingers around it, released a demonic laugh and threw the ball towards Haydan, mouthing something Haydan could not make out. The sphere flashed and blinked as it rolled across to him and everything went into slow motion.

Tallin rushed forwards. Sandau grabbed Haydan's shoulder and tried to push him away along the wall. Realising too late there was a problem, Arianna met Haydan's panicked stare with a questioning, uncertain look. There was a moment of total silence and the innocent glass ball exploded turning everything white.

∾

₥aya

Coldness and fear flooded Maya's mind. Tears poured down her cheeks, mingling with the mask she wore.

"What the hell is wrong with her?"

Maya had no idea who Kai was talking to or how long she had been out cold for. It could have been seconds or hours.

"Her soul has been cut off from Haydan's. This is what happens. That's the least of my problems right now." That sounded like Theander.

"You can tell me later. I have to go. Playing games for a woman is not how I roll, Theander, but this one … this one can push buttons."

"Are you developing an attachment to something other than your fleeting liaisons, library and hammock, Kai?"

Maya could hear the humour in Theander's voice as he sat beside her. The padding moved as he made himself comfortable. The sounds of the party increased, so it was not that late and Kai must have opened the door to leave.

"Not likely, but I have to check her future mate is okay. The things I get myself into … the things I let you get me into."

Theander laughed as the pod closed and silence returned.

"Listening in on other people's conversations is rude whatever realm you are in, Maya."

Maya wiped her eyes, pushed herself upright and rewarded Theander with a glare. "I wasn't listening in, I just happened to wake up at an interesting point. What else is wrong?"

Theander turned away. "I can't discuss that with you." He rubbed his hands against his thighs and looked a million miles away. "Having said that, you have a female perspective on things … Maya, imagine someone captured your soul and tortured you, hurting you in all manner of elaborate ways. Then they took from you your memories, your connections to your past and present, leaving you with only the here and now. What would you do?"

For some reason Maya couldn't breathe properly. Ice settled around her neck, chilling her bones. "What do you mean? What are you talking about? Is this something to do with the soul Haydan found last time we were here? The one he had in his altera?" She remembered the feelings of anger and betrayal that had surfaced inside her when she had detected that soul. They were her strongest and purest emotions to date and she had hated every second of sharing Haydan's soul with another whether he was claiming her as his or not.

"Yes. What would you do, Maya?"

"I'd run to the only thing that made sense to me regardless of the consequences. I'd seek safety."

Theander's face crumpled and he banged his fists against his forehead. "Of course you would. It all makes sense now. Except Diego won't understand."

If nothing else, Theander's odd behaviour distracted Maya from her own problems. She tucked her knees underneath her, resting on her haunches. "I have no idea what you're talking about, but if I can help in any way, let me know."

"Which is who exactly? Who is your point of safety? If you had nowhere else to go, who would you choose to protect you from harm?" Theander glared at her with his brows furrowed behind his mask. He resembled a formidable beast, one that was about to go hunting. "You're a lost soul and you suddenly escape the sea. You have no idea who you are or what to do. If it was you, where would you go?"

Haydan, Isaac? What about Alex? No, he wasn't a point of safety for Maya. Alex was controlling. Alex was needy and distracting – a friend, but Haydan? Haydan was her safety and so was Isaac. Isaac didn't have a soul, she couldn't choose him, but they both offered her a security that no other did. "Haydan, or Isaac," Maya said. "I know Isaac doesn't have a physical soul as such, but he's also a safe spot."

Theander released a cry of pain, like a wounded animal, and pressed his fist against his mouth. "I didn't see this. I can't predict the anomalies. If you had no one else and Haydan was with another woman would you still go to him, knowing that?"

"If there was nowhere else to go?"

Theander nodded, the feathers on his mask bouncing as he did so. "If you had nowhere else to go and that was the only place, would you go?"

"Yes, without hesitation."

Theander slammed his fists down on the padded floor. "Falling angels and dancing devils." He erupted into a further explosion of curses.

"What are you trying to say, Theander? Are you trying to say that Rebekka…?" That was a real head mess for Diego for sure. Theander had to be referring to Diego's chosen one. "Oh no, surely not, that's cruel."

Theander's expression remained pained. "I didn't check after the storms, but her soul would have already gone by then, so now Rebekka is pregnant." He appeared to be talking to himself. "The sea I keep links to the one on Storm Lands. That goes no further, is that clear? I control the link, or at least I thought I did, but then maybe Storm Lands intervened to release a distressed soul. What do I do? Diego will have to be told at some point. Better that I tell him than him finding out for himself. His world will be reeling. I was meant to keep her safe. I try to help, but end up making it ten times worse."

"It's not your fault, Theander."

Theander still looked distraught. "I should stop interfering. I should walk away, but I can't. That is what Kai would do. Now I understand why, the guilt…"

"You are not Kai. Kai is the loneliest figure I have ever met. Do you want me to talk to Diego?" Diego frightened Maya with his flares of anger and his mood swings. She often antagonised him with her cheekiness and belligerence, but she would not be intimidated by him and it made sense for her to tell him, especially given the nature of her unusual relationship with Haydan. Perhaps Diego would come to understand her a little more than he did if she explained to him the reason why it had happened. Accepting that his former chosen one was now going to be his daughter, however, would be a totally different matter.

"I should tell him," Theander said. He didn't sound overly convinced.

"He will want to kill you before he lets you explain or understands."

"I can't say I blame him."

"Let me talk to him. I'm chosen one. It will be easier if it comes from me," Maya said, before adding, "It's good to know you care so much."

Theander smiled bitterly and turned his head to study her. "You know, every time you evolve I find you fascinating, yet I am told evolution is a bad thing. How can it be a bad thing when you look so innocent and speak such sense?"

Maya had no idea what Theander was talking about. She scratched at her neck, which felt like a block of ice. Something was wrong with her link to Haydan. It left her with a sense of abandonment. "What's taking Kai so long?" She needed Haydan back. The waiting was driving her crazy. "Why is my neck so cold? Why am I so cold?"

Theander's expression didn't fill Maya with much reassurance. He scowled and leant in. "Because this is what happens when you don't protect your storm rider as you're supposed to. He's cut off from you. Alone. Are you missing him yet, chosen one?"

Thoughts of never seeing Haydan again skittered through Maya's mind, leaving a sense of dread in their wake as desolation wrapped around her soul. She had to reach him. She had to tell him how much he mattered to her and start opening up to him more. He was her whole world and regardless of what he thought, that was never going to change.

Chapter 34

Isaac

Isaac smiled politely at another drunken courtier with too many demands to place on the king and fidgeted. Pretending to be in love with Lavinia was hard work. At first the pretence had been fun, but now he wanted to move away from all the scheming which seemed to ooze off everyone in Tallin's court and focus on the woman he adored. As expected, Tallin had abandoned Katherine earlier. She had been talking to Si, who looked as though he was having a fabulous evening, much more so than Isaac.

Isaac scanned the crowds and a gap opened as a group of cackling women moved off. He caught sight of Katherine in profile and his breath faltered. She seemed as bored as he was. She checked on the baby, smiled at Si and searched the room. She became aware of Isaac's intense stare resting on her. Her eyes met his, her lips curled upwards and she lowered her gaze. The fact he still had that effect on her even after eight years of marriage made him grin like a fool.

Lavinia jabbed her elbow into Isaac's arm. "Well, Tallin, what do you think?"

A light cough drew Isaac's attention to a male who had barged into the space beside him. He moved with a certain amount of swagger and Isaac had noticed the man staring at Katherine earlier. In Isaac's experience, the man was either wealthy and obnoxious, or wealthy and overconfident, but most definitely used to getting his own way. In either case, he didn't like the man even if his face was mostly concealed behind a fox's mask and headdress. A fox was close enough to a wolf to annoy Tallin. The subtle goading amused Isaac, whilst also irking him. Tallin didn't have things easy.

"My Lord, I was hoping for the honour of being permitted to dance with your lovely *wife* when the music improves."

His arrogant little smirk confirmed the man was an obnoxious little skunk. Isaac's hackles rose as he stared at the man. The tone he used suggested the word 'wife' was a dig of some sort at Tallin, as though implying Lavinia wasn't really his wife at all. In fact, Tallin and Lavinia were not married in the traditional sense. Lavinia rested her hand on one of Isaac's arms, which he had crossed without even realising.

Lavinia leant in and lowered her voice to a discreet whisper. "Play nice, darling. I know Milo Balcarres is not your preference, but since he knows how to dance, perhaps you would permit the request to pass with your approval."

Lavinia batted her eyes a few times as Isaac's attention flitted from her to Balcarres. Tallin hated the man. The feeling was mutual. There was a smug, self-assured cockiness about him that made Isaac want to punch his lights out ... or maybe the man was a little too perfect; either way Isaac was siding with Tallin.

Isaac inhaled and pushed his shoulders back to

make himself look more imposing. Lavinia reached into his pocket and pulled the gloves free. "Please, I do enjoy this bit." She leant right in and whispered loud enough for others around them to hear. "I'll make it up to you later."

Isaac suppressed a shudder and locked stares with Milo, who apparently had a knack for terrorising Tallin's staff on a regular basis. "He had better keep his hands to himself." That applied to Katherine as well.

The edge of Milo's mouth twitched, but his eyes told a darker, more sinister story. "I always do, My Lord. Thank you."

Had Isaac just given his approval? He was certain he hadn't, but that didn't seem to faze Balcarres, who held out his hand to Lavinia with unnecessary flamboyance. "My Lady, would you like to dance The Vanquish?"

Lavinia reached behind her and fastened up the train on her dress, before pulling up the front part of her dress so that her legs were on show and less restricted. Isaac inhaled and his face flushed. The display was unbecoming in public, so how Tallin permitted it he did not know. She slid on the gloves with a flourish and took Balcarres' hand, letting him lead her across to the dance floor.

Of course, if Lavinia was dancing with Balcarres, then Isaac was dancing with Katherine. She was already passing the baby to Si to hold. His evening was improving.

঱৽

*A*rianna

The explosion of light proved an unexpected, nasty surprise. Magellan's parting shot threw all of them off their feet, Tallin included. He had been by Arianna when the ball detonated, but the blast had launched him further away. The air in the room shuddered.

"Haydan! Sandau!"

Tallin's shout warned Arianna that the men were still in danger. Haydan was being pulled towards the halo in the corner. Sandau appeared to be caught in it too. Neither of them seemed to be able to stop themselves. With nothing to grab hold of they were both dragged closer. Arianna rushed across and threw herself to the floor with her arms out. The momentum carried her across the polished floor and she managed to seize hold of Haydan's outstretched hand and the underside of Sandau's knife holster on his back as he slid past. The problem was Sandau and Haydan didn't stop moving. She was going to have to take the burden of both of them as they fell into the trap in the halo and Haydan was carrying extra bulk around his altera. Magellan had probably activated the trap before dying. This was the fallout.

The pain as they both dropped like lead weights was unbearable. Arianna grimaced and regretted grabbing the strap of Sandau's sword carrier. Her fingers burned. Sandau had wrapped his arms around Arianna's neck and shoulder, which gave her a small amount of respite, but he was a big man and the downward pull of his body hurt. Haydan captured her arm with his spare hand, which was something they had covered in training and she was grateful now for all the times Teeam had insisted they practise the fall hold.

The magic Magellan had used was strong. Arianna had been taught that magic use eventually subsided, but its potency was based on a number of factors, such as the skill of the wielder and the time and effort put into the creation of the magic. She could still feel the relentless pull of the magic, which showed no sign of easing, and she had no idea how much longer she could hold on for.

Leylani landed beside Arianna and extended her hands to help hold Haydan. For a moment Arianna feared she had come to help finish off what Magellan had started. "No, stay back."

"I'm not going to watch Haydan die. The magic isn't designed to affect females. Magellan's never seen women as worthy. It'll wear off in a moment."

The magic did begin to ease off. The constant draw of air abated. "Tallin, help. Get Sandau." Arianna was finding his weight unbearable and he was pulling her towards the drop as well. Tallin rushed across and helped pull Sandau out first.

Sandau cleared the halo and crawled around to haul Haydan out. He grabbed Haydan's top and dragged him up to safety, landing him on the floor nearby.

Haydan collapsed on the floor, his breathing heavy. Tallin remained focused on Leylani. "You will never breathe free air again after this stunt. I trusted you. I believed everyone mistaken."

Leylani shrank back looking terrified. "I'm sorry, he made me do it. You have no idea what it's been like being married to that. After losing his wife and child all those years ago, he turned to drink and violence. He is a hollow shell of the man he perhaps once was."

"It's not Leylani's fault, Tallin. Leave her alone. You saw the way Magellan treated her and she's just helped me." Haydan sat up and glared down at the surround on his altera, which still looked too heavy for his arm. "That wolf that you're connected to, it saw everything. He hit both of us, so I can appreciate how terrified Leylani must have been. You would be surprised what someone beaten and mistreated is capable of doing in the name of fear."

"Speaking from experience, Haydan?" Tallin's look was sharp. He stepped across and dropped down to examine the altera. "You put this infernal device on him. Do you know how to remove it?"

Tearful and looking more than a little wary of Tallin, Leylani slid her hand over the metal that surrounded Haydan's altera. A few incantations later it slipped off his altera and along her arm, settling back into a piece of serpentlike jewellery around her neck.

Haydan appeared to be relieved at the release of his altera. He pulled his arm against his front and ran his fingertips across it a few times as though checking it was all right.

"No, you are not keeping that." Tallin held out his hand to Leylani.

Leylani took off the necklace and passed it across to Tallin. "That was the only time he gave me anything nice. Then I discovered what it did and that the only reason he gave it to me was to capture you." She gave Haydan a forlorn look. "I am sorry."

Tallin huffed and moved across to the broken body of Magellan. "Sandau, would you be good enough to escort Leylani to my guards and have her locked up. I need to decide how I deal with her and until I do…" He lowered himself down and lifted Magellan's mask up before inhaling softly through his teeth. "Yes, I can see how that would make you irritable, you pathetic excuse for an elf. It seems Magellan was one of the woodland lurkers who encountered my magic. That's why he has been absent from court."

Tallin's magic had left Magellan's gaunt face disfigured. Dark stains ran from his eye to the edge of his jaw.

Haydan winced and looked away. "Tallin, you should let Leylani go…" Haydan fell silent, focusing his attention on the ring on his finger. It had turned almost jet black.

Haydan was not leaving Arianna's sight, not now. Tallin followed Haydan's stare and straightened up. "Suffering pixies, that's all I need right now." He glanced around at them all. "Get yourselves ready, trouble has arrived."

Maya

There was no sign of Kai, and Maya was not going to be hidden away all night. The cold, icy feeling lifted from her neck, calmness washed over her and she breathed a sigh of relief as she began moving to the exit. Whatever danger Haydan had been in, it had passed.

Theander sprang to his feet. "Where do you think

you're going?"

"I feel much better and since I'm with you, you may as well chaperone me back to the hall. I'm sure now Haydan is okay he will come and find me," Maya said. The earlier episode was caused through their connection. Something had happened to him. She was well again, so he was out of danger.

"Kai left us here for a reason." Theander sounded surprisingly dull for once.

"Really? It's a ball and you want me to hide in here? Not likely. Kai has probably forgotten, or been distracted by one of his fleeting liaisons." With a smirk of delight at her new game of discovering how protective Theander was prepared to be, Maya continued her escape, forcing him to follow. He grumbled as she left, clearly unhappy at her diversion.

Maya returned to the main hall to a bizarre display. The music had changed to a more flowing, lively tune. The flutes, drums and string instruments were out and Lavinia was on the dance floor with a fox, a surprisingly capable dancing fox who knew how to use his body to full effect. Tallin was dancing with Katherine, and to say that they were causing a stir was an understatement. The dancing was a combination of graceful elegance and smooth internalised movement rather like salsa dancing. Lavinia and Katherine would break off every now and again and dance solo in a style that reminded Maya of Egyptian dancing. It was a riveting display and she wanted to join in. She had always enjoyed the fluid style of dancing.

Haydan had disappeared and any contact she had with Theander's skin would drive him crazy. This was one way to grab his attention back. Wondering if Theander would play along, she took a deep breath.

"Do you know how to dance?"

Theander's grin of amusement vanished as he stared at her, looking horrified. "Oh no, no way. Haydan will be after my head for a stunt like this."

"I like to dance, come and join me. You're not a very good chaperone if you don't."

Theander rewarded her with a murderous look. She slipped her arm through his and pulled him towards the dance floor as she slid her gloves off. "We have an audience, and he'll get over it." She quickly released Theander's arm as the familiar, woozy, uncomfortable sensations assaulted her. Perhaps the more she was in contact with others, the more that feeling would wear off.

Theander didn't have a problem with moving on the dance floor either. He kept up with Maya and made up his own moves when she separated off and freestyled. The gathered crowd appeared to be enjoying the display. Maya caught a warning look from Si as she gyrated. Holding the baby, he made a cutting motion with his index finger across his throat, leaving her with the uncomfortable thought that he was warning her Haydan would be livid. He probably would be, but he had abandoned her for a good hour or so.

When Maya didn't respond further, Si mouthed 'Haydan won't like it' to her. It was an odd warning from a man who never concerned himself with understanding the strange relationship she shared with Haydan. Clearly his protectiveness of her overrode all other priorities and he comprehended their relationship far more than he ever let on. She shrugged and ignored him.

On the stairs Isaac moved into view. He spoke to one of the king's guards and scanned the hall. The guard rushed off. Something was happening. Haydan followed Isaac, his gaze locked with Maya's. She could detect Haydan's eyes on her even at a distance with his face hidden by his mask. Disapproval rolled off him as he stared across at her, his attention not leaving her. The icy feeling around Maya's neck earlier confirmed Haydan had been in danger. If that was the case, Isaac would not have been able to help him, only Tallin.

Haydan's mask had been spoilt. The finish wasn't as pristine as earlier and one of his wolf ears looked deformed, but other than that he seemed to be physically unharmed. Maya's heart sank as she fixed her forlorn gaze onto him wondering what had happened and if he was indeed okay. A small headshake from him indicated either disapproval of her dancing or that she was to stay put and not try to reach him. She discreetly slid her gloves back on, not wishing to irritate him any further.

Isaac didn't seem concerned by Katherine dancing with Tallin, but he shot daggers at Lavinia cavorting with the dancing fox. A tiny voice in Maya's subconscious told her that Isaac at the top of the stairs in the lizard attire wasn't Isaac.

Arianna flanked Haydan and remained there, alert to everything around her. She was no longer hiding in Haydan's shadow; there was significance in her bold stance at his side.

Sandau spoke to Diego and Rebekka. Maya hadn't noticed them at the top of the stairs. Diego straightened up and watched Isaac descend the stairs. Mist released from Isaac's neck as he moved. The man who appeared to be Isaac was Tallin, which meant the Tallin dancing with Katherine was actually Isaac. They had swapped identities so that Tallin could move freely through his own court for the evening.

That was clever.

Maya's moment of admiration for Tallin's stunt was short-lived. There was a flash of colour to her side and Kai walked across the room, straight up to Theander. He leant in and said something to Theander that she could not make out, but she did hear, "You might want to warn Maya's family."

Theander pulled a long, flowing piece of material out of his pocket and dragged it around Maya's shoulders. The material was lightweight and warm. He walked across and tapped the Isaac who looked like Tallin on the shoulder. "Get ready for the darkness."

It was happening; the dark gods were about to arrive. The hall shuddered. The huge antler chandeliers suspended from the ceilings and draped with lights and crystals shook, releasing an eerie tinkling noise. The music tailed off. A few murmurs of surprise released from the back of the room as dark mist began creeping in through the doorways. No one moved, the guests no doubt thinking this was all part of Tallin's usual theatrics. All the creatures that were on the loose in the hall stopped moving and Maya held her breath, a feeling of dread engulfing her.

The air filled with a low, sinister growling noise and the mist melted into figures, the darkness only receding from them once they had fully taken form. Each one had a snarling, ferocious-looking beast by their feet.

A man appeared on the staircase a few steps down from Tallin. He lowered his head and inky black strands of hair fell over his face. "A masked ball, how ironic." He scanned the room. "Someone had better tell me where the mask that I am looking for is, or you will all die. Where is the king?"

Silence descended, the atmosphere tense. A few of the courtiers stared at who they believed to be Tallin and a slow clap broke out from the staircase, diverting everyone's attention back towards the sinister new arrival.

"That all depends on which king you are talking about," Tallin who looked like Isaac said. "You will have to be more specific as you have a couple to choose from, so who do you want?"

Maya met Haydan's stare and took a deep breath in. Tallin's magic was building around her, its presence a comforting reminder of his abilities and the reason for his choice of location. She had to place her faith in him and believe this was a battle the fae king could win. Theander's warm fingers around her arm reminded her that the battle was not being fought alone, but there would be no understanding or compassion from the darkness for any of them.

Chapter 35

Haydan

The dark god standing on the stairs with them looked ready to start a war. His intense, dark stare clashed with Tallin's and his lips thinned further.

Being so close to Tallin and under the scrutiny of a dark god was uncomfortable. A certain amount of tension emanated from the king and Haydan's ears kept popping as though the air pressure was shifting around them.

Tallin's diversion gave Theander time to switch back from Isaac's to Maya's side. Katherine edged closer to Si and the baby. Haydan was less concerned about everyone else; they could handle themselves. The exception was Isaac, but he was certain Isaac could move quick if he needed to.

"Who do I want?" the dark god said. He assessed Tallin, his eyes travelling slowly across his attire. "You are not the king." His tone dismissive, his attention moved to Haydan. "You are more likely to be the king, although you look a little the worse for wear, but there are two other wolves in the room and the wolves like their games." His eyes narrowed and he glanced at Diego, then Isaac before returning his attention to Tallin, peering up at him with a menacing expression on his face.

The dark god wore black. The shoulders and chest plate of his outfit were formed from what looked like a liquid metal. Perhaps intended to denote rank, the metallic sections were in a constant state of flux as though they couldn't quite take form, reminding Haydan of Tallin's reason for choosing the summer court. It interfered with dark magic and its ability to work correctly. The dark gods were going to be in for a shock when Tallin made his presence felt. He gave a wry smile. Entering the court of a master game-player came at a price and Tallin was an expert games master.

"I want to know where the king of this realm is. Then I want to know where the mask of my people is and who its master is. Do I detect other darkness in the court as well?" The dark god raised an eyebrow. "That's interesting." He scanned the room and settled his attention on Maya, who stepped behind Theander.

After resting his eyes on Maya a second longer than Haydan was comfortable with, he continued to track the room. "So, I repeat my question one final time." He turned to address the room. "Who is the king of this realm and where is he? You have five minutes to find him before the blood starts to spill, and I do hate making magical things bleed…" Once again, his eyes conveyed a contradictory message. "Five minutes, the clock is ticking."

He slid another discreet glance towards Maya, confirming Haydan's worst fears, before dropping back into the smoke and sweeping out of the room. The doors slammed shut behind them and the sound of other doors closing echoed throughout the court.

Everybody turned towards Isaac and waited for him to speak. Isaac looked like a naughty schoolchild as he lowered his head, met Tallin's eyes and said, "King Tallin, this is way beyond my pay grade, so I think you can have your identity back now."

❧

Arianna

Tallin descended to the ballroom floor. Diego rushed past Arianna and blocked his way, the expression on his face wary.

"There are twenty of them," Tallin said. He spoke to Diego, but loudly enough so others could hear. The mist released from his neck. It swirled and drifted in continuous plumes. "No one can leave the court, as in exit the building. They have sentries at every route out. They will kill anyone who tries to leave. Consider this a big game of kiss chase, except the outcome, if anyone gets caught, will not be a happy one."

Tallin addressed the room. "I chose this location for a reason. Have faith in your king, I do not intend to let you down. For now, no one can leave."

The thrum of angry voices indicated the inevitable unrest from his court. Tallin raised his arms in a pacifying motion. "You have all witnessed the magic within these walls, but tonight we hunt dark gods."

"We can't kill dark gods," the mocking voice of a courtier announced to the room.

"No," Tallin said, "but you play games and fight as well as they do. You cannot kill them, but you can make them hurt. They can be caught and do not forget my guards are here too. I just need a bit of time and the dark gods will finally understand that they are too late to stop what has already begun." Tallin glanced at Haydan, who nodded his understanding.

Perhaps aware of Arianna's eyes burning into him, Haydan stared out across the hall. *I need to get to Storm Lands and claim the third kingdom. There is a halo in Maya's bedroom that links to one near the portal.*

You know where you're going on Storm Lands to lay claim?

You know it too. It was where you found me when I was younger.

Of course – the flecky beast. It injured Haydan when he was a child. Lavinia had saved him by throwing magic at him. She had come to Earth to find Arianna looking beside herself over Haydan's disappearance. Via their connection, Arianna had found him in a strange abandoned hall. That incident had disturbed him. He would never talk about it. Even now he looked uncertain at the prospect of returning. Or perhaps he felt uncomfortable laying claim to their homeland. That was the more likely scenario.

Maya is coming with us. She is in danger. That is the only exception to her entering Storm Lands unbonded.

"We need to spread out," Tallin announced. He moved up the staircase. Sandau slipped past on the bannister and jumped off at the end, falling into line behind Diego, who moved through the crowd to take up a position on the staircase at the far end. The crowds parted as he swept past.

Haydan opted for the balcony overlooking the hall, halfway between the two staircases. Arianna followed him. Maya appeared to be with another male, who exuded a powerful aura, but Haydan didn't seem to have an issue with that. A cape sat around Maya's shoulders. For a moment she felt certain that the cloak moved, or had she imagined that? She assumed Haydan knew the male in question and wondered if it could be one of his friends. He had a few in other realms and, of course, there was the mysterious Theander, whom she had never met.

Si passed the baby back to Katherine and moved her closer to one of the halos. Isaac looked like a tiger waiting to be released for hunting season. He paced, his expression intense and focused.

Rebekka and Lavinia had moved to stand closer together and back to back. The brief display of female bonding brought a flash of humour to the moment. Given that they hated each other, it was funny that they chose to defend each other. It was also interesting to note that Lavinia was closer to Tallin's end of the hall and Rebekka to Diego's.

The doors banged open and a gasp went up from everyone gathered as the dark gods returned. The male from earlier took up his position on the stairs below Tallin, with his hellhound at his feet. Other dark gods stood near each doorway and hallway.

"So, are you going to answer my question?"

"I am King Tallin," Tallin said. He looked unconcerned by the presence of so many dark gods.

The dark god pursed his lips and assessed Tallin. "You are not dressed like the king. Is this a game of some sort? Games with me are *very* unwise." He emphasised 'very' as if to make sure his meaning was understood. His menacing eyes scanned the room, settling on Diego, Haydan and Isaac in a move clearly intended to convey his awareness of all the wolves in the room.

Mist exploded out from Tallin's neck. "Given that I like games, I just changed the rules about royal dress codes. I like to keep everyone on their toes."

The dark god looked bemused. "Are you not going to formally welcome us to your realm, King Tallin?"

"No, Iskar, I am not going to formally welcome you. Your very presence here offends me," Tallin said.

Iskar smirked. "So, I have the king of the realm. Now, where is the mask of my people? I want that item and I want the one who wields its power. I want them on their knees pledging allegiance to me, or they will die a martyr to their cause."

Tallin folded his arm across his front and tapped his palm against his elbow looking agitated. "I have no idea what you mean. What mask of your people are you talking about?"

An ominous smile glided across Iskar's face. "The mask of the gods. Don't play this game with me. I will wipe out every generation of your family in front of your eyes if you do not give me what I seek."

Haydan rubbed his hand against his jaw. Arianna glanced across as he reached up and dragged the wolf mask off his face by the ear. His other fingers hooked around the edge of Kaleshar and he pulled the mask free. He hooked his fingers through the eye holes on the mask and leant across the balcony.

"You must mean this one," Haydan said.

"No. I don't think he means that one. I think he's talking about this one," Diego said. Diego held up the exact same mask as the one Haydan had.

Isaac erupted into laughter. "Well, how does that work?" He pulled his wolf mask off and unhooked his mask in the same manner as Haydan. "Did we all get one?"

"You again," Iskar said, spitting the words out as though even the sight of Isaac offended him.

"Afraid so." Isaac settled an amused, playful look on Iskar. How typical of Arianna's father to goad the dark god.

Maya tutted loudly, distracting Iskar. A vein throbbed in his forehead as he turned his attention to her.

"Boys, you know I can't let you have all the fun." She threw her feathered creation off her face. "I mean, if everybody else has a mask, well, I want one too." She pulled her mask off with one hand in an elegant sweep that suggested she had practised the move to perfection. Her mouth fell open and she gazed down in mock surprise at what she had found. "Oh look, lucky me." She fixed a sassy stare on Iskar, who clenched his jaw and fists. He looked ready to tear someone apart.

Arianna slow clapped and leant over the balcony, resting her arms by Haydan's on the edge. She pointed at Maya. "Oh no, you're not outdoing me, lady. I rock this look." She threw her feathered mask into the crowd below. Pulling the mask from her skin with a flourish, she captured it in her open palm. "It would appear you have a problem, Iskar." Arianna passed her mask to Haydan. Playing along, Haydan let her take his from his hand and swap them. "It seems it's not only Tallin who likes to play games."

Tallin coughed. "Well, now that you mention it, I have got this in my pocket." He produced his version of the mask and held it up, before flicking it with his finger. It made a beautiful tinging sound. Tallin shrugged. "I guess this means I am playing too. I like new games – the rules are so open to interpretation."

Iskar growled, the sound echoing around the hall.

One of the other dark gods, a female with long, almost white-blonde hair burst out laughing. "I vote we kill them all."

"No." Iskar surveyed the room as if deliberating his next move. Frustration pulled at his face. "I want the mask wielders alive. Catch them and bring them to me, along with anyone out there who is leverage. They have partners. Find them. Hurt them. I get to kill them, no one else does that. The rest of them–" he cast a disgruntled glance around the room "–are fair game." He inhaled a deep breath and chuckled, the sound coarse and vulgar. "I can still smell a new darkness." His eyes narrowed. "A vulnerable darkness … one in need of corruption. One that likes these games, but is currently shrouded in light. Come to me and I can offer you so much more than the light."

He was talking about Maya. Arianna knew as she watched Maya shrink back behind the man in the brightly coloured outfit that Iskar was after Maya. His eyes tracked the room again, staying a second or two longer on Maya than anyone else.

Arianna hadn't thought her evening could get any worse but now it had. Iskar knew. That was a new problem, one none of them had seen coming. Now they not only had the mask problem, but they had a dark god on the prowl for Maya because of her unusual heritage and Haydan appeared oblivious.

Iskar released a haunting, eerie howl of delight, his eyes taking on a sinister glint. "It's hunting time, mask bearers. Better run and hide." His gaze locked back on Maya's before he turned and lunged for Tallin.

&❧

Maya

Iskar's invitation sent a shiver coursing down Maya's neck. Grateful she had put her gloves back on, she rubbed her left hand. Her skin would be the same colour as her glove, she felt certain of that.

His threat issued, Iskar charged for Tallin. Tallin sidestepped him with the agility of a mountain goat and kicked the approaching hellhound in the head. Iskar crashed into the staircase and the hound rolled down the stairs. By the time Iskar and his furry friend had rounded on Tallin, he had already dived into the nearest halo and vanished.

Pandemonium broke out around Maya, and she lost sight of Iskar in the bedlam.

Guards rushed in. Si dragged her mother and the baby into the nearest halo. They disappeared. Isaac ducked as a goblet sailed overhead then he checked on Maya. His route to the halo was cut off as a dark god took on a number of the gathered courtiers.

Close by, another dark god struggled to fully materialise. He darted past as part man, part smoke and it didn't look as though it was deliberate, judging by the look of frustration on his face. Surrounded by light magic it appeared some of Iskar's party were already feeling the effects.

"Protect Isaac," Maya said. "Kai's behind me," she added as Theander hesitated, probably more concerned for her safety than anything else.

Kai grabbed Maya's arm as Theander ducked low.

Theander kicked a dark god's feet from underneath him as he rushed to Isaac's side. The unfortunate god landed face first into the back of a group of indignant revellers, who turned on him with all the intensity of a drunken mob in the midst of a brawl.

An arrow skewered a nearby hound with a hard thunk. Kai floored another dark mass of writhing smoke with a swift punch to its stomach. The woman he hit flew across the room into the wall with a loud thump. Hauled into the nearest halo, Maya didn't have time to consider her options.

"You just hit a woman."

Snarling as though possessed, Kai said, "She's trying to kill me, so yes, she's fair game. I've already told you the darkness destroys everything it touches. It doesn't play nice."

The halo landed them on the upper level of the hall. "Move, Maya." Kai grabbed her arm, dragging her towards another halo at the end of the balcony area. The route was blocked by more courtiers fighting with a dark god who had part materialised. Pulling chunks of dark smoke away from him in massive swathes, they cackled and hollered in delight. One of them smashed a tray of goblets on his head. Kai changed his route and veered off, steering Maya into one of the corridors. Halfway along he shoved her into another halo.

They emerged nearer the entrance hall. Kai glanced around and raised his hand, indicating Maya should wait.

"I need to get to Haydan," Maya whispered.

"Yes, but I have to find Haydan first," Kai said. He pulled Maya towards a nearby room, opened the door and peered inside. "Hide in here, under the desk. Do you have a weapon?"

That was a ridiculous question, which made a lot of sense. "No, I haven't got a weapon. That would be useful."

Kai reached behind him and passed an ornate blade to Maya with a nasty-looking serrated edge. "Maya, meet Devil's Curse. A slash to an attacker's body from this and any magic within their system temporarily shuts down. You have about a minute from contact with it before it reactivates. Keep in mind you are unlikely to kill much with it. Oh, and the hellhounds will be livid once they come around from a swipe with that. Get away as fast as you can."

"Right, I can do that." Maya pushed the blade into the loop on the back of her dress that held up her skirts. The cape tickled her hand. She gave a chuckle of amusement but it was cut short.

"Why does Theander keep gifting you things? Haydan won't like it." Kai grabbed a handful of the cape in his left hand and studied it. The fabric fondled his wrist. Kai released it in surprise. "Keep quiet in here. That cloak is activated by light magic. It moves you short distances and is especially active around light magic." Kai spun around.

"Hang on, where are you going? Why can't I come?"

"To find Haydan," Kai said. He looked exasperated with Maya. "You will slow me down. Plus, Iskar noticed you ... more than once. He is curious about you. He will be searching for you. Only run if attacked first. I will come and find you. Do you understand?"

"Yes." Maya nodded.

"Do not get caught."

There was a note of finality about Kai's statement. Before Maya could say anything else he made for the door, which closed softly behind him.

The silence once Kai left felt suffocating. Maya's mind swept into overdrive, imagining things happening elsewhere in the summer court as she hid under the desk. Reliant on just her hearing, she became aware of all manner of new noises, as though things were scuttling about. Her breathing sounded so loud she was certain half the court could hear it. Si was with her mother and the baby. Haydan and Arianna had made themselves targets, as had Isaac. What would happen if they got caught? That didn't bear thinking about and all whilst she was stuck under a desk, cowering like a small child.

Things were creeping in the silence again. Pawing and whining at the door broke the illusion that Maya had imagined the sounds. The door clicked open. One of the hellhounds entered the room with a low snarl as it searched.

Her blood pulsed in her ears, making a soft whooshing noise. Maya tightened her fingers around her blade and pulled it free of its fastening.

Chapter 36

Haydan

Kaleshar clung to the contours of Haydan's face, basking in his moment of glory as Haydan slid the real mask back on. He had swapped the main mask with Arianna earlier and just as well, too, otherwise she might not have been able to save Sandau and him when Magellan attacked them. Holding her hand as he hung over the pit full of jagged metal edges pointed at the sky, waiting for him or Sandau to drop, had been a stark reminder of why she was such a strong warrior. He had chosen her for a reason.

Tallin dived for the nearest halo as Iskar tried to grab him on the stairs and Haydan reminded himself of Tallin's carefully orchestrated plan, which involved them all splitting up. The main battles would not be fought in the great hall; that's why Tallin hadn't concentrated his magic there.

Twice that evening Iskar had been drawn to Maya. She was with Theander, but that didn't guarantee her safety. Haydan had to reach her and get to the throne room on Storm Lands as fast as he could. The thought of abandoning everyone to their fate didn't sit well with him, but he could only see off the dark gods with a show of strength if he took the third kingdom in the chain and returned.

Arianna grabbed Haydan's arm and pulled him away from the balustrade. Iskar had focused on the nearest masks and the two of them.

"Better run, boy. I can smell your fear from here," Iskar said as he rushed up the stairs.

Arianna pushed Haydan into the nearest halo and followed close behind. Arriving on one of the lower levels, they both ran towards the end of the corridor and turned the corner to find their route blocked by a whip-wielding dark god with dirty blond hair tied up in a top knot and a scar running down his cheek.

"Oh look, two mask wielders, lucky me."

He cracked the whip at Haydan, narrowly missing his body. The air shifted around Haydan as the snakelike magic creation shot past him. The tip of the whip, which looked like possessed leather because it was so slippery, slithered to the floor. Arianna pounced before the dark god had a chance to withdraw the whip and try again. She jumped on the end of the whip using both her feet as though she was surfing.

The dark god yanked on the handle twice, trying to wrench it free. Arianna ran along the whip towards the god and distracted him with a devious smile. "Well, hi there, gorgeous."

His rapid blink of surprise gained him two punches in the face, followed by two hard knee strikes to his stomach. He doubled over and Arianna reached for her blades, grabbed them and sank them into his back. The god vanished in a blast of dark smoke which dived off up the hallway.

Arianna watched it go, but it turned back at the end

of the corridor and joined with another ball of smoke. Spinning towards Haydan with a fierce expression on her face, Arianna pushed up from her crouching position. "Middle halo, now."

That contained a trap. Haydan turned and fled towards the halo trying to remember how the trap worked. Smoke wrapped around his foot, pulling it from under him. He landed heavily on his shoulder on the floor. Pain lanced down his arm and he continued sliding into the halo on his side. The god part materialised. His ghostly half mist, half skin hand gripped Haydan's ankle. Haydan kicked out to free himself of the dark god's hold. If he was still attached they would end up trapped together. A quick glance confirmed Arianna had made her halo safely.

Remember to identify yourself and shout out who he is as well.

Of course, this trap was voice activated. "Haydan – dark god." The darkness that had followed him into the trap vanished into a hole in the floor that opened near Haydan's feet and he heard the trap slam shut and a loud curse from the god.

Still on his side momentum carried Haydan out of the halo and he sprang to his feet as Arianna did the same. They were now up a level, near the main staircase. A low growl alerted them to the hellhound with glowing red eyes that had reached the top of the stairs. Its drool dripped onto the polished floor.

"Storm alive, I had forgotten about those things," Haydan said.

The hound padded onto the landing. Its paws tapped on the polished floor.

"We've found another mask bearer." A woman's voice broke the silence and the blonde-haired female god appeared on the stairs. "Ooh look, I've found the handsome one and his warrior bitch," she said. Looking smug and satisfied with her achievement, she took a step onto the landing. "There's a name for women like you, sweetheart – the other woman. I don't know how you put up with your status. You get to die for him, but you don't get to love him." She gave Haydan a lewd look. "Or maybe that's just what you want us to think."

Arianna turned side-on to check the corridor behind them. She turned back, making brief eye contact with Haydan first. "Maybe we wanted you to find us, bitch." Replicating the smug smirk on the blonde god's face, Arianna grinned in delight as the woman's face fell. "Besides, I prefer being in charge of who I love in this form, thanks very much." Arianna moved her arm out as she edged Haydan back down the corridor.

The blonde god started striding towards them. Arianna turned with Haydan and fled to the nearest halo. This one would split them, sending Arianna one way and Haydan another. None of this was getting him any closer to Maya and he had no idea where everyone else was either. Cursing, he rushed into the halo, feeling the pull of energy against his skin as it transported him across the court.

Diego

Diego turned with Sandau and ran up the staircase behind him as the hall erupted into a war zone. Sandau landed his weight on Diego, pushing him to the ground as a bolt of dark magic slammed into the wall of the walkway above Diego's head, scattering fragments of stone everywhere. They rolled to a halt on the landing and Sandau whacked his hand down on Diego's shoulder and dragged him up. "Up. Keep low, that halo, go." Sandau pointed at the nearest one, shoving Diego along.

Diego was so busy trying to track Haydan, who had been targeted by Iskar on the other side of the hall that he missed another magical assault. A yank on his sword strap brought him to a halt and ensured he kissed the floor again as Sandau threw him down. This bolt of dark magic split and both parts smashed into the wall. They were so close to his head that he heard the wail as they rushed past and felt the shudder as they pounded into the marble.

"Concentrate, storm rider."

Sandau's shout by Diego's ear hurt his head. Refocusing on the halo and the dark god who was attacking them from the stairs, he rushed into the halo, welcoming the momentary respite from the chaos of the hall.

They landed in the room with the pods hanging from the roof. The halo deposited them straight into the pods, which had all joined up and formed a type of tunnel across the room. Sandau laughed wildly and scanned the area, before indicating to Diego that the room was clear and he should follow him. They leapt across each of the pods, reached the end and ran into Si and Katherine as they made their way in through the door. Katherine was clutching the baby.

"Are you both okay?" Diego asked. Si appeared uncomfortable and a look passed between him, Katherine and Sandau that aroused his curiosity. He made a mental note to pry into that when the madness ended. Sandau refused to meet Diego's eyes and he knew Sandau well enough to know when he was hiding something.

"We're all fine, but you should be worrying about the others. Those creatures are freaks of nature and Tallin has disappeared," Si said, issuing a shudder as he ushered Katherine ahead of him into the room.

Diego barged past Si, annoyed by his dig at Tallin and the obvious secret between the group that he was not party to. "Doubtful. Tallin is always in the midst of the bedlam. He did warn you about the dark gods and how unnatural they are."

"Yeah, well we can agree on that," Si said. "Do you know where Maya is?"

"I would expect her to be with my son. Get into one of these pods and stay there until Tallin finds you. The pods are private and soundproofed. You are protected once inside – go." Leaving Si and Katherine, he swept back into the corridor with Sandau at his side. "We need to find Haydan."

𝒯allin

Iskar was a fool if he thought Tallin would be easy to capture. Not only had the dark gods had the temerity to invade his realm, but they appeared to assume the task would be simple. Sidestepping Iskar and kicking the hound in the face was easy enough to do, but he hadn't even warmed up yet.

The halo close by pulled Tallin away and landed him

in the nearby hallway. From there he would make his way back to Iskar. Dark gods descended the moment he stepped out of the halo. He punched the nearest one in the face and kicked his feet from underneath him. The creature melted back into the smoke form as though that would fool him into thinking the god was dead.

Are you okay? Tallin asked Lavinia.

Lavinia's chuckle reverberated through Tallin's mind. *Of course, what a total hoot this is. Best party to date, I think. Oh, I'm with Rebekka. You're going to be a grandfather again.*

Power released from Tallin's hand, the mist a powerful lure to the darkness around him. The dark god took human form again and Tallin reached for his dagger, burying it in the god's chest before he took on the next one.

Wonderful news, my sweet. Aaushk had unofficially informed me. It would be nice to know one of them whilst they resemble children.

Tallin darted away and dodged the punches thrown by the woman who attacked him. This one had flamed-red hair. The hair didn't fool him; it looked harmless enough, but it flailed about of its own accord and would no doubt throttle him if he got too close. She tried again to punch him, then angled a blast of magic from her hand at Tallin's chest. He deflected it, enjoying the flare of displeasure that crossed her face.

Tallin's magic could lure or deflect dark magic depending on his need, which served him well given the current situation. Close by, Tallin's magical creatures had adapted to their surroundings. The hummingbirds zipped around and jabbed at one of the hounds with their sharp beaks, and a couple of weasels jumped onto the hound's flank and dug sharp teeth into the fur.

The creature snarled and spun around as Tallin's magic seeped into its flesh. He estimated the hound might manage another half hour of being tormented, but it would be dead soon enough.

Tallin let his magic drop from his fingertips down into long whips. He drew both hands back, delighting in the sound as the whips cracked on the floor. The red-headed god had to work hard to avoid the whips and even harder to get close to Tallin.

His guards had trapped a god in one of their magical nets. They dragged him towards the trap halo and delivered a swift kick to send the god head first into it. It slammed shut and the god's yell of fury added to his satisfaction.

Tallin flicked the whips from a vertical to a horizontal position, wrapping one around the redhead's neck and the other around her arms. The woman gasped and choked. Her face turned the same colour as her hair. Now he had to get her into the nearby trap.

Theander strode up behind her, swung his blades and solved the problem for Tallin by decapitating her. The ending was rather more dramatic than Tallin would have liked, but it was equally effective.

Isaac scurried along behind Theander and held a blade in his hand, although he looked clueless as to how to use it. He stared at the dead red-headed god, then ducked as Theander launched a ball of magic at a dark god who ran up behind him. The magic exploded in the dark god's face and he staggered about as though blinded.

Theander led Isaac out of the main war zone and towards the room with the pods where he was to rendezvous with Katherine and Si. Tallin had agreed that earlier with Isaac, even though the human had been put out at being hidden away from all the action.

A group of courtiers jumped at the opportunity to launch their own attack and Tallin left the dark god to his fate as he went in search of a central location in the palace from which he could lure the dark gods.

കൈ

Maya

The snarling hound moved closer to Maya's hiding place. She could defend herself in a fight, but since she had no idea who she was fighting against or how to use the magic that they could, she felt outmatched and that scared her. Her hand tightened around the handle of Devil's Curse and she pointed the blade outwards ready to attack. She trained and she was fast; that had to count for something. Her free hand pressed against her chest and she remembered the chain that she still had in her possession, the one with the portable halo inside. Perhaps that was an escape route she could make use of. It was still hanging from her neck on the chain.

The creature stank of burning and wet dog, making Maya gag. She placed her free hand over her mouth and willed herself not to retch and give her location away. The snarling sound stopped. The seat covering her hiding place was moved away by a paw and a gaping, slobbering muzzle full of jagged pointed teeth moved into her line of vision. The stench was overwhelming. The creature bristled and growled low in its throat as it glared at Maya, its nose within reach of her hand. Maya removed her glove and raised her left hand in the darkness. The snarling stopped so abruptly all the hairs on Maya's neck rose up. The teeth disappeared from view and the nose of the hound twitched as it sniffed the air. Its head turned towards her right hand and she struck out with the blade, pre-empting the hound's change of mood as it realised she was not as she seemed. She jabbed for its neck. A minute was enough time to get away.

The hound collapsed to the floor and Maya dived for the gap, praying its master wasn't far behind it. At the door, she peeked out. The corridor appeared to be quiet. None of the shadows moved. She took one hesitant step out of the room and awareness of another presence close by raced through her mind.

"So, there you are, little innocent one."

That term sounded sullied coming from the voice in the shadows. Its owner seemed curious and intrigued, but the soft tone carried an edge, suggesting he was not normally so careful about being gentle with anything. From the deepest, darkest recess of the corridor a figure unveiled himself. He stepped towards Maya, taking his time. It was difficult to see him, but her subconscious screamed at her to get away. She had a horrible feeling she knew who it was and if her suspicion proved correct she was in big trouble.

It wasn't the poor lighting that hindered her ability to see him properly. His skin changed from the same blackness that currently enveloped her left hand to a more normal colour as he drew closer.

"Iskar."

It was him: Maya's worst nightmare come true. He had cornered her and now she had no escape. He was too close to run from and he was studying her with the intensity of a panther hunting prey.

"So…" his attention flitted to Maya's left hand, then back to her face "…either that is very good make-up on your hand, or you are all or part darkness."

That sounded like a statement rather than a question. Maya's mouth was so dry she could barely speak. "I don't know what you're talking about."

Iskar gave Maya a sneaky, playful grin that turned her stomach. "Your hand matches mine. What's your name?"

Did she want to answer that question? In an effort to act normal and calm her pounding heart, Maya swallowed a few times, trying to stop her mouth feeling so dry. "I would rather not tell you. You could just let me go, seeing as I match your hand. No one needs to know about this. I won't tell anyone."

The edge of Iskar's mouth twitched. "It could be our little secret? I let you sneak off and we pretend this never happened?" he said.

Iskar looked as though he was giving the suggestion serious consideration. Maya moved past him, trying to get far enough away to make a run for it. Iskar followed her movements.

"There's a small problem with that suggestion, little innocent one."

The edge was back in Iskar's voice, a sharpness that suggested he was going to turn on Maya any moment and was toying with his new plaything. She tried to sound calm as she said, "Oh? And what's that?"

Iskar moved closer to Maya, watching and perhaps analysing her responses. "I'm not known for letting little innocent things go. I prefer to corrupt them." He inhaled and his powers intensified. The waft of darkness slid into her being like the slow, insidious stench of evil. "And if I can't corrupt them, I tend to

… break them."

That was a challenge Maya couldn't refuse. She lowered her head and stared off with Iskar from beneath her furrowed brows. "You can't corrupt me any more than I have been previously and as for breaking me – you can't make me any more broken than I am already. I've been broken many times and that's made me the strongest creature you could ever meet. I am the biggest contradiction you will ever encounter. Even I don't know who or what I am."

Iskar appeared fascinated by Maya as he studied her with a ferocious intensity. Two more dark gods rushed up. Iskar moved his attention to them. "I am busy. This interruption had better be good."

"The elven king is running rings around us. His magic permeates everything. The rest have all escaped and hidden and I am hearing rumours of there being traps in this hellhole. Ones designed to capture us in the ball contraptions."

Iskar looked livid. "This is the incompetence I have to deal with," he said. He sounded apologetic as he switched his focus to Maya, then concentrated on the other man. "So, keep the elven king occupied. Stay away from the ball things and continue searching … in small groups if you are being picked off. I only want to hear from you when you have found me a mask wielder, is that clear? There are a number of them, it shouldn't be this difficult."

The god nodded. Looking disgruntled, Iskar waved a hand at him, dismissing him, and the man ran off. His stare returned to Maya. "Speaking of which, where is your mask and what is that clutched in your hand?" His expression switched to a scandalous one as his eyes narrowed.

Maya had Devil's Curse clutched in her left hand. She had forgotten that was on show. It appeared foolish to attack Iskar unprovoked. She held up her hand and shrugged dismissively. "You didn't expect me to be unarmed, did you?"

Iskar chuckled and smacked his lips together in a manner that Maya found disconcerting. He wasn't eating anything so the gesture seemed odd. "No, not really. At least now I know how you took my hound out. Show me."

Maya hesitated. Passing Iskar her blade left her vulnerable, but so far he had not attacked her.

A smirk of displeasure pulled at Iskar's face. His hand raised and Maya felt the tug of his energy. Her hand rose involuntarily and she released the blade into his hand with a small cry of surprise.

Iskar pursed his lips and studied the blade, angling it around to gain a better look at it. He sniffed at it, as though from the smell alone he could discover all sorts of secrets. "This is a nice piece of work. Who gave it to you?" His intense, beady eyes locked back onto Maya's.

"Oh just … someone I know. He's not important."

Iskar dropped the blade down to his side and held out his other hand, offering it to Maya as though about to start arm-wrestling with her. "This is our formal greeting handshake. Since I don't know your name, I'll just call you little innocent one, and I am Iskar, leader of the dark gods. I want you on my team."

Maya shook her head. The darkness might be calling out to her, but she was not interested in forging an alliance and certainly not with Iskar. If Iskar didn't kill her for it, Kai would. "Not interested in forging alliances with anyone. I'm on my own team."

Iskar gave Maya a coy look and intensified

his powers, forcing her hand into his. The odd combination of both their hands together made Maya feel uncomfortable. He was up to something. Nausea roiled through her body at the contact. A moment later he released her hand and brought the blade up, slicing it across her dark palm. The sting took her by surprise. She gasped as Iskar slammed his hand back into hers and studied her.

"That's not possible. What are you? Are you dark, or are you light?" Iskar looked part curious, part furious as he stared into Maya's eyes. "I should be able to read you from contact with your blood, yet I cannot tell what you are. Do I kill you, or do I corrupt you?" After a momentary pause where she could see his mind working away behind his sinister eyes, he asked, "Were you blessed at birth?"

Maya couldn't fight Iskar. The knife wound to her hand drained her of any ability to respond and would do for the next minute or two. The cut stung as he tightened his grip on her. If Iskar found out who she was, Kai had warned her that he would kill her himself.

Iskar gave a stealthy grin of amusement. "Who are you? I command you to answer. Only when blessed will you answer the true call."

Now Iskar had Maya trapped. She had to answer the call; she couldn't fight the words as they rose up within her and spilt out of her mouth unfiltered and uncensored. "Dark to light. Light to dark. Where both merge…" she tried to suppress them, to push them back down inside but nothing worked "…both take flight. I am the light and I am the dark."

Now she was in all manner of trouble.

Iskar's face distorted into a mask of fury. "That's not possible. There is only one other who is both and blessed at birth and I should know given that my brother got to carry that badge of honour."

The female god with the blonde hair approached. "Let's kill her."

"No. I'll take a chance." Iskar's attention focused off into the hallway. "Does he know about you? Is he here? Is Kai the one who attacked my youngest child earlier? Did he give you this blade?"

"Kill her and you're even."

"No, not even close. This one is something else. I'm not killing her…" Iskar's beady eyes returned to Maya. "Not yet anyway."

Releasing Maya's hand, Iskar grabbed her neck. Flexing his fingertips, he gazed into her eyes like a serpent trying to hypnotise its prey. "Scream for me, little innocent one. Bring my brother out of hiding. He likes the shadows, but the light calls him and makes him weak."

It took Maya a moment to realise Iskar was looking for the mask on her face. He would be searching for a while. The small piece of Kaleshar was nestled in her bra. Maya reached her dark fingers out, took hold of Iskar's arm, the one holding the knife, and dug her nails in. The nails extended out as she gripped him harder. He appeared oblivious as he lowered his arm and the knife.

"Iskar, you're bleeding," the blonde god said.

Maya stamped out, kicking the knife towards Arianna, who crouched undetected and in her stealth mode in the shadows behind Iskar. It bounced and skittered across the floor coming to rest by her feet

Iskar glanced at the blade, apparently deemed it to be of no immediate importance and moved his other hand across to Maya's neck. She brought her right hand up, letting it illuminate in her glove, which lit up and glowed. Pressing the fingertips of both hands together, Maya smiled at him.

Iskar studied the development, looking as though he had been drugged, his eyes glassy and unfocused.

Maya dragged her arms down and shot them rapidly into the air, breaking Iskar's hold on her throat. Once free she slashed his face with her left hand, raking her nails down his cheek, and punched his face so hard with her glowing hand she heard bone crack. Iskar roared in rage and staggered backwards holding his face.

Arianna threw Devil's Curse with the dexterity of a professional sword thrower into the back of the blonde god, who collapsed to the floor and drifted into her smoke form.

Maya dropped down, grabbed Devil's Curse and slammed it into Iskar's shoulder before he could recover from her attack. "Consider that payback, freak." She rushed towards Arianna and concealed the blade again.

Haydan was waiting further down the corridor; his expression was one of relief. Maya and Arianna ran towards him and they dived for the nearest halo. Two halos later and they were in Maya's room.

"What are we doing?" Maya asked.

"This takes us out into the woodland near the portal," Haydan said. He looked on edge, although given everything that had happened that evening it was no great surprise. "You have blood on you, are you okay?" He gently captured Maya's face in his hands and moved her head this way and that as he searched her neck trying to find her injury.

"Iskar cut my hand. I'm fine, don't fuss." She pushed his hands away and winced as the gash on her palm started stinging again. Haydan grabbed her hand to study her wound. He tilted it about. The cut had stopped bleeding but he was going to have questions. "It was a clean cut with a sharp blade. I'll heal. There are more important things to worry about. What about the magical creatures hiding out there?"

Haydan released her hand and scowled.

Arianna stood on guard behind them. She leant in. "Every magical thing will be here tonight. The forest should be empty."

Screaming and shouting further down the corridor returned Maya's attention to the imminent danger.

Haydan grabbed her arm. "As to how we get back we'll worry about that later. I've got to get to Storm Lands and lay claim to it. You're both coming with me."

Chapter 37

Haydan

The short journey from the halo in Maya's room to the one in the woodland provided a moment of clarity for Haydan. He had to lay claim to his home realm to hold the power that he needed to defy the dark gods, yet the thought of doing so concerned him. The idea of claiming a realm that was home to their elders, who were far more experienced than him, proved alarming. Teeam and Diego might treat him differently and that was not a pleasant thought, plus he had no wish for anyone to bow to him.

Maya remained quiet. She would be worrying about how much of her conversation with Iskar Haydan had listened in on. He had heard enough to admire her bravery, but was struck by Maya's moments of total defiance. He would never have imagined she could stand up to someone like Iskar in such a way before, but hearing her utter the statement she had made about being a contradiction and that she had been broken already made his soul ache with the need to protect her. Somehow he had always felt she didn't need his protection, not really.

The woodland was quiet. Arianna moved ahead, stepped out of the halo and scanned the surrounding area. They had arrived inside a network of bamboo stems that interlinked, forming a cage around them. Maya smiled and raised her hand to poke the nearest stem.

"Don't touch anything," Haydan said. He felt and sounded irked at her, although he didn't have the faintest idea why.

The plants around them were bamboo, interspersed with older trees. Some of the more ancient-looking specimens had white trunks which glowed in the darkness as though providing a route out of the realm. In the distance Haydan could see the path up to the portal.

On edge and nervous, Haydan moved them towards the portal. He would only relax once they had cleared the portal and reached Storm Lands. The clock was ticking and the longer he was away, the more chance there was that Iskar would catch one of the mask bearers.

Reaching the portal provided a small amount of relief. "I'm sending you first, Arianna. Maya, you're next then I'm following. I can't risk going first and getting cut off from you," Haydan said, running his fingers along the smooth surface of the portal. Kaleshar activated the runes to connect them to Earth. Each one made a soft thump as it locked into place on the silvery ring.

Arianna rolled her eyes at Haydan. "My thoughts exactly. See you in a minute."

Without questioning Haydan, without causing an argument, Arianna stepped into the portal and disappeared. In stunned silence Haydan waited a moment before turning to Maya.

Maya fidgeted, her expression one of discomfort. "I don't know how much you heard of what I said to Iskar—"

"I heard enough. If it's not Arianna challenging me, it's you providing the distractions. I feel like a fleeting source of amusement to you this cycle. Like you grew bored and found me to play games with. Do I entertain you?" Surprised at his own flare of anger, Haydan inhaled and focused back on the portal. "Who gave you the blade? Who gave you the cape you're wearing? Gifts from gods? If I shake your family tree who falls out? Are you ready to tell me yet? You're an eternal contradiction. What's more, you like the challenges you pose. In fact, I often feel caught in your web of deceit. Is that intentional? Do you like making me feel so insecure? I think you thrive on it. I think you delight in making me as uncomfortable as you can."

Maya inhaled softly, her eyes widening. She reached a hand out towards Haydan, her movements tentative.

Haydan brushed her hand away. "After you, Maya." He indicated the portal with a flick of his hand.

Maya's gaze rested on Haydan for a moment longer, her eyes full of hurt, conveying pain. "I am what I am." She released air through her nose and stopped at the edge of the portal before entering. "You're angry, I understand that. You have to love all of me, even the broken parts. Can you do that, Haydan? Can you love the darkness that resides within me? I'm not sure you can." Her expression hardened. "Mind you, all you want from me is the bond. That's all I'm good for, isn't it? So, who is really playing games with who, Haydan?"

With a final glare, Maya stepped into the portal, leaving Haydan with a sense of total desolation. He inhaled and fought back the emotions trying to claw their way into his mind, which would not help him that evening. They were fighting again, but that kiss in the lounge at her house stayed with him. There was no way that kiss was a pretence. She had been as caught up in the moment as he was and he had loved every second of laying her soul bare.

Haydan cast a glance around the portal room and considered his options. This was the only one. He could deal with Maya if he remained calm and played her at her own games. He could charm what he needed from her, so long as he gave her the space and respect she craved. The fact that he had to do so sent his emotions into free fall again. Taking a deep breath, he concentrated on the next realm and reminded himself of her promise to find a way to be there for him. That response should have been a given not something she needed to figure out.

❧

Diego

Tallin was in the central part of the court. Diego sensed the elven king's presence as he moved through the building with Sandau. Watching Sandau defend him was always a pleasure. The big man ducked, dived and when necessary used brute force to smash a dark god out of the way. He was a skilled fighter and had the same knack that Arianna did for changing his approach to suit any occasion with a fluid ability and quick-thinking plan of attack, which came to the fore in times of challenge.

A dark god materialised in front of Sandau and he barged into the creature with a yell of fury, sweeping him off his feet to land him in a heap on the floor. Winded and caught by surprise, the god switched back into his smoke form. Sandau muttered something under his breath, which sounded like, 'Numarya'. The god struggled to change back, now trapped as a writhing mass of swirling, churning air. Diego presumed that Sandau had trapped him in the smoke form for a reason.

Sandau continued with his previous route, rewarding Diego with an innocent stare. "He's stuck like that for a while, which they hate." A hellhound lunged for Sandau. He grabbed his smaller blades in his fists and punched the creature's muzzle, sending it sprawling sideways, before slamming his blades down into its neck and throat. Diego ducked to avoid another stream of dark magic that blasted past. Locating the god who sent it, Diego returned the favour, sending an arc of fire towards the figure, who tried to hide in the shadows. The god attempted to push the magic away, which didn't work as expected. The stream hit the floor at his feet, then surrounded him. Diego was rewarded with a cry of frustration.

"He'll tire himself out before long. One of the others will have to rescue him and that takes them time to sort out," Sandau said.

It took Diego a moment to realise Sandau was still on their previous conversation. "Neat trick," he said.

They passed a group of courtiers who had cornered a god by using small blasts of magic to encircle him. They didn't hold the same strength as the royal line and Tallin's magic surrounded them, which no doubt helped, but even their combined efforts proved effective. It had created a barrier that looked like a fine-glowing fabric in the air around him. The trapped god was tiring. Diego could see it in his face as he rushed past.

Entering the main room at the centre of the court, Diego took a moment to appreciate the size and scale of the centrepiece before acknowledging the chaos around him. Tallin stood in the middle, at the heart of the court, on a plinth that was home to a huge halo on top of a large water feature. Water cascaded out underneath his feet.

The room was full of dark gods, perhaps lured by all the energy which flowed out from the room like the scent of freshly baked goods. Tallin produced huge swathes of it as he ducked and dodged any attacks that the dark gods managed to launch in his direction. A large number of Tallin's magical creatures had congregated there. Earlier, the creatures had been a cute form of entertainment as they ambled around the court, now they had become feral, wild things. Any god within arm's reach of them was under attack as they stung, bit and terrorised anyone who was close by.

Rebekka and Lavinia were working together to round up the more vulnerable gods and kick them into a nearby halo. Another woman, with blonde hair, stood close to them. She released her own unusual aura and Sandau focused on her.

Another trap slammed shut.

Sandau stopped at Diego's side and glanced around, his unusual eyes glinting in silent approval. "Ever the showman," he said. A hint of sarcasm laced Sandau's voice as his eyes tracked the blonde woman. "That's Leylani, seems we might have got her wrong."

Diego smiled and picked his space, partway between the two women in his life who always provided him with the most challenges. Sandau nodded his agreement and backed up against him. His face had flushed.

"Is that a glint of approval I just saw in your eyes for Leylani, Sandau?"

Sandau snickered. "I don't know what you're talking about, Diego."

It would be better for everyone if Sandau ceased his pursuit of Arianna. Diego had seen the god who stood watching her earlier, the one hidden behind the bright, garish mask, with the vibrant blue eyes. The blue eyes denoted the favoured line of the gods. Diego had his suspicions about who the secret addition to the court was and if it was who he believed it to be, Theander, Sandau could not touch Arianna without sealing his fate.

"When I was in the Pool of Sorrows I saw one of Arianna's futures." The Pool of Sorrows contained predictions of the future. They were possible futures, but Diego had seen enough to convince him Arianna would have a much happier future with the blue-eyed man from the prediction. "You do know that Arianna will never fall for you the way you want her to, don't you?" Diego sensed rather than heard Sandau's sigh of regret. "You're a teenage girl's passing fascination, nothing more. She looks up to you, idolises you, but that's where it ends. She acts mature, often beyond her years, so I can understand why–"

"I know, but there was a tiny part of me that hoped one day she might just let me under her armour. What a place to be…"

Diego smiled wistfully. "I know that feeling, my friend, but sometimes things don't work out the way we hope." After a moment of silence, Diego added, "So, are you going to talk to me about Si?"

A hellhound lunged for Diego as another dark god entered the room. Diego muttered a low curse and prepared to fight.

৵৹৵

Maya

Freezing cold, tired and bedraggled, Maya waited for Haydan to haul himself out of the water. There was no comfort or warmth in his eyes when he reached her; instead she met with a look of total disdain. Her soul quailed at the realisation that he was on the verge of losing faith in their unusual relationship; she had pushed him too far. She reached for his hand to help him out. Haydan brushed her hand away.

Arianna moved off to scan the surroundings and keep watch. She returned as Haydan stood and beckoned them both closer. He would not look at Maya, adding to her sense of utter abandonment.

Glancing around, Arianna rocked on her heels and wrapped her arms around herself to keep warm. "Well, this is nice and awkward again. Are we going?"

Haydan's tornado dropped around them. The breeze brushed Maya's skin, sending a little thrill coursing through her body. If it was deliberate Haydan didn't appear to notice. He was concentrating on something straight ahead as though his thoughts were somewhere else entirely.

The dark cavern they arrived in felt warm, and

the air smelt earthy and damp. Haydan surveyed the immediate vicinity and moved off without acknowledging Maya or Arianna. He halted as the cavern began glowing, the walls providing an iridescent light. He stared up towards the ceiling, focusing on a section where a series of ancient-looking banners unfurled. The last of the banners unravelled. Haydan inhaled and exhaled slowly through his mouth as though calming himself.

"Have you worked out the last banner yet?" Arianna asked.

Haydan nodded and focused on the path that led up to the throne. "It says 'the hall of the forgotten king'. She knew. I'm convinced Lavinia knew, even then. She wanted me to find this place. She wanted me to know I was destined for something else." He walked off.

Arianna locked eyes with Maya and flicked her head towards Haydan, as though suggesting Maya should talk to him. Maya followed Haydan at a jogging pace. He was moving fast. "You've been here before?"

"When I was a child, yes. I had an accident. Lavinia sent me here to protect me. I couldn't find the way out so Arianna had to find me. I couldn't read the last banner properly. This place has always haunted me." Haydan stopped at the bottom of the steps and finally met her eyes. "Rather like you. It seems we both carry hidden secrets, chosen one."

Before Maya could respond, Haydan climbed the stairs. "Stay down here, you can't follow me, and right now I'm not sure I want you on the platform with me."

The coldness remained. Maya's body temperature plummeted as Haydan walked away. One day he might walk away from her forever. That broke her heart and brought desolation to her soul.

"You can't dismiss and ignore me and not expect me to work my way back underneath the barrier you've placed around your soul."

Arriving on the main platform, Haydan strutted across to the throne. The back of the obsidian seat was covered in arms that reached out towards him. As he moved closer the hands stretched out as though welcoming him and trying to console him.

Maya hated the throne on sight.

She wanted to be the only person to offer Haydan solace and the hands reaching towards Haydan suggested otherwise. Haydan interlinked his hand with the one closest to him and stepped in towards the throne, before sweeping around and taking a seat. The obsidian hands glided around his torso as he pulled the blue keystone from his pocket.

Maya lurched forwards, finding her route blocked by Arianna. "Haydan doesn't want you up there with him. I can't let you through."

"Are you serious?" Maya couldn't get past Arianna and she stood like a sentry on duty, refusing to move.

Haydan slid the stone around in his hand. Maya's vision blurred with tears as she watched his new game. "Haydan, don't push me away. You're breaking my heart and my soul with this."

Haydan stared down at Maya, his intense green eyes full of pain and loathing. "You promised me you would find a way, but every realm I claim takes me further away from you and our future together. If we can't be honest with each other, then I have to wonder what all of this is for." Haydan glanced around at the obsidian hands. "I knew when I found this temple that I might have to walk a lonely path alone. My soul rebels at the thought, but I feel like it's my destiny … mine alone,

Maya."

Maya folded her arms. "Haydan Leon Xander Tournadir, I made you a promise and I don't make those easily. In fact, I have made two promises to you, one to your soul and one to you in the flesh. If you are upset because I won't share my family tree with you then so be it. I can't talk about it and I'm not ready to discuss it, even with you. That does not mean I love you, or your soul, any less." Maya inhaled sharply. Haydan was pushing her to her limits. "If you are upset over what I said to Iskar, then I don't know why. I had to sound convincing to him."

Haydan leant forwards and rested his arms on his knees. The dark, mysterious hands released him, but remained close. "If we make it home in one piece, unscathed by all of this, I want you to tell Alex to stay away."

Maya couldn't do that. She had tried so many times, but the right words wouldn't form. It should have been something so easy to deal with, yet it was the most complicated issue in her life. "He's an echo of my past. Something awful happened to him and I can't do that to him. He's a lost soul. I love you. I'm here with you."

"Or am I a game to you? A piece in a puzzle?" Haydan asked.

Her family was trapped on Aveyamara. Haydan's family was trapped there too. "Haydan, I love you, heart, body, mind and soul, but if any harm comes to either of our families because you're delaying with this, I'll never forgive you. What's more, you will never forgive yourself either."

Haydan's nose wrinkled.

Maya kept her tone playful. "I'll agree to a date and a kiss." That was what Haydan had been after before all of this happened.

Arianna looked mortified. She rolled her eyes and huffed at the awkward atmosphere.

Maya sensed Haydan's resolve weakening at her capitulation to his previous request. He lowered his eyes to the floor by his feet, swallowed and flicked one of the obsidian hands away as it tried to grab hold of his shoulder. He cut a handsome but lonely figure on the platform and her soul longed to be close to him again and bask in the knowledge that he still adored her. After a long, drawn-out pause, Haydan raised his head and beckoned her up to the platform.

Maya smiled in delight before giving Arianna a sassy look. Arianna checked for Haydan's approval, which he issued with a nod. She moved away to let Maya past.

Maya bounded up the stairs and landed herself on Haydan's lap with a dramatic swagger to highlight her achievement. He smiled but still regarded her with wariness as he passed the blue stone across to her. He was allowing her to activate the next realm for him. That was unexpected.

The stone felt warm. The lights reflected in the glossy surface as though it had liquefied. Haydan slid his hand along the arm of the throne and pointed to the jagged recess designed to hold the keystone.

"Taking this realm bothers you the most. Why?" Maya could tell from Haydan's agitated state since they arrived that he didn't want to claim Storm Lands.

"I'm claiming my home world. I don't feel like I have a right to do this and I have no idea how the elders will respond."

"You have no choice though and we have to get back."

Haydan sighed and wrapped his arms around Maya's

waist. "Let's just get this done and return to the castle."

Maya nodded her understanding and dropped the stone into place.

Chapter 38

Haydan

Instead of feeling jubilant at claiming Storm Lands, the sensation Haydan was left with after the initial thrill had subsided was that of disharmony. Or perhaps it was more to do with his discomfort at having riled Iskar a little more. It was doubtful that a god as powerful as Iskar would leave without making his fury felt throughout the court.

A yellow keystone lifted up from the other throne arm. Haydan slipped his fingers around it. This one was rougher, the surface full of tiny striations like the bark of a tree.

"We have to get back to Aveyamara," Haydan said.

Maya nodded. "The water book has information inside it about which realms correspond with which keystones. I have yet to understand it, but when I have the deciphering glasses and more time, I'm sure we can figure it out."

The woman Haydan doubted and felt unsure about was helping him to find the next realm. Maya cared enough to do that at least. The unusual addition to Maya's neck glinted in the light. Haydan reached out and caught the odd little cage between his fingers. "What is this?"

Maya frowned and peered down. "Oh, that's a gift from Lavinia, I think. It helped me get into the library when it was locked. That's when I found the water book."

"It has three balls in it."

Arianna ventured onto the platform and moved across to him. Her skirt had been abandoned, and she wore trousers in a complementary shade to her dress. "So how are we going to get back?"

Maya fiddled with the chain around her neck. Releasing it, she held it up. "It's a mobile halo."

Haydan's smile widened. Lavinia had helped them find their way back. "I think that's how we return. We take the portal to reach Tallin's realm, then use that to get to the summer court."

Movement erupted in Arianna's trouser pocket. She sighed as though a little embarrassed. A purple head appeared – Aaushk. "What do you want?"

The shock of purple hair surveyed the cavernous room and scowled as though the surroundings displeased him. "The portable halos won't get you back to the court. They'll get you close, but not out of the forest."

Haydan slammed his hand down on the arm of the throne. Both girls jumped. Maya's cape brushed Haydan's face. He flinched, pulled away and studied it more intently. "What the hell is that?"

Maya shrugged. "It was a gift."

Her defensive answer drew Haydan's attention. He wasn't going to like her answer. "A gift from whom?"

Maya searched for an answer.

Aaushk reached a hand out towards the cape and

giggled as it caressed his hand. "It's a bewitched cape. Theander wore it when he came to talk to Tallin. This will get us from the triple halo into the court. It will probably take us to the library. He arrived and left from the library as well."

Haydan stared at Aaushk in delight. The pixie grinned as he basked in their attention. "You're welcome. You can reward me with crisps and jelly sweets. I like them."

"Aaushk, you're a genius," Arianna said. "Let's go and kick Iskar's butt."

With a flourish, Haydan picked up the yellow keystone, slipped it into his pocket and stood. The summer court was going to be in chaos when they returned, but he was more concerned about his family and whether they were safe or not. Hopefully they would not be too late. Maya and Arianna rushed ahead. His evening was far from over. Now he had to finish what he had started.

❧

Tallin

The plan to lure the weaker of the gods into the room Tallin occupied at the centre of the court had been successful. He had a grand finale planned. It was daring, it was dangerous, but having assessed the court over the last few weeks, he was certain he could make it work. He would rebuild the court stronger than it was before.

The closest dark god was fixated by a stream of light that Tallin released. It drifted towards him like the mists across the Varza Swamp. The local inhabitants used the mists to their advantage to capture anyone who wandered into their territory, and they then fell under their spell. Like the creatures that lived in that swamp, Tallin had a nasty surprise waiting for the god. The light transformed slowly into a huge serpent and drew itself up before striking the god and catching his shoulder. The man shuddered and twitched as he dropped to his knees and stopped moving. He would be trapped like that until one of his kind rescued him and worked on releasing him from the light magic that trapped him within his own skin.

Since meeting Kai and Iskar one thing had become apparent to Tallin. They were well matched and if they fought, neither would win. The only way Iskar might be able to swing things in his favour would be if his pack of dark gods were able to overcome Kai. Kai worked alone and that was his weakness. Tallin intended to make sure that did not happen.

A flick of Tallin's hand sent the magic swirling around them. Caught in a vortex it spun wildly. Taking the cue, Diego, Sandau, Rebekka and Lavinia began moving towards the central halo as they battled with the hounds and the numerous dark gods who filled the room. The pressure in the air increased. Tallin rubbed at his ear to release the build-up and focused on completing the task.

A shudder ran through the building and Tallin's subconscious, confirming another realm had been claimed. Haydan had reached the vault on Storm Lands. Now they stood a fighting chance.

Each time Haydan claimed another world, the rulers of the realms already claimed felt the calling. Tallin was certain the gods knew as well. Confidence was key now.

Haydan had to start believing in his future and acting like a ruler. If his performance in the corridor the other day was anything to go by, that needed work.

Diego's smile was brief, perhaps in recognition of Haydan's achievement, then he looked more serious. The claiming of Storm Lands was something new to Diego. He apparently bowed to no one and Tallin wondered how he would deal with his own son holding a more senior status than he did as elder.

Lavinia's face illuminated and she shared the news with Rebekka, who looked delighted. Tallin and Lavinia had been able to grow used to the idea of Haydan's status and whilst they would never bow to Haydan, they would both defer to him with the appropriate amount of respect due to his position in the realms.

Now Iskar would be livid, not just because he had been outmanoeuvred by them and the mask bearer had escaped, but because he had underestimated everyone in Tallin's court. Tallin was about to inflict more suffering on the dark gods, who should never have set foot in his realm. If the darkness was in chaos, Iskar did not have a plan, and that was a good thing.

Everyone stepped into the halo as sections of plaster began breaking away and became caught in the powerful blast of energy that filled the room. Tallin let the magic finish its task. The halo dropped as the roof began shaking and the building trembled. The shouts of trapped dark gods and the howling, churning wind filled the air. His soul thrilled in response. He didn't need to be storm rider, he was so much more.

꙳

Theander

Isaac was safe with Si and Kat. Si wasn't happy about being left babysitting, but he would have to get over his childish and juvenile responses to things he was not happy about. Theander had endured numerous lifetimes of growing accustomed to that feeling of irritation at being ordered by Asanda to do something. Even now annoyance roiled around his mind at the latest instruction to take Haydan's female warrior as his mate. Asanda didn't suggest it. He didn't ask if he wanted to meet someone new and different. No, Asanda told him with his usual directness to make it happen. Theander had been alone too long after Ashuri. It was time to move on.

It sounded like a transaction, or a deal. Move on from the past and acquire something new, but Theander's heart didn't work like that. He still hid one of Ashuri's feathers away in his private vault on Acquorous. It no longer smelt of her, but he could remember the feel of Ashuri in his arms. Their time together had been far too fleeting and now Asanda expected him to just forget the past.

Studying Arianna earlier as she surveyed the court, oblivious to Theander's attention, he had noticed numerous things about her. She was beautiful in a distinctive and striking way. Her huge eyes were an intense hazel colour; her skin, visible beneath her mask, flawless. She scanned the court with a keen, astute gaze that saw everything but gave away nothing. She definitely hid mysteries deep down inside. Catching Si messing around, she smiled, the edge of her curvy mouth pulling up. Her smile lit the room around her.

That was the moment when Arianna ensnared Theander's interest. He would love to be able to make her smile like that. He challenged her to notice him when her eyes tracked back across the room again. She missed him on her first perusal, but her attention returned to him with the precision of a finely honed predator. Captured in his intense stare she blinked a few times then lowered her gaze to someone closer to the balcony and finished her sweep.

Theander had counted down from ten. By the time he reached four, Arianna had cast another furtive look in his direction. He let his mouth curl upwards and waited for her to break the contact. Her fingers were suddenly the focus of her attention as she fiddled with them as if she didn't know where to look. He could sense her unease and it somehow thrilled him. Maybe he could enjoy this pursuit more than he thought and still keep her emotionally at arm's length.

Arianna had reappeared on the stairs just before Iskar arrived, moving with poise and ease. Her confidence was increasing all the time. She struck Theander as a young woman growing comfortable in her own skin and aware of a world shifting around her that she never let brush her heart or soul. He had to find a way beneath that to fully possess her attention.

Arianna would not be easy to win over. In fact, Theander wasn't even sure he wanted to win her heart. The idea of loving another and giving her a route to hurt him made all his defences rise. He kept himself apart from the pain a woman could cause for a reason.

Asanda had told him that had to end. Apparently Theander was growing cold like Kai. Asanda did not find that development to his liking.

Theander left the room with the swinging pods inside it, grateful for the relief from looking after Isaac. He hated babysitting anything, but when the man in question made him think about Arianna yet again, it became too much. He was ready to battle. It wasn't often that he was presented with the chance to demonstrate his fighting prowess, but the opportunity to run rings around dark gods was a rare opportunity, one too good to miss.

Moving into the darkness of the nearby corridor, Theander stayed in the shadows. The magic permeating the air around him provided him with cover as he edged towards a figure further down the corridor.

Iskar stood in the gloom, staring out of the window. "I knew you would find me. Darkness always has a habit of dragging you out of the gutter where you hide."

For a moment Theander thought Iskar was talking to him, which made no sense. Then he realised someone else was with them.

"You feel it calling to you." Iskar kept his voice low and teasing. "It slides through your bloodstream. It seeps into your mind. It plays with your subconscious. I like to think sometimes you commit hideous, dark acts that you hide away in shame in the name of the darkness."

"That's the difference between me and you, brother. I have a conscience that stops me from realising those acts." Kai shuffled about as though uncomfortable in the darkness. He had removed his mask although the feathers across his shoulders and back remained.

Theander had often wondered about the dynamics between Kai and Iskar; now he had a front-row seat of what they really thought of each other and their past. He remained hidden, not wanting to intrude or make his presence known.

"I was not the one who murdered our mother." For once emotion rippled through Kai's words. His voice cracked as he added, "She did not deserve what you did to her."

Iskar turned, giving Kai a sly look. His beady, dark eyes glinted in the darkness. "No, but she wasn't gifting him any more children. I made that mistake, letting her give you life, little brother. I knew the moment I laid eyes on you that you were not worthy. You didn't get there quick enough to save her though and he will never forgive you for that."

That explained the reason why Kai never talked about Iskar, or Theander's grandmother, and why Asanda and Kai hated Iskar so much. Theander had always known something awful lay at the heart of that hatred; now he knew what. That was why his father never let anyone too close. Perhaps the only woman Kai had ever cared about was Silvera, Theander's mother, but even that was something Kai never made clear to anyone.

"Not for want of trying. At least I gave her and our sibling a proper burial."

Iskar's bark of laughter echoed around the corridor. "Like a good little boy. Yes, I'm sure she would be proud of your failings. I despised you from the moment I laid eyes on you. That hand you're afflicted with makes you weak."

"I was a boy and you made sure I would be too late." In response Kai's right hand glowed in the darkness, illuminating his face as he held it up. "This makes me weak? I disagree. This is my strength."

Iskar's lip curled into a sneer of disapproval. "You might see it that way, but he never has and never will." He cast a dismissive glance around the corridor. "You run here when you're in trouble? That's pathetic."

Kai returned Iskar's disapproval, looking equally menacing as he clenched his fists. "And you hide from the light, remaining unable to deal with its beauty and strength. Your world is dark. Your partners are dark. You will never know any joy or happiness." Almost as an afterthought, he added, "Not that I do either, but at least I recognise and can identify with those emotions."

Iskar shook his head. "You're lying to me, little brother. I can sense the deceit. You do know those emotions, but you try to hide them from the darkness, and I know everything when I stand this close to you."

A shudder rippled through the building around them, as though something ancient was stirring from its slumber. Haydan had made it to Storm Lands and claimed the realm. Storm Lands was always going to be the hardest realm for Haydan to claim. He would struggle to deal with the change in his status and the elders would have to adjust to the new balance as well.

Eerie whistling sounds were creeping through the building from the main room where Tallin had trapped a large group of the gods. Their shouts mingled with the howling gale building to a crescendo.

Iskar growled. "No! How is that even possible? I had all the mask bearers here – trapped. Did you play a hand in this?"

Kai chuckled and shook his head. "No, brother, but I am glad the mask bearer succeeded where you failed."

Iskar roared in fury and slammed his fist into

Kai's stomach as the pair took to resolving their disagreement with brute force. This was Asanda's worst nightmare realised and as Theander watched the two men destroying each other and the corridor around them, he could appreciate why.

Chapter 39

ᗰaya

The return journey was faster than Maya expected. The portal took them back to Aveyamara. Her portable halo landed them by the drawbridge that led across into the summer court. She had no idea where they would end up once they activated the cape. Haydan caught it in his hand and ran his fingers over the surface.

"So, how does it work?"

Before Aaushk could respond, the cape slid around their shoulders, enveloping them all. Haydan stilled, as though in surprise.

In a swift downwards pull, the forest was left behind. Maya scanned their new surroundings to find they were back inside the summer court and enclosed on all sides by bookshelves.

Arianna grinned in delight. "That was cool. This way, follow me." She ran across the room towards the door. Haydan held out his hand, letting Maya move ahead and give chase.

The building shuddered as though an earthquake had hit and a loud crash emanated from deep within the court. Arianna skidded to a halt and looked across at Haydan as the rumbling continued for a moment. "Please tell me that was the plan."

Haydan nodded and indicated Arianna should continue. "Yes, Ari, that was the plan. Keep moving."

The hallway was quiet. They reached the main stairwell without incident, only to run straight into a masked Theander, who moved out of the darkness and attempted to herd them back in the direction they had just come. A loud crash behind him indicated why.

Kai flew backwards across the stairwell and slammed into the wall with a sickening thump. Rubble cascaded all over the floor. Maya stifled a scream, clamping her hand over her mouth to keep herself quiet. Arianna backed up against Haydan with her arm out to protect him.

Iskar strode out of a corridor to the stairwell and surveyed the damage. Kai picked himself up, dusted himself off and bounded back up the steps. Moments later and it looked like they were trying to kill each other with their bare hands. Kai ploughed his full body weight into Iskar. In the blur of movement Maya couldn't tell who was hitting who and who was damaging who, but she had never before seen such violence. Gravity didn't seem to bother them either as they threw each other about. The scent of destruction, sweat and testosterone flooded the air along with an occasional waft of chocolate.

"Stop them. Help Kai," Maya said. Her voice sounded tiny in the wake of the devastation being wrought around her.

"Are you crazy?" Theander snapped. "They have unfinished business and I will get my own kicking from Kai if I dare to interrupt this. Even Tallin won't step between these two."

Theander flicked a hand gesture down the stairs. Tallin rubbed the dust out of his hair. His face etched with concern, he peered up at the carnage. He no longer released huge streams of mist. In fact, Tallin looked tired, and that suggested Theander's theory was correct.

Springing up from a crouch, Kai smashed his fist into Iskar's face and kicked him hard in the stomach. Iskar sailed through the railings and plummeted onto the floor below. The stairwell shuddered from the impact.

This was a brutal fight for supremacy.

"They're going to kill each other," Maya said.

Theander moved to the top of the stairs and surveyed the brawling gods. "The darkness has been badly damaged today and another realm has been claimed. What did you expect, a party to celebrate?"

Arianna followed Theander's movements as though fascinated. She stared back at Haydan. "Who is that?"

Maya resisted the urge to tell Arianna she was in the presence of Theander.

Haydan scowled and shook his head. "Not now." He returned his attention to Theander and bounded up the steps. "If I show myself, will I distract them from this?"

Reading into Haydan's suggestion and apparently aware he meant to announce himself as the mask wielder, Theander clutched Haydan's jacket and yanked him forwards. "No. That would be unwise … tell your warrior to point her blade somewhere else, before I get annoyed."

Defending Haydan, Arianna had drawn one of her main swords and rested it on Theander's shoulder, by his neck.

Looking uncomfortable, Haydan pulled his jacket out of Theander's grasp. "Stand down, warrior," he said.

Kai ran down two levels to the bottom. Iskar charged as Kai arrived, slamming him down onto the ground with a sickening thump. Iskar grabbed a handful of Kai's hair and smashed his head against the floor. Kai retaliated by punching Iskar's head with his right fist. Maya heard bone crunch. Kai hit Iskar so hard that he stunned his brother, who slumped on top of him. Kai threw Iskar off and leapt up. Taking hold of Iskar's foot, he dragged him through to the main court, bouncing his head down every step along the way.

"Iskar doesn't need to know who you are yet," Theander said. "Besides, I'm hoping for another form of intervention, one that will sort this problem out in its entirety tonight." Theander ran to the stairs and followed Kai.

No one else moved. Maya wasn't missing the show. She chased Theander before the others could stop her. Haydan and Arianna would stay close to her no matter the consequences.

Kai kept dragging Iskar until he arrived near the main part of the court, which lay in ruins. Maya knew Tallin was okay and gathered that he had played some part in the carnage in front of her, but the main hall was completely destroyed.

Dropping Iskar's leg, Kai stalked around him and kicked his stomach hard. "Do you hear that, big brother? That's the sound of all the dark gods trapped in the rubble." Kai took a step back.

Shouts could be heard from beneath the debris. Kai fell silent as if to let Iskar enjoy the full effects of his actions.

Maya came to a halt behind Theander. Haydan
and Arianna stayed further back, but Haydan grabbed
Maya's arm, pulling her further away than she would
have liked. She glared at him whilst prising her arm free.

Behind Kai, in the darkness, the blonde-haired
woman from earlier slid into view. Maya tugged on
Theander's sleeve and flicked her head in that direction
when he turned his head towards her.

"You brought them here. This is on you," Kai said.
"The light drains their powers further. Then there
are the ones in the traps, who are now our prisoners.
Tonight, you entered a realm you should not have
entered. You crossed a line you should not have
crossed."

Iskar laughed, pushing himself up from the floor.
"Did I really? Maybe I had my sights set on someone
else altogether. Perhaps you just think you've won. I
would wager that our master and commander would be
a little more upset about losing his most favoured heir,
wouldn't you?"

Kai tracked Iskar's every movement as he advanced.
"What are you talking about? Asanda doesn't have a
favoured heir. I was the runt of the litter."

The blonde wrapped her arm around Kai's neck,
dragging him backwards. Kai tried to fling her over his
head as Iskar punched his stomach. She tightened her
grip on Kai's neck as he went down. She cackled in
delight as Iskar took hold of Kai's left arm and forced
it up around his back in one deft movement before
dropping to his side.

Theander lurched forwards. A sly glance from Iskar
towards Theander confirmed Maya's worst fears. He
was playing right into Iskar's hands with this, because

Iskar now knew Kai was significant to Theander. Plus, he was a fully light god and Iskar being able to identify him wouldn't bode well. Iskar now had a route to hurt both Kai and Asanda. Maya grasped Theander's arm. Haydan grabbed for hers.

"Oh, I think he does and I think it's you." Iskar glanced up at Theander as his free hand formed into mist and slid across Kai's face. "Say hello to the darkness. It's missed you and you'll be spending a lot more time suffocating in it, little brother."

སྐ

Haydan

Kai jolted and his chest and shoulders shuddered as though he was choking. There was something undignified about watching Iskar tormenting his own sibling. Witnessing his torture made Haydan feel ill and Maya clutching Theander's arm wasn't helping.

"No. Get. Up," Theander said, straining against Maya's tight grip on his arm. "Get up, Kai. Fight the darkness."

Iskar's intense stare settled back onto Theander. Maya jerked forwards to warn him. She appeared to understand the darkness and its intent. Iskar was identifying who the players were; that much was clear from the way he homed in on Theander. He was seeking anyone who he could use as leverage to hurt Kai. Haydan tightened his grip on Maya's arm, restraining her. She was not stepping into this battle.

"Watch your back, but do something," Maya said,

glaring up at Theander.

"He can't," Haydan said. He pulled Maya back against him and said, "Stay out of this." Theander could not step between Iskar and Kai without making himself a target and identifying himself in the process. Asanda had sworn long ago that Theander would not be known to the dark gods.

Something slid out of the darkness and the curling black mist from around Iskar shattered as a large, bulky male strode up to both men and grabbed them before hauling them apart. Brightness flared around him.

Haydan instinctively knew who it was.

Iskar flew across the rubble into the wall, the force so great more masonry fell. Thrown backwards Kai sat on the floor looking as livid as the new arrival. Caught in the release of energy from the new arrival the woman who had been fighting alongside Iskar slammed into the wall behind Kai and collapsed to the floor, stunned.

Iskar made another attempt to reach Kai. He launched himself forwards with a snarl, stretching his arms out to grab at Kai. Kai reciprocated, pushing up from the floor as though he was possessed. The air around Haydan stirred as the new male moved. His presence palpable, he shoved the men apart before they could reach each other, his expression one of total fury. His blue eyes glinted and Haydan knew he was staring across at the ancient and formidable Asanda, who had come to protect his boys from harm.

Haydan still had nightmares about those eyes at night when he fought with Maya. They reminded him how it had felt to be plunged into the deceptively deep water of the oasis on Acquorous. Haydan met Maya's eyes as she turned to him and winced.

"Ouch, that hurts."

Haydan had dug his fingers into the top of Maya's arm. He released his grip. Scowling, she yanked her arm free and turned her back to him as she watched the show in front of them. Asanda now held her enthralled.

Theander glanced over his shoulder at Haydan, as though assessing his response to the new development, before turning back.

"I do not expect to find my family brawling like village idiots, especially not in front of so many spectators." Asanda glared up at the gathered audience. Tension rolled off him as he fidgeted backwards and forwards, flexing and releasing his hands, like a cornered beast ready to fight. "Yet here you are and I am having to intervene like I did when you were children. Get up." Asanda kicked at Kai's feet. "Is this what you wanted, Iskar? To remind the twelve kingdoms we exist? Or were you hoping for something more spectacular?"

Iskar shrugged and shot a sly look at Theander. "No, I wanted the mask bearer and a fight. The mask bearer will keep for another time and I'll settle for killing one of your favourites instead. There must be someone very special here for you to turn up because I don't think it's just on account of my presence, is it?" He threw a ball of darkness out of his hand in Theander's direction.

Theander ducked and tried to dodge it as another figure moved across with lightning-fast reactions.

Haydan didn't know if Iskar had found his mark. Theander crashed to the ground. Arianna's wail pierced the air as she dropped down to check on who had been injured.

Theander picked himself up, looking stunned by the

development.

It was Sandau who had sacrificed himself. He lay on the ground at Theander's feet, with Arianna at his side, shaking him in an attempt to wake him. His body twitched as he reached up to his injured shoulder and groaned as though in agony.

Asanda focused his attention on Iskar. "You had better run, Iskar, because tonight I am hunting dark gods and I won't rest until I tear you apart." With a ferocious roar Asanda grabbed the blonde god and dragged her to his feet before sliding his hand across her face, as Iskar had done to Kai. His hand illuminated as a beacon in the darkness and mist glided into her body through her mouth, nose and eyes. "Let the light in and it'll be so much easier."

Her body convulsed and twitched as it shuddered from light to dark and back again. Haydan had heard of that magic before. It was ancient and powerful. If the woman survived, her mind would be ruined; she would descend into madness.

Iskar ran. Asanda gave chase and everyone returned their attention to Sandau.

There was no sign of Diego or Tallin. "Find Leylani," Haydan said. He shouted it again to a gathered group of Tallin's guards who hadn't moved. "Find Leylani, now. That's an order from your prince."

The men rushed off.

Ironically Haydan would have to ask a woman he previously despised for help, because if anyone could save Sandau, it was Leylani.

❧✦❧

Tallin

Tallin gave chase as Kai and Iskar started fighting and destroying the building around them. His court was in a state of total chaos; his people were injured, scattered and scared. He didn't know how many dark gods had been caught in the flood of magic he had released into the main hall. At least eight were in the traps. A large number were buried under rubble which would take them a while to move. One had been killed by Theander. No doubt a few would still be lurking, but they were much less confident now. His show of strength had been a huge shock to them.

Tallin was exhausted. He would never outwardly admit that, but he needed rest. That would not happen until he knew his court was clear of the darkness.

Haydan had claimed another realm and returned with Arianna and Maya. That fact alone suggested that leaving Aaushk with Arianna had been a wise move. Together they had worked it out and had figured out the clues and hidden help he had provided, managing to claim three of the twelve realms and return without issue. The rest of the realms would be harder to acquire.

Diego distracted Tallin from his fragmented thoughts and the fighting between Kai and Iskar. He moved closer as Asanda arrived and pulled Tallin to the side. "The court needs to be cleared of the remaining dark gods and I need to check on the Earth visitors,"

Diego said. His gaze travelled over Tallin and he added, "You're tired. Are you sure you're up to this?"

Tallin huffed and ran his hand over his face. "My magic is tired, but I have no intention of resting until my court is unsullied. Besides, I have a room full of whirling dervishes downstairs courtesy of Maya. Shall I unleash them?"

Diego's mouth twitched upwards. "That would be a help, yes. We can check on the Earth visitors on the way. I'm leaving Sandau here with Rebekka and Lavinia." He glanced across to check on Haydan, who was standing close to Arianna, Maya and Theander, then moved off. Tallin followed.

The court was quiet as they swept through the hallways. Tallin's courtiers were all gathered in groups and everyone seemed subdued as the enormity of that evening's events sank in. A couple of the repulsive hounds lay dying, their bodies twitching and convulsing.

The dervishes had already freed themselves from the confines of their suite and made their way into the court. That didn't surprise Tallin. The dervishes were not known for their ability to listen or take heed of instruction. They had surrounded two dark gods in the main hall. Both had given up on trying to escape and now cowered on their knees in quiet resignation of their fate.

The sound of fighting reached Tallin as they approached the room with the pods hanging from the ceiling. He heard a loud bang, followed by a whump noise and the sound of scuffling and snivelling.

"So, if you ever do that to me again, what's going to happen to you?"

That sounded like Si. Diego narrowed his eyes, slid the door open and peered inside.

"I told them to stay in the pod and not venture out," Diego said. "What part of that did they not understand?"

Not to be outdone, Tallin jostled with Diego to get a better view. This was a most intriguing development and one he was very curious about, because the sight greeting Tallin was bizarre to say the least.

༺·༻

Diego

Si gripped a glowing stick in his hand. The bang was the sound of him slamming it down on the ground to catch it on its return journey. He spun it in his hand like an expert swordsman before using it to beat the dark god who cowered by his feet on the floor. The dark god had a scar down his face and greasy-looking, scraggy blonde hair dragged up on top of his head. The whump sound was Si swinging the stick at the god's stomach. Doubled over on his hands and knees the dark god struggled to draw breath.

"Have you had enough yet, or shall I go back to the beginning, you pathetic excuse for a god?" When the god remained silent, Si raised his voice. "Answer me, or we go back to the start and I do some damage to your knuckles."

Tallin's eyes widened as he watched the development. "That's an interesting weapon for a human," he said, his tone low as they continued to spectate. "In fact, I'm not sure it's one I'm familiar with. Maybe I can find it in my library."

"What do you suggest I do?" Diego asked. Torturing a defenceless being was barbaric and cruel, but the dark gods had descended into the realm with one intention and that was to cause total carnage. They had not worried about a body count, but if Diego did the same and let Si continue with his form of justice, that made Diego no better than the monsters who had invaded his father's realm. Tallin yanked Diego back out of the room and pulled the door to.

"What do you know about Si?" Tallin asked, keeping his tone low.

"Enough! Please, no more. I'll do whatever you want," the dark god said.

Diego strained to hear Si's response from by the door. Leaning in, Tallin angled his head as though he was listening as well.

"What do I want from you? Now there's a question." Si's voice lowered but the menacing edge remained. "I want you to apologise to my friends for trying to attack them and their child."

Diego could just make out a snivelling apology from the god, directed at Katherine and Isaac.

"So … what do I do with him, angel? Do I kill him, trap him or let him go? He could be a useful informant."

Tallin's scowl took on the same intensity as Diego felt. "Does Si know about Katherine?" Tallin asked.

Diego shook his head. There was no way Si could know about that. It was doubtful that even Katherine knew about her own heritage, so how could Si know? "Isaac refers to Katherine as angel and Si has heard that many times, but that's simply a term of endearment, a human pet name."

"Is it? You're sure about that?" Tallin's expression

was sharp as he leant in. "But Si is, as I understand it, unreadable. In fact, I know he is, I have met him."

"Yes, but so is Isaac, and I don't see him in there wielding an ominous-looking stick."

Tallin looked thoughtful. "Could he be a guardian? A protector of some sort, one hidden in plain sight?" A sly smile slipped across his face.

"What does that look mean?"

Tallin folded his arms. "Si does not want anyone to know who he is. He is hiding close to all the interesting parties: Haydan, Maya, Arianna. What does Haydan make of him?"

"Haydan can't stand him. Actually, that's incorrect, Haydan is wary of him. He's unreadable, but Haydan has warmed to Isaac much more so than to Si."

"Hmm." Tallin frowned. "There is a folk tale amongst my people about a farmer, a shapeshifter and a herd of lynx cats."

Diego grinned. "A herd of lynx cats?" He had no clue where Tallin was taking this, but he was intrigued. "Okay, this should be good, go on then."

Looking perturbed, Tallin huffed and appeared to ponder his response a moment before continuing. "He had kept lynx cats for a long time. Their fur and meat was prized amongst his people. He became aware that his large flock was being depleted. Some nights by an animal or two, other nights three or four of them vanished without a trace. Becoming suspicious, the farmer set up watch from a suitable vantage point and kept lookout into the night. That night he noticed one of the lynx cats was not as he seemed. Hidden beneath a lynx cat pelt was a night stalker, a ferocious creature with long claws and fangs that attacked two of his lynx cats and dragged them off into the night. But the farmer knew that night stalkers could not do such a thing, so he waited patiently. On the third night, the night stalker finally revealed his true identity. It was the farmer's friend, a shapeshifter. The farmer challenged his friend and asked him why he had done such a thing. If he wanted meat all he had to do was ask. If he was cold, the farmer would have given him pelts to keep him warm. The shapeshifter chuckled and replied that he had stolen for two reasons. Firstly, the farmer had trusted him and by default given him permission to steal, and secondly, it was in his nature to thieve. Since he had no idea what he was, he had no conscience about such things." Speculation burned in the look Tallin focused on Diego.

Diego debated his response. "So, the moral of that tale is what? Don't trust a shapeshifter?"

Tallin pursed his lips. "You are mocking me. No, that is not the point. Shapeshifters have their uses. The moral is that trust is a matter of perception, which is not always real. Sometimes those who are hiding and manipulating things to suit themselves are showing you who they really are, and there are those who play others because they do not know any different."

Diego risked a cheeky retort. "Like you, for example?"

Tallin's playful smile dropped like a stone. "No, I know different, I just choose to play certain games depending on my mood. My realm is riddled with mischief, what do you expect? This is no laughing matter, Diego. You have a night stalker amongst your son's pack. The question is why? What is he up to and more importantly when is he going to reveal himself as the shapeshifter?"

"Si's a shapeshifter?"

Diego must have looked stunned or confused or both. Tallin shook his head, looking exasperated. "No, you fool, I'm speaking figuratively. The night stalker is out tonight, but when is the shapeshifter going to reveal himself? I would wager when we announce ourselves, Si will pretend this never happened."

That was a valid point and Diego wondered if Tallin was correct. "Isaac and Kat know then?"

Tallin shook his head. "No, perhaps not, but tonight they know he is different. He is their friend, they will believe whatever he tells them and keep his confidence. That will give him the security he needs and maybe at some point he will trip himself up because of it. Keep an eye on him and do not trust him. Si is enjoying torturing that god in there and hides the same coldness as they do."

That much was true. There was a certain amount of glee evident in Si's torture of the dark god. Diego nodded his understanding and walked back down the corridor with Tallin before returning to the room in a more obvious manner.

Diego would find it difficult to act normal around Si knowing the man was full of deceit. The thought did not sit well with him, although a tiny part of him hoped that it was a misunderstanding and Si was on their side. However, he couldn't shake the thought that Si, for all his tomfoolery, was something more than he appeared. A devious man, playing his own game with all the pieces on the board.

Chapter 40

Maya

Leylani rushed into the room and assessed Sandau. She cut away his clothing to examine the damage to his shoulder. The skin there had turned as black as Maya's left hand. Within seconds Leylani was insisting Sandau was moved to a more comfortable room where she could tend to him. "What happened to him? Where is Diego?" Leylani asked.

Lavinia had entered the destroyed hallway with Rebekka and loitered by the stairs. Haydan beckoned Lavinia across. "Find Diego. Is he with Tallin?"

"I need to know about his family history," Leylani said.

Lavinia nodded. "Tallin confirms Diego is on his way back. He can tell you about Sandau's bloodline better than I."

Haydan ruffled his hair. "He told me his mother was a dark god and that he saw the light because of his father."

"Really?" Leylani looked fascinated as she crouched next to Sandau. "So, he's half dark, half light god?"

Diego entered and his face fell as he took in the

sight of Sandau collapsed in front of Leylani. "No, he's not a pure-blood god. His mother was a dark god. His father was a hybrid or chimera, part light god, part something else. That's why his irises are ghosted. Even Sandau doesn't know who his father is. Can you help him? Will he be alright?"

Leylani stepped back as Sandau was lifted onto a stretcher and carried off to another more comfortable location by a group of guards. She spoke to Diego with a lowered voice. "If his mother was a dark magic wielder there's a good chance he can fight this. I'm hoping that when the magic that did this to him was created, it was designed to hurt the light rather than the dark and he's biologically more dark than light. I may need some assistance from another god who is both though, if we can find such a being."

Kai stepped back from the gathered group and loitered next to Theander as though leaving. Maya moved away from Haydan, with a dismissive flick of her hand before he tried to stop her, and across to stand by them. "You need to help Sandau," she said.

Kai pursed his lips, raised his chin and surveyed Maya. "The only thing I am doing is getting out of here. Asanda will be in even more of a bad mood when he returns. The dark gods captured here need moving back to our vault. He will not allow me to be involved in that now."

Theander raised his hand up and rested it on Kai's shoulder. "That man just sacrificed himself to save me because of your brother. You are going to help him, out of gratitude for what he did."

Kai's body tensed and he gave Theander a withering look. "Are you asking me to do that, or telling me?"

Theander's mouth twitched upwards. "I don't tell

you to do anything. I'm appealing to the conscience that you claim you don't own. You need to make friends. This is a good way to do that. Maya and I would appreciate the gesture. Plus, it will surprise Asanda and that can only be a good thing."

Theander's eyes clashed with Maya's as if a look of understanding passed between them. She had unexpectedly gained his support; the realisation made her smile inwardly at her achievement.

After a moment's silence, where nobody moved, Kai clenched his jaw and glared at Theander. "Fine, but you owe me." He followed Leylani and Diego out of the room.

Maya grinned as she returned to Haydan. Perhaps she had some of her mother's skills of persuasion after all.

Haydan

It was going to be hours before they knew how Sandau was doing. Haydan checked in with Diego to see if there had been any further developments, there hadn't, then returned to Tallin with the rest of the party.

Theander remained close by. Haydan guessed he would stay until Kai came back from helping Leylani and that they would then both melt away.

Asanda returned with an army of winged creatures to collect the trapped gods. They marched into the court in an impressive display of force and separated off into groups who then rounded up the prisoners and moved them off. In the midst of all the activity Asanda walked up to Tallin. After a moment of staring at Asanda as though dumbstruck, Tallin dropped to a knee.

"Get up, Fae King. I am not here for worship. I wanted to thank you," Asanda said. "Iskar has evaded me this evening, but their entrance to your court has been sealed off. He will not be so foolish as to attempt to return. This realm is well guarded and tonight I have reminded him of my interest."

Asanda surveyed the hall, his eyes sliding across everyone gathered. He concentrated on Haydan for a second longer than Haydan was comfortable with. His mouth dried the moment Asanda's gaze slowed and his heartbeat stuttered as the weight of all that power and energy focused on him. The relief he felt when Asanda's attention moved on was immeasurable.

"You have the heart of a forest wolf, the agility of a mountain gazelle and a strong soul, King Tallin, but do not forget that I keep a close eye on the aberrations." Asanda's attention flitted to Arianna, Maya and Haydan again, before returning to Tallin. "Today you proved yourself worthy of your position at the centre of Aveyamara. I would like to reward you with two things."

Asanda held out his hand and a large ball of light formed. The surface danced with explosions and pulses of energy. "Firstly, a way to replenish yourself. This evening has taken its toll on you and I would hate to see the more devious of your people take advantage of you under such circumstances. I think this will give any of your detractors a very clear message." Asanda passed the ball of light across to him.

Tallin peered at it, his expression one of delight at the gift. "Thank you, My Lord. This is most kind of you."

Asanda lowered his head by way of acknowledgement. "As my next gift will be." He turned and two angels stepped forwards. "I am leaving two of my angels in your care. They offer hidden abilities that are for you alone to discover. I think you will find them useful."

Tallin studied the man and woman in surprise. "Well, yes, I am sure I will. I have no idea what to do with them though."

A bemused look crossed Asanda's features. "My advice is do not corrupt them and as long as you let them ride the evening air currents, they tend to be content." Asanda moved off. "This is the last of the darkness."

A dark god was dragged past in heavy chains which thrummed with the type of energy that only the gods could create.

"Our time here has come to an end. Good luck rebuilding the court. I advise keeping the foundations untouched when you renovate. That way this stronghold remains exactly that." With a look at Tallin that conveyed so many potential messages, Asanda swept away, following the angels as they marched through the nearby doorway.

Asanda turned back before he crossed the threshold. "I almost forgot. I will have the protective guards around the human properties extended. Iskar would never be so foolish as to return, but I will make sure that cannot happen."

Tallin's surprised expression fell on Haydan, then he recovered himself and refocused on Asanda, who was disappearing into the darkness. "Thank you, My Lord."

Asanda had already gone, leaving Haydan with the uncomfortable reassurance that it was Asanda who protected Isaac's property, for reasons that he couldn't begin to fathom. The unsettling mention of more than one property being involved was more intriguing than alarming. Who else was Asanda protecting?

☙❧

Diego

The last person Diego expected to see as he waited in the corridor near Sandau's room was Maya. She wandered across to him with a pensive look on her face and sank into a nearby seat, patting it to indicate he should join her.

He settled next to her and rested his elbows on his knees, which earned him a gentle smack on his arm. "Do you have to do that – spread out like that? It's vulgar."

Feeling like a scolded child, Diego moved his arms and straightened up. "Watch who you're speaking to, Maya." Pausing for a second, he then said, "Does Haydan know you're here?"

Maya looked unconcerned as she stared at the door to Sandau's room. "Haydan is with Tallin. Theander escorted me." She indicated Theander with a wave of her hand. He was waiting discreetly nearby. She flicked her head towards the solid, ancient-looking door. "How is he?"

"Theander escorted you? You're on first-name terms with a god? That's an interesting development." Theander was a friend of Haydan's, but it still seemed odd. This was Maya though and she had her moments

of unusual behaviour. Diego let the incident pass
without further comment in front of Theander.
"Sandau's fighting it, but it's going to take time. I
suspect I will be returning without him. Leylani seems
to think his recuperation will be lengthy, and it will be
good for him to be away from Arianna for a while.
She does not welcome his attention. She never has."
That was for Theander's benefit. He needed the god to
understand that Arianna was unattached. The last thing
he wanted was a challenge from Theander to Sandau
and all of the trouble which would accompany that.

Theander's head turned towards Diego at the
mention of Arianna, confirming Diego's suspicions
about the blue-eyed Adonis. Haydan would not
welcome the news. In fact, Diego disliked the idea as
well. A merger of god and warrior wasn't something he
was keen on. The gods had a lot of enemies, remained
oblivious to the devastation they caused and were
disinterested in dealing with the aftermath of their
involvement and meddling.

"Plus, I think Leylani might be sweet on Sandau. He
likes her a little as well and he understands Arianna is
off limits. Haydan will not tolerate another touching his
warrior, and he knows if anyone does, even when they
train together."

Theander appeared to relax. His head lowered
and his attention shifted elsewhere, suggesting the
announcement about Sandau and the reminder of
Haydan's awareness of what Arianna was up to had
pacified him.

Maya nodded her understanding and studied the
ornate door. "You think the world of him. That's
wonderful to see."

Diego ruffled his hair. His shoulder ached from the

earlier exertion. He sported countless cuts and bruises from all the fighting, and his body ached with the need to sleep. "He's my best friend. I rescued him from his abusive mother when he was a child. Well, I say that, she traded him. I could sense the light in him even then. She tried to beat it out of him, but that never worked. He was a frightened, injured, scared little boy and I took him under my wing and raised him." He shuffled in his seat unsure why he had just shared that with Maya. "You have something to say to me."

"I owe you an apology for my behaviour in the kitchen before all of this." Maya fiddled with a charm bracelet covered in hearts on her wrist, most likely a gift from Haydan. Contemplating Theander for a moment, she turned towards Diego, her expression so serious that his heart thrummed. She looked like the bearer of bad news and that alarmed him.

"To my knowledge my soul has never been wiped clean, or reset in the sea, but if it was…" Maya swallowed hard and focused on her slender fingers for a moment. "If I was reset, trapped in the darkness and I could not remember who and what I was, I would run to the one place where I felt safe and protected. Well, in actual fact, I have two places I would run to. Haydan and Isaac."

Diego narrowed his eyes and pursed his lips as he leant forwards. "Not Alex then?"

Tears brimmed in Maya's eyes. "He's an echo of my past. A loud echo, one I can't ignore. He wants something from me. I don't understand what yet and maybe I don't want to know. In truth, I can't figure out if I can bring myself to ever give him what he needs – the sea, before you jump to conclusions." Maya's mouth thinned. She brushed her dress down and straightened up. "It's about the soul, not the physical form, Diego. If I was broken and in need of understanding and the storms happened, that is where I would go. Your chosen one is no different. She will have sought safety." Maya placed her hand against Diego's knee in a concerned manner as she studied his responses and searched for understanding in his eyes. "I believe the storms always change things for us, sometimes in unexpected ways. Please don't be angry at Theander. It's not his fault. He didn't anticipate this and Magellan was playing a cruel, twisted game with you."

What did Magellan have to do with this? Diego tried to make sense of the hidden thread of Maya's message. "Why was Magellan playing a game with me?"

"Haydan has filled me in. Apparently, you refused to take the souls of Magellan's wife and child into our care. I'm guessing this happened in a previous cycle."

"I don't remember," Diego said. "I don't bring everything with me when I resurface. That explains why I didn't like him though."

"This has all been about revenge. He wanted you to suffer. Leylani was working for him under duress. He did something to your chosen one's soul and stripped her of any connection to us. Then Leylani scuppered whatever he had planned and let her go. Haydan found her last time we were here. She was safe for you, but she doesn't remember you right now."

Now it made sense. Diego cupped his hands over his nose and mouth. "Are you trying to tell me that Sasha left the sea in the storms and found me?"

Maya nodded, her expression pained. "It looks that way."

"Storm alive." Diego slid his hands into his hair and dropped his head. "Rebekka's pregnant. Are you suggesting that the baby is—" a snarl of anger erupted from his mouth "—no! It can't be true."

Maya sighed and twisted the bracelet about again. "I think you might find it is. She fled to you for safety, just not in the way intended. Take some time to come to terms with it."

He had understood that Sasha was safe. He had trusted Haydan and Theander, believing that she would be protected. Theander had failed in that duty of care. He was out of his seat and heading towards Theander before he had thought through his actions.

Maya dived into the space between them. Diego advanced until he was close enough to Theander to force the god to acknowledge his presence and meet his eyes. "I trusted you with her and you allow a chosen one to tell me that you failed to protect her? Now you're allowing her to defend you?"

Theander's head tilted back, defiance flashing in his glowing eyes. "I'm not allowing it. Maya is what she is. She felt it would be better if she told you. I asked her for advice on this subject. This is hardly my forte, sharing bad news. I never intended for your chosen one's soul to escape. She was safe, it's … well, perhaps Storm Lands helped her flee. It was not something I was aware of, or had control of. I am sorry."

That apology sounded odd coming from Theander, forced, as though even having to state the words was alien to him.

"I didn't know Magellan had messed with a soul. That is not something normal, or acceptable. The souls of your people are sacred, to us as well as you. Rebekka is a strong choice. Is she not enough, storm rider?"

That question silenced Diego. He didn't have an answer. After a moment he managed to say, "Her soul is different. It's not the same. You wouldn't understand."

"You love her."

"Yes."

Maya pushed Diego away and he stepped backwards as desolation swept his mind. That was it. Decision made.

"Rebekka gets her wish then. No more chosen one to worry about." Staggering backwards, he landed back on the seat and tried to compose his shattered emotions.

Maya's sad smile hinted at how much the news affected her as she returned to the seat next to him. "Oh, I don't know. Our souls have ways of finding their way to where they truly belong. Be patient, Sasha may well surprise you."

"Well, she's already managed that. This is going to break my heart." Diego's voice cracked.

Maya nodded. "I know. If you ever need to talk about this, you know where I am. Just remember what I said about the soul."

Kai slipped out of the room and left with Theander. Leylani came to the door. "He needs rest but he has improved. I'm going to stay with him. You should get some sleep."

Diego stood. "I'll walk you back to the others." He needed time to clear his head.

Maya fixed a wistful smile on Diego. "It will be okay, you know."

She had progressed from pushing Diego to his limits before they reached Aveyamara to now offering him support and understanding in his time of need. That was the thing with Maya, she was always unexpected.

Chapter 41

Tallin

Lavinia walked towards Tallin and wrapped her arms around his waist. He smiled and pulled the gift from Asanda from his pocket. Holding it where she could see it, he allowed her to study it. Light gently illuminated the soft velvety skin at the base of her neck. Even though her mask was tattered and feathers hung off it at jaunty angles she still looked beautiful as she basked in his adoration.

"Well, go on then, activate it," Lavinia said, her voice soft and breathy. "I know you want to. The one good thing to come out of all of this is I get some of your attention back."

Tallin huffed in a playful manner. "You are so greedy, my sweet, but you will have to share me for a short while longer. No one is going home until I have got to know my family a little better. Plus, I will have to check that the wards on the properties where they all live are reset by Asanda to my satisfaction."

Lavinia tightened the squeeze, showing her approval with a delightful smile.

Tallin could enjoy being Lavinia's focus for hours,

but there was still work to do. He drew on a tiny amount of the power Asanda had provided. He closed his eyes and his body tingled as the energy he had expended replenished itself.

Asanda had mentioned that Tallin would be able to deal with his detractors effectively. He could not resist the urge to announce his victory to the realm.

Lavinia released her hold and stepped back, her face a mixture of awe, delight and fascination.

The scent of powerful magic flooded Tallin's mind and body, refreshing and revitalising as it flowed. It permeated his entire being, leaving him with a feeling of utter ecstasy. He pushed the energy out, gently at first, then with more force when the ball of energy did not appear to bear any ill effects. If anything, it glowed brighter in response.

The summer court began its regeneration with a light shudder. Tallin took his time triggering off the process, exploring his connection to the magic that thrummed from the centre of the court before allowing it to gain momentum. It would be rebuilt to look even more spectacular than previously.

Now Tallin's realm knew he was untouchable and held in great favour. The fresh, zesty scent of vitality overwhelmed him. He allowed his lands to thrum with the force of the magic. All his subjects would feel that. They would understand the powerful message hidden within. The magic wielders who had been hiding their talents in his forest would know that the king was back, blessed by the gods and confident in his abilities.

Tomorrow evening the two angels in his care would take flight, announcing their presence to his people. This was something new, something his realm had never before been granted and his soul buzzed from the thrill of it all. This was even better than the tiny piece of the mask that still nestled in his pocket. It was addictive. It was mesmerising. It was everything Tallin could have hoped for and more – approval from the gods.

☙❧

Maya

Something disturbed Maya's sleep. Bleary-eyed she cracked an eye open and reorientated herself. She was back in her own bed – of course.

After a couple of extra weeks in Tallin's realm, he had at last allowed them to leave. It had been accompanied by much huffing and sulking from the king, but with promises of return visits he had begrudgingly agreed to their return to their respective homes.

Watching Tallin prowl around the garden checking on the wards had been the most bizarre experience ever, but finally satisfied by the changes, he had wished them well and stalked off. Haydan had surveyed the odd display with an apologetic look on his face and a headshake, as though exasperated by his grandfather, but resigned to his strange behaviour.

Katherine had smiled at him. "At least you know he cares," she had said.

Maya wanted to tell her mother about their family tree. It had played on her mind ever since, but she could not bring herself to do so and Kai would be livid if she did. She often wondered what her father and grandfather looked like. Did her grandfather know about Maya? Did he think about her and her mother and wonder how they were? Did he care at all?

One thing Maya knew for certain, she had not seen the last of Kai. She had not seen him since the night of the fight with Iskar, but she knew he was about. His scent was distinctive and she would catch wafts of his spicy, chocolatey scent in her home when she wandered around.

Movement on the bed confirmed Maya had company. With a whimper of fear, she reached for the bedside light and switched it on illuminating a small shock of purple hair that dragged something onto the bed beside her. "Aaushk, you gave me a heart attack." Her thundering heartbeat hammered in agreement.

He was returning the water book. The purple shock of hair squinted in the brightness and folded his arms. "It's on loan, courtesy of Tallin."

That meant only one thing, because Aaushk had struggled to get the book onto the bed. Tallin was in the property. Tallin had expressed more than a passing interest in her siblings. "Why is Tallin in our house, in the dark?"

Aaushk shrugged and refused to meet Maya's gaze. "Please tell me he's not after the kids." Grabbing her torch from the bedside table, she pushed off from the bed and rushed to the door, praying she was mistaken and that her siblings were still tucked up in bed.

The lights recessed in the stair treads illuminated the carpet as she descended to the first floor of the house and opened the doors into her siblings' bedrooms. Every bed was empty.

Haydan, get here right now. Maya issued a low growl. "Mum! Dad! Arianna!"

The main landing light switched on as Isaac and Katherine left their bedroom and wandered onto the landing looking half asleep. Haydan arrived a moment later. He meandered onto the landing from the staircase down to the ground floor and nothing could have prepared Maya for the effect he had on her as the thump of his arrival resonated in her chest making her gasp. Her soul shuddered in delight at his proximity and lurched towards him. It was an irritating but reassuring reaction to his presence, one that was growing stronger as she matured during her teenage years.

"Evening all, or should that be good morning all?" Despite the obvious panic around him, Haydan seemed remarkably relaxed. He ruffled his tousled hair as he blinked and fixed heavy-lidded eyes on her. He hadn't bothered to sort out his facial hair, something he could easily have done with his magic, and his appearance struck her as sinful. The top two buttons on his crisp white shirt were unbuttoned, giving her a brief glimpse of his chest beneath. The sleeves were rolled up past his elbows, revealing his forearms and altera. He stretched. The lazy motion reminded her of a beast stirring from its slumber before leaving its cave and surveying its empire. All that muscle and power wrapped up inside a handsome, mysterious package that was as stunning on the inside as he was on the outside. It gave the false impression of a man at ease with everything around him, but his sleep-hazed eyes told her an entirely different story. He was toying with her, feigning disinterest whilst knowing that every time he did so, it lured her just a tiny bit more, and curse him to Storm Lands and back, this was a game he was very good at. His shirt lifted as he finished his stretch. His fingers extended right out, then slid behind his head and his arms folded back. Her gaze settled and lingered a little bit longer than it should have on the flat expanse of stomach and dark hair that had appeared above the fastening on his jeans. Haydan never let anyone else see his body. That had been done purely to tease her and goodness, it was effective.

"Well? Earth calling Maya?"

Maya blinked a few times and composed her thoughts. Isaac was speaking to her and she was gawking at Haydan open-mouthed. Her heart thudded loudly and her mouth had dried. To make matters worse, Haydan had noticed, because he dropped his arms back down, shot a sly look at her and leant back against the bannister with his arms folded. His right foot pointed straight at her as he lazed back and waited for her to recover.

"So, what has happened? Are the children missing again, or is it something more serious?" Haydan asked as Arianna bounded down the stairs. "Arianna, good of you to join us. In the event of an emergency, it's reassuring to know you are alert and on form at all times."

Arianna wrinkled her nose. "I was forced to play a game to escape my room that I would rather not have."

Isaac scowled. "Is there someone else in the house, Arianna?"

Arianna's face flushed. "Hell no. Not anyone invited at least. What's going on?"

"The children have been taken whilst we slept." Isaac's voice cracked. His eyes looked glossy in the dim lighting before settling back to their normal appearance as he quelled the flood of emotions no doubt surging inside him. "Haydan is about to explain how he's going to help to get them back."

"What? That's not possible. The wards were tightened to keep others out," Arianna said, looking distraught, "unless Asanda made a few exceptions. How did Maya find out?"

Everyone turned their attention to Maya. She cleared her throat and tried her best to ignore Haydan. He had fixed one of his smouldering looks on her, which was definitely intended to distract her, and now rested his arms out along the bannister with his altera on show. The surface roiled like a turbulent sea and all Maya could think about was how she wanted to move closer to him and calm the unease that stirred around his soul. His woodsy pine and cinnamon scent reached her, calming her own soul and reminding her of how much he affected her, even though she tried to deny the intensity of the attraction between them.

"Aaushk has just returned the water book to me, meaning Tallin has been in the house and the children are gone. All of them. He's taken them."

Haydan tilted his head right back and closed his eyes, giving Maya a view of his throat, which bobbed as he swallowed. His head lowered and his eyes slid open as he leant his body forwards. "You know that for sure, or you're assuming that?"

"Assuming. You know what he's like. Will you take this seriously, please?" Maya glared at Haydan. He was being annoying, which was probably his intention.

"You want me to do what about this exactly?"

Indignation flared through Maya's mind and she folded her arms, mimicking his earlier pose. "What do you mean by that? Go and get them back, of course."

Isaac drew himself up, his brows furrowed and he folded his arms, reflecting his displeasure at Haydan.

Haydan lowered his head and met Maya's eyes with

the most mischievous and taunting look she had ever seen. "What's it worth, beautiful?"

Maya huffed and scowled at Haydan. His behaviour was infuriating. "What's it worth? My eternal gratitude, how about that?"

Haydan appeared to consider her answer, the edges of his mouth turning down even though his face remained relaxed. He leant in closer. "I would prefer the kiss and date night you promised me. Grant me that and I might consider it."

"Are you serious? He's kidnapped my siblings."

Haydan's eyes narrowed and he straightened up, relaxing back against the bannister. "Yeah, but this is Tallin you're talking about. He doesn't see things as being kidnapped. His world is more varying shades of grey depending on your viewpoint. For all I know, he's not after the kids, he's after all of us, or me. There is also the possibility that he sent Lavinia back with Aaushk, and Tallin doesn't even have your family. If he has them, they're safe. He won't harm them." His shoulders raised dismissively. "I actually don't think he does have them. Check again and you'll find a feather in each of their beds. Someone else has them, someone who is a close blood relation. He's taken them before at this time of night. He always returns them. I think the being who took them wants Tallin to know he has them, however. This is a game between Tallin and your mystery bloodline. The question is, do you wish me to play the game? Knowing my grandfather, this is some ancient feud and he's waiting for me to take the bait."

Maya tapped her foot. "I suggest you quit seeing this as a game and do something about it before I rattle the family tree." She held up her hands, letting them slide into their unusual colouring. She had become better with practice, and when sleepy, she found the transition easier to manage, perhaps because she wasn't as focused. The bracelet on her wrist jangled at the same time.

"I second that." Isaac wrapped an arm around Katherine and pulled her closer. "Why would Tallin, or this other being, want the children?"

Haydan scowled, his brow lowering in disapproval, no doubt at Maya's goading, and he finally began to look more serious. "That's a new trick, Maya. We need to talk about that." He let his words sink in for a moment, then continued. "Diego has a theory that the birth rate is low in Tallin's realm because they have been isolated for too long."

"They're children." Katherine looked furious.

Haydan massaged the sides of his temples with his thumb and index finger. "Technically so are Maya and Arianna. Look, Tallin doesn't see the world like you do. Time means nothing to him. He sees the world in terms of games, tricks and sleight of hand. Children fascinate him. They see the world differently. He was taken with the baby when you entered Aveyamara. If he bewitches them as children, they will return to his realm when they are adults and that is probably his end goal. You have a big family and you have a bloodline that he finds fascinating. If there is a feather in the bed, as I suspect there is, then this is a battle of wits between Tallin and someone he has encountered before, someone ancient, powerful and linked to the gods and angels."

Maya went to check the nearest bedroom. She grabbed the small feather that was left on the pillow and returned to the landing, holding it out for everyone to see. "Haydan's correct. What does this mean?"

"If my theory is correct, it means your siblings

should be back shortly."

Isaac grinned in his usual mischievous way and held up his piece of the mask. "Does this help at all?"

Haydan fixed his attention on the piece of Kaleshar. An almost indiscernible flitter of annoyance shot across his features as he straightened up. "Yeah, that changes things somewhat. You're enjoying this, aren't you?" he said.

Isaac nodded his agreement enthusiastically. "Yeah, stirring you up is great fun. Are you bringing Diego?"

The lines across Haydan's forehead deepened. "Are you suggesting that, or telling me that? I am more than capable of–"

"I don't doubt that for a second, Haydan, but if Tallin is involved, it's usually wise to bring his first heir along – just to be on the safe side."

Haydan ruffled his hair again as though agitated. "Diego and I are not getting along at the moment. I knew when I claimed Storm Lands that this would happen. You are not coming, Isaac. You have a business to run and a family to provide for."

Isaac looked incensed and he turned as though intending to return to his room and get dressed. "Yeah, you're right – *my family* – that's just been kidnapped by your crazy grandfather, or some other lunatic. I'm not going to manage to focus on anything until the kids are back. I'm getting dressed, then we're going."

"I don't think the mystery visitor will thank you for calling him a lunatic," Haydan said. "Not to mention that you're human." Irritation flashed across his face. "And go where, Isaac? Have you listened to anything I've said?"

Isaac stilled, a sure sign that he was running out of patience with Haydan. "Tallin's realm."

A breeze swept through the house. It skittered over Maya's skin, buffeting her hair.

Haydan's jaw clenched. "As I said, you'll find the children back in their beds. Safe."

Katherine rushed to the nearest bedroom and glanced inside. Her hand fluttered up to cover her mouth and she nodded, confirming Haydan's comment as fact. "They're back." She checked on the rest of their brood. Isaac remained still like a sentry as he waited for her to make sure all the children had been returned.

Maya grinned at Haydan. "Don't look like that, so put out. Whilst you're gone I'll try and work out the clues for the next realm in the water book."

Haydan turned to Arianna. "You're not coming with me. Sandau is already there. Keep an eye on Maya."

"You're not serious, are you? I'm being left babysitting?" Arianna's glare of annoyance confirmed that news pleased her as much as it did Maya.

Maya smiled sweetly. "Oh, come on, I'm not that bad. We can figure the water book out together." She settled a sneaky look on Arianna. She had no intention of staying put and behaving; it would be easy enough to convince her stepsister to join her.

Arianna's eyes narrowed in understanding as she fought back a grin of amusement. Katherine looked as though the sleight of hand from Maya had not escaped her attention either.

Haydan was underestimating Maya again. This time she would not be behaving like she did normally. The darkness within her didn't like doing as it was told. It never had and Kaleshar agreed. A piece of him was still nestled in her drawer upstairs where Haydan couldn't find it.

ॐॐ

𝒟iego

The village was still destroyed. His people had seen off the warlord after Diego drew the mage away, but he would be back. Diego had set up a team to help with the rebuilding. The female shreken warrior was leading the team in the realm. Progress was slow, but they had made a start on helping the villagers who lost everything.

Teeam was helping to train the villagers so they would have a chance of surviving another attack. Defences were being built, they were planting new crops and an air of optimism hung over proceedings rather than the fear and gloom that had prevailed when he had last been there.

Now he had to visit Touranga to check on his mage friend. This was going to be interesting. He had to apologise to the queen for his brief visit and for depositing a problem, in the form of the mage, into her realm. He needed to explain things to Keilty and he was never very good at this part. Bracing himself for an uncertain welcome from her, he dropped his storm cloud, letting the breeze and flood of energy from his altera calm his soul.

It was evening when he arrived. The scent of campfires permeated the air, punctuated by the smell of flowering plants. Nearby, waterfalls cascaded down to the main river, the roar of the water unmistakeable. He had forgotten how much he enjoyed the evenings of dancing and merriment on Touranga. Like his own people, Keilty's enjoyed the simple pleasures in life and this was the time of day when they relaxed.

He was close to the training ground. Vibrations flooded the air, warning the guardians of his presence. He waited for the formal welcome. Who would be on duty? Perhaps it was Keilty's shift. A rune flashed across the ground in front of him and an arm wrapped around his throat from behind. Diego raised his hands as a blade flashed in the corner of his eye. It stilled close by, glinting in the light from the distant setting sun.

"You have the audacity to land us with your problem, then take off again without a chance for us to follow? I expected better, storm rider Diego."

He would recognise that feminine, angry tone anywhere. "Keilty, let me explain before you judge me." There was no give in her arm. The blade remained poised and ready to inflict injury.

"Hmm, then there's the issue of your broken promise, storm rider. I thought you had more honour than to do such a thing. Submit to me and at least bestow upon me this privilege."

That accusation stung, as did the suggestion of Diego acquiescing to her demand.

"I always did enjoy this moment," Keilty whispered close to his ear.

Diego could hear the poorly concealed humour in her voice at the reminder of their playful banter and games, however. Historically, they never submitted to each other in public, but in private it was a different matter. Inhaling, Diego tapped her arm, requesting release. He had no wish to fight her. They had always been evenly matched, although his elven and elder status would now change that. He had no intention of adding to her list of grievances or irritations that evening.

"I brought a storm rider mate out of the sea with me. I had an ancient vow to uphold, it superseded yours, and I was told to follow the anomalies, so I did. I haven't forgotten our pact, but now that I am captured in my father's web, I may never taste freedom again. I did not forget our agreement, or dishonour it, Keil. I wouldn't do that to you. I am, however, currently unable to fathom how we can ever fulfil our promises to each other." This was harder than Diego had expected. He hated letting her down and his storm rider sense of honour railed against the idea that he had failed her.

Her arm remained tensed. She pulled him back harder against her body and pressed her forehead against his head. "Why is nothing involving you ever simple? You always make it so complicated and I'm the one who is immortal. Does she know when you touch someone else?"

Shaking his head, Diego sighed and turned towards her. Keilty's arm lowered, permitting him to fully turn around and face her. Keilty's now silvery-white hair was loose, suggesting she wasn't on duty that evening. It was always braided so she looked more formidable when she was working. She lowered the blade and returned it to the holster carried around her waist.

"My soul doesn't link with hers. We don't share that type of connection."

"How many children again, remind me?"

"Including the one on the way, eight and an adopted one." He was trying not to think about Sasha. He cleared his throat and ruffled his unruly hair.

Keilty's eyes narrowed. "The one on the way

bothers you for some reason. Why?"

Astute as always, nothing escaped Keilty's attention. Diego had not forgotten that. He would end up telling her about Sasha at some point. She would tell him that was karma, but at least she would understand how he felt. "Enough of the questions. I came to explain myself to you and to deal with the mage that I dumped on you. I also need to apologise to the queen."

Keilty smiled and turned, a flick of her head suggesting Diego follow her. Leading the way, she walked down to the waterfalls and selected the path that led to the queen's residence.

"What happened to my irritating friend anyway?" Diego asked as the spray from the waterfall brushed his skin.

Keilty smiled and some of Diego's tension eased. "Your mage friend likes it here. I don't think he wants to leave. His home world is not so accepting of his unique abilities. Here, he is with those who value and welcome his gifts and he is quite talented. Not as skilled as us, but nevertheless, he is comfortable and can hold his own amongst our kind. The queen has offered him the chance to stay, but that would, of course, require your blessing."

That was an unexpected turn of events. He had anticipated finding the mage wallowing in the prison. The walls of the corridor to the queen's residence glowed and they walked alongside the internal river that flowed underground before meeting with the river that flowed above ground. "Has he talked about the warlord?"

"He has been more talkative of late, yes."

Keilty turned towards Diego, trapping him against the wall as she stepped closer. "I'm certain you're not just here to talk to me about a broken promise and to discuss the mage who was chasing you. There's more to it than that. Darach mentioned a mask. I know you well enough to know when you're up to something."

"Darach? That's his name, the mage?"

Keilty nodded and waited for his response.

"The mask of the gods has surfaced. I know who its true master is and the dark gods are hunting him. This is a battle of epic proportions, one I need help with."

Keilty glared at Diego in the glowing ambient light. "You are one of my dearest friends. I would do anything for you, but what you ask is too much. The queen will not allow it. No one can unite the twelve kingdoms. It's not possible."

"You would rather the dark gods ruled over all?" Keilty hated dark gods, so Diego already knew her answer, but the subject matter would rile her enough for him to get under her skin and irritate her further.

Keilty's brow furrowed. "Filthy dark gods are not walking this realm."

"Keilty, this is already in motion. With your people onside, it would be a whole lot easier to make sure that can never happen."

A couple of guards approached. Keilty turned and nodded in greeting to them as they walked past grinning at her. The last thing Diego needed was rumours springing up amongst her people that he was back and close with her again. She turned back and narrowed her eyes. "Why are you involved in this anyway? It's not your battle."

This was the part which he had been dreading. She wouldn't like his answer. "It kind of is my battle. He has claimed three realms so far. He will have to come for yours. There is no intent to rule, he's as caught up in this as the rest of us. I would rather he claimed the realms than dark gods, and given his success so far, they will not cease in their hunt. They will come back more determined than ever to stop him."

Keilty inhaled sharply as awareness reached her. "Your son. Your son is the one destined to rule."

"Yes, Haydan, my son, is the one recognised by the mask as its true master. He did not choose this destiny. Give him a chance."

Keilty's headshake confirmed that the news wasn't well received. "The queen will not bow to anyone." Her tone contemptuous, she drew herself up. "Especially not to a male."

"Haydan has a female chosen one and you've met Arianna. He's surrounded by strong women. He's my flesh and blood. Have I ever given you cause to think I disrespect you and your queen?"

"No, but—"

"Don't back the wrong side, Keil. Between dark gods and my son, I know which I would prefer. There will be no bowing or kneeling involved with Haydan, he has no interest in ruling. He will respect your people and your customs. Dark gods will destroy everything."

"It's not my decision, but he will have to prove himself worthy before any of us even consider it and given your track record of keeping to your promises…"

Diego inhaled at her barbed comment and tried to ignore the unease that shuddered through his mind at her words. "I didn't make this decision lightly, Keil. I don't regret a moment of the time I spent with you, but please don't judge me on this. I have responsibilities to my people and that has to be my main priority. You know how few of us remain."

"Which realms are already claimed?"

"Aveyamara and Storm Lands."

"Do you kneel to him?"

"No, you know my views on that. Plus, I'm elder, I don't bow to anyone." He didn't add that he had knelt for his father under duress when he first met him.

Her eyes narrowed. He knew that look well enough to understand he should divulge everything and quickly.

"I'm heir to Aveyamara this cycle. One day I will be king."

Throwing her head back, Keilty burst into laughter. "Full disclosure, wow. Well, aren't you full of surprises today. Tallin is your father this cycle then? Tell the queen all of that before adding the information about the mask."

Nodding his understanding, Diego braced himself for speaking to the queen.

"Oh, and for the record, I still consider you my husband, whether you like it or not."

Diego suppressed a wry smile. That was a secret he had never shared with anyone. Keilty had understood it was a once in a cycle event. That had turned into two cycles. Perhaps that had been unwise.

"That Diego crossed over and returned to the sea," he said. It was doubtful that argument would hold any sway with her, but he would try it first. "Oh, and I need your help with how to charm a pixie post. Any underhanded tactics would work a treat as the creature knows what I'm up to."

"You're reborn, that argument doesn't carry any sway with me, not after two cycles together. That means you're living in sin with another woman. Naughty Diego." With a sly grin at her tormenting of him, Keilty spun around and stalked off. "Why would I help you with a pixie post?" Her voice echoed around the cavern they were walking through. "You would have to persuade me and right now you're not in favour."

Fighting back his irritation at Keilty's new game, he walked after her. He had to persuade the queen to help him and Haydan. Her response made a big difference to how this all played out.

❧

Katherine

Her youngest was still asleep. If lucky she had twenty minutes to grab the washing from the line, put it away and prepare lunch. The breeze picked up as she rushed out into the garden and started hauling sheets from the line. Whipping the nearest sheet back, she stifled a scream. A man was standing a metre away from her on the other side.

The breeze buffeted his dark hair. His arms were folded and he surveyed her with a contemptuous look. His clothing was dark, but the shoulders of his jacket displayed silvery crests that made him appear regal. He projected an air of intimidation.

Composing herself, Katherine swallowed her fear, cleared her throat and backed away. "Hello. You frightened the life out of me. Can I help you?"

"I don't know, Katherine. I think it's time you provided me with a few answers though. You hide in plain sight, with a human mate. Explain yourself."

Hysterical laughter bubbled up from her throat at his strange demand. This man was not human. She had a sixth sense about these things and he exuded an authority that even storm riders didn't possess. "I'm not explaining myself to anyone, least of all a stranger. How can you be on this property? The wards were strengthened."

A knowing smirk suggested the stranger would have some sort of smart answer to her question.

"By my father, yes. Certain individuals are allowed special access. I'm one of them."

"And you are? It's polite to introduce yourself first, before making demands."

"I'm Kai. Do you know what you are? Were you blessed at birth? Do you know *who* you are? I command you to answer. Only when blessed will you answer the true call from another god."

An oppressive force pushed against Katherine's chest. Magic of some sort. She struggled to suppress it. Inhaling, she shoved it aside and scowled at the stranger. Words bubbled up inside her mind, words that she couldn't ignore or deny. It felt like being possessed. They demanded release and she couldn't fight or stop them.

"Light to dark. Dark to light. Where both merge, both take flight. I am neither."

"That makes no sense. Only those who are blessed at birth respond to the call and you have given me your answer. How can you be blessed, but be neither?" Kai frowned, as though unsure how to proceed, or perhaps he was disappointed. "You have to be something." He erupted into laughter before composing himself a moment later and looking more serious. "Is this some kind of joke? Are you mocking me?"

He looked furious. His arms unfolded, his hands clenching into fists at his side.

"I don't know what you're talking about, and why

would I be mocking you? I'm smart enough to know an alpha male when I'm staring at one and I understand storm riders enough to know that you don't irritate an already angry man, god, whatever you are. It's like poking an angry snake. Unwise. Foolish. I am none of those things."

Kai blinked a few times as though surprised by her response and deliberating her answer.

Katherine detected movement in the corner of her vision. Captured by the breeze, something small scuttled along the grass, coming to rest near Kai's feet.

A beautiful black and white feather.

What kind of an answer was that supposed to be?

He crouched down and picked the feather up between his thumb and index finger. Twirling it around, he studied her intently. "A wild angel, in her natural habitat with an unreadable male as her mate. How interesting." His voice had softened, all of his earlier aggression evaporating. "You appear to have evaded the flock." His tone chiding, he was watching her like a science experiment. "Naughty, wild angel."

Si

Morning light crept into the lounge as Si sat on the leather corner sofa with the doors open surveying the view. The scent of the waxed floor mingled with the earthy, sweet smell of petrichor. The rainfall remained light, but he could hear it gaining momentum as it thrummed harder on the ground and the nearby ferns.

The sight of the woodland and loch always calmed Si's soul and after his recent journey into Tallin's realm he needed that grounding influence. It helped him to think.

The elven king was powerful and protective of his family. His show of unity had surprised Si as much as the dark gods. That was an unforeseen glitch, one that Si had not fully considered before. His own family tree was causing him enough of a headache.

Si had always found his father fascinating, yet somehow distant. Interestingly Kai didn't invite Si onto Acquorous, it was Theander who had sought him out and introduced himself. Si remembered that meeting vividly. It had been when the girls were nine years old.

Si had returned home from work late one night, with his usual act of throwing his car keys on the kitchen island. Arabella, his wife, was at her parents' house for a few days with his children. He had grabbed a beer from the fridge, opened the can, turned towards the lounge, taken a mouthful of the cool liquid and promptly frozen at the sight of a figure with glowing eyes standing in his lounge by the window.

An expletive had exploded from Si's mouth as he spat the drink everywhere and his heart started hammering in his chest. He had even glanced back at the can, wondering how much he had actually had to drink.

The figure in Si's lounge had turned from the window. "That view is impressive, brother. I kind of understand why you live here. I'm aware you know you're different. I don't understand why you remain amongst humans when you're fifty per cent a god though."

Si's voice had sounded calmer than he felt. "Get

the hell out of my house and don't come back. I don't know who you are, but I don't want you here. This is total bull. I'm human, my parents are human. This is a head mess. Isaac signs up for this weird stuff. I don't. There's the door."

In response, Si's mystery guest had tutted. "That's not nice. Kai is a god and your biological father, as he is mine. We share the same mother. Eve didn't feel you were ready to know the truth until now. You don't need to physically leave by a door, Si. You can jump worlds at will. Your grandfather is Asanda, the most powerful god in existence. This is why Lucas didn't initially like you and why Haydan doesn't like you. You're hard for storm riders to read. Isaac likes all the weird stuff that goes on around him and the women in his life. He finds it intriguing, yet you're terrified of it. Why?"

Interestingly, his mystery guest, who he later found out was his brother, Theander, had sounded fascinated by Si's utter rejection of him. Si had felt his world spiralling out of control around him. The figure had disappeared and reappeared closer to Si, who had cursed and stepped away.

"How do you know about Lucas, Haydan and Isaac? Get out of my house right now or I'll call the police and have you arrested."

Theander had smiled. "To explain to them that a man has appeared in your house out of thin air? Good luck with that. I'm friends with Haydan, so of course I know about him. Si, stop acting like a child. You're a god. Act like one. You need to meet Kai and I need to introduce you to our home world."

"No. I'm going for a shower. When I come back I want you gone." Si had turned and stormed out of the lounge, placing the can back on the kitchen unit on his way past.

Once in the shower Si had calmed down. There hadn't been a man standing in his lounge earlier, there really hadn't. He was working too hard, or was having some kind of episode. He had tipped his head back, closing his eyes to let the water run off his face. The shower sounded different and the water echoed more. Opening his eyes, he had almost had a heart attack. He was standing under a waterfall – a loud one – and he was surrounded by steep rocks on three sides. The other side led into a large canyon.

"Ah hell, what are you playing at? Take me home," he had shouted, aware his mystery visitor was nearby and enjoying his game.

Standing on a ledge higher up, Theander had laughed and shouted back. "Get yourself home, then you'll believe, brother. I'll find you later. We'll talk, once you believe."

The downpour outside increased. Rain dripped off the roof, bouncing off the patio. Si cursed, feeling overwhelmed. The idea of him being different had been something he had been aware of since he was a child. His eyes glowed in the dark for a start, which wasn't normal, but until the evening Theander landed in his life, he had always chosen to push all the strange things that happened away, to act normal.

Now Isaac and Katherine knew Si was different. Katherine had witnessed him fighting twice: once, before they bumped into Diego and Sandau on the night of the ball after Iskar arrived, and the second time, when the dark god with the scruffy hair cornered him. Si had left the pod to check if it was clear and the dark god had trapped him. Si had no choice but to fight and blow his cover a second time. Isaac and Katherine would keep his secret though. He felt confident of that. They were good friends and he could, to his great shame, use that to his advantage.

Si hadn't realised that Diego's warrior was part light god and Sandau had figured out the moment they met in the corridor of the summer court that he was a god. Light gods could recognise each other easily enough. That didn't concern Si, because his other secrets remained hidden and he had two major ones.

Asanda had a real aversion to creatures evolving. Ironic then that he had missed two major evolutions that had taken place right under his nose.

Si presented as a light god. He had been blessed at birth by Asanda, but evolution had found a way and the darkness surfaced on demand for him. The rest of the time it remained hidden away from detection.

Too focused on his primary plans and his main goal, Si had taken his eye off the minute intricacies of leaving the sea – although he had not had much choice in the matter. That was the other secret that he carried around inside. He had a physical soul … well, he would have once he figured out how to retrieve it.

When Diego left the sea with Rebekka, Si knew it was time to make his move. He had to follow the anomalies, because they all led back to the most interesting part of all of this – Maya and Arianna.

Si was now confident that the girls did not belong to Haydan. They had another owner, Alex. He was going to make sure that they were returned to that owner. None of their families and a mask were going to stop him.

Now that the main game-players were out of the sea, Si just needed the catalyst. Maya and Haydan needed to bond. Then his main game plan would kick into operation, because whether Haydan was an elven prince or not, Si was going to bring Haydan's world crashing down from within. Not out of hatred. The boy had understood what he was getting embroiled in when he found and forged an alliance with Maya and Arianna in the sea. Finding souls in the deepest part of the sea always indicated baggage and complications. They were on temporary loan. Haydan wasn't keeping them. Of course, Haydan didn't know any of that. Si had been careful to hide the plan from him and wipe any memory of it from his mind within the sea.

Promises forged in the sea were never forgotten and evolution had at long last found a way. This was all on Maya and Arianna. They were going to deliver for him with Haydan, as promised before they left the sea.

To Be Continued…

ACKNOWLEDGEMENTS

I have to start by thanking Susan Cunningham who is by far the best editor, proofreader, supporter and friend any author could ask for. We laugh about the 'Tallinism's' and Sooz will tell me if something isn't 'Haydanesque' and I can't get over how much she gets the world I have created and the characters who inhabit it. I always say I like the writing part the best, but Sooz makes the editing part fun too and the finished draft is always so much more polished once done.

To Reuben Lane who brought the water book to life for me on the cover, big thank you. You have probably forgotten about this design by now as you created it a while ago, but I love it so much and you captured it so perfectly, it's an absolute masterpiece.

Many thanks to Si for the cover layouts and Yvonne for the wonderful formatting, I appreciate the work that you do so much and final touches matter as much as everything else in the book giving it a professional finish.

To my beta readers, for all your feedback, the good the bad and the ugly. I always appreciate everything you pick up on. Your support and enthusiasm is also much appreciated.

My real-life whirling dervishes, Joshua and Nathan get a special mention. They know that their mother writes books, they love the dervishes, recognise my character names and cherish their copies of my debut book…even though they've never read it from cover to cover and maybe never will. Love you more boys!

I've been married eighteen years this year, so I have to mention my wonderful husband. He knows my cast as well as I do. He tolerates my crazy side, my urge to write and create and he supports me every step of the way. He also suffers my epic meltdowns half way through an edit and buys me chocolate. That's true love that is!

Finally, to my readers, bloggers, instagrammers, writers, friends, fans and supporters of my work, thank you. Writing a book is a huge undertaking and a massive slog and knowing I have you alongside cheering me on is humbling and I am so grateful.

If You Enjoyed This Book...

I hope you have enjoyed reading *Mask of Deception* as much as I have enjoyed writing it. I am an independently published author. I take pride in the standard of my work which I believe reflects in the high quality of this story.

Reviews really help with how a book ranks and ensure a title is more discoverable for other readers. If you enjoyed this book and would like to read more about the adventures of the characters in Mask of Deception please share the joy by leaving a review and helping to encourage others to try out a new indie author.

Join the Adventure

Which is only just beginning and find out more about the author, Karen Furk, by visiting:

www.karenfurk.co.uk

Sign up to receive author updates on forthcoming and new book releases. Ensure you don't miss out on blog articles, cover reveals and releases of concept artwork that bring the characters from the series to life. Plus you can read short stories about the characters introduced in the Mask Chronicles for free.

You can reach Karen via social media on Twitter, Facebook and Instagram under the user name: Karenfurkauthor
Plus, you can find visual inspiration about the world and characters on Pinterest by searching for the user name: Karenfurkauthor

MASK OF DECEPTION CONTINUES…

BENEATH THE MASK

Coming Soon

Book 3 – Preview

Chapter 1

Haydan

The nightmare had returned. It hadn't happened for a number of months, but that night it had consumed Haydan's mind. Now he was awake, and the idea of sleep had long been abandoned. He wrapped a blanket around his body, slipped out of his sleeping compartment and made for the doorway which led from his snug into the woodland. There he walked to the highest cliff overlooking the sea with Kaleshar clutched in his hand. He picked his spot, a sheltered rocky outcrop and settled down to stare out over the icy landscape.

The three Storm Lands moons were all on display, although the chosen one moon had slipped behind the storm rider one, the only hint of its presence an aqua tinge bleeding into the edge of the silvery storm rider disc. The white warrior moon shone bright like a moonberry tree glimmering in the darkness, lighting his route. Haydan scowled. The formation merely reminded him of his own dysfunctional set-up with a mouthy, disobedient warrior and a difficult and often rude chosen one. His father's warning about throwing him back in the sea if he disappointed, surfaced.

Winter winds swept in at night now as the seasonal changes over Storm Lands took hold. Another few weeks and they would be in the depths of winter. Frigid waves crashed and thundered on the rocks below, and Haydan sought consolation in the desolate sounds. An owl hooted somewhere deep in the woodland behind him. Haydan would be content with a fire crackling in the hearth back in his snug and Maya's arms around him offering comfort, but he feared he would never experience that. Maya's affection seemed further away than ever. Even conversation with her was strained, and now Kaleshar was disturbing the little peace he had left, with nightmares of a figure running in the woodland, pursued by someone who remained shrouded from his sight.

More secrets.

He wanted peace, but in his current state of limbo he would never find it, so he had come here to think. The idea of launching the mask into the water had occurred to him a while ago, and on nights such as these he considered it more frequently. If Kaleshar could read his thoughts, the mask never let on, but stayed shut down and unresponsive in his hand as though it too felt lost and adrift. Perhaps the nightmares terrified Kaleshar in the same way that they bothered Haydan. In fact, maybe the link wasn't something Kaleshar controlled and his silence was related to his shame.

The outcome, however, was always the same.

A wall of silence.

Then Haydan would pry, the mask would shut down and he was no closer to getting any answers. It continued to be that way. Every time, Haydan grew more irritated by Kaleshar's lack of response, and they would freeze each other out for longer. It started at a day or two. Last time it was over a week, and it took Maya's intervention to prise Kaleshar out of his shell and get them talking again.

He gave a heavy sigh. "You wake me with this and then you shut down, Kal. What am I supposed to make of that? It's like you're torturing me with your past. Your past, not mine. It's nothing to do with me. You need to make peace with that and stop harassing me with it, because until you're ready to share more, I don't need this storm show. I have enough of my own problems to deal with." He glared down at the mask, which glinted in the light from Storm Lands' three moons but offered up nothing in return. "It's all on me, isn't it? The pressure. You know I have Maya and Arianna running rings around me. Diego's on my ass most of the time because I'm failing to live up to expectations. Tallin dips in and stirs things when it suits him, but he seemed keen to be rid of you from his realm, and then you go and lumber me with your night terrors. I'm not your storm-blessed babysitter, and if you can't get your god-touched magic around that, maybe you should find someone else to inconvenience. I never asked for this. I want you gone." He growled. "You can't even apologise, can you? I mean an. 'I'm sorry, Haydan, for disrupting your sleep with my unresolved previous life issues' would be great, but no, you just freeze me out. It's the story of my storm-damned life."

Nearby, a twig cracked.

Haydan inhaled a shaky breath and pulled Kaleshar back under his blanket. The wind picked up and he yanked the fleecy blanket closer. A familiar woodsy, cinnamon and earth-infused smell brushed his senses. "It's rude to creep up on people, Diego."

His father stepped out from the nearby trees. He was wrapped in a thick fur-lined cloak with a scarf anchored around his head and tied at the back to protect his face and ears from the cold. His breath formed plumes in front of his face as he approached Haydan and ducked down to shelter with him. "I wasn't creeping about. Storm Lands made me aware we had a lost soul loitering up here and I came to check on its well-being. I didn't expect it to be you. Why aren't you asleep?"

Haydan didn't want to divulge details. He wouldn't get anywhere talking to Diego about it. "Nightmares. I came up here to clear my head. I'm fine, go to bed. Storm Lands needs to mind its own business and stay out of mine."

Diego pulled his hands out of his cloak pockets, cupped them to his face and blew on them. "Storm Lands sensed desolation from you. I'm not leaving you out here alone, son. Come back to my snug. I'll make you a warm drink and we can talk."

Haydan remained silent but could tell Diego wasn't going to leave him. He hadn't moved from his side.

"I'm not out here as elder. Well, I was, but tonight I can just be your father, with no judgement. We can go back to your snug if you prefer."

A tiny part of Haydan's soul thawed in response and he angled his head towards Diego.

"Haydan, you're freezing," Diego said in a gruff tone. "How long have you been out here?"

"Long enough to recognise that even the moons are tormenting me and adding to my misery tonight." Haydan glanced back to the night sky. The warrior

moon appeared brighter and fuller than earlier and the
chosen one moon was peeking out from behind the
storm rider moon as though teasing him.

"The moons stand as guardians of our realm.
Anything else is you projecting your own insecurities
onto them. On your feet, storm rider," Diego said,
pushing up from the ground.

Haydan reluctantly rose from his spot and shivered.
Diego raised his arm and swept his cape around
Haydan's shoulders. The cold retreated from his bones
as Diego hauled him closer.

"Freezing yourself to death isn't a good plan. Are
you out here brooding on warriors and chosen ones,
the mask or me?"

Haydan chuckled. "The first two, and the third a
little. Why would I be brooding on you?"

Diego shrugged as he walked, the frozen ground
crunching beneath his feet. "I give you a hard time,
but I don't remember having clashed with you recently.
I was just checking. You do know you can talk to me
about anything, don't you?"

Haydan grunted. "Easy enough to say but those are
empty words."

Diego stopped walking. "They aren't empty
words. Storm alive, Haydan, you're my son, my flesh
and blood. You and your siblings are mine and your
mother's greatest creations. I always have to act as elder
in public, but in private I'm your father ahead of all
else."

They reached the snugs and Diego raised his hand
to usher Haydan ahead of him. "You don't have to deal
with all this alone. I know you feel as though you do,
and as elder I give that impression as well, but in private
you aren't alone. If you want company or a listening ear

I'm always here."

Haydan stepped into his father's snug. "You're often busy and I don't want to add to your problems. Plus, since I claimed Storm Lands … well, it's been awkward between us." Diego's eyes already reflected a hint of hostility as they shone in the firelight.

Haydan's ears and nose tingled in the warmth from the central fire basket. He sank into a nearby seat and huddled up, his hands thrust out towards the fire to absorb the heat as he waited for the backlash he would receive in return.

"If the alternative is you freezing to death on a hillside, I would rather you burdened me," Diego said. Seating himself next to Haydan, he held out a mug of something that smelled strongly like hot chocolate. "A peace offering, for being a poor excuse of a father, who piles pressure and expectation on you to the point where you can no longer cope."

Haydan released the mask into the folds of his blanket, wrapped his fingers around the warm ceramic and smiled inwardly. This was preferable to suffering in silence. He scoffed. "You're being ridiculous. Ow! Is that punishment?" He burned his lip on the scalding liquid. "Next time ease off on the heat," he said, blowing on the drink to cool it.

Diego shrugged and rolled his eyes. "Ridiculous, am I? You've just burnt your mouth on my peace offering and you would rather freeze to death than talk to me. I'd say that's a fail."

"You're not a poor excuse for a father. Arguably, I'm a poor excuse for a son, and it's not that I didn't want to talk to you, I just don't know what to say." That sounded pathetic, and Haydan drew the drink closer to his body to steal some of the warmth it exuded and try to lift his mood.

Diego's eyes reflected the mesmerising flames that licked up the side of the fire basket. He straightened himself up and pushed back against the plush snug seat before turning his head to study Haydan. "You stop talking that way, do you hear me? You're an incredible son. I'm in awe of you on a daily basis, and no, I will never publicly admit that, but I am." He sipped his drink and fell silent for a moment. "You're the only storm rider I know who hid in the depths until he could lure out two of our lost and most confused souls. You deal with so many weird occurrences on a regular basis and juggle them so effectively. I don't know anyone else who responds to the challenges they face like you do. Let's not forget the mask either."

"Really?" It was odd to hear Diego speaking so highly of him. His father was usually ranting at him, telling him to take control or sort things out, depending on his mood.

"Yes, really, Haydan. Maybe you just need a new adventure to remind you of all that you have and all that you've achieved." Diego sipped his drink again and grinned. "It might do you good to claim another realm."

Haydan shifted in his seat and placed his drink down on the arm of the chair. He had heard enough. "Why would you assume I want adventure? Perhaps I just want some peace and quiet without everyone else's expectations burdening me!"

Diego's eyes widened and he raised his hand as Haydan leapt up from the seat. Kaleshar bounced onto the floor and mist poured from the back of the mask as it lay face up as though taunting him. He resisted the urge to kick it into the fire.

Diego's gaze lifted to meet Haydan's. "So, this issue tonight is related to the mask, not me or the girls."

Haydan sighed and nodded. He couldn't lie about it. "I have nightmares."

Diego eyed the mask for a moment. "If you claim another realm, you move closer to freeing yourself of the burden. That's got to be better than sitting on a hillside freezing your behind off."

Drained and tired, Haydan gave a weak smile, sank back down into the seat and hung his head. Diego spoke sense, but he wasn't in the mood to feed his father's ego by agreeing with him just yet.

Diego sipped his hot chocolate. "There's a realm on the list that Tallin reckons you can claim easily enough. You could bring Arianna. Plus, I have a few guests in mind, and Kai has been making noises about joining us. Not sure I want him along, but I can hardly say no, and at least he's extra protection."

Haydan slumped lower in his seat. "Tallin downplays everything. You sound like you've got this all planned out. What do you need me for?"

Diego rolled his eyes. "Oh come on, you complain about not joining me when I go off on adventures. This time we go together. Think of all the fun we could have."

Diego had that devilish look in his eyes that always signalled trouble. Haydan would end up joining him whether he wanted to or not. "Tearing up another realm? Yeah, sure that'll be fun. Sign me up."

Diego gave his shoulder a playful thump. "See, I knew you'd come around to this. Arianna will love it too."

Haydan grunted and grabbed his hot chocolate. Diego had given this adventure far too much thought for his liking. His bad mood was already worsening like a gathering storm cloud. Diego's eyes glinted. This was the excitement he lived for. It made Haydan feel more than a little ill.

His father's storm cloud died back with a blast of cool air and rush of energy, revealing black obsidian buildings that stretched for the sky. The low sunset added an intensity to the purplish hue of the atmosphere, making Haydan squint. His skin prickled from the warmth, and he slipped off his jacket. Turning, he surveyed the city that sprawled out behind him. It was built on vast terraces and the views from the top levels out to the ocean were spectacular. Heavily textured steps on either side framed walkways, and chutes ran down the centre, channels for all the water that fell during monsoon season. The salty air reminded him of the Scottish coast and the saltwater lochs near Maya's home, and as usual his mind wandered its favourite route to his chosen one, like water trickling along a rill.

He missed Maya already, especially her incessant chatter and constant questions, but he suppressed his unease at leaving her behind. Despite her loud protestations to the contrary, it was too much of a risk to bring her, and Isaac, her stepfather, was better left out of this as well. If Isaac had joined them he would have bombarded Haydan with even more questions. The irritating human was forever a challenge.

They had come to check out a realm that his grandfather, Tallin, had indicated would be easy enough for Haydan to claim. Arianna was by his side, but the amount of additional backup Diego forced him to bring added to his growing unease. Diego had overruled his argument that only Arianna and Xavanchi, his adopted brother, accompany him. As a group, they stood out, and although this was a realm where they could freely use their abilities, he was uncomfortable in the presence of an elder and a god. Kai had invited himself along and Diego wasn't going to argue with a god. The guest list had then extended to include Keilty, because, according to Diego, she knew the realm well and Haydan needed to get to know her better.

Kai and Arianna had disappeared up front, where she would scout the area ahead of them. Diego marched ahead with Keilty beside him, chatting to the pretty mage as they walked. She had joined their party because Diego thought it would be good for Haydan and Arianna to spend some time with her. Haydan was certain her inclusion was more to do with his father's needs than his own, but Diego was insistent, and he knew better than to argue with him when he was determined about something.

Xavanchi was at Haydan's side. He hadn't said much since they arrived, but he was a reassuring presence and someone Haydan trusted.

Arianna and Kai reached the dark stairwell that disappeared into the underground club, scanned the area and waved the rest of the group forward to join them.

Runes of protection and welcome covered the dark walls overhead, glowing and enticing them in. Haydan tried to suppress the rush of apprehension that flooded over him. Here magic was embraced and magic users walked without question or confrontation.

Once inside, however, there were only a few safe routes out, and all would be guarded by enforcers: a group of elite guards who watched over all the exit points and could arrest any troublemakers who captured their attention. The trick was to enjoy yourself and not incite violence, otherwise you would spend a night in the holding cells.

A beautiful, ethereal voice called to Haydan as the pounding beat thumped deep underground, making his surroundings vibrate as he descended the wide stairwell. It was similar to the clubs on Earth. He could do this. He braced for the swell of crowds and the overwhelming scent of magic mingling with perfume, sweat and alcohol.

Where the steps met the entrance hallway, the floor was gritty beneath his feet. Everything else was smooth and slippery. Raised voices bounced off the enclosed walls. The throbbing beat of the music now made his body pulse along with the surroundings. Even his soul couldn't resist the odd sensation as it danced to the same entrancing call. He could lose hours in this place; the atmosphere was so addictive.

The lulling, seductive notes of a saxophone inside the club beckoned to anyone nearby to kick back and relax.

Haydan fought back a grin. This was going to be fun.

Diego pivoted to face Haydan and smirked as he strutted backwards into the cavernous club and began to move in time to the music. He spun away as Keilty joined in, dancing close against Diego. Haydan sucked air in hard against his teeth and turned away, determined not to let her spoil the evening.

Xavanchi grunted and cursed low under his breath

with what sounded like, "Son of a storm." His eyes didn't leave Diego's gyrating figure. "Is that display necessary?"

Haydan trusted his father, but there were boundaries, and Keilty was testing those to the limits. The two definitely had a shared history, because he felt like a chaperone looking after two teenage delinquents who couldn't keep their hands off each other, and Diego had been insistent that Rebekka, Haydan's mother, wasn't to come. She needed to keep an eye on the family apparently. That seemed very convenient, although some of Haydan's irritation at Diego could be down to the fact that the next portal stone and throne were nearby. This realm was supposed to be one of the easier ones to acquire – he wasn't convinced. Nothing about what he had to do felt simple, and he was certain that he would meet resistance in any of the realms he tried to claim on behalf of the mask.

The hall reminded him of a place of worship. High vaulted ceilings stretched out of sight overhead. Diego bounced around in front of him, showing off whilst throwing small tornados out from his hands into the crowd. No one seemed bothered, even though he was garnering a lot of attention and plenty of admiring glances.

Sprites had been activated and they glowed, releasing light from their bodies as they moved around the club. They were all waiflike and a similar height to Haydan, who was over six feet tall. The colour indicated their core abilities. Red could use fire; blue, water; green, plants. White connected to the air; yellow to the weather; orange to the earth.

Mysterious sylphs, who were shorter and far curvier than the sprites, floated on top of tall pillars and pushed fire or swirling purple air out from their hands, creating columns of light.

Smoke rings and balls of light drifted into the hall from a curvaceous and bulbous central column that rippled as if alive. A lady captured the balls of light in her hands and released them to dance. The lights followed her as though attracted to her movements, which were fluid, beautiful and mesmerising.

Tallin would love this place, so would Maya.

Xavanchi smacked Haydan's shoulder playfully and raised one of his eyebrows in a disapproving manner, maybe as a result of his staring. Xavanchi leant in and shouted, "Not you too. Diego's bad enough. Stop sightseeing the illuminations and focus on the task, storm rider."

Haydan grinned and shook his head at Xavanchi's banter before turning his head from the light show and focusing on the rest of the room.

Magical creatures fluttered about, lighting up the air as they moved. Wolves snaked their way in among everyone. Their fur glowed, adding an otherworldly quality to the evening. Haydan caught glimpses of wings, fangs, pointed ears, blue skin, horns; so many magical creatures frequented this place, each with their own unique appearance and abilities.

Large alcoves lined with seating were tucked into the sides of the space and provided privacy. That was where underground activities occurred – drinking, gambling, drugs and purchasing the services of the magical creatures floating around the establishment. They could be hired for anything from entertainment at parties and tracking down missing persons to more unsavoury activities such as assassinations, smuggling, stealing, kidnapping and prostitution. You could acquire most of the abilities flying around the room if you were prepared to pay enough. How much were a storm rider's services worth? A shudder passed through his body. That didn't bear thinking about.

A few of the guards loitering around the alcoves tracked him as he stalked through the hall with his party. He didn't want their kind noticing him, but then Diego was hardly blending in; in fact, Diego was ensuring he was the centre of attention as he showed off his dancing prowess. Facing Haydan, he was jiggling about as if possessed. His father could move on a dance floor if he needed to, but that's not what the show he was putting on right now was all about. Diego was deliberately making a spectacle of himself with Keilty and he seemed disappointed Haydan wasn't dancing too. He turned his back, punctuating his displeasure with a disgusted look thrown over his shoulder in Haydan's direction.

Xavanchi nudged Haydan's arm before casting a wary glance at the alcoves. Haydan nodded his understanding. That was why Diego had insisted on bringing reinforcements, although why Kai was necessary Haydan didn't know. He had never liked the arrogant god who thought he was better than everyone else. The sullen deity had stayed up front with Arianna, as though holding court with her, ignoring the rest of them. Haydan gritted his teeth and refused to dwell on that unwelcome thought. Kai was there for reasons that he was keeping to himself, and Haydan didn't trust him at all.

Valendri, a frequent visitor to the realm, was lurking in the archway nearest the door. Xavanchi suspected Valendri acquired a lot of objects and slaves whilst visiting. A shiver crept down Haydan's neck in spite of the comfortable ambience. His reputation preceded him. Valendri had access to numerous portals in his home world, so was adept at shifting realms. Haydan wasn't trying to claim Valendri's realm yet, but when he did, the creature wouldn't make it easy for him.

Diego had encountered Valendri when he attempted to enter the Pool of Sorrows hidden in Valendri's world. That hadn't gone so well for either of them, but Diego had managed to escape with more than anyone had bargained on. Valendri was unlikely to have forgotten or forgiven that. The tense glare in Diego's general direction confirmed that suspicion.

The raised throne platform dominated the end of the cavernous space. That was his throne. He wasn't sure he wanted it with so many eyes burning into him. What was a storm rider who was also a mask bearer worth? He snorted to himself. Let them try to lay a finger on him. He had an elder, a god, a mage, a storm rider and a warrior in tow. He glared across at one of the more aggressive-looking men, and the mask on his face glowed. The man turned to another guard close by and yanked on his sleeve.

The steps in front led up to the platform. Haydan spun away and focused on that. Kai halted by the guard standing at the bottom. The guard didn't move, but stared directly ahead. Kai raised his hands. The left one matched the surroundings, the right one illuminated, creating a beacon in the darkness. A surge of energy whooshed into the air around them and Haydan's ears popped at the change in air pressure.

The guard was quick enough to recognise the warning that he was in the presence of a powerful god. He blinked a few times, and after another few moments of staring off with Kai, he stepped to the side, offering

Kai access to the platform.

Still glaring at him, Kai swept ahead, only turning away when he raised his foot to ascend the steps. The guard was lucky to have survived the encounter. Haydan felt certain Kai had killed people for lesser slights to his superiority.

Arianna followed Kai then turned back and waited at the bottom of the stairs for Haydan to catch them up. She exuded an air of confidence, which had grown since her time in Tallin's realm. It suited her and her flares of rebellion had calmed of late, meaning relations between them were much improved. Diego had started giving her more breathing space as well, letting her spread her wings. She met Haydan's eyes and dipped her head as he strode past.

That evening she had gone for a tribal look: heavy on the smoky eye make-up, with dark stripes across her flawless cheekbones. Tiny beads and feathers were anchored throughout her hair. Layers of curved metal panels shrouded her décolletage, reflecting her fierce energy and defiant beauty. They were emblazoned with protective charms and runes, a stark visual reminder of the dangers his warrior presented. Her outfit was an unusual combination of mesh fabric that hugged her body in the right places but flared out around her legs, and a flesh-coloured layer underneath which protected any exposed flesh from view. Her arms were bare, but silver and tribal leather bracelets protected her wrists.

Xavanchi halted by Arianna's side with Diego and Keilty loitering close by. Diego scanned the club for anyone who might interfere in their plans.

Haydan bounded up the steps leading to the ebony throne at the top, passing Kai on the way. The god had stopped at the top of the steps and stood like a silent sentry, staring ahead with his arms folded behind his back. He didn't even acknowledge Haydan as he sauntered past. No one else walked on the platform. Presumably that was because it was off limits to most, save those who were brave enough to stake a claim and try acquiring the throne as theirs. Nothing called him to the throne. It gave no hint of it being his. He skirted around it, taking another moment to scan the club. Nothing seemed out of the ordinary. Several men in the shadows kept an eye on him, but no one had ventured any closer. Flicking his coat-tails back, he settled onto the throne and searched for the recess for the stone he held in his hand. Nothing denoted the stone belonged there. Something felt off about the whole thing.

From the corner of his eye, Haydan detected movement on the ground by the recesses. A flicker of weapons being retrieved. Diego, Keilty, Arianna and Xavanchi all sprang to life as fighting erupted around them.

Kai silently choreographed everything as he bounced about on the steps, launching balls of energy out from his hands to throw off anyone who ventured too close to the group. A female approached him and he held his hands out, letting them darken and glow before deciding which magic she was drawn to – the light – and using the other type to fling her backwards across the room. His magic releasing sent everyone on the dance floor into a frenzy. If anything, the beat picked up in response.

Kai tracked Haydan over his shoulder and shook his head as Haydan pushed up from the seat. Something dark fluttered to Haydan's side. Kai's eyes narrowed and he shouted words that Haydan missed as the ground pulled away from him and the throne plummeted into darkness. His stomach lurched at the sudden drop and he gripped the arms.

One thought was clear in his mind – this wasn't part of the plan. He'd walked straight into a trap.

❧❦

Maya

The water book wasn't giving up its secrets easily.

Maya trailed her fingertips against the sunken relief on the ancient cover and once again marvelled at how smooth it was. There was no sign of the cold water that filled the cover when she discarded it, or the locks that appeared as soon as it flooded. She groaned in frustration, then, throwing herself back onto her bed, stared up at the solid oak roof trusses. At this rate, she would never help Haydan obtain the next realms. He was off somewhere with his father. Recently, they had been creeping around more, and she was certain it was connected to him claiming another realm, but Haydan wouldn't divulge details and Arianna was also being stubborn about sharing anything. Maybe a change of scenery would help. She grabbed the book and made for the stairs.

Cool mist covered the garden in a thick blanket that left dew on the grass. The loch was veiled from sight, but given the still, silent air, the water would be calm. Unconcerned, Maya pulled her jacket closer around her and ran for the trees at the bottom of the garden. Feathers fluttered around the side of a tree as she approached the woodland, giving the odd impression that a bird was hiding there. She gasped and came to a halt, unsure whether to ignore the intruder or bolt back to the safety of the house. The air around the tree shuddered. Whoever was concealed there was powerful.

"Hello." Maya clutched the book closer against her front. Tallin could be in the area, but he didn't have wings. She couldn't see anything. Had the prowler gone? Her sixth sense told her someone was still lurking in the forest. "I know you're there. You're not welcome. I know martial arts and I'm not afraid to use it."

Soft laughter filled the silence and a man stepped out from behind the tree, dark wings rising up from his back, arched either side of his head, framing him. Vibrant purple and red feathers lined the bottom of them. His shadowy jacket and trousers matched the unusual angelic addition. He was tall, gaunt-looking, with a long face and pronounced V on his top lip. Black hair tumbled across his forehead.

"You're an angel."

A sly smile tugged his thin lips upwards. "Not really, but whatever." His lyrical, richly toned voice added to his air of mystery.

"Our garden is off limits to intruders, but whatever," Maya said, mimicking his sarcastic word choice.

"Yes, the wards protecting this property are powerful." The creature took a bold step closer. "But when you're as gifted as I am, they pose little threat, and family are exempt." His eyes twinkled as he leant in. "Tiny snag in the plan that whoever set them forgot to tell you about."

That was unlikely. Asanda set the wards. "No. The person who set them wouldn't have been sloppy. If you can breach them, they want you here."

Uncertainty flickered for a moment across the intruder's face as his confidence retreated.

"I doubt that." His eyebrows raised as he stared at her as though surveying a special prize. "I'm not usually welcome anywhere."

He was smug and arrogant, but intelligence simmered in his intense gaze. Maya hugged the book closer as his eyes swept across the back cover.

"Who are you and what do you want?" she said.

"I'm Lawson. Some know me as Dark Angel. What I want is you."

Maya's mouth had dried and she gripped the book so tight it hurt her knuckles. Her jaw hung open before she caught herself and stopped her gawking. "Why would you want me?"

"It's less about you," Lawson said, his voice low, "and more about him."

Maya wasn't sure she wanted to know what that ominous statement meant, but she had to ask. "Him?"

"Your storm rider."

His threat against Haydan and the accompanying scowl sent her heartbeat racing.

"I want his attention. How do I get that? I take from him the thing he cares about more than life itself and make him come to me."

What was it with non-human creatures? They had such a strange way of approaching problems. His proposal was ridiculous.

'I've got a better idea. How about I ask Haydan to come over and you can talk to him, as any sane person would?"

The edge of Lawson's thin mouth twitched. "You're assuming I'm sane. That's interesting. Given who his grandfather is, I have no interest in talking to him until I have made my position clear. I currently have the upper hand and I intend to keep it that way. Last time I talked to Tallin, he tricked me, so you'll forgive me for being wary of anything that descends from his bloodline."

"That's my future mate you're bad-mouthing."

"I know." Lawson leant in. "You should be careful about what you share and with whom. You don't know me, yet you've already furnished me with plenty of information that I can use to my advantage. Much of what I know is guesswork. Now I know for sure that your future mate, Haydan, is Tallin's heir, meaning his father is Diego, and I would wager that's an elven trick you're clutching in your hands, suggesting you've met Tallin, so you know exactly what I'm talking about."

Maya's mouth opened and closed again. She wasn't about to say anything to him that would reinforce his views.

He chuckled. "Thought so. Tell me–" Lawson moved in closer still, now within arm's reach. The air around him shimmered as though a heat haze had erupted from his wings "–has he pulled you into his games and web of deceit too?"

"Why is everyone so obsessed with Tallin?" This creature was strange and his presence was beginning to concern Maya.

"Oh, Tallin has a way of getting under your skin."

He was correct, but for some strange reason his accuracy riled Maya, and she hugged the book hard, trying to ignore his tormenting. She liked Tallin, and listening to Lawson's digs felt disloyal.

"What is that book?" He flicked his hand out in an irritated gesture.

"None of your business. It's mine."

His laugh lacked any hint of warmth or humour. "If you're my prisoner, that makes anything in your possession ... mine."

Maya's heartbeat was pounding so hard in her chest she was certain he could hear it.

His eyes narrowed. "Including your storm rider and his soul."

Maya whimpered and stamped her foot into Lawson's chest with so much force that he staggered backwards. She spun and fled, vaulting the fence and sprinting up the grassy meadow to the house, confident he was close on her heels. She risked a glance over her shoulder.

He hadn't followed.

Relaxing, she exhaled loudly and turned back to the house, running straight into a warm, tall, dark body that appeared out of the mist. The book she was clutching slammed into her chest and cold water sloshed all over her. A yelp of surprise escaped her as wings closed around her with a whump, and a power as ancient as the creature that had grabbed her dragged her away from Earth.

If Haydan tried to blame her for this debacle he would get a piece of her mind.

Theander

The water was cool, the sun hot and nearby, crickets chirped. Splashing in the private and sheltered lagoon,

Theander stretched out and enjoyed the moment. Soon enough he would have to return to the main beach and speak to Kai about accompanying Diego and guarding Haydan as he searched out the next few realms. Since the episode in Aveyamara, Kai had warmed to the idea of helping Haydan, he had even offered to visit the next realm with them, but Theander suspected that was only because Haydan was a direct route to shelter Maya. He hadn't failed to notice the protective streak that Kai was displaying towards her, the way he would occasionally ask after her. He was certain Kai visited Maya from time to time, although he never admitted it when asked. Maybe he had warmed to her because she was the same blend of magic as him and demonstrated the same feisty attitude that he did. Regardless, Kai expressing interest in anything was rare, but Theander had no intention of focusing on it too much; he knew better.

His swim finished, Theander dried himself and slipped his clothes on again. The route back to meet Kai was a casual meander through the surrounding forest, and the dappled shade provided some refuge from the baking midday sun.

The muted sounds of the stream faded. Something was approaching. Something dark and menacing. Spinning around, Theander tried to assess where the movement had come from. Nothing stood out, but everything felt wrong. The crickets had fallen quiet. No birdsong filtered through the tree canopies. Nearby, reeds rustled, drawing his attention to their incessant swaying.

He sensed the sudden shift behind him as he turned, and something pounced. An icy and unforgiving sensation wrapped around his bare wrists, overwhelming him so rapidly that it almost snatched his breath away. Restrained by the sinister energy, he struggled to break free. He was Asanda's heir, a strong and gifted god of the light. Nothing was capable of attacking and overpowering him.

Except perhaps a powerful dark magic user such as Iskar, his uncle.

The pain within his body amplified, flooding through his system with so much ferocity it wiped out any sensible thought. His arms burned from the exertion of fighting his unseen assailant. The more he fought, the more it overwhelmed him. He roared as he once again tried to fend off the attack. He could not admit defeat, but the intensity of the assault grew with every attempt he made to evade it, as though his fighting back provoked his assailant even more.

Only when he had depleted his emergency energy reserves and no more strength remained in his body, did he accept that the dark magic besieging him had won. He could do nothing but withdraw his light energy, shut it down and embrace the black void that swamped him as he collapsed to the ground.

The darkness brought relief but also the horrific realisation that he was about to find out what it felt like to be tortured by a merciless power that would bring him pain. It was the only time he had ever wished for the same balance of light and dark powers as his father. At least with his father's curse, he might stand a chance against his assailant. He feared he would never taste freedom again as his world spiralled into darkness and the pitch-black menace snatched him away from Acquorous.

Chapter 2

Haydan

The darkness disorientated him. The high-pitched whistle of total silence overwhelmed Haydan's senses, and even with his finely tuned hearing, the noises from the club had vanished. He clicked his fingers and blue flames erupted from his fingertips, adding a frosty glow to his surroundings.

He was alone.

He must have imagined the feathers he had seen before, or it was a trick deployed by the venue to deceive revellers. Smooth walls enclosed him, their surface as black as the building above and the streets beyond. A tunnel ran away from him to his right-hand side. The only exit. With no other option available, he followed the route. It descended for what felt like forever, eventually opening out into a larger room with another inky throne in the centre. This one was raised on a platform, with steps leading up to it. Around the perimeter of the room a number of large plinths extended up into the vast space overhead.

The throne in the club had been a decoy, a false creation to detract from the real throne hidden away in the bowels of the building, because this private area seemed more genuine.

The yellow stone with the tiny striations on the underside drew his attention. He slipped his hand back into his pocket and grabbed hold of it. Revelling in the warmth releasing from the chunk of rock, he pulled it free. As though in response, the jet-black throne pulsed and bright blue light travelled through the surface, reminding him of lightning strikes erupting in a night sky. The flashes focused on a location at the top of the throne, and a stone that perched there glowed.

The next keystone.

Transfixed, he struggled to move. The thrones in Aveyamara and on Storm Lands hadn't done that, giving the impression that the mask and the thrones were learning about Haydan as quickly as he was learning about them. That suggested there were layers of secrets still to be revealed to him. Unease rolled through his mind at the prospect.

He didn't have time to dwell on this. He needed to claim the throne and leave.

An explosion of dark feathers blasted outwards from one of the plinths, cutting him off from his target. The glowing crystal vanished. That was Haydan's prize. He wasn't having it snatched away from him at this stage. He rushed forward, releasing a powerful blast of magic at the intruder. An arm flicked the flare of energy away as if swatting a fly, before the owner's hand closed around the jewel that Haydan had spent months tracking down.

'That's mine.' That came out harsher and more commanding than Haydan intended. Powerful creatures rarely responded well to aggression. He winced as the hand stilled and the blur of feathers disappeared — a clever illusion. The figure now holding the jewel turned slowly around and positioned himself between Haydan and the throne. His face was lean and framed by high, angular cheekbones and dark hair. He was taller than Haydan had expected. Menace oozed off him.

"So, it's really you. I heard rumours you existed, but to find out you're real, well, that's unexpected." Haydan rubbed his hand across his jaw, his anxiety growing. If this was who he suspected, the creature rarely showed himself. This was a bold display of dominance. "That's still mine. I worked hard for that." He indicated the stone clutched in the creature's hand with an agitated flick of his own.

"It's not yours if I'm holding it, grandson of Tallin."

Haydan's breath caught. "How do you know that?"

The creature gave a devious smile. Arrogance and power flooded from him as he closed his hand around the jewel, obscuring it from Haydan's sight.

"I'll consider a trade. Tallin has something of mine and I want it back. Get it for me and I will give you this pretty chunk of rock."

Laughter burst from Haydan's mouth. "I don't involve myself in games with Tallin. I'm not that stupid. Is it really you? I think you're an imposter."

A sneaky glint in the creature's eyes suggested Haydan's challenge had landed him in even more trouble.

"You doubt me? But you can sense the power I hold. I know you can, as can your father and your grandfather. Fine. You leave me no choice."

"What the hell does that mean?" Haydan took a step back and raised his hands in a conciliatory gesture.

Wings pushed out from the creature's back, large ebony wings edged in purple and a vivid red.

It was true.

The legend that was Dark Angel was back.

Panic snatched the air from Haydan's lungs as he turned and tried to drag himself away from the creature's magic. It clawed at his legs and feet, anchoring onto his light magic and bringing him under its control. Darkness swept in and the last thing that entered his mind was a vision of dark feathers and the haunting words, *Now you're my prisoner, grandson of Tallin.*

ॐ

Maya

Something soft brushed Maya's face and she pushed up from the fluffy blanket she found herself lying on. She was alone on a bed covered in teal and grey throws and pillows. The bed didn't bother her though; it was the only normal thing close to her. A wall of layered aquamarine glass surrounded her. Curious to know more, she nudged her hand out to touch it, and the surface flowed like liquid towards her fingertips. Squeaking in surprise, she withdrew her hand as though scalded – that wasn't glass. It was something she had never encountered before, and whilst she had no idea what it was, it detected her presence, as if she was in a prison that was alive or, more probably, imbued with magic.

She slipped her feet over the side of the bed and dangled them for a moment. The smooth white stone floor didn't try to touch her feet as the wall had. That seemed safe. She wriggled to the edge and placed her foot on the warm ground. Opposite her, bars blocked the entrance and a soft glow emanated from beyond.

That was her escape route. She pushed off.

"You're awake then." Lawson's soft, resonant voice broke the pervading silence.

"Where's my book?" Maya couldn't see anything beyond the bars of her cage except for swirling dark smoke. "Why have you locked me up?"

"I have the book, a curious object wrapped in ancient and powerful magic. It refilled with water when I grabbed you, almost as though it was trying to protect its secrets. Tallin's full of those."

Lawson was angry with Tallin or he had a major issue of some kind with the elven king.

"You really don't like Tallin, do you?" The bars vibrated. Maya reached her fingertip out and touched the nearest one. It was warm. She gasped as her surroundings closed in, pressing her against the bars, not squashing her, but making it clear that touching the bars was a bad idea. Lawson was a talented man. Her fingers withdrew from contact with her prison and the dark green surroundings pulled back, reminding her of an ocean parting. She released a shaky breath.

Lawson's soft laughter filled the air.

Maya balled her hands into fists. He had the upper hand and she could do nothing about it. "So, that's it, I'm your prisoner and I have to accept that? Well done, Lawson, you win. What do you want?"

The swirling smoke snapped back to the wings on Lawson's back. The edges of the unusual adornments twitched as his dark eyes clashed with hers, suggesting he was finding the games with his new plaything entertaining. He sat across from her prison on a wooden stool in a dark corridor of some sort, which gave her little to go off. She had no idea where she was.

"You can't outsmart me," Lawson whispered. "Tallin thought he could, but I'm now letting him know that's not how this is going to work."

Maya bumped her head against the metal bars, ignoring the pain that lanced through her skull at the contact. "I'm not interested in outsmarting you. In case you hadn't noticed, I'm not the one gifted with abilities. I asked what you want. I don't think that's an unreasonable question given the circumstances. Are you going to hurt me?" Her bottom lip quivered at the prospect of being tortured. Knowing martial arts was one thing, but being up against a magical creature with powerful capabilities was another.

"No, I'm not going to hurt you. I want back what Tallin stole from me."

Maya inhaled sharply and focused on trying to get Lawson to talk rather than her own irrational fear, which had receded but still pulled on the edges of her consciousness. There was no guarantee Lawson was telling her the truth. "Tallin isn't a bad man. He sees things from another perspective, that's all. Not everything in his world behaves, so he overcompensates. Mum says that sometimes our differences are what truly bring us together." She eyed his wings. They were beautiful but intimidating. "Why are your bottom feathers not the same colour as the rest?"

Lawson gave an angry hiss. "You do like to talk. I preferred you when you were asleep."

Maya glared at him. "You kidnapped me. You're getting what you deserve. I do talk a lot, deal with it. If it's any consolation, Tallin doesn't enjoy my sass either.

He got plenty last time I saw him."

Lawson smirked. "You love the sound of your own voice, don't you? Keep talking. You forget yourself and share lots of information that way. It's going to land you in plenty of trouble."

It frequently did, but Maya preferred it that way. "That suits me fine."

"So much fire burning inside. I wonder what fuels it." Lawson kept his eyes focused on something to the side of Maya's prison bars. She couldn't see what it was but it felt as though he was taunting someone.

"So, why do you have purple and red feathers at the bottom of your wings when the rest are black?" Her hand would fit through the bars if she kept it vertical and her arm away from the metal. She slipped her fingers through the gap. Lawson remained oblivious. She snapped her fingers and his attention sprang to her as if he were magnetised by her.

"The bottom feathers changed colour when I broke my curse." Cunning glinted in the depths of his intense stare. "I'm not interested in a therapy session."

"No. You're a cursed thing. My father always left small piles of feathers around the house as a gift for my mother." Silence resonated back at her, so she risked a little more. "Tallin thinks a cursed thing with feathers is my grandfather." His wings thrummed and he blinked rapidly. "But if you've never loved a woman and had a baby daughter with her then I guess you have nothing to worry about." She withdrew her hand from the bars and took a step back. The dark swirling cloud returned beyond the confines of her prison boundary, but she could still sense his presence. "Nothing in my family behaves. It runs in my blood."

Lawson stepped up to the bars of her prison and

stared across at her. "You think I don't know who you are, little girl?" There was a hint of playfulness in his tone. At her prolonged silence, he widened his stance so he filled more of the doorway. "It seems sass runs in your blood too. Your future mate has trouble running in his blood. Perhaps we can talk about this at some point soon." He raised his hand and pressed something against the bars. The metal meeting metal emitted a soft ting.

The object's surface rippled under the unusual lighting emanating from her prison's walls. She could see two eyeholes and the outline of what could only be the mask. Her eyes clashed with Lawson's and a euphoric grin slid across his gaunt face.

"This is a most interesting and ancient artefact."

Maya's throat ached as she swallowed hard and glared at him. "That's Haydan's. Is he here? Whether you're family or not, if you've hurt him to get that, I will never forgive you." If Lawson had managed to acquire the mask, she didn't want to think about the state Haydan was in. She moved back towards the bars and returned Lawson's menacing glare.

Lawson's fingers threaded through the eyeholes of the mask and he withdrew it from the bars. "You have no idea what this piece is, do you?"

"I do know what it is, and it's not yours. You've stolen it."

Lawson stared down at the mask. "Yet it lets me hold it without attacking me, and this relic is perfectly capable of defending itself if it needs to. If I were to return it, Asanda would welcome this item back with open arms." He winced and dropped the item into his other palm. "I don't think that suggestion went down too well." He flexed his fingers. "Duly noted. I have no intention of returning you to Asanda."

The idea of Lawson communicating with the mask didn't sit well. Maya growled low in her throat. "You're taking liberties. It's Haydan's, not yours. It doesn't want to go to Asanda."

"I don't blame it." His eyes crinkled as he grinned at her. "This object is of my people. Haydan is not of my people, therefore I am not the one taking liberties. Asanda and this object have interesting history. I guarantee that if Asanda gets this back, it will never be heard from again." Lawson tilted his head back and surveyed her. "I had forgotten how powerfully your souls link. Your need to protect him is strong. That's good." His voice was soft and lyrical now, all traces of the earlier aggression gone. "Whatever you think you know about this object, you're wrong."

"Have you hurt Haydan?" Maya demanded.

Lawson shrugged. "He's unbonded, so what do you care? You leave him vulnerable. Does that make you feel more powerful, knowing Tallin and Diego's heir is on his knees at your feet, defenceless?"

Amusement rippled through his voice as he said it, but then the tension between Lawson and Tallin explained the reason for that misplaced humour and his taunting. Silence returned, and Maya clenched her hands so her nails dug deep into her palms.

"I snatched him from under the watchful eye of his own father and a god, and not just any god. I believe the one present was called Kai. Not even his warrior was able to challenge me. My magic is undetectable to their kind. She won't have realised I snatched him until it was too late. Now I'm guessing she's frantic to get to him, but has no way to do so. Frustrating for her, I imagine, although I'm less interested in the warrior's relationship with him and more intrigued by you." Lawson's lips curled up into a wicked grin. "The grandson of the great King Tallin, grovelling in my prison cell with his chosen one locked in my other cell and his new toy in my pocket." He sucked air in between his teeth, creating a soft hissing noise. "He's not having a very good day now, is he?"

"Lawson—" She had no idea what this creature was capable of. He had the advantage, and challenging him was pointless. "Is Haydan being held next to me? Is that who you keep looking at? Can I see him?"

"No."

"Why not? You have us both held here. We aren't going anywhere. What difference does it make? I want to know he's okay."

"Your soul links to his, so you already have your answer." His brows furrowed as he assessed her. "Pressure creates the hardest of diamonds. Consider this a test of your love for him." Lawson glanced to the side again, implying Haydan was listening to this conversation and Lawson was taunting him. "You do love him, I assume."

"Yes." Her vision blurred as warm tears surfaced, threatening to spill down her cheeks. "Of course I do."

"Good." He returned his attention fully to her. "Then even when he's begging for your affections you have nothing to worry about."

"He doesn't beg me for anything. You need to check your facts before throwing accusations around."

Lawson burst out laughing, the rich sound echoing off the walls. "You haven't gifted him the bond. You don't even enjoy spending time with him, from what I can tell. I have eyes and ears. Anyone who knows about storm riders and chosen ones is aware that the bond is the most critical part of your relationship. An indication of trust, respect and ultimately love outside the confines of the sea. You offer none of that to him, just antagonism and disinterest. You have a strange relationship. Feel free to disagree. I'll wait…" He tilted his head again.

Tears pricked at Maya's eyes. She wouldn't show him weakness, but found herself unable to deny his accusations.

"As I thought," he said.

"Tallin will go crazy when he finds out about this—"

"I'm counting on it." Lawson's smile melted away. "Tallin will do nothing, because he knows that I have the moral high ground. I stole two of his most treasured possessions from under his nose, and now he has to figure out how to get them back unharmed."

"Lavinia will go crazy as well." Maya was certain that was true.

Lawson sighed. "No, she won't, because I know secrets about her that she never wants Tallin to know, and that gives me a certain amount of room for manoeuvre."

"For an ancient, highly intelligent creature, you behave like a small child yourself."

Menace surfaced in Lawson's eyes. "Watch that sassy mouth of yours or I'll work on finding those shared soft spots with your storm rider. I know you have them and I know his soul resides in his altera. I have plenty of ways to demonstrate how vulnerable he is right now. Start this game with me and I'll make you very sorry." His threat issued, he banged his hands against the bars and stepped back into the mist, melting out of sight.

Left alone, Maya wrapped her arms around herself and paced. Lawson had drawn her attention to her strong link with Haydan. It was the only thing keeping her focused on how to get through her current predicament. Their link was silent, as though blocked. She glanced around her prison. This place was disrupting their telepathic connection, meaning Lawson was playing games with them, and she didn't like it.

There was no doubt in her mind her goal was to find Haydan and get away from their captor. She had no idea how to achieve that, but she latched on to Haydan as she pondered her next move, and an idea began burrowing into her mind. Haydan was close by and he was vulnerable, but together, united, they were stronger than when apart.

The story continues in Beneath the Mask…

Milton Keynes UK
Ingram Content Group UK Ltd.
UKHW021849110424
441013UK00007B/12